John Trueman

Grass Roots

Published by

**MELROSE
BOOKS**

An Imprint of Melrose Press Limited
St Thomas Place, Ely
Cambridgeshire
CB7 4GG, UK
www.melrosebooks.com

FIRST EDITION

Copyright © John Trueman 2011

The Author asserts his moral right to
be identified as the author of this work

Cover illustration by John Trueman
Cover designed by Jeremy Kay

ISBN 978 1 907040 91 7

Printed and bound in Great Britain by:
CPI Antony Rowe. Chippenham, Wiltshire

MIX
Paper from
responsible sources
FSC® C013604

For all the past players, officials and supporters of Alanbrooke Football Club, but especially to Nigel Jordan and Barnie (Reggie) Wirdnam, true gentlemen both, now playing in the big Sunday League in the sky

Thanks to my wife and best friend Sue, who has lived with the Poachers Arms Football Club for the last two years whilst this book has been written (and rewritten and rewritten)

One

Football Notice

Downham and District Sunday Football League
Poachers Arms Football Club
Registered Players

Surname	First name	Known as	Position	Age	M/S
Cornwell	Matthew	Matt	Midfield	18	Single
Cornwell	Paul	Paul	Ball manager	41	Married
Clutterbuck	Vivian	Viv	Midfield	32	Married
Crosswell	George	George	Goalkeeper	23	Married
Farr	Joseph	Gunner	Forward	27	Married
Gaye	Gordon	Gordon	Forward	24	Married
Millmore	Michael	Billy	Defender	39	Married
Oakley	Thomas	Paddy	Forward	24	Married
Plumb	Barry	Barry	Goalkeeper	41	Divorced
Raisin	Daniel	Razor	Forward	25	Married
Smith	Brian	Big Smithy	Defender	21	Single
Smith	Derek	Little Smithy	Midfield	19	Single
Statham	David	Dave	Manager/Secretary	39	Single
Tippling	Steven	Steve	Defender	22	Single
Tocket	Wayne	Tocks	Midfield	21	Single
Tomlinson	Daniel	Tommo	Midfield	17	Single
Woodman	Percival	Percy	Defender	32	Married

- Please note that teams for each match will be posted on the door of the Poachers Arms (Public Bar) each Friday evening prior to the Sunday game.
- Players unable to play should contact Dave Statham as soon as possible.
- Subs will continue at last year's rate of £3.00, to be paid after each game. Substitutes not used and players not selected need not pay.

Signed: *D. J. Statham* (Secretary/Manager)

Football Notice

Downham and District Sunday Football League
Poachers Arms Football Club
Fixtures

September

7	Lower End W M C	H	Tenacre Recreation Ground
14	Hearty Oak, Downlea	A	Downlea Sports and Social Club
21	AFC Cummiston	H	Tenacre Recreation Ground
28	Downham Churches	A	St. Mary's Recreation Ground

October

5	J G Tanner & Co	H	Tenacre Recreation Ground
12	Sunday League Cup (preliminary round)		
19	Shellduck Inn	A	Back of the Shellduck Inn
26	Sunday League Cup (Round 1)		

November

2	Pickled Herring	H	Tenacre Recreation Ground
9	No games played		
16	Lower End WMC	A	Tenacre Recreation Ground
23	AFC Cummiston	A	Cummiston Recreation Ground
30	Sunday League Cup (Round 3)		

December

7	Sunday League Cup (Round 4)		

January

11	Jones Juniors FC	H	Tenacre Recreation Ground
18	New Inn, Gorton Down	A	Gorton Down Club
25	Hearty Oak, Downlea	H	Tenacre Recreation Ground

February

1	Downham Churches	H	Tenacre Recreation Ground
8	Tanner and Sons	A	Tanner's Sports Ground
15	Shellduck Inn	H	Tenacre Recreation Ground
22	Pickled Herring	A	Tenacre Recreation Ground

March

1	Jones Juniors FC	A	Gas Board Social Club
8	New Inn, Gorton Down	H	Tenacre Recreation Ground

April

5	Sunday League Cup Final		

Signed: *D. J. Statham* (Secretary/Manager)

Sunday 7th September

Downham Sunday Football League, Division Two
The Poachers Arms v Lower End Working Men's Club
Tenacre Recreation Ground – Kick-off 10.30

THE POACHERS ARMS

1 George Crosswell

2 Steve Tippling   4 Percy Woodman   5 Brian Smith   3 Billy Millmore (Capt)

8 Matt Cornwell   6 Vivian Clutterbuck   10 Wayne Tocket

7 Gordon Gaye   9 Daniel Raisin   11 Paddy Oakley

Substitutes
12 Danny Tomlinson
13 Derek Smith
14 Gunner Farr

Reserves (Please bring boots)
Paul Cornwell
Barry Plumb
Dave Statham

Manager
Dave Statham

All players, substitutes and reserves to turn up at 09.45

Dave turned over and looked at his bedside digital clock for the umpteenth time that morning. The large, aggressive green numbers glared at him. 08.23.

Oh bollocks, another seven minutes before getting up. He waited and looked again.

08.24. Six minutes to go.

08.27. Dave scratched under his pyjamas. Sunday mornings during the football season were always special, but today was very special: the first day of the Downham Sunday Football League season.

08.29. *Just one more minute.* He watched the clock carefully, anticipating the change. *Come on, come on.* The numbers suddenly flicked over to 08.30. Dave immediately leapt out of bed and bounded out of his bedroom and into the bathroom. He stood by the toilet and aimed his first pee of the day into the centre of the water, the strong smelling, yellow stream causing the water to froth and bubble like a steaming cauldron of, well, piss. A steaming cauldron of piss; what a lovely term. He was determined to remember that one and use it during the day.

First day of the season. The thought made him shiver as he moved the two steps across the bathroom to the sink and turned the hot tap on, staring into the mirror. He scrutinized his face for spots, blemishes and dry spittle, somewhat disappointingly none of which he could find. He washed his hands, drying them in his hair and considered his Sunday ablutions complete. As he crossed the landing back to his bedroom he caught the first, slight smell of cooking bacon as it wafted up from the kitchen. He knew that his mum would have been up for an hour or so and that a full English breakfast would be waiting for him on the kitchen table.

Dave drew open the curtains in his room and gazed out into the road below. He had been standing at this same window looking out at the same road, the same row of shops, the same pub, the same miserable weather for thirty years, since his parents had decided that they would prefer to sleep in the back bedroom of the semi-detached house on the Poachers Estate. They had carefully explained to the young David that the back bedroom was a tad quieter, that Dad needed his sleep and David may like it in the front bedroom. But Dave did not need to be convinced about the move. He loved watching the neighbours in the flats above the row of shops opposite, especially in the evenings when curtains were left open and lights left on. He would stay awake until pub closing time, watching the front door of the Poachers Arms, hoping that there would be a drunken fight. Perhaps the scrap would boil over into Pete's Chinese chip shop and onto the grass verge, where he could get a really good view. He had seen neighbours rowing, wives screaming, men staggering drunk. He had seen young men and women leave the Poachers Arms and project vomit across the pavement, across the road and across each other. He had seen local youths smashing up the bus shelter and young couples in passionate embrace, bodies locked together before sneaking into the dark corners at the back of the pub for a drunken knee-trembler. For a few glorious years, he had watched Mrs. Barnes in the flat above the paper shop take off her bra and wander half naked around the bedroom.

Now all was quiet, apart from one or two early risers strolling to the paper shop or standing with hunched shoulders in the chill of the morning and light-ing up the first cigarette of the day. Mrs. Barnes had long since moved away, although the impression had remained strong enough in his mind to be the source of imaginative masturbation over many years since. The mental image returned, as he imagined her offering herself to him, massaging her large breasts and whis-pering, 'Come on, big boy,' just like the plastic breasted women on the Internet. He wondered if he had time for a quick one.

'Breakfast's ready,' his mum called up the stairs. He looked at himself in the mirror, checked his penis, smelt the bacon and thought that, on balance, a good fry-up took preference over a good J Arthur.

He pulled on an old T-shirt and an even older tracksuit, once a bright, royal blue but now fading to a patchy grey. He slipped on his football socks, red and white hoops like the rest of the Poachers Arms team would be wearing, and an old pair of once-white trainers. As he rushed downstairs into the spotless kitchen, his mum, small and rounded, smiled a lovely mum-smile and said, 'You took your time this morning, David, what have you been up to?'

Just having a quick wank, Mum, he wanted to reply, but instead said nothing. He sat down opposite his father and emptied great dollops of HP sauce over

6

his meal. His father, looking older than his sixty-two years, had already made half a dozen Old Holborn roll-ups. They were lined up like a neat row of white-uniformed soldiers, guarding his tobacco tin by the side of his plate. He never looked up or stopped chewing as Dave entered the kitchen.

'Who is it today, David?' he asked.

I told him that last night, and about seven hundred times during the previous week, Dave grumbled to himself, but calmly replied, 'The Club,' trying hard not to dribble sauce down his chin.

'Good one to start the season, aye,' Dave's dad said pensively, still chewing on a mouthful of Tesco quality sausage and runny egg. 'The Poachers Arms versus Lower End Working Men's Club. Local derby. Good start to the season. You home?'

'Yeah, pitch three at the rec.'

Dave's dad Eric was known to everyone as Tonker and Dave had never had the nerve or, indeed, the inclination to find out why. It was rumoured that it was something to do with the size of his penis but Dave did not want to know. Mind you, his mum did smile a lot.

Tonker had played for the Poachers Arms in the sixties and seventies when they were first formed. 'Just a bunch of lads wanting to play football,' he never tired of telling Dave. 'Just a bunch of lads, formed our own team, no help from the pub even though we used their name and spent all our money there.' He shovelled another forkful of Tesco bacon and the last of the sausage into his mouth. 'Just a bunch of lads and look what we achieved.' His mind drifted away to the Sunday League cup final of 1973, chewing noisily and swilling down the last of his full English with a gulp of sweet, milky tea.

What you achieved, dear Father, was next to fuck all. A couple of division two and three runners-up medals and one Sunday League cup win in twenty-odd years. What the current team has achieved however, Father, is, well... also next to fuck all. But just wait; this could be our year. Then you might stop rambling on about what you achieved in the ancient days of Beatles, miniskirts and free love.

'I'll probably look out later, David,' said Tonker. 'Watch the second half.'

'Good, I'll see you there,' Dave replied, knowing that his dad would use any excuse to get out of the house on a Sunday morning to be first into the pub.

'Thanks, Mum,' he mumbled through a final mouthful of bread and butter, used to wipe his plate clean. 'That was historic. Shall I wash up?' and he squeezed her gently on the arm and kissed the top of her head. She smiled like a child who had been given a new bicycle and tapped her son lovingly on the bottom.

'You go and get ready for your whatsname. I'll see to everything in here. Oh, and I've made up your flasks of tea ready for half-way,' she grinned, thinking how lucky she was to have such a loving and thoughtful son.

'Thanks, Mum, and it's half-time, Mum, half-time,' Dave called back as he left the kitchen. Always works, never washed up yet. He quickly bounded back up the stairs to prepare for the imminent game against the Club. It was also important to beat Tonker to the only bathroom in the house. It was important on any morning, but particularly on Sundays after Tonker's regular Saturday night of six pints of bitter and a chicken curry from Pete's Chinese chip shop. And he always lit an Old Holborn roll-up on the toilet – it was important not to be second in line to the throne.

9.15. On schedule. Dave switched on his PC which was supported on a small Ikea desk in one corner of the bedroom. He opened the team sheet file and studied the screen carefully. He was meticulous in his preparations for football, as he was at work in the Downham Borough Council Information Technology Department. He had been in the job for almost fifteen years now and, as he openly admitted, understood very little about the computers and the way they worked, but he was organized and meticulous. The housing database was always up to date and he understood enough about the way things worked to continually offer suggestions for improvement. He was also a master of report writing, and had impressed a series of senior managers with his ability to investigate a problem and produce a detailed report on the matter, backed up by impressive spreadsheets and graphs. He knew that it was 75% bullshit, but it kept him employed and well-paid.

Dave quickly gathered the rest of his Sunday morning kit, stuffed each piece into his old plastic sports bag and checked his watch again. 9.30 – time to go. He bounded down the stairs two at a time and shouted, 'Bye, Mum, see you later.'

'Dinner's at one thirty, David,' she shouted back and Dave could hear her banging various cooking implements about in the kitchen. Sunday dinner was always at half past one but Dave never returned from the pub until two o'clock.

He jogged across Poachers Drive, the main arterial road of the estate, towards the shops, carrying his sport bag and trying to look as athletic as an overweight and unfit forty-year-old could, before stepping into Muzzy's paper shop. He picked up the *Sunday Times* from the small pile on the floor, dwarfed by stacks of the *Sunday People* and the *News of the World*. He took the paper to the front desk and stopped and stared. Muzzy wasn't behind the counter. Muzzy had served him his paper every Sunday for the last ten or so years without missing a day, but today, the first day of the season, he wasn't there.

In Muzzy's place was a girl; or a woman. It was impossible to guess her age; somewhere between twenty-five and forty, he supposed. She was very pretty in a sort of plain way, no wrinkles but a tired face, as if she had seen a bit of life. Pretty hair, nice eyes and lovely smile, he noted. And it looked like she could have nice tits under her new, blue nylon overall.

'Oh hi, Dave. Muzzy said you'd be in at this time. *Sunday Times* and a pack of Hamlets isn't it, Dave?' she said as she took his five pound note and rang the amount up on the till. Dave was stunned. He didn't know this girl/woman from Adam, or more correctly, from Eve, but she had called him by his first name.

'Er, yeah,' he said, feeling his face flush.

'Still playing football then, Dave?' she questioned as she handed back his change.

'Er, yes, but no, well sort of...' His voice trailed away to nothing.

'Don't tell me,' said the girl/woman. 'Vicky Pollard.'

Dave grinned but didn't understand what she was talking about.

'You know, that little fat man on the telly who dresses up as the little fat tart and says "Er yes, but no, but yes, but no" – Vicky Pollard.'

Dave forced a smile, nodded, and quickly stepped out of the door, the cool morning air a relief against his burning face. Who was she, this girl/woman with the pretty face, who knew his name but he had never met?

He wandered back across the road to his Volkswagen Polo which was parked on the drive to his house. Dave opened the car door and reversed gently off the drive into the main estate road. His mind was still on the girl/woman as he eased the car into first gear and headed for the rec. By the time he was passing the cemetery, Dave had almost forgotten about his embarrassing encounter with the girl/woman and his mind was again fully focused on the match. The hollow feeling in his gut returned and he whistled to try to calm his nerves. The only tune he could think of was the theme tune to Match Of The Day. He arrived and parked his car, first in the car park as usual on Sunday mornings. He checked his watch. 09.42. Two minutes behind schedule but never mind, still first on parade. Dave grabbed his bag and jogged the few paces to the changing room door.

'Morning, Lightning,' he called joyfully to the odd-looking youngster in the small, cramped office at the entrance to the changing rooms. Andrew had been known as Lightning for as long as anyone could remember. He was proud of his job as Assistant to the Groundsman; not Assistant Groundsman but Assistant TO THE Groundsman, as he would explain to anyone willing to listen. His head wasn't quite right. What went on inside Lightning's head was not right at all, but physically his head wasn't quite right. It looked as if it had been squeezed in at both sides so that it was very narrow, and the squeeze had pushed his nose out in front like a long, thin beak. His eyes were placed on the flat sides of his face so that they seemed to be looking in opposite directions. It was a wonder how Lightning ever managed to focus on anything in front of him with sideways-looking eyes.

'Mornin', Mr Statham,' replied Lightning, standing to attention and just avoiding banging his head on the ceiling of his office. He always called Dave 'Mr Statham' at the rec on Sunday mornings, although for the rest of the week, when they met in the street, it was 'Dave'. This was work and, as such, called for a formal address.

'What number today, Lightning?' asked Dave.

Lightning checked his changing room allocation sheet, neatly held on the clipboard in front of him, and replied, 'Number three, Mr. Statham.'

The twelve changing rooms were housed in a roughly-built concrete block building and were positioned six either side of a long, narrow corridor. Ten changing rooms were for the football teams and two allocated to referees and, on Saturdays, to referees' assistants (although everyone at the rec still called them linesmen). At the end of the corridor was a communal shower block with eight showers and two toilets. Hardly enough for ten football teams, fifteen match officials, assorted managers, trainers, supporters, groundsmen, and one assistant to the groundsman. Lightning passed Dave a large key attached to an even larger piece of wood onto which had been crudely etched "CR 3".

'Please sign here, Mr Statham,' he said as he held the changing room allocation sheet under Dave's nose. Dave knew that the sheet would later include the signatures of Osama bin Liner, Napoleon Boneyfart or Arsene Wanker, but he signed neatly and correctly "D. G. Statham, Poachers Arms FC".

Dave quickly checked round the changing room. The high window, its thick glass reinforced with metal mesh, had been replaced during the summer. The

seating, which consisted of wooden slats screwed onto concrete
been freshly stained and varnished. The changing room smelled of pa
and a lingering odour of sweat from the Saturday footballers. Ther
coat-hooks at each side of the room and another three under the window. Fifteen
hooks, perfect for eleven players, three substitutes and one manager. He removed
the team sheet from his bag and pinned it to the front of the open door, then sat
down to wait. He checked his watch. 09.50. He knew that the players wouldn't
turn up until ten at the earliest, and some not until a quarter past, but Paul and
Billy should be here by now. He checked his team sheet again and noted that it
definitely said "All players, substitutes and reserves to turn up at 09.45".

As he looked out of the door, panic just beginning to set in, his two right-
hand men came ambling into the changing room block. Paul Cornwell looked,
as always, as if he had the cares of the world on his shoulders. What he actually
had on his shoulders was a large net bag containing half a dozen footballs. Billy
Millmore followed directly behind Paul and was also carrying a large bag, this
one containing the football kit.

'Well done, lads. Well done,' said Dave as he took the bag from Billy and
opened it. Dave loved everything about the routine of Sunday morning football,
but best of all was preparing the changing room for the team. Starting at the first
hook to the left of the door, he hung the shirts in numerical sequence, ensuring
that the numbers were clearly visible. He then placed a pair of white shorts and
red and white hooped socks, neatly folded, on the seat below the shirts. When he
had finished, he looked round to check that all was in order. Number 1, a yellow
goalkeeping shirt, then red and white hooped shirts, numbered 2 to 14, around
the wall.

Paul and Billy sat beneath the spare hook, Paul lighting up a cigarette and
both men looking morosely at the changing room floor.

'Come on lads, it may never happen, cheer up,' Dave stated cheerfully. 'Try
to look a bit happy and confident for the young players.' Billy gave a weak
smile and Paul coughed, bringing up a wedge of phlegm which he immediately
swallowed. Neither spoke.

10.10, and suddenly there was bedlam. All the players arrived at once, having
met at the Poachers at ten o'clock. Everyone was talking at once, generally about
the previous night out, the beer they had drunk and the girls they had pleasured.
Not one mentioned the imminent football match.

Dave's neatly positioned shirts were now spread haphazardly around the room as the players grabbed their kit and moved to be next to their mates or into the positions they had used for years, irrespective of team numbers. Dave tried to check that all the players were present, knowing that any attempt to organise the chaotic scene would be useless. As Dave ticked the team sheet, Vivian Clutterbuck burst suddenly and noisily into the room. Viv couldn't do anything quietly.

'Sorry I'm late, lads, bit of trouble with the missis this morning. She wanted a shag. I told her no at first , I haven't got time. I'll be late for the game if I give you one now, I said. For goodness sake Viv, she says, it's only seven o'clock. So I had to stay and give her one. By the time I'd done the business, wiped the old man on the curtains and got dressed, it was ten o'clock. That's why I'm late.' Everyone laughed, but none louder or longer than Viv.

'OK, OK, lads!' Dave clapped his hands to gain the team's attention. 'This game will not be easy, but we can win this morning. The Club are a good team, but not as good as we are. You all know what you're doing, or you should do by now, so let's go and kick some ass out there. Firm but fair.'

Dave realised that the lads were continuing with their own conversations and not one player was listening to him. He raised his voice. 'This is a local derby.' Still no one listened. 'So it's gonna be like a cauldron of piss out there.'

The players stopped talking and looked at Dave.

'A what?' asked George Crosswell. 'A what of what?'

'A cauldron of piss,' replied Dave. 'You know, like steaming and frothing and…'

The team burst out laughing, Viv shouting out, 'Come on, you steaming whatsits of piss,' and they pushed each other out of the changing room door towards the playing field, still laughing at Dave's team talk. Paul looked up from his position on the bench as the last of the team left, giggling as they went. 'A cauldron of steaming piss-takers, I reckon, Dave,' he said before tagging along behind the team.

Dave checked that nothing had been left in the changing room. Kickabout balls, match ball, first aid kit. Nothing left as far as he could tell, so Dave grabbed his sports bag and strolled out into the sunshine which had now enveloped the playing field. He carefully locked the door and placed the key in the side pocket of the bag and trotted off towards pitch number three.

By the time he arrived, Billy was shaking hands with the Lower End Working Men's Club skipper in the centre circle. He was pleased to see that the referee was Rabbit Warren, an old friend and work colleague. *Might get a few decisions going our way this morning.* He trotted stiffly towards his usual position on the halfway line. As well as the substitutes and reserves, Barry Plumb was also in position as chief supporter of the Poachers Arms Football Club. Barry was a big man, about six feet four and sixteen stone, who had played for the team in goal during the years that Dave and Paul also played. He had spent many years in the police force and now ran his own business as a security consultant. Although he had signed on for the team and was officially a reserve, Barry did not bother getting changed as he was only likely to play if three of the team failed to show, and even then he would be third in line. But he enjoyed being involved and was never backwards in coming forward with his opinion on the team selection, the team tactics, the team kit, the government policy on council housing, the war in Iraq, homosexuality, real ale, the smoking ban, sexual positions, foreign travel, television programmes and other topics which had grabbed his fertile imagination at the time, preferably involving football, sex, politics, television or, preferably, all of them.

The game kicked off like any Sunday league game with some long punts towards the opponents' goal, and crunching tackles on any player who tried to do anything other than thump the ball first time. Dave liked the game to start in just this way to raise spirits and tempers before settling down after a few minutes. It was certainly not a classic example of 'the beautiful game', the ball being belted from end to end and being chased by little groups of three or four players at a time, but it was certainly red-blooded and not a game for the faint-hearted. A cauldron of piss, alright, this morning.

In what seemed like no time, Rabbit blasted his whistle for half-time. No score and, much to everyone's surprise, no broken bones, bookings or sendings off.

Dave had poured tea from the three flasks made up by his mum into plastic cups taken from the Civic Offices canteen, and handed them round to the team. By now the sun was beating down and the players were drenched in sweat, many ignoring the tea and grabbing the water bottles that some of them had thought to bring along. As they stood around the halfway line, swigging tea or water, a few lighting up a well-earned cigarette, the light-hearted banter was gone. They drew in deep breaths and wiped sweaty foreheads with their sleeves. Dave lit up his first Hamlet of the day and faced his weary troops in the lull before returning to battle. He thought hard about the right words, to lift them, to stir their hearts so that they would be prepared to die for the cause.

'Fuckin' brilliant,' he said finally. 'You're playing fuckin' brilliant. Keep it going.' That should do it. He poured a final cup of tea from one of the flasks, grabbed a water bottle and walked briskly to the centre circle where Rabbit was standing, studying his notebook.

'Morning, Rabbit,' Dave greeted him and handed over the tea. 'Going well this morning.'

'Yeah, enjoying it, Dave,' smiled Rabbit. 'But tell your number 2 to calm down. I should've booked him three times already.'

'Sorry about that, Rabbit, but you know young Steve – gets a bit carried away – just over-enthusiasm really.'

'Over the bloody ball, more like.' Rabbit laughed.

Dave added, 'I'll have a word,' before collecting the emptied cup and jogging back to the huddle of red and white. Rabbit blew his whistle and Dave tried again to grab the team's attention. He blurted out, 'Fuckin' brilliant. Keep it up. And, Steve, Rabbit says watch them tackles.'

Steve smiled as the lads trotted out to resume combat. He liked to be considered a hard man even though he was only five feet six, and he took the warning as a compliment. He turned back towards Dave and shouted, 'It's a saucepan of hot piss out here, remember!'

The second half continued in much the same vein as the first, but with both sides tiring in the late summer heat and last night's lager slowly seeping from their pores. Vivian, skilful if rather slow in midfield, began to make an impact on the game after spending the first half watching the ball sailing over his head. He encouraged the other players to play the ball to him, and he was sweeping good passes out to the wings to allow Gordon Gaye and Paddy Oakley to make dangerous runs and crosses. As yet, this had brought no real chances, but Dave felt confident that it was just a matter of time.

Dave looked at his watch. Twelve o'clock. About ten minutes to go and still no goals, although young Steve had tried Rabbit's patience once too often and earned a yellow card for a tackle where his boot had made impact far closer to the winger's left testicle than the football. Dave substituted him for Gunner Farr.

'For your own good, Steve. We don't want you suspended, do we?' explained Dave with a pat on the back. Steve was pleased with the action as being taken off for being too tough was a proverbial feather in his cap. Besides, he was knackered.

Dave would have settled for a draw when Gordon suddenly burst into the Club's penalty area before glancing up just as the big, heavy lad at centre half came in for the tackle. Gordon obviously did not fancy the challenge, pushed the ball past the defender and tried to jump out of the way of the lunging fifteen stones of blubber. Suddenly, Gordon was in the air, producing a credible impersonation of the Fosbury flop before landing in a heap on the edge of the goal area. Almost before Rabbit had whistled, Vivian grabbed the ball, pushed Gordon out of the way and placed the ball on the penalty spot. The team had never discussed who would be responsible for penalties, because Viv always grabbed the ball and took them. No discussion.

The ball thumped into the net off the underside of the crossbar as Viv turned and held both arms aloft, waiting to be mobbed by his team-mates. The players were too shattered in the heat to do anything but wander back to their line-up positions, although Dave, Barry and the substitutes managed a cheer, and a fairly rousing cheer considering the heat and the fact that the pub was open. Just as the Club centre forward kicked off, Rabbit blasted his whistle for the end of the game. 12.05. Five minutes early.

The players shook hands and trudged back towards the changing rooms, all of them satisfied with the outcome of their travails. The Lower End players could go back to their club and complain about the last-minute penalty: 'never was a penalty, referee blew up early, we were all over them apart from that', and drown their sorrows happily. Poachers had three valuable points.

The players were waiting in the changing room corridor as Dave fumbled in his bag to retrieve the key and open the door. 'Come on, Boss, the pub's open,' shouted Vivian, 'and my mouth's as dry as a nun's snatch.'

Dave opened up and all the players squeezed past him, hurrying to get changed as quickly as possible. Few Poachers players bothered with the showers as there was no time to wash when you had a real thirst and a nice cold lager was waiting. Dave eased his way past the other changing rooms, past players, trainers, assorted hangers-on, kitbags and footballs into the referees' changing room to seek out Rabbit. Rabbit was sitting on a bench, not yet beginning to change but taking a deep swig from a water bottle. He looked up as Dave walked in. 'Reckon it was a penalty then, Dave?' he asked.

'Looked like it from where I was standing, Rabbit,' Dave replied.

'Oh good.' Rabbit looked relieved. 'Only I couldn't see fuck all. Got a job keeping up with play these days and the sun was in me eyes anyway. I don't want to cheat, just be fair, and I see that big lardbucket coming towards your bloke and next thing he's on the deck, so I thought he must have brought him down somehow.'

'You done right.' Dave patted him on the back. 'Definite pen.'

Rabbit smiled and was happy with his morning's work, especially when Dave gave him his twenty pounds refereeing fee.

It didn't take long for the throng of sweaty footballers to remove their smelly football kit, drag on their normal clothes and make a beeline for the pub, leaving Dave, Paul and Billy alone to collect the kit and clear up the room. The kit was bagged in Billy's laundry sack, various pieces of detritus: old plasters, cigarette stubs and, strangely, two empty condom packets, were collected and placed in a plastic carrier bag, and the three stragglers left the room, Dave locking the door as he left. He returned the key to Lightning, who was sitting in his office poring over the allocation sheet.

'Thank you, Mr Statham,' said Lightning, hanging the key on hook number three and ticking the allocation sheet under "RETURNED".

'Going to the pub, Dave?' he continued. For Lightning, business was now officially complete as the key had been signed back, so there was no need to be formal.

'Is the Pope Catholic?' replied Dave, before realizing that this was not a good response to a question from Lightning, who looked confused, staring at Dave as if he had been asked to define quantum physics.

Last to arrive at the pub as usual, after parking his car on the drive of his house and running across the road, Dave saw Barry holding court with three or four of the younger players, all of whom looked like they wanted to get away but didn't quite know how. 'Trouble is,' he could hear Barry sounding off, 'trouble is, the BBC uses our money, yours and mine, but don't understand what we really want to watch. All we get is fucking poofs looking at antiques, shirt-lifters cooking and fucking foul-mouthed so-called fucking comedians…'

Dave thought about avoiding Barry, but he knew that Barry would have bought him a pint, and he was very, very thirsty. As he walked across the public bar, Barry took a full pint from the top of the one-armed bandit and passed it to Dave without looking and without stopping for breath. He was on a roll with a captive audience and wasn't going to be stopped in mid-rant now.

Dave took a long draught from his pint and looked around the bar. He felt proud that the lads, his lads, were happily quaffing beer and talking about this morning's game. They all made a point of speaking to him or acknowledging his presence as he made his way into his normal corner, where his seat was free. His seat was next to his father who had been sitting in the same corner, playing cribbage with the same mates, every Sunday since he was married. Dave had joined him on his eighteenth birthday, since when his seat had become *his* seat. Dave nodded at the four old men playing cribbage as they followed their Sunday routine. 'Fifteen two, fifteen four, pair's six and six is a dozen,' he heard his father say and the other three players begrudgingly pushed a fifty pence coin across to Tonker. Dave looked completely baffled at the ritual and pulled his notebook from his pocket.

'Subs, everyone, please,' he shouted and waited while a few players threw three pound coins at him, Dave carefully recording all receipts in his book. After a few minutes, he had only a couple of subs to collect; Vivian was too busy telling jokes to bother with anything as mundane as money, whilst Billy, as usual, was hiding in a corner trying to avoid paying. Dave caught them both, accepted the money and updated the book. As he was returning to his seat, he glanced out of the window. Someone was waving to him from outside. Not an ostentatious, showy wave, but just a little movement of her hand as she left Muzzy's paper shop. He almost stopped dead in his tracks, and everything around him was suddenly detached and his heart seemed to thump a little harder; he felt a little dizzy even, as he raised his hand to acknowledge the girl/woman. She smiled and climbed into a small yellow car parked outside.

'Get us four pints, David, while I go out for a smoke. Get yourself one.' Tonker's voice broke his trance. Dave took the twenty pound note from Tonker and moved to the bar. By now the clientele were divided into four distinct groups: the old boys in the corner, including Tonker and his cribbage mates; a group of footballers happily chatting about football and sex and listening to Viv's jokes; another smaller group trapped by Barry and listening to his views on the world in general and the BBC in particular; and a final group of oddballs and loners at the bar.

Dave looked at each group as he took the first two pints back to the cribbage table and felt content. It was going to be like this pretty well every Sunday for the next six months or so, during the duration of the football season. It was what he knew, what he understood and could relate to, except that he had an uneasy feeling at the back of his mind. Who was the girl/woman in Muzzy's and why had she made him feel so uncomfortable?

Dave finished the last of his five pints and placed the empty glass on the bar. Viv followed his lead, finishing his sixth pint and joining Dave in saying goodbye to the stragglers before leaving the pub and strolling home together across the road. Vivian lived next door to Dave and they had known each other since Vivian moved in to the house a dozen years before. 'I'll try not to wake you this afternoon,' said Vivian as they parted, 'only I'll probably have to service the missis again later,' and laughed loudly as he went. Dave stared furtively at Muzzy's shop, half hoping that the girl/woman would return, and then glanced up in the vain hope that Mrs. Barnes may also appear.

Downham Sunday Football League, Division Two
Results for Sunday 7th September

Poachers Arms	**1**	**0**	**Lower End WMC**
New Inn, Gorton Down	4	1	Shellduck Inn
Jones Juniors FC	5	3	Downham Churches
J G Tanner and Sons	1	2	Pickled Herring
AFC Cummiston	3	3	Hearty Oak, Downlea

League Table

Team	Pl'd	Won	Drew	Lost	For	Ag'st	GD	Points
New Inn, Gorton D	1	1	0	0	4	1	3	3
Jones Juniors FC	1	1	0	0	5	3	2	3
Pickled Herring	1	1	0	0	2	1	1	3
Poachers Arms	**1**	**1**	**0**	**0**	**1**	**0**	**1**	**3**
AFC Cummiston	1	0	1	0	3	3	0	1
Hearty Oak, Downlea	1	0	1	0	3	3	0	1
J G Tanner and Sons	1	0	0	1	1	2	-1	0
Lower End WMC	1	0	0	1	0	1	-1	0
Downham Churches	1	0	0	1	3	5	-2	0
Shellduck Inn	1	0	0	1	1	4	-3	0

Sunday 14th September

Downham Sunday Football League, Division Two
The Hearty Oak, Downlea v. The Poachers Arms
Downlea Sports and Social Club, Downlea – Kick-off 10.30

THE POACHERS ARMS

1 George Crosswell

2 Steve Tippling   4 Percy Woodman   5 Brian Smith   3 Billy Millmore (Capt)

8 Matt Cornwell   6 Vivian Clutterbuck   10 Wayne Tocket

7 Gordon Gaye   9 Daniel Raisin   11 Paddy Oakley

Substitutes
12 Danny Tomlinson
13 Derek Smith
14 Gunner Farr

Reserves (Please bring boots)
Paul Cornwell
Barry Plumb
Dave Statham

Manager
Dave Statham

All players, substitutes and reserves to turn up at 09.45

Elaine had been lying awake for an hour, warm and cosy in the king-size bed as the sun began to filter its watery light through the curtained window. She was enjoying the peace, a rare pleasure for a thirty-two-year old working wife and mother of two lively schoolchildren. Her head felt a little heavy and her mouth dry, although she seemed to have avoided the full-blown hangover that last night's gin and tonics and red wine could have, and probably should have, inflicted. Perhaps the refusal to open a third bottle of Rioja was a sensible move.

She turned over and looked at her husband sleeping gently beside her where he had been every morning for twelve years since their marriage, and a couple of years before that if truth were told. He was barely snoring, but his mouth moved slowly as if he was trying to suckle. Like a little baby sometimes, she thought, and carefully moved a strand of wayward hair away from his eyes. Even after fourteen years, she loved him deeply and had never wanted another man, although the last few weeks had been difficult. She enjoyed sex with him. She wanted sex with him. She wanted not just the physical pleasure that he gave her, but the comforting feeling of knowing that he loved her and wanted her too. But it had been almost a month now since they last made love, since that hot August night when he failed to, well, come up to expectations.

Last night, she had taken the two children to her mother's house and cooked him his favourite meal: medium rare steak, peas, mushrooms and a big pile of crispy golden chips, preceded by half a dozen cold lagers and washed down with a couple of bottles of Rioja. This was normally an unfailing aphrodisiac in the Clutterbuck household.

Elaine rested her head on his muscular shoulder and her fingers traced the blue lines of a tattoo across his chest with her fingernail until it rested on his left nipple. She gently toyed with the nipple, a little pink button hiding underneath the straggly chest hair. As he stayed sleeping, she moved her right hand slowly down his body. Her fingertips tenderly stroking the coarse hair on his belly, she felt like a naughty schoolgirl as she carefully lifted the quilt and stared at his penis lying softly beneath the thick blond pubic mat. She stealthily moved her hand towards his genitals and cautiously cupped his testicles.

'Unhand me, woman, for thou art but a wanton wench, tickling me in the testicular area,' he roared, and leapt out of bed. 'Besides, 'tis football I crave this morrow, not rumpy pumpy.'

'Viv,' she said, watching him scan the airing cupboard for a clean towel, 'come back to bed. It's OK, lover, we can sort this out, you know.'

'Nay, nay, and thrice nay,' Vivian answered. 'For football is of more import this day.'

'Please Viv, I—'

'Be a good girl and do me a bacon sarnie while I have me shower, 'Laine,' Viv interrupted, 'and this afternoon we shall indulge in one long shagfest.'

Elaine's face broke into a broad grin. God, how she loved this man, half he-man, half Carry On film. Who else in the world could turn everything into a joke? Even something as serious as having no sex for weeks.

Viv jumped in the shower and let the hot water rain on the back of his neck. What the hell was wrong with him? An offer of Sunday morning sex and he turned it down. Bugger, bugger, bugger! He looked down at his penis. *And don't think I've forgiven you, you useless bloody… bloody… bugger, bugger, bugger!*

Viv stepped out of the shower and dried himself on the large bath towel, rubbing it energetically across his back and shoulders. He dressed quickly and ran down the stairs two at a time.

'Just going for me paper,' he called to Elaine as he opened the front door and strode down the garden path, leaving the door ajar. He took a deep breath at the garden gate and enjoyed the late summer air, smelling of flowers and mown grass with just a hint of exhaust fumes. He trotted across the road and into Muzzy's paper shop. As he bent down to pick up a copy of *The People*, he noticed Dave standing and staring at the newspapers piled neatly on the floor.

'Bloody hell, Boss, you're early this morning. What's up; shit the bed?' he asked, laughing loudly.

Dave looked and felt very uncomfortable and tried to think of a witty riposte. He opened his mouth but nothing came out except a sort of *uuummm* sound, like a moped struggling up a hill. He caught sight of the lovely girl/woman out of the corner of his eye and couldn't be sure, but thought that she was looking at him and laughing. He felt his face burning and still his brain could not connect to his tongue. Not that it would have done much good if it had as his brain was like a wordsearch puzzle which would not sort itself into a coherent sentence. All he could think of to do was to cough. He hoped that this would both cover up his inability to communicate in an intelligible way and also give an excuse for his suddenly scarlet visage. He coughed loudly into his hand, first just once, and then a few more times until a great heavy thump on the back returned him into the land of the living and the paper shop.

'Sorry, Boss,' he heard Viv's booming voice. 'Did I make you jump?'

'Too many of them Hamlets, that's your trouble, Dave.' The beautiful voice drifted like the tinkle of a summer stream from behind the counter. Dave turned and looked through watery eyes at the girl/woman, who was smiling at him sweetly. He returned the smile and was immediately lost again; nothing else but the smile seemed to exist for a few seconds.

'Come on, you old fart – wake up! More like too much muff diving,' he heard, as Viv gave him another mighty blow on the back and chuckled loudly. He was immediately dumped back into the world of reality and began to regain his not too steady composure, feeling the burning on his face diminishing. He took three or four deep breaths.

'That's better,' he said. 'Sorry about that. Asthma. Comes and goes. Lots of pollen about. Sorry about that. Trouble with asthma. Comes and goes. No control over it. Pollen. Phew, that's better. Sorry.'

There was silence in the shop as Viv, the girl/woman and a couple of other early morning shoppers stood and looked at Dave quizzically. He grabbed his *Sunday Times* and moved towards the counter.

'Packet of Hamlets, please,' he said, not daring to look at the girl/woman again. She handed over the cigars and took Dave's ten pound note. As she rang the money into the till and counted the change, she asked, 'Your team playing today, Dave?'

Dave took another deep breath. 'Yes,' he answered as calmly as he could. 'Out at Downlea. The Hearty Oak.'

'Nice morning out in the country, then, Dave. I must come along and watch you one of these Sundays, if Muzzy ever gives me a day off.'

'Yes. Thanks.' Dave had no idea what to say next and his mind was turning to mush again. 'Yes. No. Thanks. Vicky Pollard,' he mumbled and hurried from the shop.

He was just crossing the small green in front of the row of shops, when Viv's voice boomed behind him, 'Oy, Dave, what about your change?' and Dave turned to see Viv waving at him from the shop doorway. Viv trotted across to Dave and handed over the change.

'That asthma must be some disease,' said Viv. 'Makes you cough, go bright red, get tongue-tied AND forgetful. Glad I've only got a dose of the clap.' They both laughed as they continued their way across the road.

'What time you leaving this morning?' Viv asked as they reached Dave's gate. 'Only I might as well go with you as I'm up and I've already done a bit of horizontal jogging. Might as well go in one car and help save the environment, eh?'

Dave nodded. 'See you here at half past nine, spot on, mind. Don't go having another shag and make us late.'

'Can't ever promise that, Boss,' chuckled Viv as he turned and walked briskly towards his own house. 'You know that most of my brains are in my knob.'

As Viv pushed open his front door and walked into the hallway, he could just see Elaine in the kitchen. She had on her pink dressing gown and fluffy slippers with a rabbit on the toe. She stood over the hob, turning the hot spitting bacon in a frying pan. Vivian entered the kitchen and saw the big pile of thick white bread and butter on the table, waiting to be filled with the sizzling bacon. Viv stared at her dressing gown stretched over her well-rounded bottom. It was true that, up to a few weeks ago, he may have tried his luck there and then: he would at least have grabbed her buttocks or tried to slide his hand into the front of her dressing gown and give her breasts a squeeze. But today, he just sat down and turned to the back page of the *The People*.

Elaine emptied the hot bacon onto a plate she had been keeping warm under the grill and placed it on the table alongside the bread and butter and extra large bottle of tomato ketchup. As Viv took a large slice of bacon, placed it on a slice of thickly buttered bread and poured on a generous helping of sauce, Elaine sat down and watched him for a minute, then slid her hand across the table and rested it on the back of his hand.

'Vivian,' she said, 'we really must talk about this problem. Is it something I've done? Don't you, you know, love me any more?'

Viv couldn't look her in the face. 'Course I do,' he replied quietly. 'It's just that I've been working so hard lately and I really have been knackered. Don't worry, it'll be OK soon, honest.'

It was unusual to see Viv quiet and serious and Elaine gave his hand a loving squeeze.

'I know, Babe,' she said, 'but if there's anything I can do, you know, anything. Tell you what, I'll leave the kids at Mum's this afternoon and we can go to bed like we used to on Sunday afternoons before they came along. What about that?'

'It's not the bloody kids, 'Laine, it's just that I'm a bit tired, OK. Now just drop it, please.'

'OK, Babe. I just thought that if we had some time on our own…'

'I said bloody drop it!' Viv shouted. Elaine sat there in shocked silence. Viv never shouted. He told dirty jokes, very loudly, but never shouted.

'I'm going to football, so bloody drop it!' he added and stormed out of the house slamming the door behind him.

Elaine sat in stunned silence. It just wasn't like Viv to raise his voice. She looked at his plate. And it certainly wasn't like Viv to leave a bacon sandwich half-eaten. This really was serious. She heard the key in the front door, which brought her round immediately. He was coming back to apologise. He would probably grab her roughly, squeeze her breasts and bottom and say something about a 'shagfest' after football, and then leave for football, happy and laughing like he always used to. The door opened and Viv entered. 'Forgot my boots and stuff,' he said sheepishly, grabbed his sports bag from the hall and immediately left again. As she watched him go, tears began to roll down her cheeks.

Viv arrived at Dave's house and checked his watch. Quarter past nine, fifteen minutes early. He may as well go in. He walked up the drive, past Dave's Polo, and rang the bell. Dave's mum answered the door.

'Hello, Vivian.' She looked genuinely pleased to see him. 'Have you come for our David? He's almost ready. Come in, love, come in.'

Vivian looked very serious. 'I don't know that I should, Mrs. Statham,' he said. 'Only you know what you do to me when you've got that pinny on. I may not be able to control myself if we're left alone, me being a sex machine an' all.'

Dave's mum laughed. 'You're a naughty boy, Vivian,' she said as she led him through to the kitchen. Dave and Tonker were sitting at the kitchen table, Dave gulping the last of his tea and Tonker rolling his Old Holborn into neat, uniform cigarettes in readiness for the pub later.

Dave got up. 'You're early Viv,' he said. 'I won't be long. Just going for a quick pony, and I'll be with you.'

'How's Elaine, Vivian?' Dave's mum asked.

'Oh, you know, tired after a night of passion,' replied Viv. 'But I just can't stop her. But then, what woman could resist me, Mrs S?'

Dave's mum liked Viv. He was the only one who spoke to her like this and the only one she would tolerate speaking to her like this. 'If I were a few years younger, I couldn't resist you, Vivian,' she laughed, surprised at her own daring and audaciousness.

Dave poked his head around the kitchen door. 'Ready then, Viv?'

'Bad timing, Dave,' Viv replied. 'Me and this gorgeous creature here was just about to get it together, wasn't we, Mrs S? Just about to make beautiful music together.'

'Get away with you, you naughty boy,' chuckled Dave's mum as the two left the house and opened the doors to the Polo.

Downlea was a small village about ten miles from Downham, or rather it had been a small village until a large housing estate had been constructed five years before. The village centre remained much the same as it had been since Dave first went there twenty years ago to play football or, more often, to visit the five pubs in the small, twisting High Street. The pubs had now been changed from dingy ale houses into bright and brash pubs, one even being renamed Downlea Wine and Tapas bar. Dave had never been in there and never intended to. The Hearty Oak had remained more or less faithful to the idea of a village pub, except that renovations over the years had given it a false, plastic feel. Beams had been exposed, floorboards stripped, cleaned and polished, and old prints of hunting scenes hung on the walls. Dave preferred the old pub of cracked and nicotine-stained ceilings and sticky carpets smelling of stale tobacco and spilt beer. He wondered if, in a few years' time, theme pubs would emerge with this format, complete with smelly outside toilets and a miserable old bastard for landlord.

The football team was no longer made up of rough local lads who followed their fathers, and perhaps their grandfathers, into the team, but was almost exclusively the preserve of men from the new estate: thirty-year-old commuters who were something in the city, spending the week on a train between Downham and Paddington and playing soccer for the village pub on Sunday mornings. They could then regale their work colleagues on the following Monday morning with tales about "the village lads and I... game of soccer... damn good fun... few pints of Gruntley's Old Speckled Dogs' Piss afterwards." A right load of merchant bankers. The one good thing, the only good thing, about the influx was that they were all pretty poor footballers. They had little idea about the game, even calling it "footy" at times, having been brought up on rugger and tennis and other sports of the upper classes. But they were always ridiculously keen and very, very fit, so were no walkovers.

Both men were quiet in the car as they travelled through the Poachers Estate, through the adjacent council estate, past the old power station and into the country, deep in their own thoughts. Dave was imagining what he would say to the girl/woman next week and how he could bowl her off her feet with wit and wisdom such that she could not resist his charms. Viv was wondering what to say to Elaine. He loved her, really loved her, and had never wanted or needed another woman, so what was going wrong? A few times they both felt the need to talk to someone, but men didn't talk about affairs of the heart and certainly not about failing to raise an erection. They were both glad of the time to think with no interruptions.

Dave parked the Polo in the spacious car park next to the sports centre and both men grabbed their bags before ambling into the light and spotless changing rooms. Unlike the rec, teams shared the single large hall for changing and the intimacy of an individual private space was lost. The room was empty except for Paul Cornwell, Billy Millmore and Barry Plumb who had taken their places in the corner, Paul puffing away on a cigarette and Billy reading the team sheet which Paul had brought from the pub. Barry was expounding his theory on why there are so many homosexuals on the television to no one in particular. 'Take that ugly little Irish bloke, face like a bulldog chewing a wasp,' he was saying. 'No talent. Not good for anything, but because he's a bender he gets all the prime jobs introducing the best shows, y'see, it's because they're all chutney ferrets…'

Dave took the team sheet offered by Billy and pinned it on the wall, then laid the shirts out in strict numerical sequence in the Poachers corner of the changing room. Surprisingly, the next to arrive were the team's younger lads. Stevie Tippling, Brian Smith and his brother Derek, Wayne Tockett, Matt Cornwell and Danny Tomlinson swaggered into the changing room and threw their bags nonchalantly onto the benches running around the edge, ignoring Dave's shirt layout, and chatting loudly about their Saturday night out. Dave tried to listen but could only pick up the fact that Brian and Wayne had ended up with a 'right coupla goers' and 'shagged the arse off 'em'.

As the changing room filled up with excited, noisy footballers, a tall thin gentleman with a bald head hidden beneath a carefully engineered comb-over came across into the Poachers area and introduced himself to Dave. He was the sort of chap who probably played bridge, held dinner parties and ran half marathons. A tosser.

'I'm skipper of the Hearty Oak. Welcome,' he said, shaking Dave's hand a little too vigorously. 'I note that a couple of your chaps are smoking and this is, in fact, a smoke-free zone—'

Dave didn't quite know what to say, but the conversation was overheard by Viv, who interrupted. 'You'd better go and tell them then, mate,' he offered.

'Yes, yes I shall,' said the skipper and, with a determined look, moved into the corner where Paul and Razor Raisin were drawing deeply on cigarettes. 'I'm skipper of the Hearty Oak. Welcome,' he began. 'And, actually, this is a smoke-free zone, so if you wouldn't mind.'

Both smokers looked at him for a few seconds, looked at each other, then looked at their cigarettes. 'Fuck off,' Paul replied and took a drag from his cigarette.

The skipper looked shocked, angry and then scared. His courage returned and he continued. 'Look, you chaps, you must put your cigarettes out as this is a smoke-free zone and smoking is not allowed.'

Paul and Razor ignored the plea and carried on smoking. Barry Plumb was taking a great interest in the conversation at this point, having finished his homophobic rant. The skipper's voice was strained and raised an octave. 'You really must put your cigarettes out,' he squeaked.

Barry stood up and looked the skipper directly in the eye. 'That, young man, is not strictly correct,' he stated in his authoritative manner, usually reserved for teenagers appearing in local courts for shoplifting, caught on one of his company's security cameras. He kept his hands behind his back in a non-threatening manner as he had been taught when he was a police constable, although the fact that his face was within six inches of the skipper's face somewhat negated the principle. 'I am most experienced in matters of law,' he continued, 'and I am here to tell you that, in order to adhere to the law and ban smoking from this area, as it is not strictly a public area but a private members' club, you must display notices to that effect for a period of one month before a ban can take effect and I see no such notices in these rooms.'

The skipper looked stunned. 'I-I-I see,' he stuttered. 'Right. Thanks very much for letting me know. I'll get on to it right away. Committee meeting on Tuesday evening. I'll raise it there as an extraordinary item. Yes, thanks very much.'

Tosser.

After the skipper had made his way back to his own corner, Paul looked up at Barry who was standing smugly watching the skipper explaining the situation to his team. 'I never knew that about the month's notice, Plumby,' he said. 'When did that law come in?'

'It didn't,' said Barry. 'I just made it up.' They all laughed and said, 'Tosser.'

The game finally got under way at 10.32 according to Dave's watch. From the first whistle, the Hearty Oak immediately threw everyone into all-out attack. Their style of play was based on the ability to thump the ball as far as they could and chase it frantically until another hefty boot changed their direction. After the first fifteen minutes of frantic action, the Poachers discovered how to gain a tremendous advantage over their adversaries. They began to play football.

The pattern was set for the remainder of the first half, with the Poachers' better skills and organization resulting in two headed goals for Razor, and the Hearty Oak's enthusiasm and energy being rewarded with a scrambled goal. At half-time, the lads trooped off the pitch to the halfway line where Dave, reserves and substitutes had made their usual untidy encampment. By this time the sun was high in the sky and beating down with unseasonal strength. The players took advantage of the ten minute break by rolling down their socks, some taking off their boots and shirts, and all were sitting or lying on the grass, sweat dripping from their reddened foreheads. Dave passed out bottles of water and lit his Hamlet. He reviewed his troops proudly, reminded of a painting he'd once seen of some famous general overseeing his troops part way through an historic battle, probably Waterloo, he thought… or maybe it was Agincourt; anyway it was probably somewhere we beat the Froggies.

'Bloody well done, lads.' Dave began his familiar and ignored half-time pep talk. 'Just keep it going out there. I know it's hot, but they'll crack first, running about like a load of mad bastards. Just keep your shape.' Dave was never quite sure what 'keep your shape' meant exactly, but Alan Hansen always said that teams should do it on Match Of The Day, so it was probably a good thing.

'Boss.' Viv sat, sweating, looking up at Dave. 'Boss, is it a cauldron of steaming piss today?' he asked innocently and the whole team burst out laughing, rolling around on the grass. Dave gave an embarrassed grin.

'Viv, any more piss-taking and you'll be substituted,' he said, only half joking.

Viv looked up in mock horror. 'Oh no, Boss. You mean you're going to pull me off at half time?' Everyone knew what was coming next. 'Lucky me. I usually just get an orange.' Even Dave had to laugh.

The only person who did not join in the half-time banter was Barry, who had commandeered a local pensioner taking his dog for a walk through the sports field and was unlucky enough to engage Barry in conversation. His innocent question of 'What's the score, mate?' somehow led him into a one-sided debate on the influence of homosexuality on television. Dave looked over and noticed Barry's preoccupation with some relief; he found it difficult to give pep talks with Barry mounting his high horse at the same time.

The team had settled down just before the referee whistled the start of the second half. They replaced boots and shirts and pulled up socks, re-tying their tie-ups before taking the field again. Surprisingly, Dave's half time prediction was correct and the Hearty Oak simply upped their work rate and ran faster and more furiously. This had the reverse effect with Viv, Wayne and young Matt revelling in their midfield mastery and creating another three goals for the forwards, one each for Razor and Gordon, and a speculative lob from the halfway line by the commanding Viv. The only danger from the Hearty Oak came from a long-range shot from a defender which goalkeeper George Crosswell missed altogether as it crashed against the crossbar. Dave reminded himself to have a word with George about lighting up during the game. 'Five–one. What a result. Bloody well done, boys,' Dave enthused after the game, pleased with the team, but even more so with himself.

'Fag, Dave?' said Paul, handing out cigarettes to the whole team. 'Celebrate with a smoke, eh?'

Dave noted that most of the team were lighting up, even the non-smokers, and making a point of blowing the smoke towards the area of the dressing room where the Hearty Oak players were dressing, looking absolutely shattered. Even Billy, who had never smoked in his thirty-nine years, accepted a cigarette as he was collecting the kit discarded on the changing room floor. Dave noted that he had not lit the cigarette though – he was probably going to sell it later.

George, always last to get changed, was sitting on a bench in the corner, dressed in just his jockstrap and socks, drawing deeply on a large roll-up, when he called Dave. 'Can't play next week, Dave, gotta go to a team building weekend with work.' For a moment, Dave was stunned. George had not missed a game in years. He was the best goalkeeper in the league and so reliable that the Poachers had never bothered to sign another goalkeeper although Gunner could do the job at a push.

'Fuck me, George, can't you get out of it? Say you're ill or going to a wedding or something?' Dave asked with genuine unease.

'Not this one, Dave. Could mean promotion if I do OK. We could do with the extra cash.' At twenty-four years of age, George had three children, so the rationale was undeniable.

'OK, George, thanks for letting me know. And good luck.' Dave was turning over the options in his mind. He had planned to play Gunner up front next. But, no problems, just ask Gunner to play in goal. Rest of the team as was.

'I won't let you down, Dave. Feeling fit as a fucking fart.' Barry's voice assaulted Dave's senses. 'You see, George may not even get his place back after next week.'

Dave was momentarily stunned. He gained some composure. 'I was thinking that maybe Gunner could…' he started.

'Good idea, Dave. Gunner up front, me in goal. Good idea. Should be a walkover against Cummiston.' Barry would not give up this chance of playing. 'Call themselves AFC Cummiston now. Load of nancies anyway, bloody AFC Cummiston, half of them probably work in bloody television. Nancies.' Barry marched out, mumbling something about even having brown hatters in soaps nowadays, leaving Dave wondering how on earth he was going to get out of this one.

Vivian could not wait for Dave to be ready, so he took a lift back to the Poachers with Gordon and Paddy, whilst Dave, Paul and Billy collected and bagged all the smelly, sweat-stained kit, gathered up the balls, rescued an additional ball carelessly left by the Hearty Oak skipper, checked the dressing room to see if there was anything else worth salvaging (there wasn't) and left for the pub. Dave thought that he should really pick up all the cigarette and cigar butts left in the Poachers' Corner, and said to Paul, 'I'll be a few minutes, just going to pick up these fag ends.'

'Yeah,' Paul replied. 'If you leave them, that snotty skipper will probably get a right bollocking from his committee.'

'Quite right,' said Dave. 'I'll leave 'em.'

Dave felt extraordinarily happy on the drive back to the Poachers. His team had won five–one away from home, he'd dropped the Hearty Oak tosser in it, he was going for a few pints to celebrate, and he may get a glimpse of the lovely girl/woman as she left Muzzy's after finishing her shift. Life didn't get much better than this.

Back at the Poachers Arms, Dave ordered five pints and carried three to the old boys' corner, placed them on the cribbage table and sat down. 'Where's me old man?' he asked.

'Where do you fuckin' think?' answered Tommo Tomlinson, Tonker's mate of the last fifty years. 'Outside, having a fuckin' roll-up. Fuckin' ruination of fuckin' crib, this fuckin' smokin' ban. Fuckin' Tonker's got to go and have a fuckin' fag between every fuckin' game. Makes you lose fuckin' concentration.' Tommo quaffed his pint, belched and started shuffling the cards. Dave returned to the bar to collect the remaining two pints and waited for his father to return. As Tonker came back into the bar, coughing and wheezing, Dave passed him his pint and said, 'Five–one today, Dad. Good result. Eh?'

Tonker allowed a glimmer of a smile to show. 'Did you get a pint in for the lads?'

Dave made his way back to his seat, looking out of the window towards Muzzy's, but the girl/woman did not show. He hadn't been sitting long when Tommy finished his pint and banged it noisily on the table.

'My fuckin' round,' he said. 'Same again?'

'Stay there and play crib, Tommy. I'll go up again. After all, it's my old man who's ruining your game by going off for a fag every five minutes.' Dave gathered up the glasses and made his way to the bar, ordered the refills, then turned to look out at Muzzy's while he was waiting. The girl/woman did not leave the paper shop.

As the time reached two o'clock, the bar emptied, everyone going home for their Sunday roast, until there were only three men left, Dave, Barry and Vivian. Apart, that is, from two young couples, late arrivals who took over the vacated old mens' corner. It amused Dave that, an hour before, Tonker, Tommy and company had been effing and blinding, coughing and farting on those same seats which were now being used for gentle courtship.

All three were a little the worse for wear after a couple of hours of beer drinking and were a little louder than usual, which for Barry and Viv meant very loud indeed.

'Late on duty, Viv. Not going home to pleasure Elaine, then?' Barry enquired.

'Tell you the truth, we were at it all night last night like a couple of rabbits. I need a break,' Viv answered. 'Mind you, I reckon our Dave here might be at it this afternoon, from what I saw in the paper shop this morning. What do you reckon, Dave?'

It took Dave a few seconds to understand what Viv was talking about. When the penny finally dropped, he shrugged, blushed and said, 'I dunno what you mean, Viv.'

'Come, come, David, my randy little chum,' Barry joined in. 'What's this I hear about you and our lovely little sales assistant from Muzzy's?'

Dave wanted to run away. He couldn't go home yet – after all, he had three quarters of a pint left. He considered saying that he had to go the gents but, again, his brain and tongue seemed to be wired on completely separate circuits. He smiled the smile of the mentally challenged before Viv felt sorry for him in his obvious state of distress and rescued him.

'Don't worry, Dave, old son. Only me and Barry know. And she's a cracking girl, our Mandy.'

Mandy. Dave now knew her name, Mandy. It suited her. Sort of pretty and innocent with just a hint of naughtiness. He wanted to say that he hardly knew Mandy but he had to admit that he found her a little attractive. He opened his mouth and a sound like bath water draining away came out. Barry and Viv held on to each other as they laughed at Dave's obvious embarrassment, but again Viv came to the rescue.

'At least we know he's not queer,' he laughed. 'We were beginning to wonder.'

'Don't you start me on uphill gardeners,' said Barry, the mood suddenly turning very serious. 'If I had my way…'

'Time we all went home,' said Dave, who finished his pint in one long guzzle and headed for the door. As he was crossing the road, he turned for one last look at Muzzy's. Mandy was just leaving. She looked over and waved at him, making his insides turn inside out with her lovely smile. He was about to shout 'hello, Mandy' across the road, but his nerve failed just as he opened his mouth. Mandy started her car and drove past him, looking just a tad quizzical as Dave stood there in the middle of the road staring at her with his mouth wide open. Viv and Barry watched the scene unfold, laughing loudly again before setting off for their respective homes.

Viv let himself in to the house but it seemed strangely quiet. There was the normal agreeable smell of roasting meat and boiled vegetables but the house was empty. He realised that he had only eaten half of a bacon sandwich since nine o'clock this morning and was ravenous. Where the bloody hell was Elaine? On the kitchen worktop was a note. He picked it up, his hands trembling slightly, and read:

> Gone to Mum's to pick up kids
> Dinner in oven – very hot – use oven gloves
> Back at 5 ish
> Laine
> PS I love you very much

Viv stared at the note and read it again. He slipped on the oven glove as instructed, opened the oven door and reached in for the plate containing his steaming hot roast beef dinner. The pain caused him to drop the plate which smashed on the tiles of the kitchen, splattering meat, gravy, roast potatoes and vegetables across the floor. He stood and looked at the remains of the repast in disbelief, then looked at the oven glove on his left hand and a growing red mark on his right hand.

'Oh bugger,' he said. 'Bugger, bugger, bugger!'

Three

Downham Sunday Football League, Division Two
Results for Sunday 14th September

New Inn, Gorton Down	4	0	Lower End WMC
Hearty Oak, Downlea	**1**	**5**	**Poachers Arms**
Pickled Herring	2	2	AFC Cummiston
Downham Churches	2	4	J G Tanner and Sons Ltd
The Shellduck Inn	0	3	Jones Juniors FC

League Table

Team	Pl'd	Won	Drew	Lost	For	Ag'st	GD	Points
New Inn, Gorton D	2	2	0	0	8	1	7	6
Jones Juniors FC	2	2	0	0	8	3	5	6
Poachers Arms	**2**	**2**	**0**	**0**	**6**	**1**	**5**	**6**
Pickled Herring	2	1	1	0	4	3	1	4
J G Tanner and Sons	2	1	0	1	5	4	1	3
AFC Cummiston	2	0	2	0	5	5	0	2
Hearty Oak, Downlea	2	0	1	1	4	8	-4	1
Downham Churches	2	0	0	2	5	9	-4	0
Lower End WMC	2	0	0	2	0	5	-5	0
Shellduck Inn	2	0	0	2	1	7	-6	0

Sunday 21ˢᵗ September

Downham Sunday Football League, Division Two
The Poachers Arms v AFC Cummiston
Tenacre Recreation Ground – Kick-off 10.30

THE POACHERS ARMS

1 Barry Plumb

2 Steve Tippling   4 Percy Woodman   5 Brian Smith   3 Billy Millmore (Capt)

8 Matt Cornwell   6 Vivian Clutterbuck   10 Wayne Tocket

7 Gordon Gaye   9 Daniel Raisin   11 Gunner Farr

Substitutes
12 Paddy Oakley
13 Derek Smith
14 Danny Tomlinson

Reserves (Please bring boots)
Paul Cornwell
Dave Statham

Manager
Dave Statham

All players, substitutes and reserves to turn up at 09.45

Barry had been up since 6.30 and was sitting on the settee, idly using the remote control to move around what seemed like hundreds of channels on the television. He wasn't looking at, or even for, any particular programme, just flicking round and round, pausing momentarily on BBC1 Breakfast News before starting again. Monica always said that it was a "man thing". He was waiting for the repeat of Match Of The Day at 7.35. As he changed the channels, his mind was a jumble of thoughts about playing that morning and his bowels were in overdrive. He felt mildly nauseous and hadn't slept much the previous night. Why the hell did he volunteer, no, insist, on playing today? He hadn't played for over four years and then only in an end of season friendly. The last time he had tried to catch a football was at a Poachers Arms match last season when he was standing behind the goal as a spectator, explaining to a fellow supporter why we British were too soft on immigrants, when a shot flew towards him, just wide of the goal. He missed it completely, to hoots of laughter from the lads on the halfway. Worse was to come. He retrieved the ball from the brook running behind the goal and, after slipping into the water, tried to return the ball with a hefty punt towards the pitch. His wet boot caused the ball to be erratically miscued and it had landed on an adjacent pitch, where it was immediately hammered into the net by an enthusiastic forward who then ran the length of the pitch, arms raised in triumphal celebration. The "goal scorer" was finally caught and told by the referee that it was not a goal as it was not the correct ball, resulting in a mass melee, at least three red cards, and the game being abandoned, with the referee striding away, mumbling 'No one calls me a blind cunt and gets away with it!' as he tripped over the guy-rope holding up the nets.

Barry decided that Match Of The Day may calm his nerves as he flicked onto the BBC repeat. 'Bloody hell, Monica. Have a look at this. Bloody hell!' he erupted. 'How can anyone enjoy football any more? All bloody foreign posers, acting like tarts and diving about like, well, like bloody divers. I'll tell you what, Monica, it was a better game before all these Dagos, Spicks and Wops came into the game. What's wrong with English players anyway? Look at him, bloody Tevez. Not a patch on…er…Rooney…er…Crouch…er… Defoe. OK so he's better than any of ours, but there's no need to go on about it.'

Monica wasn't really listening to Barry's ranting as she busied herself in the kitchen. 'Please try not to swear, darling,' she added.

'It's enough to make a saint swear. It should be a man's game, football. It always was in my day. No diving and prancing about like a bloody great poofter then. It was more about kicking great lumps out of each other. Real football. Never mind fancy tricks and stepovers and bending the ball. The only balls that got bent in my day belonged to the wingers when the full backs whacked them in the knackers.'

'Swearing, darling. No need for it. Not for a man with your position in the community.'

Barry liked that. He was very proud of his rise in life, from rough council house lad with ragged clothes, little food on the table and scraping every last penny together for a sack of coal to keep warm. The truth was a little different. It *was* true that he been raised on a council estate although his parents were relatively well off and, as an only child, he was very spoilt, having the best of everything. He was first in the street with any newly introduced toys, a shining bicycle from Halfords every couple of years, even a second-hand car when he was seventeen. But he loved the image of poor boy done good. After a short spell in the Royal Air Force, he had joined the police force at the age of twenty-two, where he stayed for fifteen years working his way up to station sergeant. He now ran his own business as a security consultant, specialising in surveillance equipment in retail shops. The business was going well and he made a very good living. A pillar of the local community, he had recently applied for a position of magistrate at the suggestion of Charles Harris, chairman of the local Conservative Association and a current magistrate, which would underline his rise from poor council house boy to a man of some standing. But he still kept his old friends, still drank pints of bitter at his local pub, still stood in the cold and swore at referees on Sunday mornings. Barry always said that it was important to remain true to one's roots to keep his rise to the middle classes in perspective. The truth was that he felt more at home in the company of builders, postmen and factory workers, and in the unchallenging world of pubs and local football, than he did mixing with his social peers with their wines and dinner parties and charitable events.

Monica brought a cup of hot, strong coffee and a bowl of muesli over to the settee. She placed the breakfast on the coffee table in front of Barry, turned and kissed him on the forehead. Barry caught a glimpse of her cleavage as she bent over and was tempted to suggest a morning quickie, but the forthcoming game was still worrying him.

'Is the football over, darling?' Monica asked politely, wiping lipstick from his receding forehead with a paper handkerchief.

'Not yet. Half-time. Pundits blabbing on about bloody Tevez being a genius. Bloody Argie. Listen to that Alan Hansen. Bloody centre half for Liverpool. Kick anything that moved, Liverpool did, when he played, and he tries to talk about tactics. Their tactics were to hack lumps out of the opposition, then thump the ball upfield for Kenny bloody Dalglish to chase. Great tactics they were. And he's bloody Scotch. Now there's a nation who can't play football, the bloody Scotch.'

'Please don't swear, darling, and it's Scottish. Scotch is whisky. The people are Scottish.'

'Bloody fucking Scotch twat,' mumbled Barry under his breath.

He looked at his breakfast on the coffee table. Muesli and coffee. Why couldn't he have toast and tea like everyone else? Perhaps with a rasher or two of crispy bacon or a bright, golden fried egg. He would even settle for cornflakes or Weetabix but bloody muesli. Sawdust and rabbit shit. He stirred the cereal around the dish for a while and sipped the filter coffee, which he always thought tasted like mud, but consumed very little of each.

'I know what's troubling you, darling,' Monica breathed in her husky, sultry voice as she moved into the lounge and sat next to him, holding his hand. 'It's this football thing this morning, isn't it? You're nervous. Look, why not cry off and come back to my place. We can go for a nice long country walk, and then I'll prepare lunch on the terrace. It's supposed to be another sunny day so it should be fun.'

Walk in the country, lots of flies and stinging nettles and cowshit. And lunch prepared by Monica. Bloody salad and couscous. No thanks.

'I would love to, Monica, really love to,' he lied. 'But you know that I can't let the lads down. It's a matter of honour. They really need me, be lost without me. They look up to me as their leader and, after all, we should all try to put something back into the community. It's not all about ourselves and our pleasures, is it?'

'It was all about our pleasures last night. You were like a young buck,' Monica laughed, and went to the kitchen knowing that trying to separate Barry from Sunday morning football was a lost cause. 'But just think about it, darling.'

'I will, my sweet, I will.' Barry wandered into his bedroom, undressed and entered the shower. *I'll phone Dave straight away. Tell him that I can't make it because Monica's ill and I have to take her home then nurse her for the day. That will have to do.* It was not very convincing, but the best he could come up with. As he was getting dressed, he reconsidered his options. If he did not go to football, how could he avoid being stung to within an inch of his life by wasps and nettles and be forced to eat more rabbit food. If he played, he was liable to make a complete fool of himself and would not live it down for years, probably never being able to go to the Poachers again. Or he could do neither and hide in his bedroom until midday, then rush to the pub and tell everyone that Monica had been taken ill suddenly and he didn't have time to phone, but now she needed to be left alone to recover from her illness, probably food poisoning or similar. But Barry knew that he could not let Dave and the lads down that badly. He would have to phone through with an excuse or play.

'It's nearly half nine, Monica,' he called. 'Don't you have to get going?'

'Are you trying to get rid of me, you brute?' Monica replied. 'I'm just off anyway. And remember, if you want to come over for lunch, no need to ring; just turn up. Love you, darling,' she added as she closed the front door. Barry watched her walk down the drive, ease herself into the small, red Japanese sports car and roar off up the road. He hoped that the neighbours had noticed her go. It was good for the ego when they talked about it, Barry Plumb's posh bit staying overnight again. Dirty, lucky bastard.

Dave had already had two calls this morning and it was putting him behind schedule. The first call was from Billy Millmore, the Poachers' veteran defender and kit man.

'Dave, Billy here. I've just heard that you're playing Plumby in goal. For Christ's sake, Dave, you can't be serious. Bloody hell, Dave. Come on, Dave, think about it.'

Dave knew that Billy was right. Plumby would be a disaster and he had to tell him that the team had changed. He'd do it immediately. Or perhaps later, when he reached the changing rooms but before Barry left from home. Or perhaps in a few minutes. Dave was still wondering what to do when he was taking a long time to select the *Sunday Times* and watching the lovely Mandy from the corner of his eye. His second call was from Gunner.

'Dave, Dave, Gunner here. Dave, I'm going to have to cry off this morning. Fucking knee's up like a balloon again. Got to go, Dave, sorry.'

Oh shit, but at least that means that there's no choice but to play Plumby. First and second choice keepers out. What else can I do? Match Of The Day played again from Dave's tracksuit pocket. He took out his mobile, pressed the green button and again put it to his ear. 'Dave Statham, Poachers Arms FC,' he answered. No one would phone him on a Sunday unless it was about football.

'Dave, it's me, Barry. About the game this morning…'

'Great, Barry, no changes, you're still playing. Well done. I know you won't let us down. Thanks for ringing. See you there in a few minutes.' Dave switched his mobile off, grabbed his *Sunday Times*, took it to the counter and handed over a five pound note.

'You've been busy this morning, Dave. Football business I suppose, is it?' Dave was sure that Mandy deliberately made her breasts stick out. 'You must be very important.'

'Well, you know, manager, problems, match day,' Dave stumbled. 'Thanks, better go. Goodbye, Mandy.'

Dave scurried out of the shop. He had called her Mandy. He actually had the courage to call her Mandy. As he skipped across the green in front of the small row of shops he felt as if he could fly; he was young and light and slim and blissfully happy. Mandy, he'd called her Mandy, and he hadn't blushed or stammered. OK, so he stumbled over his words a little but she wouldn't have noticed that. What a great day. The sun was shining again, the Poachers Arms Football Club had a game against AFC Cummiston, a Sunday lunchtime beer or two to follow, and he called her Mandy. Dave all but floated off the kerb and into the road, when there was a loud blast from a car horn and a small red sports car roared past him at a ridiculous speed. Dave jumped back, just in time to see Barry's latest woman zoom past him.

'Stupid cow!' he snarled as he resumed his trek across the road. 'Stupid fucking cow! Trust Barry to ruin my fucking day. First his tart tries to kill me then he's going to make us a laughing stock in this morning's match. Stupid fucking cow!'

'I saw that.' Viv's annoyingly cheerful voice blasted in his ear. 'She nearly had you. Plumby's bit, wasn't it? Come on, then, give us a lift to the rec.'

Barry gathered up his kit, resigned to the fact that there was no way out of playing. Dave and the team really did need him this morning and, although his insides were turning somersaults, he felt excited and proud to be needed. In the bottom drawer of the chest in his bedroom, he found his goalkeeping jersey, shorts and socks, all in black. He used to revel in the nickname of the Black Cat and felt that it reflected his ability and persona – lithe, agile and instinctive. He would be all right. After all, what could go wrong? He was still a good goalkeeper even after four years of inactivity. He was the Black Cat.

Barry stuffed the kit into an old carrier bag and made his way out to the garage to find his boots. The boots were hanging where he had left them, in a well-worn leather bag hanging on a hook at the far end of the garage. As he lifted the bag from its hook and opened it, a distinct odour of mould seeped up and assaulted his nostrils. He peered more closely into the bag and could see that his boots were covered in a coating of grey/green down, the furry veneer giving them the appearance of studded carpet slippers. By now it was too late to do anything about the growth, so Barry shoved the furry boots into the carrier bag and set off for the rec, ruing the fact that he had not prepared his kit during the previous week. Something he would rue even more in twenty minutes' time.

Lightning stood to attention, with his usual 'Good mornin', Mr Statham' and pointed towards his changing room allocation sheet. 'Changing room number three, Mr Statham,' he added, passing the key with its heavy wooden block to Dave. 'Please sign here between Peter Pissflaps and David Fuckham. Thank you.'

'You're very efficient today, Lightning,' Dave complimented the Assistant to the Groundsman. 'What's up?'

'Mr Carter is very poorly with his head this morning,' replied Lightning, standing even more straight and upright. 'And Mr Bridges has given me the opportunity to prove my worth by giving me complete control this morning, so I don't have time for socialising this morning, thank you, Mr Statham.'

'Well done, Lightning, I'm sure you'll do very well,' said Dave as he signed the sheet, then patted Lightning on the arm.

Lightning saluted him. 'Yes sir, Mr Statham,' he added as Viv sniggered and made his way to changing room number three.

As he unlocked the door, Dave was aware that Billy Millmore was standing directly behind him with the bag of clean football kit.

'Did you tell him?' asked Billy as the men entered the stark changing room and began hanging the kit out in numerical sequence.

'I was going to, honest,' Dave stammered, 'but then I had a call from Gunner. His knee's gone again. Up like a fucking balloon, he said, so we've got no choice, Billy, we've got to play him.'

'Oh bollocks.' Billy sat down and put his head in his hands. 'Surely we can find someone to play in goal. Anyone's better than Plumby. And he's probably been shagging his new tart all night. Come on, Dave, there must be a way round it.'

'Sorry, Billy, he's playing,' declared Dave, surprising himself with his firmness. Billy had a sulky look and went to sit beneath his number 3 shirt, refusing to even look at Dave again.

Within a few minutes, the changing room was full of bodies in various stages of undress, and the customary excited chatter about yesterday's football and last night's exploits filled the air, alongside the smell of sweaty bodies mixed with aftershave and deodorant. Billy sidled up to Dave. 'He's not here yet. Perhaps he isn't coming,' he said a little optimistically, before his face dropped as the large shape of Barry entered the room.

'Worry not, my noble comrades,' bellowed Vivian from the corner. 'The Black Cat is here to save us all from defeat and dishonour. Welcome, my liege.'

Barry could only smile nervously and dare not admit that he was late because he had to return to his house twice to satisfy his bowels' unstoppable urge to open in a flood of nervous diarrhoea. He began to undress, carefully hanging his clothes on the only remaining spare hook, and trying not to think too much about what was going to happen. It was only a game, he told himself; he had played on hundreds of Sundays in similar games. There was nothing to worry about. He took his kit from the bag and stepped into his black shorts which had stayed neatly pressed in his bottom drawer for four years. With a little difficulty, he managed to pull them up to his thighs before coming to the awful conclusion that the two and a half stones that he had gained since his last game may just restrict his ability to get his kit on. After a violent struggle, he was just able to pull the shorts up so that they stretched across his behind and cut into his ample frame at the front somewhere well below his belly button. He could feel his genitals suffocating and he looked down at his legs, bulging like fat, pink sausages from the shorts, but they were on. Bottom half covered, now for the top. He tried to pull on his black goalkeeping jersey, but struggled to get the garment over his head, past his broad shoulders and down over his body, wriggling, writhing and pulling until, finally, the jersey was sort of in place. The main problem was that there was a large expanse of wobbly pink flesh between the top of his shorts and the bottom of the jersey, an expanse filled by a bulbous belly swollen by four years of inactivity, beer and takeaway curries. Just the socks and boots to go. He was pleased that the socks were less trouble as he pulled them on, every seam of his shorts and shirt stretched to the absolute limit. Now for the boots. As he dipped into the carrier bag and pulled out the boots, he was aware that everyone in the changing room was staring in open-mouthed amazement at the circus unfolding before them. A huge man, in skin tight shorts and a shirt several sizes too small, his belly uncovered and hanging obscenely over the shorts, about to don a pair of furry grey slippers. Barry put on the fuzzy boots and tied up the fuzzy laces. Nothing was said until Viv blurted out, 'Fuck me, Plumby, did you make them rabbit skin moccasins yourself?'

The team had never gone out to a game in such high spirits, laughing and giggling as they trotted across the rec towards pitch number three, Barry waddling along behind them like a giant panda with furry slippers. Before the game started, Dave called all the players together at the side of the pitch. He had missed giving his usual team talk as both he and the players were so intrigued by Barry's antics in the changing room.

'Right, lads.' Dave always started with 'Right, lads'. 'AFC Cummiston are a good side but we are better. Just make sure that we give Plumby a bit of protection and we can win this comfortably. Concentration. Keep your shape. Protect Plumby. Let's go, lads, and remember, firm but fair!'

The team looked at each other, looked at Barry and trotted out to take up their positions. Not one of them understood how they should protect Plumby and from what, how they should concentrate or what keeping their shape meant, but none of them cared. It was another fine Sunday with a game of football to enjoy.

Barry was pleased that for the first two or three minutes the play was concentrated at the opponents' end, so he was able to prowl about the goalmouth, yelling instructions to his team-mates and trying in vain to stretch his jumper enough to cover his belly. He no longer felt nervous and the more time he went without seeing the ball, the more he grew in confidence. That was until Percy Woodman ignored Barry's shouts to 'belt the bloody thing away' and turned to give a soundly struck, but slightly mis-hit, back pass just to the right of the goal. Barry scrambled across to reach the ball and, as he dropped to one knee to get his body behind the ball, there was a terrible ripping sound, and his huge, pink behind appeared to explode from the back of his shorts like the inner tube bursting out from a split bicycle tyre. As he booted the ball clear, Barry could feel that his tight-fitting shorts had now loosened. It made movement easier and he had no choice but to carry on playing with his backside hanging out. For a brief moment, the referee was going to stop the game and not allow the goalkeeper to continue, but he was worried about completing his match report. "I had occasion to send the goalkeeper from the field of play for being ill-dressed and exposing his backside" did not seem to be a reasonable reason for dismissal, and would have caused potential problems with the league executive if Poachers had appealed.

As the game continued, Poachers gained control with the experienced defenders controlling the rearguard tightly and encouraging and cajoling the younger defenders into a disciplined resistance. The benefit of the scrappy, midfield struggle was that Barry had very little to do and, apart from two or three back passes and several goal kicks, he had not touched the ball. He had not had to make one save, which was just as well because with his jumper now riding up to his armpits and his shorts beginning to cut off the flow of blood to his legs, he was not feeling too inclined to dive about.

Half-time came and went. The players continued their personal battles, the referee allowed all kinds of pushing, pulling, kicking, tripping, elbowing and kidney punching. As long as there was no swearing, complaining, diving or other forms of "simulation", he appeared to be thoroughly enjoying the general thuggery around him. Towards the end of the game, as legs became tired and bruises became more tender, as players tended to ignore the ball more often and concentrate on their personal skirmishes with their opponents, the Poachers' defence began to come under heavier pressure. With just ten minutes until the final whistle, a Cummiston forward managed to slip clear and let fly with a cannonball shot from the edge of the penalty area which deflected slightly from the back of Billy's boot. Barry raised one arm casually, shouting 'It's wide' as the ball thundered against his crossbar, bounced down onto the goal line and somehow rebounded out of play.

'Bloody lucky there, Plumby,' Billy panted as he came back to take up his position in readiness for the resulting corner.

'Lucky, my arse,' said Barry. 'Judgement, m'boy, just fine judgement.'

The corner was floated in dangerously towards the waiting heads of the Cummiston front line, when there was a sound like a herd of wildebeests thundering across the savannah as Barry left his goal and ran in the general direction of the ball with a deafening roar of 'Keeper's ball!'

Predictably, he missed the ball by some feet but the Cummiston forwards and, indeed, the Poachers' defence, were so amazed by the noise and the vision of Barry crashing around the goal area, that they all left the ball and allowed it to run gently out of play for a goal kick. The goal kick from Barry was not good. In fact it barely cleared the penalty area before being intercepted by the Cummiston centre forward, who headed for the goal before unleashing a rocket of a shot, heading directly and inevitably past Barry towards the net. The striker had started to raise his arm in triumph when suddenly Barry threw himself towards the trajectory of the rocketing ball, arms above his head and fists clenched, like a bloated black and pink superman. His outstretched arms and fists predictably missed the ball, but such was his leap that there was a piercing slap as the ball met his face in a whack of leather, skin, blood and snot. The ball dropped to the ground, closely followed by Barry's belly and another noisy thump, then a whoosh of air. Barry lay there, still, the ball lost under his ample midriff and blood and mucus dripping from his nose and mouth. Everyone else stopped in their tracks looking at the great heap of black, white, pink and red heaving up and down. The referee tried to think back to his training course and the rules of association football, but nothing quite fitted the scene before him. He was about to blow his whistle to save the goalkeeper further punishment when Barry hauled himself to his feet, took two paces forward and thumped the ball towards the opposing half. He then stood at the edge of his goal area, his face scarlet with passion, excitement and blood, his fists clenched and raised like a victorious gladiator and bellowed, 'Bring it on, bring it on!'

But there was no time to bring it on as the referee had had enough for one day and whistled a halt to the proceedings. Barry looked a mess. His boots had lost most of their grey mould but were still badly stained, his socks had slipped to wrinkle around his ankles, his big, blotchy pink legs and knees were grazed and criss-crossed with green grass stains. His shorts were barely hanging on, the waistband stretched to its limits below his large belly and the shorts themselves torn in several places with his large backside trying desperately to escape. His special Black Cat jersey remained stretched across his upper torso like a sleeved sports bra, flecked with blood and snot. But this was nothing compared to his face. His nose was bright red and swollen, and trickling yet more viscous liquids of varying hues down into his mouth, whilst dark rings had started to appear below his eyes, which were watering furiously, tears joining the other juices dripping from his nose. And yet he was beaming with a wide, bloodstained smile of victory. He accepted the plaudits from his team mates with a nonchalant shrug, as if he was used to being treated as a hero.

'Well done, Barry. Bloody well done.' Dave added his congratulations. Barry sniffed, loudly snorting the contents of his nose into the back of his throat before regurgitating the gunk and spitting it like a slimy multi-coloured meatball onto the ground.

'Thanks, Dave,' he muttered humbly. 'It was nothing.'

As Dave, Paul and Billy walked through the front door of the Poachers Arms, Billy decided he needed to urinate and diverted into the gents, leaving Dave and Paul to go to the bar. They pushed their way through, finally catching the barman's eye and shouting, 'Two pints of bitter, please,' just as Billy caught them up and stood at their shoulder. 'And a pint of best for me,' he added before slipping back into the crowded bar. Dave paid for the three pints and looked at Paul, shaking his head, resigned to the fact that Billy had caught him again.

'One day, we'll catch the tight bastard,' said Paul, taking a long draught from his pint.

Dave squeezed his way through the crowded bar towards the old men's corner and sat next to Tonker.

'Good result wasn't it, David?' his father stated rhetorically. 'Thanks to Plumby, from what the lads have been saying.'

'Fuckin' Plumby, fuckin' amazin', that fat bastard, fuck me, who's fuckin' round?' Tonker's mate Tommy contributed his usual eloquent summary of the proceedings. Barry moved across and sat quietly next to Dave, sipping his pint between great snorts, using the beer to help swallow the globules of phlegm from his nose.

'You're quiet, Barry,' said Dave, more used to Barry holding court, ranting about some perceived injustice than sitting serenely and saying nothing. Barry took out his mobile.

'Just got to phone Monica,' he said, his big sausage fingers banging clumsily down on the keys. 'Hi, Monica. Just ought to let you know that I definitely can't make it this afternoon: bit of an accident at football this morning... Not really serious, no... Broken nose, that's all. I really can't, my love. I'm there now. I may be some time. No, no need, my love. I'll call you later.'

He turned to Dave. 'Daft cow only wants to pick me up from the hospital.'

'You going to the hospital, then?' Dave asked.

'Am I fuck.' Barry replied. They both smiled and took swigs from their glasses.

Four

Downham Sunday Football League, Division Two
Results for Sunday 21st September

Downham Churches	3	3	New Inn, Gorton Down
Pickled Herring	2	1	Shellduck Inn
Hearty Oak, Downlea	2	4	Jones Juniors FC
Lower End WMC	P	P	J G Tanner and Sons
Poachers Arms	**0**	**0**	**AFC Cummiston**

League Table

Team	Pl'd	Won	Drew	Lost	For	Ag'st	GD	Points
Jones Juniors FC	3	3	0	0	12	5	7	9
New Inn, Gorton D	3	2	1	0	11	4	7	7
Poachers Arms	**3**	**2**	**1**	**0**	**6**	**1**	**5**	**7**
Pickled Herring	3	2	1	0	6	4	2	4
J G Tanner and Sons	2	1	0	1	5	4	1	3
AFC Cummiston	3	0	3	0	5	5	0	3
Hearty Oak, Downlea	3	0	1	2	6	12	-6	1
Downham Churches	3	0	1	2	8	12	-4	1
Lower End WMC	2	0	0	2	0	5	-5	0
Shellduck Inn	3	0	0	3	2	9	-7	0

Sunday 28th September

Downham Sunday Football League, Division Two
Downham Churches v Poachers Arms
Saint Mary's Recreation Ground – Kick-off 10:30

THE POACHERS ARMS

1 George Crosswell

2 Steve Tippling   4 Percy Woodman   5 Brian Smith   3 Billy Millmore (Capt)

8 Matt Cornwell   6 Vivian Clutterbuck   10 Wayne Tocket

7 Gordon Gaye   9 Daniel Raisin   11 Gunner Farr

Substitutes
12 Paddy Oakley
13 Derek Smith
14 Danny Tomlinson

Reserves (Please bring boots)
Paul Cornwell
Dave Statham

Manager
Dave Statham

All players, substitutes and reserves to turn up at 09:45

Billy Millmore was listening to "Weekend Breakfast" on Radio Five Live as he went to the refrigerator to find fillings for the girls' sandwiches. He had been up for an hour: an hour which offered him peace from his wife and twin teenage daughters. He felt happy and relaxed because he was to be left alone, all day. His wife, Louise, was playing in a hockey tournament somewhere, along with the twins, and would not be back until late afternoon, which meant that he could spend the whole day doing just what he wanted to do. Football this morning, pub at lunchtime, snooze on the settee this afternoon. The Poachers Arms were near the top of the league and playing Downham Churches – an easy three points. The weather was windy but fine. Days didn't come better than this.

He found a pack of outdated processed ham and some cheese slices from Aldi tucked away at the back of the fridge and checked the sell-by date. Only a few days over so they'd be OK. As he was spreading the cheap margarine onto the even cheaper bread, he ran through his morning's tasks in his head. Cup of tea for Louise in bed – done. Lay the table for breakfast – done. Team football kit ready and bagged up – done. His own football kit ready – done. Prepare sandwiches – in process. Everything running like clockwork and no scolding from Louise this morning.

'Do you have to listen to that awful noise at this time in the morning?' Louise's voice blasted behind him. 'For God's sake turn that radio down, or preferably off.'

'Of course, my sweet. Are you all set for the tournament? Where is it again?' Billy asked, glancing over his shoulder at his wife as he turned the volume button a fraction.

'Melksham,' Louise snapped as she took a piece of toast from the rack. 'Don't you ever remember anything?'

'I do now that you've said. What time is it you're going? Don't tell me. You're leaving here at ten and the tournament starts at eleven. Right?'

'We are leaving at nine thirty and the tournament starts at eleven fifteen,' she corrected him. Billy knew the exact times but enjoyed deliberately getting things wrong and receiving the subsequent chastisement. He reasoned that if he lay down small traps and accepted minor punishments, any serious misdemeanours may go unnoticed or, at least, unchallenged.

'And don't forget that I'm taking the car, so you'll have to get a lift to football,' Louise snapped as she sat at the kitchen table waiting to be served.

One of the twins staggered wearily into the kitchen, rubbing her eyes. 'What time is it?' He was so proud of his teenage daughters, especially now that they were growing into beautiful young ladies. He wanted to grab her and give a huge cuddle, but cuddles had been outlawed by the twins since the onset of puberty.

'Time you were getting ready, young lady. And your sister too. Go and give her a call, get dressed both of you and come down for breakfast. We are leaving here at half nine, on the dot,' Louise stated firmly.

Billy finished the picnic lunch for his family and placed it in a cool box, adding the ice packs. He had forgotten about the lift so rushed to the telephone in the hall and rang Dave's number.

'Dave Statham, Poachers Arms FC.'

'Dave, it's Billy. Any chance of a lift this morning? She's got the car to go to some hockey tournament in Melksham, so I'm stuck.'

Dave looked at his watch. 09.25. He had time if he left now. Billy's place was more or less on the way to St. Mary's Rec.

'No trouble, Billy. Be there in about ten minutes.'

Dave had made his mind up that this week he would ask her out. He had practised what he was going to say and was confident that his nerve would hold. He would march straight in, collect his *Sunday Times*, walk directly to the counter and say, '…and a packet of Hamlet, please, Mandy. And I was wondering if you'd like to come out one evening?' Easy. Just like that. No messing. He wasn't quite sure what her reaction would be but he would play that by ear when the time came. He grabbed his sports bag and headed for the door.

'Don't forget your flasks, love,' Dave's mum said as she walked into the hall from the kitchen wiping her hands on her pinafore. 'They're on the telephone table there, look.'

'Thanks, Mum.' Dave looked at his lovely little mum, smiling like the picture on the packet of Aunt Bessie's Yorkshire pudding, her round face glowing pink as usual from the morning's exertions in the kitchen. Dave put his arms around her and kissed the top of her head. 'You're the best mum in the world,' he added. And he meant it.

He rushed across the road to the paper shop and stood outside the door for a moment. He rehearsed his lines in his head, took a deep breath and entered the shop. He grabbed his *Sunday Times*, turned and walked to the counter and said, 'And a pack…'

Muzzy's happy brown face was grinning at him from behind the counter. 'Hamlets, Dave? Still on the Hamlets, isn't it? No good for you, you know. Look, "Smoking Kills". It says so here on the packet.'

Dave was shocked, shaken that Mandy wasn't there. He quickly gained his composure. 'Bloody hell, Muzzy. You're a tobacconist. You make a living out of selling people tobacco, not trying to stop them smoking.'

'Only you, Dave. I worry about you. The rest of the people here can smoke themselves to bloody death for all I care, but you are a good man and I don't want to see you die.' All the while, Muzzy was beaming like the – what was it? – Cheddar cat or something. 'I returned yesterday from the island of Tenerife. What a place, Dave,' Muzzy continued. 'Sunshine all day, and cheap. Everything is so cheap. And the hotel. What a hotel. High on the hill with magnificent views over the sparkling blue sea…'

'Must rush, Muzzy. Big game this morning. Tell me about your holiday next time, eh,' Dave said as he took his change and rushed out of the door. 'Bollocks and more bollocks,' he said out loud as he made his way back across the road to his car, parked on the drive of his house. Vivian and Paul were waiting for him by the car.

'Something wrong, Dave?' Viv asked, also grinning like Dave's Cheddar cat. 'Didn't see someone you were expecting in Muzzy's?'

'Fuck off, Viv!' said Dave as he opened the car door.

Billy had everything ready and was waiting at his front gate for Dave to collect him, when Louise came rushing out of the front door. 'And don't think that you're going to spend the afternoon boozing with those useless mates of yours down the pub,' she said, handing Billy a piece of paper. 'I've made a list of jobs that need doing, starting with the vacuum cleaning, dusting, mowing the lawns, cleaning out the garage – and make sure they're done by the time we get back.'

With no further conversation, she turned and went back to her breakfast.

'Stick your vacuum up your ass,' Billy mumbled under his breath as Dave's Polo turned into the Close. Billy opened the boot and squeezed the bag of clean kit in amongst the rest of the football paraphernalia. No one spoke except for a brief 'Mornin', awright.' Each man was deep in his own personal little world. Paul was dreaming of the day multiple marriages would be legal and he could have both his wife and his lady friend living with him. Perhaps he should become a Jehovah's Witness, or was it a Methodist? Anyway, one of those sects that allowed you to have lots of wives. He wondered how to go about becoming a Methodist.

Viv's erection problem had not been mentioned in his house since the last row, but he was determined that this afternoon he would only have two pints and then go home and ravish Elaine. Or maybe three pints. The thought had caused a slight erection to begin. *Fucking typical, can't raise one with the missis but get a lazy lob in a car with three fucking ugly blokes.* He hoped he wasn't turning homosexual, but smiled to himself at the thought. Anyone who had ever seen Percy Woodman in the changing rooms, could never be homosexual. Scrawny, spotty body and a sagging hairy backside. The slight erection immediately subsided.

Dave's thoughts were concentrated on the forthcoming game. The team looked good. George Crosswell back in goal, thank God; Gunner Farr in for his first game of the season; confidence running high as a result of being near the top of the league; playing against Downham United Churches who were not a good side. Surely a relatively straightforward three points and perhaps top of the league by this afternoon. As Dave pulled into the small car park next to Saint Mary's recreation ground, a red sports car roared through the entrance gate in the opposite direction, causing him to brake quickly.

'Fuckin' mad cow,' he shouted, and Monica smiled and waved to him as she blasted past.

'That's Barry's bit of stuff.' Billy immediately brightened up. 'She's a widow. Her old man used to run Goodprice Motors and Luxbuild Developments before he snuffed it. In strange circumstances too, I've heard. Didn't take her long to cotton on to someone else, did it? Old Barry's shagging seven colours of shit out of her, I reckon. Stays in his place every Saturday night even though she's got this big place in the country somewhere…'

The other three were out of the car and walking with their kit towards the church hall, which doubled as changing rooms on Sunday mornings. Standing outside the door was the large forbidding figure of Barry. He was wearing a white shirt with a red tie, a dark blue overcoat and smart pinstriped trousers with shining black shoes. Not a pretty picture at the best of times, he looked even more menacing with his nose swollen, bent at a slight angle, and his eyes ringed by yellowing bruises as he stood, arms crossed, like a washed-up heavyweight boxer minding a Mafia boss.

'Morning, Barry. Fuck me, you look well,' laughed Viv.

'Dinner party at her place last night,' Barry explained. 'Put my best whistle on and the others turn up like they're going gardening. No manners. Typical of the attitude of people today. No standards. Anyway, fucking disaster. I couldn't breathe properly because of this nose and got bollocked for making snorting noises when I ate, then I got pissed on the wine and brandy and got another bollocking for calling her mates scruffy pikeys, then had to stay at her place because I couldn't drive, then she wouldn't let me have a leg over because she was sulking. Then, to cap it all, missed Match Of The Day last night and this morning. Fucking disaster.'

They entered the old church hall, the players arriving in dribs and drabs. Dave's pre-match talk to the team was ignored as usual except when he finished with '…and remember, firm but fair,' when the whole team joined in at the top of their voices.

The game began slowly with the Poachers' team knocking the ball about rather too casually, perhaps believing Dave's inspirational team talk that they should win this one easily; after all, they were almost top of the league and the opposition was only a bunch of Holy-Joe pansies. As it turned out, the Downham United Churches players were anything but pansies. They were a fit and muscular bunch who spoke only in low whispers, just a gentle murmur against the noisy profanities of the Poachers' team. Dave had put this down to the fact that they were probably religious fairies. The truth was, however, becoming apparent as the game progressed. The Church players were all babbling and calling in languages which sounded like Polish or Russian and they all seemed to be called Ivan or Igor.

'What's all this about? Paddy, go and find what's happening, will you?' Dave asked, and Paddy trotted off to talk to the church trainer. A few minutes later he was back.

He explained. 'It's a bit complicated. The vicar, old Phillips-Clarke, has signed on a bunch of immigrants who work in supermarket warehouses, you know, pickers, cleaners, fork-lift drivers and general labourers, for the minimum wage. He promised them a beer and a sandwich at the Horse and Jockey if they attended the early morning service and played football later each Sunday. This way, his congregation was increased which keeps the bishop happy, he's got a decent team, the landlord of the Horse and Jockey's happy, and the players are happy. Everybody's happy… except us.'

After fifteen minutes of defensive play from the Poachers with the church team having more and more possession, one of the Polish (or Ukrainian or Georgian or Russian) midfielders easily stole the ball before threading an inch-perfect pass to one of the Polish (or Ukrainian or Georgian or Russian) strikers who lashed the ball past George and into the Poachers' net. The spectators on the Poachers' side of the pitch stood and looked in disbelief as the Polish (or Ukrainian or Georgian or Russian) centre forward, a big, burly blond player who looked as if he should be playing a baddie in a Bond movie, trotted quietly back to the centre circle, shaking hands with one or two of his team mates on the way. The rest of the church team applauded politely and resumed their positions ready to re-commence play.

Within five minutes of the restart, it was two–nil and the polite routine following the goal took place once more. The Poachers' players looked at each other in confused disbelief; there was no one to blame, no one to shout at or complain to; it was just a brilliantly created, brilliantly taken goal. They looked at Dave on the line but he had no real clue as to what to do. All he could do was call upon his years of tactical experience and nous, shouting, 'Whack the fucking ball upfield – and give that centre forward a good seeing to.'

This tactic unsurprisingly failed to work and Poachers were soon three, then four goals down. The half-time whistle came as a huge relief and the players traipsed off, heads down and not a word spoken. Dave looked at his dispirited troops, sitting round with socks rolled down and faces red through exertion and the cutting wind. Some gulped from water bottles whilst others shielded lighters by cupping their pink, wind-chilled hands and tried to light a comforting cigarette. Dave was unsure what to say to his shell-shocked troops and had just begun to stutter an unconvincing 'Welt the thing down the middle…' when Barry stepped forward.

'Respect, lads, that's what it's all about, respect. See them Russkies, Jam Rolls or whatever they are, they've got respect. No bawling, no screaming, no play-acting. They're smart, respectful lads. Just look at them now. No long hair, socks still pulled up, not lounging around like they're at bloody Glastonbury. Respect. You lot could learn from them.' Barry folded his arms, looked around the team and nodded. 'Fucking respect.'

No one argued, no one laughed or made fun. No one told Barry to fuck off. The team just stood up slowly, looking very embarrassed, pulled up their socks and stood waiting for further instructions. By now, however, Barry had marched off to harangue two teenagers cycling across the goalmouth about respect for their elders, their parents, their bicycles, and the pitch.

The second half started much as the first half had finished, with the Poachers' defence struggling to hold the slick passing church team and reduced to banging the ball away anywhere to relieve the pressure. But they held out, more by luck than judgement, with the ball hitting the crossbar twice and sizzling just past the post on a number of occasions. After twenty minutes, with the score remaining at four–nil, Steve hacked the left winger across the thigh as he was sprinting at full speed down the left wing. The Pole flew acrobatically into a surprised dog which was sniffing the corner flag. As the dog ran off yelping, the referee had had enough and blew his whistle loudly before running across towards Steve and feeling in his pocket for the inevitable yellow card. His third booking in four games meant that a suspension was due very soon.

As the referee was pulling the card from his pocket, the Downham United Churches' trainer called out to him 'Subs, ref' and, without waiting for permission, five of his players trotted off and disappeared into the church hall. They were replaced by three pimply young lads who ran on to take up their positions, causing a delay whilst the confused and overworked referee tried to resolve the disorder. He was a picture of bewilderment as he tried to sort out and document one caution, five players leaving the field of play without permission, and three players joining the field of play without permission. He was, however, nothing if not determined and took each action slowly but carefully and thoroughly.

'You, number 2,' he said, pointing towards Steve, 'are being cautioned for violent conduct. Now run along before you get a red card.' He raised the yellow card with an exaggerated theatrical flourish. He then summoned the church team trainer onto the pitch. 'Right, I need the names of those players who left the field of play and the names of those who replaced them. OK, first one to leave and his replacement, please.'

The trainer took out a tattered notebook and ran his finger down a list of names, and said, 'The first one to leave was Wlodzimierz Szymanowski.'

The referee, his pencil poised above his notebook, looked blankly at the trainer. 'I think we'll stick to numbers and sort the names out later,' he said with a nod of self-congratulation. After five minutes he was satisfied that all was in order and the game was restarted with only nine players for the United Churches.

'What's that all about? Paddy, go and find what's happening, will you?' Dave asked, and Paddy trotted off to talk to the church trainer again. A few minutes later he was back.

'Bit complicated, Dave,' he explained. 'Seems that when the vicar signed the Russkies and whatever, all his old players left in a huff, so he had to sign these young lads as cover; they're all from the choir at Saint Mary's. Anyway, turns out some of the Russkies have to go to work for the twelve o'clock shift, so the trainer waits until the morning church service kicks out when the choirboys are ready, then the Russkies go off to work, then he brings the lads on as subs, but he's only allowed three subs but there's five that goes off to work, so he's got to finish the game with nine men. So I reckon that we've got a chance. Half an hour left, send young Smithy and Danny on and take Wayne off and Steve before he gets sent off, put Viv into defence, move Big Smithy up front to play four-two-four and we've got half a chance.'

'Just what I was thinking, Paddy. Right, Paul, wave that flag and get the ref's attention. Smithy and Danny, get ready to replace Wayne and Steve. And tell Viv to move into defence and your brother to go up front, Smithy.' Dave stood with his arms folded across his chest, feeling like one of the great generals in history, Montgomery, Patton, Custer. Perhaps not Custer, on second thoughts.

The changes were made and the game changed accordingly. The choirboys were only there to avoid choir practice after church, and the rest of the team were tiring after working a night shift and didn't really care whether they won or lost anyway so long as they got their beer and sandwiches. The goalkeeper had been replaced by a five feet six soloist whose voice sounded as if his testicles were in the process of dropping. The Poachers scored very quickly, Gordon Gaye using his speed to break through the shambolic church defence and cross for an easy tap in for Razor Raisin. Gordon was cutting through the defence at will and added two more before passing for Big Smithy and Gunner to add to the goals tally. Razor added a sixth goal with a spectacular lob from the edge of the area, by which time the trainer of Downham Churches had wandered back to the hall, resigned to defeat and mumbling, 'Three–nil up last week, drew three each, two–nil up the week before and lost four–two. How the blooming heck can we expect to win if half the blooming team goes to work halfway blooming through. Blooming daft vicar, blooming daft ideas.' This constituted a strong indictment of the vicar from someone who had been his live-in boyfriend for several years.

As he walked across the road to the pub, Dave tried to look into Muzzy's to see if Mandy was there, hoping that perhaps she had just started later this morning. He could not see through the dark windows and was tempted to go to the shop and buy something, more cigars or another Sunday paper perhaps, but decided that the small chance of seeing Mandy was not worth listening to Muzzy talk about the wonderful island of Tenerife. He walked into the bar and pushed through the crowd of happy and excited footballers, stopping a couple of times to congratulate particular players on their earlier play and accepting congratulations from a few pub regulars. He approached the bar, pulling his wallet from his tracksuit pocket, looked up and was dumbstruck. He couldn't say, 'A pint of bitter, please,' because standing behind the bar was Mandy, a beautiful smile playing on her lips.

'Hello, Dave. You look surprised to see me – did you miss me this morning?' Mandy asked him, looking even lovelier than ever, her eyes sparkling as they caught the reflection from the Carling lager tap on the bar. 'Don't worry, love' – pretty little lines crinkled in the corner of her eyes as her smile widened – 'your dad's put one in the till for you.'

Dave grinned the grin of a simpleton and nodded, just managing to blurt out a brief 'Ta. Thanks. Yeah,' before Mandy began pouring the pint.

'I was only helping Muzzy out for a couple of weeks in the paper shop. Still looking for a proper job, but this'll do until something comes up,' she chattered, before placing the pint on the bar counter. Dave reached for the full glass as

Mandy placed it on the bar and, as he did so, gave his hand a slight but definite squeeze which made him so nervous that he could not pick up the pint for a moment. When he did, he was shaking. He took a deep breath, gained control of his trembling hand and turned to raise his glass to Tonker in the old men's corner. Tonker looked up from his cribbage and nodded in recognition.

Paul, Billy, Viv and Barry had decamped to a table at the edge of the old mens' corner, and Dave carried his beer over to join them. He tried to arrange his seat so that he could catch glimpses of Mandy as she moved back and forth along the bar, serving the Sunday lunchtime faithful. Barry was knocking his forefinger against the table to emphasise a point whilst delivering a sincere and demonstrative homily on the need for more respect in the world, whilst Viv was ignoring him and telling jokes about terrorism and blowing people up. Tonker and his mates were engrossed in their cribbage: fifteen two, two's four and a pair's six; fifteen two, fifteen four, fifteen six and six is a dozen; four for pairs, ragged thirteen. The matches in the cribbage board were shifted up and down in what appeared to be random movements. Then money was exchanged, usually with mumblings of 'Lucky bastard' before Tonker slipped outside for a smoke. The ritual had been followed every Sunday, in the same pub, on the same table, for forty years.

On Dave's table, pints were downed and Barry gathered up the empties and strode off to the bar to buy the next round, pushed his way to the front and told anyone that would listen that respect was a disappearing trait in Britain and that we should take it very seriously as it was the foundation of civilization. As soon as he had left the table, Viv immediately launched into his own impersonation of Barry, which sounded more like Ian Paisley, but it still made everyone laugh, even Paul who rarely smiled.

The drinkers in the pub began to drift away to their loved ones and Sunday roasts. Before leaving, Tommy had bought Dave's table a round from his crib winnings, Dave had bought a round, Viv had bought a round, and Paul had bought a round. The pint glasses were empty on the table. Empty that is except Billy's which still had half an inch at the bottom of the glass. As the others waited for Billy to offer to buy his round, Billy stood, drained his glass and said, 'Better get off, lads, only I've got to walk home and it takes best part of an hour.'

'Whoa there, Billy.' Barry gently gripped his wrist as he was about to leave. 'Your round, is it not?'

Billy did not flinch. 'Haven't really got time for another. She'll be waiting for me at home and it's a fair old walk.'

'Worry not, Billy,' said Viv. 'You won't be walking home. I'll see to that. Can't let an old mate walk home after a few pints. You just pop up and get the round and I'll sort out your lift home, don't worry.'

Billy decided that there was no way that he could avoid buying a round. He could make a run for the door, but that would be too obvious. Perhaps he could buy halves and say that he thought there wasn't enough time to drink a pint before closing time, but he'd done that before and besides, the pub was open all day. He could say that he had no money, but they knew that Dave had paid him for two weeks' laundry money that morning. It seems that there was no way out. As he slowly and reluctantly walked to the bar, Viv was talking quietly into his mobile. Billy returned with three pints of bitter and a lager for Viv, placed them on the table and sat down. His mates looked at the four pints for five people.

'We sharing one then, Billy? Got a couple of straws in your pocket?' asked Viv.

'No, no, I've had enough. Besides, I've got a few jobs to do later, so thought I'd better not have any more.' Billy looked at his watch. It was two o'clock. It would take Viv about twenty minutes to finish that pint, then give him a lift. He'd be home by just before three and the girls should be home about five. This would give him about two hours to do his jobs. Pushing it, but he may just make it. The four drinkers made great play of sipping their pints slowly and sighing with a satisfied 'Aahh' after each swallow. Billy looked at his watch.

'Don't worry, Billy.' Viv patted Billy on the arm. 'I won't let you down. A couple of minutes, honest.' As he finished speaking the door of the pub opened and a short fat man leaned into the bar. 'Taxi for Billy Millmore,' he shouted.

'There you go, Billy. Told you I wouldn't let you down, didn't I?' Viv said with a beaming smile. 'Go and get your taxi.'

Paul and Barry finished their beers, said their goodbyes and strolled out ready for the walk home, still laughing at Billy's nerve. Viv and Dave sat there for a moment with their own thoughts, and then Dave, by now feeling just a bit the worse for wear, suddenly blurted out, 'Viv, can I ask you something, you being, sort of, good with women and that?'

Viv wondered what was coming next, but enjoyed the compliment. 'Course, mate, ask what you like, but I'm not telling some of my best sexual positions in case you take over as the estate sex god.'

'No, it's not that.' Dave wished he hadn't said anything but it was too late now. 'It's Mandy. You know Mandy. From Muzzy's. Well, from this pub now, I suppose. It's just that, you know…'

'Wait a minute,' said Viv. 'Don't move from that seat,' and he left Dave and walked across the almost empty bar and whispered in Mandy's ear. Mandy ducked under the bar hatch and put her arm through Viv's and they walked towards Dave's table. He watched this taking place as his throat dried up and his head started slowly spinning, the couple seeming to float towards him like an old fuzzy film. Then Mandy sat down at the table.

'I think you two need to talk,' Viv said. 'I'll look after the bar for a minute.'

Mandy reached across the table and held Dave's hand. 'What do you want to say, Dave?' she asked, looking directly into his eyes. Dave couldn't speak. He just looked at her and thought that he'd never, ever, seen anyone or anything as beautiful in his life. 'It's about time you asked me out, Dave.' Her voice seemed to surround him like the sweetest of love songs. 'Now I'm busy most of this week, but I'm working here on Friday so you can walk me home then, and I'll get Saturday off and we'll go out on a proper date. Is that OK?'

Dave nodded. He wanted to laugh, or cry, or shout, 'I love you, Mandy,' as loud as he could, but he just nodded. Mandy gave his hand one more squeeze, then returned to the bar.

'Thanks, Viv,' she said as she took her place behind the bar. 'I thought he'd never ask.'

Five

Downham Sunday Football League, Division Two
Results for Sunday 28th September

New Inn, Gorton Down	4	5	Hearty Oak, Downlea
Pickled Herring	P	P	Lower End WMC
Downham Churches	**4**	**6**	**Poachers Arms**
Shellduck Inn	3	0	AFC Cummiston
Jones Juniors FC	7	1	J G Tanner and Sons

League Table

Team	Pl'd	Won	Drew	Lost	For	Ag'st	GD	Points
Jones Juniors FC	4	4	0	0	19	6	13	12
Poachers Arms	**3**	**3**	**1**	**0**	**12**	**5**	**7**	**10**
New Inn, Gorton D	4	2	1	1	15	9	6	7
Pickled Herring	3	2	1	0	6	4	2	7
AFC Cummiston	4	1	3	0	5	8	-3	6
Hearty Oak, Downlea	4	1	1	2	11	16	-5	4
Shellduck Inn	4	1	0	3	5	9	-4	3
J G Tanner and Sons	3	1	0	2	6	11	-5	3
Downham Churches	4	0	1	3	12	18	-6	1
Lower End WMC	2	0	0	2	0	5	-5	0

Sunday 5th October

Downham Sunday Football League, Division Two
Poachers Arms v J G Tanner and Sons
Tenacre Recreation Ground – Kick-off 10.30

THE POACHERS ARMS

1 George Crosswell

2 Steve Tippling   4 Derek Smith   5 Brian Smith   3 Billy Millmore (Capt)

8 Matt Cornwell   6 Vivian Clutterbuck   10 Wayne Tocket

7 Gordon Gaye   9 Danny Tomlinson   11 Gunner Farr

Substitutes
12 Paddy Oakley
13 Percy Woodman
14 Paul Cornwell

Reserves (Please bring boots)
Dave Statham

Manager
Dave Statham

All players, substitutes and reserves to turn up at 09.45

Paul Cornwell rolled his legs out of bed and sat for a moment staring at the carpet. Sunday morning: home to Tanner's at the rec. He was substitute today so would need to change into the number 14 kit and may even have to play. Unlikely but possible. Percy Woodman and Razor Raisin had both cried off during the week, Percy with a twisted knee and Razor had to go to a christening. That meant that young Danny Tomlinson and Little Smithy had been brought in so he had been "promoted" to substitute. Better make sure that he had clean underpants on this morning.

Paul quickly dressed and made his way downstairs and outside. A fine rain was falling and he took a deep breath, enjoying the fresh, cool air before entering the garage and grabbing the large netting bag containing five footballs. He put the bag of balls into the boot of his car alongside boots and walked back into the house. He climbed the stairs once more and rapped loudly on the bedroom door next to his own.

'Shift your lazy ass, sunshine,' he bellowed. 'Tanner's at home 'smorning and I want a bit of effort off you this week. And watch that bloody temper of yours.'

He was very proud of his son Matthew. If it wasn't for his temper, he could have been playing for a better team than the Poachers, but when the red mist took over, he was uncontrollable. So far this season he had been OK with no outbursts of swearing at the referee, no wild, groin-high tackles, no punches, headbutts or kicks at opponents. But it was like watching a volcano smoking gently where explosion is just below the surface and could blow at any time.

Paul drove his car through the estate and parked outside the row of shops before going into Muzzy's. He bought two newspapers, a large bar of Cadbury's Dairy Milk, forty Silk Cut and a tube of wine gums. As he left Muzzy's, he looked carefully up and down the street, then moved quickly along the row of shops before turning right between the Poachers and the chip shop, making his way into the front of the two-storey block of flats behind the shops. He went through the front entrance and climbed the stairs to flat twelve, took out his keys and let himself in.

'Morning, Lin,' he said, and sat down at the kitchen table opposite the attractive brunette sipping tea.

'Morning, Paul love,' Linda responded, grinding her cigarette out into the ash tray. 'I'll get your tea and toast.'

'Thanks, Lin. I've got your paper and chocolate and some wine gums for Andrew,' said Paul, laying out his purchases carefully on the table. 'You all right? You look a bit tired.'

'Course I'm OK, love.' Linda placed two pieces of bread in the toaster and filled the kettle. 'I just didn't sleep too well last night, that's all.'

'Not worried about anything, are you?' asked Paul as he took a twenty pound note out of his wallet and pushed it across the table towards her.

'Thanks, Paul,' she said, taking the note and putting it in a jug on the kitchen worktop. 'No worries at all, just not sleeping. Probably women's troubles.'

Paul liked to watch her busying herself in the tidy little kitchen. He knew what people on the estate said about their relationship, but it was none of their business. It was none of their business that he saw her regularly, any more than it was none of their business that they had never once had sex in the years that he had been visiting. He knew that everyone thought that Andrew was his son and sniggered about him behind his back. But it was none of their business.

His mind wandered back to how this had all started. A Saturday night many years ago. He was in the Poachers with his best mate John Grant. They had had a few and had planned an early night before a big cup game the next day but, as more pints were sunk, John became louder and wanted to go into town 'on the pull'. Paul had refused to drive and, finally, John had lost patience and stormed out of the Poachers.

'Bollocks to you then, Paulo, I'll fucking go on my own,' were the last words Paul had heard him say, and probably the last words that he had ever said. The lads found out about the crash the next morning in the changing rooms. Barry was on duty that night and was called to the scene, but he didn't recognize John's car or John, as the body was cut from the wreckage after ploughing through a traffic island and into the solid concrete pillars supporting the cemetery gates.

Barry had announced the news to the team as they were changing ready for the Sunday League Cup quarter-final. One of the players had said, 'If you're gonna go, that's the most convenient place, the cemetery,' but no one laughed. The players just got dressed and went home without playing; most of them didn't even go to the pub that day. The Downham Sunday League Management Committee fined the Poachers Arms twenty pounds and made them forfeit the game. Heartless bastards.

Paul told Linda. He drove straight to her parents' house and told her about it at the front door. They both cried and held each other tightly, and he was ashamed that it had given him an erection. It was a couple of months later that she had told him she was pregnant with John's baby and he promised that he would look after her and the baby. He'd been true to his word. He'd taken Linda to the maternity hospital on the cold and rainy night in February and had stayed there until the baby was born at five in the morning. He'd sat in the waiting room and heard the screams as Linda strained and pushed to produce John's baby. He had been present as the doctor was called and came running to the delivery room, his white coat unbuttoned and stethoscope flying behind him. He had heard the comments about a difficult birth and recognised a degree of panic, and then relief on the faces of the midwife as the baby cried loudly seconds after birth. After the hospital staff and Linda herself, he had been the first to see baby Andrew and remembered thinking that he looked like the Mekon from Dan Dare comics, his head swollen out of proportion to his tiny wrinkled body. After the nurses and Linda, he had also been the first to hold the baby, a week later when Andrew was released from the special baby unit. He had discussed names with Linda before settling on Andrew, simply because they both liked the name. He had taken mother and baby home from the hospital to her parents' house on the estate and wiped tears from his eyes as he left her.

He had bought baby clothes and a cot, and decorated the council flat when she moved in, papering the room with woodchip and painting it a gentle, pale blue. But they'd never let the relationship go further than friends. There were times when he wanted to – after all he was a normal red-blooded bloke – and there were times when he thought that she may have wanted to, but she was John's girl and it was John's baby and it would be improper to do anything other than make sure that she was alright.

'Good morning, Paul. How are you this morning? I believe it's raining.' Lightning's voice made Paul start. Lightning carried a dirty cup and plate from his bedroom and placed them in the sink.

'Hello, Andy mate,' said Paul. 'What's this then? Breakfast in bed?'

A big grin spread over Lightning's squashed face. 'Mum says a working man deserves a little treat now and again. Ah well, best be off. Them changing rooms won't open themselves you know.'

Lightning took his flat cap and anorak off a hook in the hallway and put them on before presenting himself to Linda for inspection. She looked him up and down. 'You'll do, Andrew. Be careful.' She smiled and stood on tiptoe to kiss him on the cheek.

'I'll do. See you later,' he said and left to collect his bicycle before riding to the rec.

'I can always give him a lift, Lin,' Paul said as the front door banged shut.

'I know you would, love, but he's got to do things on his own. And besides, what about our half-hour alone before you go off playing your silly games?'

'*Our* half-hour.' Paul liked that. It made him feel special. He had always felt special when he was with Linda, as if they really belonged together. He wondered what might have been if he had only had the nerve to tell her how he felt twenty years ago, before he had met Christine, made her pregnant and drifted into marriage. He couldn't even remember proposing; the wedding just sort of happened, arranged by Christine and her mum. He had just turned up, said 'I do,' and that was that.

'Talk about me, you seem to be in another world this morning,' Linda interrupted his daydream.

'Just thinking about this morning's football. Tough game. Tanner's. Not a bad side.'

'Typical man,' said Linda, lighting up another cigarette. 'Brains only ever tuned into two things and the second one's football.'

'Oh yes, and what's the first thing?' Paul asked.

'Beer, knowing you lot,' she laughed.

They talked about the weather, about Lightning, about football, about the latest news, about last night's television. They never mentioned Christine or John.

'Better get off. Make sure Dave's OK with everything,' said Paul as he eased himself out of the chair. Linda followed him and they stood at the door, Paul feeling awkward as usual. Twice a week for twenty years, they had met and yet they still didn't really feel at ease when it came to saying goodbye. Linda grabbed his hand and stretched up to kiss him on the cheek. It was similar to the way that she had kissed Lightning earlier and yet she seemed to linger and look into his eyes. It was a brief glance, but was directly into his eyes and he couldn't remember her doing this before. It made his heart beat a little faster and he wanted to hold her closely to him and kiss her deeply and passionately.

'I'm off then,' was all he could manage.

He considered whether to take his own car to the football today. Sometimes he would go and wait by Dave's car to get a lift, listening to daft jokes from Viv as they waited, but sometimes he enjoyed being on his own, listening to his Tony Christie CD and singing along to "Avenues and Alleyways" and "I did what I did for Maria". Today was a Tony Christie day.

Dave glanced across to the window where he used to watch Mrs Barnes undress and imagined her large bosom as she stretched in front of the window. He felt a slight stirring but smiled. No need for onanism now, I've got a girlfriend. Me, David James Statham, courting a beautiful young lady. On the previous Friday evening he had waited for her in the Poachers at closing time and walked her to the house she shared with two other girls, a twenty-minute walk away on the edge of the estate. They had walked in silence for most of the way, Dave wondering whether he should hold her hand or just walk alongside her. He decided that just walking was the best option. If he had tried to hold her hand, she may have pulled away and that would ruin his well laid, and not too honourable, plans for the future.

They had made small talk about the evening. The pub was busy tonight; Viv was on good form with his bad jokes; Billy never bought a round again; Tonker spent most of the time outside smoking his roll-ups. After six pints, Dave felt at ease and was pleased that he didn't need to try hard to impress her. Mandy just thought that Dave was sweet, although it would have been nice if he had held her hand.

When they reached her front door, they chatted for a few minutes and Dave's confidence grew. He had never found it easy to talk to girls, but with Mandy it was different and he just seemed to be able to talk to her like, well, like a bloke. Except that she most definitely wasn't a bloke. She was sweet and beautiful and kind and pink and fluffy... Dave ran out of adjectives in his mind, wondering if he'd crossed the line from girls to kittens with "fluffy".

'Are we still on for tomorrow, then?' he asked.

Mandy gripped his elbow as they stood and faced each other. 'Of course, Dave. What do you want to do? Only there's a film I want to see at the multiplex. Eight o'clock. It's got Hugh Grant in it so it'll be a bit soppy, I expect.'

'Great. We'll do that then. I quite like Hugh Grant. Well, not him really, not like I like Hugh Grant, but his films are usually pretty good.' *That's good. Off to the pictures with no embarrassing silences, not knowing what to say. In the dark, bound to be all couples on a Saturday night, romantic comedy film. What a result. Even worth putting up with watching smug Hugh Grant.*

'Right, see you tomorrow, half past seven,' he added, starting to turn away, then realised that Mandy was still standing there facing him and looking at his mouth. Dave took a deep breath, leaned forward and pecked her quickly on the cheek, before turning and trotting down her garden path and back up the road towards his home, waving as he went but without turning round. What a nice gentle bloke he was. But Mandy would have welcomed a little more love and affection.

Saturday had not quite gone to plan for Dave. It was as he had anticipated except for the finale, when he imagined himself slipping naked between smooth silk sheets and making passionate love to Mandy. He had picked her up at seven thirty, on the dot, before driving to the multiplex. The film was dire, with bloody Hugh Grant stuttering his way through, hair flopping about like a tart and as wet as a Bank Holiday weekend. But Mandy had seemed to really enjoy it and had even held Dave's hand. After the film, she had suggested that they stop off for a drink and, because he was driving, Dave said what about the Poachers' lounge bar and Mandy said that would be just lovely. They only had time for a couple of drinks before last orders were called, and Dave walked her back to her house. During the time in the pub and during the stroll home, they chatted more: about the film, about working for Muzzy, about working at the pub and how she was looking for a "proper" job. She told Dave that she was thirty-five years old, that her surname was Church, like the boozy Welsh singer, and how she lived on the estate years ago but left to live in Bristol when she was eighteen, then missed her home in Downham and decided to come back. Her parents were both dead and she liked travel, evenings out, meeting people and reading; just like a Miss World entrant, they laughed. Except that, to Dave, she was more beautiful than any Miss World could ever be. When they reached the front door, they chatted for a few more minutes. Dave seemed a little lost as to what to do next.

'Why don't you come in for coffee, Dave?' she asked, with what Dave imagined to be a knowing smile, except that he wasn't sure what a knowing smile was. Dave meant to look at her in a Hugh Grant way from under his fringe, except that his hair was cut very short and he had no fringe, then say, 'Why, thanks, Mandy. That's jolly kind of you. I'd love to.' But what came out was 'Um, I'd better get off. Not keen on coffee. See you in the pub tomorrow,' before turning tail and jogging off home. And this time he hadn't even had a goodnight kiss. He heard the front door slam as he trotted up the road.

Paul was first at the rec and considered parking in Dave's favourite spot just to annoy him, but decided that he would save that for the last home game when everyone would be playing silly jokes on everyone else. He parked next to Dave's spot, grabbed his bag of footballs from the boot and wandered into the changing rooms before seeing Lightning standing to attention, ready to begin his weekly task of dishing out changing room keys in exchange for a signature. 'Morning again, Andrew,' he said, 'Number three again, is it?'

Lightning looked down at his allocation sheet, looked back up to Paul and seemed surprised that Paul knew what number changing room had been allocated to the Poachers Arms. The fact that they had used changing room number three for the previous two games and teams generally kept the same number for the season, where possible, had escaped him. 'Have you looked, Mr. Cornwell?' he asked, fixing Paul with an inquisitive look, which reminded Paul of a parrot, even to his hair which always managed to stand up like a cockatiel's crown no matter how often it was flattened.

'Of course I looked, Andrew. How else would I know?' Dave gave him a light, playful punch on the shoulder and Lightning nodded and said, 'Thought as much.'

Paul was sitting quietly in changing room number three, smoking his third cigarette that morning when Billy arrived with the kit and dumped the bag in the middle of the floor. They acknowledged each other with a simple nod and no words were spoken. Paul didn't like Billy much even though they had played in the same football team for around twenty years. He had been brought up where paying your round was a way of life, a matter of honour, and he didn't like the way Billy never paid his way. Billy considered Paul a miserable fart who was only good for providing a source of gossip about his supposed mistress and half-witted son.

Dave arrived, smiling broadly, and was followed closely by Viv who waited until they were both in the changing room before asking loudly, 'So how many times with Mandy last night then, Dave? What was it like then, Dave, nice tits or what?' as he winked at the other two behind Dave's back. Dave just smiled and shrugged, stating, 'No comment, gentlemen. If you want to know more, you'll have to see my press secretary.'

The changing room was soon heaving with naked and half-naked bodies, the atmosphere thick with stale body odours and cigarette smoke and everyone babbling away as usual.

Dave clapped his hands. 'Right lads, listen. This is important. Tanner's got stuffed last week and will be on the rebound this week. They're not a bad side despite last week, so we must work this morning. We haven't got Razor up front and Percy at the back, so Gordon and Gunner, I'll need more from you, and Big Smithy, keep an eye on your brother at the back there and...' Dave's speech trailed off with an uninspired 'firm but fair' as it was obvious no one was listening and half the team were already on their way out of the changing room and heading for pitch three.

As Dave and Paul strolled across the pitch, Barry shouted at them from the touchline, 'See who's ref, lads. Bloody Poppy.'

Both men groaned on seeing Billy shaking hands with Mr Poplar in the centre circle. Poppy was probably the best referee in the Sunday League and also handled semi-professional games on Saturdays. He was in his early twenties and had been refereeing since boyhood and was desperately ambitious, tough, and a stickler for getting things right. There would certainly be no favours from Poppy, but at least it would be the same for both sides.

Poachers kicked off and were playing some good football with Gordon Gaye tearing the Tanner's defence apart with his long, speedy runs down the right wing. His accurate crosses were not telling, however, without the rangy Razor Raisin to get on the end of them and, for all his efforts, young Danny Tomlinson up front was no great header of the ball. If he reached any crosses at all, the ball would fly off his head at any angle, usually flying harmlessly over the crossbar or towards the corner flag.

'Head like a fucking thruppenny bit,' grumbled Paul as he sprinted up and down the touchline with his orange flag signifying goal kick after goal kick.

The Poachers' defence was largely untroubled with the Smith boys strong in the middle and clearing the rare Tanner's attacks with relative ease. The only potential problem was Steve Tippling who was venturing further and further upfield in search of some excitement and had already been pulled up for two inelegant tackles. With just a few minutes until half-time the ball was deflected into no-man's-land just inside the Tanner's half. The Tanner's left half and Steve were heading towards the loose ball at full speed. Everyone connected with the Poachers' team knew what was coming as Steve's face took on the look of a snarling animal and he launched himself towards the Tanner's player with studs bared, two feet off the ground and in only the vague direction of the ball. There was a tremendous thud and crack as the two bodies collided and the ball bounced up and ran gently out of play. Both players lay together in a tangle of arms and legs as everyone stood for a brief moment and stared in disbelief until a cry of 'You dirty little bastard!' came from somewhere in the Tanner's team, and players ran towards the two combatants who, by this time, had started exchanging punches as they lay on the ground. The Poachers' players naturally ran to defend their full back with Matt Cornwell first on the scene flailing punches and kicks at anyone within flailing or kicking distance. Within seconds, a melee had started with players pushing and shoving each other, punches being thrown, some players holding others back from taking more violent retaliation, whilst Steve stood there, six inches lower than most of the other players, fists raised offering to take on all comers. Meanwhile, Poppy stood firmly at the edge of the chaos blowing his whistle loudly and trying to regain some kind of control without becoming too involved in the conflict.

When the fracas finally died down, Poppy stood straight-backed in the centre circle with his notebook and pencil in his hand and called the players to him one by one. The first was Steve, by this time sporting a split lip from a thump received at some time during the fray, with a thin trickle of blood dripping down from his mouth and onto his chin.

Dave, Paul and the team stood in a huddle watching Poppy and Steve standing face to face as Poppy wrote in his notebook before pulling the red card from his pocket and holding it in the air until Steve had slouched off the field of play. Next to be called was Matt who was still glaring menacingly at the Tanner's players whilst the referee recorded his name and again raised the red card. Surprisingly, Poppy opted not to dismiss or even caution any more players, probably because, had he done so, it would have ended up as a five-a-side game, but he immediately blew for half-time. The players walked briskly to the halfway line, some nursing bruises but all babbling excitedly about who they had managed to thump on the referee's blind side. Steve sat down dabbing at his rapidly swelling lip and pleading innocence. 'Wubble my faw,' he said. 'I wem fwu th'baw,' whilst Matt was all for crossing the pitch and carrying on the scrap where he had left off.

Dave poured the teas and walked out to the centre circle with a cup for the referee.

'Thanks, manager,' said Poppy, taking the cup. 'Silly lad, that number 2. I had no choice. He had to go. And the number 4, like a wild animal.'

'I must agree, Mr Poplar,' Dave replied. 'You could have sent more off, if you'd have wanted.'

Poppy nodded sagely. 'The rest was just handbags, something of nothing, but that tackle was dangerous and the other fellow is just mad. It may be worth your while having a word with the lads or they're always going to be in trouble. You might even think about suspending the lads for a game or two – let them think about their actions.' The fact that "the lads" were much the same age as Poppy seemed strange to Dave, but he promised to have a word and consider not playing Steve and Matt for a week as advised and hoped that the referee's report may show some leniency.

The second half began with Poachers under pressure. With nine men, they struggled to find any rhythm and the Tanner's team, infuriated by the tackle and the subsequent skirmish, had been buoyed by the sendings-off. After several spectacular saves, leaping to push the ball over the bar and round the post, the goal came from a rare error from goalkeeper George Crosswell. He came out for an inswinging corner and mis-timed his punch, the ball dropping tamely at the feet of a Tanner's forward who took great delight in banging the ball into an unguarded net. Almost immediately, it was two–nil as the home team pushed forward leaving the Smith brothers exposed at the back and, despite a valiant effort from a diving George, a second goal was gleefully taken by the Tanner's forwards. The Poachers' team rallied and put a little pressure on the Tanner's defence but the game was settled by a speculative lob which dipped inches under the crossbar for the third goal.

Dave ambled back to the dressing room alongside Poppy, following his dejected team who trudged off slowly in strict contrast to the jubilant Tanner's players who ran and skipped joyfully to the changing rooms; except for the left half who wouldn't be skipping for a few weeks after Steve's tackle.

'Any chance of not reporting the sendings-off, Mr Poplar?' Dave asked without much optimism.

Poppy shook his head slowly, and then paused for dramatic effect. 'Can't be done, manager. My job boils down to two responsibilities. One: to enforce the laws of association football. Two: to protect the players. I would be failing in my duty if I didn't report the facts fully and honestly. Honesty is the byword for referees. Honesty and integrity.' Dave knew that he was right.

The changing room was quiet and subdued. Viv was telling an old joke about an undertaker's apprentice and a prawn, but even this generated no more than a smile from the gloomy team as they sat around the room resting elbows on knees and staring at the floor. This was the time that a manager showed his mettle, when his men were down, and it was his role to boost them, give them back pride and spirit and the will to put the setback behind them and move forward to greater things.

'Lads,' Dave began, 'the first round's on me.'

Everyone looked up, smiled happily and started chatting. A free pint from Dave. Not such a bad morning after all. Billy was exceptionally happy as he figured that he could get two or three free pints if no one was counting.

Dave collected the subs and entered the amounts in his notebook before making his way to the referees' changing room. He found Poppy and handed over the twenty pounds fee.

'And two pounds fifty expenses, manager, please. That's ten miles at twenty five pence a mile.'

'Fuck me, Poppy, you only live round the corner,' Dave blurted out, his previous respectful approach destroyed.

'True, my friend,' Poppy replied. 'But I go to see my sister on Sundays for breakfast and she lives on the Marshfield estate, five miles away. And petrol's not cheap nowadays.'

What about honesty and integrity? Dave handed over the extra cash, then realised something else. 'Poppy, you've only got a fucking moped.' Mr Poplar took the money and winked.

Although the team had suffered its first defeat of the season, the atmosphere in the pub was, if not exactly jubilant, extremely relaxed and carefree. The players were comparing bruises and boasting of their prowess in the maul and exaggerating a little more with each telling until it seemed that every player had taken on the whole of the Tanner's team single-handed and given them a thrashing. Paul was giving Matt a dressing down for getting involved when it was none of his business in the first place. Matt was pleading his case. 'But Steve's my best mate, Dad. What could I do? Can't let your best mate down, can you?' Paul knew what he meant and dropped the reprimand.

As Dave went to the bar he saw Mandy. His chest immediately began thumping and the sound of the busy pub was blocked out by the hammering in his head as he gazed at her beautiful face, her lovely hair, her...

'Yes, Dave, what can I get you?' Mandy asked, somewhat brusquely, but then, she was very busy.

'Pint of bitter please, Mandy,' Dave said, putting on his best Hugh Grant look and voice, although he had to admit that it came out sounding more like Russell Grant. Mandy poured the pint and said, 'Forty pounds, please.' Dave must have looked as shocked as he felt. 'Fifteen pints at two pounds fifty a pint, that's thirty seven pounds fifty, plus yours, is forty pounds exactly, please.' Dave remembered the offer to buy the team their first pint but, even then, fifteen pints? There were only eleven in the team. Then he saw Billy with one glass half full in one hand and a full pint in the other. He'd probably ordered the four extra. Dave moved his way through the crowd and sat next to Tonker.

'Three nil, aye, David. And a punch up. Me and Tommy was watching from behind the goal. Really enjoyed it, especially Paul's youngster getting stuck in. Reminded us of when we played, didn't it, Tommy?'

Tommy looked up from working out his cribbage hand. 'Certainly fuckin' did, Tonker. And I've got twenty fuckin' four so you owe me a fuckin' quid. And it's your fuckin' round.'

As the pub cleared out, the usual three drinkers, Dave, Paul and Barry, remained, comfortably seated around one table in the old men's corner. They were joined by Viv who had been staying later over the last couple of months. Luckily, Billy had to rush to take his wife to her mother's so they were spared an extra mouth to feed, as Viv put it. Dave finished his pint and said, 'My round again, I suppose. Same again?' and walked up to the bar without waiting for an answer.

Mandy looked at him but didn't smile. 'Yes, Dave. What can I get you?'

'Four pints, Mandy, please. Is there something, you know, not right, sort of wrong? You don't seem your usual self.'

Mandy looked at him as if he was a simpleton. 'David, last night, we went out for a pleasant night out, saw a smashing film, had a nice drink. You took me home and dumped me on the doorstep like an old milk bottle. No I am not alright. That's another ten pounds, please.'

Dave paid the money and carried two pints across and placed them on the table, returning to collect the remaining beer. Mandy ignored him and continued chatting to one of the bar flies who was obviously smitten with her.

Dave sat down and took a deep draught of ale. 'Look, lads,' he blurted out. 'I'm glad that you're all here because I need some advice. It's about Mandy. Well, you know that we had a date last night and I sort of fucked up at the end and didn't quite know how to go about, you know, saying goodnight, and now don't quite know what to do about it. I mean, you know I'm not too good with women, but you, Paul, I mean, you've got, you know, your friend on Fridays and Sundays.' Paul said nothing. It was none of their business. 'And, Barry, I mean, you've been married twice and got the blonde in the sports car, and Viv, you are a sort of legend in the sex stakes, so I was wondering if you could, sort of, advise me how to go about it.'

'You, my friend, have come to the right place,' said Viv thoughtfully. 'Now, to make up for buggering up last night, you need to give her a little present. But be careful, as it's easy to offend. So just a small gift, like a simple necklace made of pearls, perhaps. But check first that it's an acceptable gift, so go up to her and say, "Mandy, I would like to give you a pearl necklace, is that OK?" and see her reaction.'

'Me, David, I would try a different tack,' added Barry. 'Perhaps she's a sports fan and would appreciate a day out in the Smoke taking in a good football match, but again, check first. Ask her if you can take her up the Arsenal next Saturday and watch her reaction.'

Paul looked a little more pensive. 'Too complicated for me. Just offer to buy her a drink. Probably a short of some kind. Just say you want to give her a nice stiff one.'

Dave was thinking about the advice and appreciated their help when he realised that all three of his comrades were sniggering and trying to suppress breaking out into full-blooded guffaws.

'Pearl necklace, up the Arsenal, stiff one. You rotten fucking bastards!' said Dave and stormed out of the pub in anger. Then he came back to finish his pint and join in the laughter.

Six

Downham Sunday Football League, Division Two
Results for Sunday 5th October

New Inn, Gorton Down	2	1	AFC Cummiston
Hearty Oak, Downlea	4	4	Shellduck Inn
Lower End WMC	0	5	Jones Juniors FC
Pickled Herring	4	2	Downham Churches
Poachers Arms	**0**	**3**	**J G Tanner and Sons**

League Table

Team	Pl'd	Won	Drew	Lost	For	Ag'st	GD	Points
Jones Juniors FC	5	5	0	0	24	6	18	15
New Inn, Gorton D	5	3	1	1	17	10	7	10
Poachers Arms	**5**	**3**	**1**	**1**	**12**	**8**	**4**	**10**
Pickled Herring	4	3	1	0	10	6	4	10
AFC Cummiston	5	1	3	1	6	10	-4	6
J G Tanner and Sons	4	2	0	2	9	11	-2	6
Hearty Oak, Downlea	5	1	2	2	15	20	-5	5
Shellduck Inn	5	1	1	3	9	13	-4	4
Downham Churches	5	0	1	4	14	22	-8	1
Lower End WMC	3	0	0	3	0	10	-10	0

Sunday 12th October 2007

Downham Sunday Football League, Knockout Cup, Preliminary Round
The Boar's Head v Poachers Arms
Tenacre Recreation Ground – Kick-off 10.30

THE POACHERS ARMS

1 Gunner Farr

2 Percy Woodman   4 Derek Smith   5 Brian Smith   3 Billy Millmore (Capt)

8 Wayne Tocket   6 Vivian Clutterbuck   10 Danny Tomlinson

7 Gordon Gaye   9 Daniel Raisin   11 Paddy Oakley

Substitutes
12 Matt Cornwell
13 Steve Tippling
14 Paul Cornwell

Reserves (Please bring boots)
Dave Statham
Barry Plumb

Manager
Dave Statham

All players, substitutes and reserves to turn up at 09.45

O8.20 The bright numbers glared through the early morning gloom, giving Dave's bedroom an eerie green glow. He stared at the clock for several minutes, watching it click silently over, minute by minute. 8.21, 8.22, 8.23. *Why bloody wait, it's only a cup game and we'll get hammered anyway, so why bloody wait? What a bloody week. Miserable bloody weather, a bloody cup game against the bloody Division One leaders and no bloody girlfriend. Bloody short romance that was.*

Throughout the week Dave had been going over and over in his mind what had gone wrong. Up until the coffee incident, it was all going so well. They had chatted like old friends and Mandy was open about her life, telling him more than he had ever known about any other woman. And he wasn't embarrassed talking to her. He didn't say anything stupid or boastful and he didn't stutter or blush. They held hands in the pictures, she linked arms on the way back to the car, and they held hands again when he walked her home. They had sat quietly having a drink in the lounge bar of the Poachers, and Dave didn't even like the lounge bar. It was all going perfectly until the coffee incident. She had asked him in for coffee and all he'd done was explain that he didn't like coffee and went home. What on earth was wrong with that? And now Mandy barely spoke to him. Even in the pub last night when she was working, she was polite enough, but treated him just like any other customer.

Of course, he knew that the invitation to coffee was not really an invitation to coffee. Mandy was probably inviting him in for more than coffee. What he should have done was to have accepted the invitation and, having finished the coffee, sat with her on the settee, put his arm around her shoulders and said, 'Mandy, I've never felt like this about anyone ever before. I know that we've only been out together twice, but I really feel that there is something special between us.' He should then have leant over and given her a long, lingering kiss, gently exploring the inside of her mouth with his tongue, then moved his hand over her plump, firm breasts, removing her blouse and bra, feeling her firm nipples, aroused and responding to his tender caress, then she would carefully have unzipped his trousers and taken his erect, hardened penis in her hand…

8.35. *That didn't take long. Only five minutes behind schedule.*

Tonker was already sitting waiting for his breakfast to be delivered when Dave finally raced down the stairs two at a time and took his seat at the dining table. His mum carried two big plates over from the hob: sausage, bacon, beans and fried egg neatly arranged on each plate. Dave's mum's face glowed pink and she offered a huge grin as she stood, chubby hands on chubby hips, and watched her men tuck into the repast. She poured herself a cup of tea and sat down at the table. She took a sip from her scalding beverage and said, 'You were in early last night, David. Didn't see that girl, thingummy, then?'

How did she know about him and Mandy? But then, the whole estate probably knew about him and Mandy. 'No, Mum,' replied Dave. 'We're just friends, just went to the pictures together the other week. Just wanted to see the same film, that's all.'

'That's right,' added Tonker. 'Always been keen on that Hugh Grant, haven't you?'

'Now now, Eric,' said Dave's mum. She looked at her son, leant a little nearer and patted his hand. 'Now don't take this the wrong way, love,' she said, 'but she's not for you. She's not really from the sort of family you want to be associated with, is she, Eric? I mean, she's probably quite a nice girl and it's probably not her fault, but she wasn't brought up very well, was she, Eric?'

Dave had never heard his mother say so much. She rarely spoke more than a couple of words at a time and here she was, launching into full sentences about something she could know nothing about.

'It's the genes, David. Her mother wasn't the sort of person that we would want to mix with, not our sort at all. When she lived opposite, she had a bit of a thing for your father – mind you, he wasn't bad looking in those days and didn't cough and splutter all day – but she, how can I put this, showed herself off to your Dad, didn't she, Eric?' Tonker continued to eat with his head down and, if Dave didn't know better, he would have thought that his father was blushing.

'Whenever he was in the bedroom, she'd, well, expose her you-know-whats to your Dad from across the road. That's why, when I found out you were seeing her daughter, I said to your Dad, I said, that Barnes girl, she's not right for our

David.' Dave's mum patted his hand again and returned to the sink, splashing around with hot water and pots and pans.

Dave had stopped eating and was sitting there trying to take in what he had just heard. Mrs Barnes had been exposing herself to his dad from over the road. Mandy was Mrs. Barnes's daughter. But her name wasn't Barnes, it was Church, which meant that she must have changed her name. Or have been married.

Dave's mum turned her head towards the table. 'That's why we had to move to the back bedroom, you know, David, and give you the front bedroom. Because of that Mandy's mother. Kept showing your Dad her you-know-whats.'

Tonker kept his head down, refusing to look up at either his wife or son until he had finished his breakfast. He got up and said, 'I'm going for a walk up the garden,' and disappeared in a haze of blue tobacco smoke.

Dave tried to gather his scrambled thoughts. Mandy, the woman he loved and adored and desired with every part of his body, was the married daughter of Mrs Barnes, the woman he had loved and adored and desired for the last twenty-five years, though only with his penis in the latter case. For just a second, he considered the masturbation possibilities of the mother and daughter combination, but quickly dispelled that idea from his mind, although he did think that he may go back to it later if necessary. He was aware that his mum was still talking. 'Of course, there was talk that your Dad and her were more than just acquaintances. They said that your Dad and her were having an affair, but I know your Dad. He was too bone idle to make the effort so I knew that it wasn't true. It was just her, you see. Fancied my Eric for some reason and tried to entice him with her bosom. And a very big bosom it was too.' Dave was aware that his mum wasn't actually talking to him but just rambling, to no one in particular. He had heard her do this before. When she was preparing a meal or doing her housework, she would often hold a conversation with herself, but she had never mentioned Mrs. Barnes before.

'And her daughter. Pretty little thing she was. That'd be that young Mandy. Then they up and left and went to live in Bristol. Why Bristol, for goodness sake? Big, dirty city, Bristol. Anyway, they do say she had another man and moved in with him in Bristol. That Mandy would have been what, about seventeen or so then, I suppose. Never seen hide nor hair of them since, not 'til that Mandy turns up a month or two back and starts work in the paper shop. Well, it was the flat above the paper shop where her mother used to show my Eric her you-know-whats.'

Dave looked at his watch, then his breakfast. 9.40. Ten minutes behind schedule. He grabbed the remaining sausage and held it in his mouth as he hurried upstairs, picked up his sports bag and ran back down the stairs and out of the house, not even bothering to close the front door. Viv and Paul were leaning on his car on the drive, patiently waiting in the grey morning mist. He suddenly remembered the teamsheet, dropped his bag and returned to the house, sprinted up the stairs and back down with the sheets of paper in his hand. His two compatriots were coolly leaning, arms folded, watching him rushing in and out, a half eaten sausage in his mouth.

'D'you want a light for that, Boss?' asked Viv as Dave searched his tracksuit for his car keys.

'Fuck it,' he shouted loudly and dashed back into the house, reappearing seconds later with his keys. He reversed hurriedly off the drive and, as he pulled away, he could not resist glancing up towards Mrs. Barnes' window.

Lightning was scrutinising his allocation sheet as the three arrived. 'Morning, Mr Statham,' he said, standing to attention and again just missing cracking his head on the roof of his office.

'Morning, Lightning,' replied Dave and Viv, whilst Paul nodded and just said, 'Andrew.'

'You are in changing room number two today, this morning, and your key has been collected by a man called Mary Hinge,' Lightning announced in his best official tone.

The lads carried their kit into changing room number two and saw Billy hanging the last of the shirts on its hook. Dave was irritated: that was his job and he enjoyed arranging the kit, but he inspected what Billy had done and everything looked shipshape.

'Do you get it? Mary Hinge.' Billy was laughing to himself. 'That Lightning doesn't see it, does he? Thick or what?' Paul started to move towards Billy with his fist clenched until Dave caught his elbow and held him back.

'Funny team today, Dave,' Viv said, tactfully changing the subject. 'But I suppose we'll get stuffed anyway.'

'I dropped Matt and Steve after last week, hoping that it might help when their case comes up at the FA meeting next week, and George is away on another jolly with his company, so I didn't have much choice really. And like you say, we're going to get stuffed anyway.'

The Boar's Head had been one of the strongest Sunday League teams for many years. Based from the pub on the Oakhill council estate across the rec from the Poachers' estate, and always known as "The Pig", they had the pick of the best local amateur footballers. They were all but guaranteed medals at the end of the season and were also paid to play, unlike the Poachers' team who had to fork out three pounds each game. The Boar's Head was frequented by local builders, tilers and car dealers, who didn't mind putting a few pounds into the football club coffers, and the brewery provided a reasonable donation each season, aware that trade at the pub was boosted by the football team's success.

Dave tried to blank visions of Mandy and Mrs. Barnes from his mind and clapped his hands in an attempt to get the players' attention. 'Right, lads,' he began, 'today won't be easy—'

'Too fucking right, we'll get stuffed,' interrupted Viv.

Dave gave him a disdainful look and continued, 'But we can still play for pride. This is our Cup Final, our Dunkirk…'

Barry burst breathlessly through the door. 'Just been talking to some of the Pig's supporters. Seems they haven't got a team this morning. Well, not a full team anyway.' He paused for breath, gasping as his reddened face looked like it was about to explode. 'They've only got nine players. Seems that five of their best lads were playing away in the Hellenic league yesterday at Newbury somewhere and the coach had a prang on the M4 coming back. They've all been kept in hospital for observation.'

'That's really good news. Hope it's nothing trivial,' said Billy, and the team left the changing room in better spirits than any of Dave's team talks could ever hope to achieve. Dave followed his upbeat team out of the changing rooms and was accompanied on his trek to pitch number two by Barry and Spadger Aitkin, the long time manager of the Pig and the husband of Paul's sister Donna.

After nodded greetings, Dave opened the conversation. 'Sorry to hear about your lads in hospital, Spadge. Not too serious, I hope.'

Spadger laughed. 'Serious be fucked. It's an insurance scam from their Saturday team. Their players are insured for travel to and from the game as well as the game itself. Apparently, the club gets paid a stack of money for every night a player has to spend in an NHS hospital 'cause it saves paying out for private. So their manager insists that the hospital keeps them in overnight for observation. He doesn't give a flying fuck about our team on a Sunday, the lads are in hospital having a laugh, and the insurance coughs up. Everyone's a winner.'

'Except you,' said Dave. 'What with not having a full team and all.'

Spadger laughed again. 'We'll have a team all right, Dave. I've got thirty players signed on, remember, and some of them are more than happy just to play now and again, 'specially in the Cup. They play half a dozen matches and get another medal to add to their collection. I just rang round a few. Good players too. All part-time pros or ex-pros. Good players. One of them just spent four seasons playing for Swindon Town, but the others are pretty good though.' Spadger laughed again and Dave groaned as they both imagined the one-sided match to come.

'National Health Service. Don't talk to me about the National Health Service,' Barry's deep voice boomed. 'Worse now than at any time since it was brought in. We were all better off before the war when there wasn't a National bloody Health Service. National Health Disgrace more like. Ruined by successive governments, what can you expect from that lot of middle-class tossers. If I had my way…'

The two managers blocked out the salvo from Barry and took up their positions on opposite sides of the pitch. As the players lined up for kick-off, the Poachers' team were visibly shaken at the line-up opposite. Rather than the scratch team of nine players they had expected, there were eleven fit and athletic young men, with another three or four knocking a ball around on the touchline with consummate ease and skill, and available to be called on at any time. There was not a bald head, a bandaged knee or a pot belly to be seen in the opposition squad. The Poachers' lads looked at Barry, and Viv shouted, 'Barry, you prat, I thought you said that they couldn't raise a team.' Barry ignored the comment and continued his tirade against the NHS to a stranger who was taking a short-cut across the playing field to visit his family. He would never take that short-cut on a Sunday morning again.

Within minutes of the game starting, it was obvious that the best that the Poachers could hope for was to keep the score down to a respectable level as the Pig's players stroked the ball quickly and accurately around the pitch, barely moving out of first gear. The ex-Swindon Town player was on the left-hand side of midfield and the ball seemed to find him, unopposed and in plenty of space, throughout the opening sparring. He controlled the ball easily, found time to look up, choose his pass and knock the ball with unerring accuracy to the selected recipient. The Poachers' midfield were chasing shadows and rarely touching the ball. When they did gain position, usually more through luck than judgement, a Pig player seemed to materialize from nowhere and take the ball from them with little effort. The Smith brothers in the centre of the defence were resolute and strong, although a little desperate in their tackling. The remaining players worked hard, but the Pig players were obviously in a different league; they were, after all, in a different league. The first goal came through a sweet flowing move of quick, first-time passes which ended with the Pig centre forward beating Gunner easily. Three other goals followed in the first forty-five minutes and the Pig players had barely broken sweat, whilst the Poachers' team looked exhausted as they slumped on the ground during the half-time break. Dave looked around at his broken troops and wondered what to say. How do you lift players who can only look forward to another forty-five minutes of humiliation?

Tonker and his mate Tommy had strolled slowly from their usual position behind the goal and addressed the huddle of despondent players. 'When we played in the sixties and seventies, if we was two goals down, our captain used to shout, "Kick anything that moves," and we did. Mind you, we did that if we was two up as well.'

'Didn't fuckin' do no fuckin' good, though, but we felt a lot fuckin' better for it,' added Tommy and the two old boys chuckled.

Barry joined in the conversation. 'It was all right in those days though, because we had a National Health Service to be proud of. Not like today; bloody disgrace.' He turned to address the team. 'Look, lads. It doesn't look good out there, I know, but it could be a lot worse. You could be in hospital like those other poor bastards from the Pig and be catching MRSA or C Dificile or syphilis or something. Those poor sods may not get out of that hospital alive.'

'And we'll have no more cup games this season,' Dave said in as positive an approach as he could muster.

The second half continued as the first half had ended, with the Boar's Head in total control and the ball being easily moved from defence to midfield to attack. The Poachers never gave in and continued to chase and harass and work hard. They even seemed to be enjoying the game. Their spirit and enthusiasm were rewarded with a delightful goal a few minutes from the end of the match when Gordon found space on the right and put over a glorious cross which Razor met with astonishing power, crashing the ball past the goalkeeper and into the net. The fact that they were already seven–nil down at this juncture did not seem important as they celebrated their consolation goal.

The players sprinted for the changing rooms at the final whistle, in a relaxed and happy mood. They had not been humiliated; seven–one against the Boar's Head was not a disgrace and they had scored a magnificent goal themselves. The opposition players had been very magnanimous in victory, thanking the Poachers players for a good game and complimenting them on the goal. And there was the pub and a couple of pints to look forward to.

As Dave was gathering up his bits and pieces from the touchline, Barry came trundling across, again red-faced and excited. 'I just been talking to a couple of blokes who drink in the Pig,' he gasped, struggling for breath. 'They reckon that Swindon Town player may not be kosher. They reckon that he only signed on Thursday and there's no way that that his form could have been registered at the FA by this morning. We could appeal and be awarded the game, what d'you reckon?'

Dave looked at his players trudging across the rec, tired but happy, cracking jokes about how they were just coming into the game when the ref blew for full time or how it was seven lucky breakaways. 'Nah, let it go,' he said.

'I blame the bloody NHS,' said Barry.

The pub was busy as usual when Dave and Paul arrived, Viv accepting an earlier lift from the Big Smithy. Barry had bought them both a pint and signalled to them to join him, squeezed onto the edge of the old men's corner. They were joined by Viv, and the four men sat there enjoying their pints in silence for a minute or two. The general clamour from the pub was an indistinct racket in the background, with the occasional burst of laughter rising above the general din. The juke-box was played very quietly on Sunday lunchtimes to prevent any chance of mutiny from the old men's corner. The calls of 'Fifteen two, fifteen four, four for a flush and one for his knob' came from Tonker's table, along with 'Fuck me, not another fuckin' fag break, Tonker. We'll never fuckin' finish this fuckin' game.'

As the time went on, the crowded pub began to empty until, at two o'clock, there were just a few regulars sitting at the bar, a couple of kids forcing down a pint they weren't enjoying in one corner, and the table of four. They had made small talk for the previous hour and Dave was a little bored and aimed to leave early himself, especially as his roast dinner would be drying up nicely in the oven.

Paul went to the bar and called Viv to help carry the four pints back to the table. Whilst they were away, Barry broke the silence. 'I've been thinking,' he began as if he was about to make an earth shattering announcement. 'We've all been thinking a lot this week, actually.'

Dave was prepared for a rant about immigration, disk jockeys, homosexuals on the television, Alan Hansen, or the National Health Service and shrugged, prepared for the inevitable haranguing.

'We've been thinking about what you said last week and what we said and, well, we think we were a bit unfair with the pearl necklace and that. So we reckon that we can help you.'

Paul and Viv rejoined the table with the four pints at this stage.

'So what exactly is your worry? Is it that you don't think that you can satisfy this woman, are you worried that you may have a smaller dick than her previous lovers, are you worried that you won't be able to raise one or find her clitoris or what?' Viv looked down at the last suggestion and hoped that no one had noticed his embarrassment. He wasn't sure what a clitoris was anyway. 'You've got three of the world's leading experts on women in general, and sex in particular, here to offer you advice.'

Dave smiled and said, 'Look, thanks, lads, but it's none of those things. It's basic really. I'm just not sure how to start.' The beer had again loosened his inhibitions and his tongue. 'I mean, do I just kiss her and start playing with her tits, then is it OK to stick me hand up her kilt and make a grab for her, you know? I mean, I'm forty, for fuck's sake, so I don't want to bugger about like a teenager with his first sniff of fanny. Should I just ask her to come to bed and, if she agrees, then what? Do I just strip off and jump into bed and wait for her to join me or do I start to undress her first?'

Viv took a drink from his beer. 'Were I in your position, I would take her out for a romantic evening, then invite her to your home for coffee. I would then pick her up and carry her upstairs without a word – they like strong and silent men, you see – throw her on the bed and gently remove her clothes, making sure that her knickers are removed with your teeth, a sure-fire winner, then enter her roughly until she cries for mercy.'

'Most enlightening, thank you,' said Barry. 'I do tend to go along with most of the Vivian method of seduction, though. Except for the knickers and teeth bit. It's far too easy to clasp an element of pubic hair in one's teeth, which can be a little off-putting for both parties.'

Dave sat for a minute whilst his advisors waited quietly for a response. 'It's all academic anyhow,' he finally mumbled. 'She's not even speaking to me at the moment.'

'Not again, you useless tosser,' said Vivian. 'Leave it to the Poachers' super-stud to get her warmed up for you,' and he strode across the bar and began talking to Mandy. She looked across at Dave who quickly looked away. Viv returned a few minutes later with a huge grin spreading across his rough, unshaven face. He clasped Dave firmly on the shoulder as he sat down and announced, 'The sex machine never fails with women, even helping his mates. Just watch, study and learn. You, David Statham, are meeting Amanda Church, barmaid of this parish, at fifteen hundred hours GMT this afternoon when she has finished her shift in this very pub. She will meet you by the front door, from where she has asked that you take her home and give her a fucking good seeing-to, preferably doggie fashion.'

Dave's eyed widened. 'You mean you asked her to, sort of, to...?'

'No, you daft prat. I made that last bit up. Your round, I believe, David. Then that just gives you time to go home and put some decent clothes on. No woman wants to be seen with a bloke in a 1980s' tracksuit.'

Dave happily went to buy the last round. Mandy moved along the bar to serve him, but still did not smile. 'Yes, Dave, four pints is it?' she asked, maintaining such a serious look that Dave wondered if Viv had been telling the truth about the date. She poured the pints and lined them up on the bar in front of Dave who handed over a twenty pound note. As she rang the cash into the till, Dave hurried across and placed two pints on the table before returning to collect the remaining beers. Viv, Barry and Paul said nothing but sat and stared at the mini soap opera unfolding to Viv's script. Dave gripped the two pints and racked his brains for something to say, but could think of nothing, so just stood at the bar, holding two pints and grinning nervously. As Mandy placed the change on the bar, she said, 'Now how are you going to pick up the change holding on to those two pints?' Dave blushed and let go of one glass to enable him to pocket the change. 'And don't be late,' she added before turning away.

As they walked across the road towards their respective homes, Dave muttered thank you to Viv again for his intervention.

'No problem, mate,' Viv replied. 'And just remember not to look like some inexperienced schoolboy. Just be yourself, but be confident and the sex will take care of itself. Besides, she shouldn't offer much resistance. Apparently her mum used to flash her tits at my Uncle Geoff on his way to work every morning.'

As they strolled silently towards Mandy's home from the pub, Dave reviewed his options silently. He almost wished that he was home with his feet up in front of the television because he just could not think how to open the conversation. He was becoming more nervous and pessimistic as they walked. Suddenly he began talking without knowing where the words were coming from or what he was going to say, but the speech poured out like a relentless waterfall.

'I really am sorry about the other week, but I just wasn't sure what to do. I mean, I didn't want to insult you or anything, that's the last thing I'd ever want to do, and I wasn't sure whether you meant coffee or something else and I thought, well if I insult her now, I might lose her, and then I found out that you'd probably been married and I didn't know what to say about that because you never told me – not that there's any reason that you should, it makes no difference to the way I feel about you... but it just made me even more nervous and I'm really, really sorry that I didn't contact you or anything, although I wanted to, all the time, but, to be honest, I'm not that, you know, experienced with women... er... girls, so I wasn't sure what to say, so I just hoped that you might call me, but when you didn't, I thought that's it, but I'm still not sure why I upset you, but I must have and I'm really sorry, I wouldn't hurt you for the world...' He paused, all the while looking ahead and not daring to look at Mandy in case he upset her again. '...And I really do love you.' The words blurted from his mouth which surprised him even more than it surprised Mandy.

They walked in silence for a few minutes, and then Dave turned his head and looked at Mandy. She was silently crying. Oh fuck me, what the fuck do I do now? He felt in his pocket for a clean handkerchief, but all he found was an old tissue that he had used to dab some blood from somewhere at some time recently. He offered her the tissue.

'It's got a bit of blood on it, I'm afraid,' he said as she shook the tissue and blew her nose, quite loudly for a woman, he thought.

As they reached her front door, she looked up at him and shook her head. 'What am I going to do with you, David Statham?' she said and squeezed his arm. 'You'd better come in.'

This is what Dave had secretly dreaded. He went over Viv's advice in his mind and hoped that he wouldn't drop her when he carried her upstairs, or get a pubic hair caught in his throat when the time came. Mandy opened the door and led him into the hall before opening the door into the sitting room and leading Dave in. Two attractive young girls, probably in their early twenties and dressed in very tight jeans and very small tops which exposed their midriffs, were lying on the sitting room floor, surrounded by magazines and sweet wrappers. The sound of some pop music was coming from the system in the corner (probably Justin Timberwolf, thought Dave) and the television was blasting away in the opposite corner.

'Hi, Mand, just having a girly day in,' said the blonde girl. The dark girl just smiled.

'Chelsey, Jo-Jo, this is Dave. We're just going upstairs for a little chat,' Mandy said, emphasizing the word 'chat'.

Dave blushed and nodded 'hi', trying to look cool but knowing that that was impossible with a face glowing like a stop sign. Mandy took his hand and led him upstairs as the girls called out, 'Be good,' and 'Don't do anything we wouldn't do,' followed by giggles.

As they entered the small front bedroom, Dave glanced round the room. It contained a single bed, a single wardrobe, a small dressing table and a wooden chair. There was no other furniture. There was no room for any other furniture. The room was neatly decorated, with new curtains which seemed too large and lavish for the room, and a couple of prints on the wall. Modern art squares and circles and splodges in different colours. Dave didn't like the pictures but at least they matched the curtains. There was a small shelf above the dressing table with a few paperbacks and a framed photograph.

So far, so good, thought Dave. At least I don't have to carry her upstairs. He took a deep breath and wondered what to do next.

'Sit down, Dave.' He turned, and Mandy was pointing to the bed. He gulped nervously and sat exactly where Mandy was pointing, thinking, this is it, David, the moment of reckoning. He started to sweat and his hands began to shake again. Mandy pulled the chair out and sat down facing him.

'Don't look so nervous,' she said firmly, reminding Dave of a schoolmistress. 'We are not going to have sex, so you don't have to worry, but we are going to talk. We are going to sort this relationship out one way or another, this afternoon, now.'

Dave nodded.

Mandy continued, 'Now do you want to start or shall I?'

Dave shrugged.

'Right, I suppose that means me,' Mandy continued. 'I'm sorry about the other week too, Dave, but you must understand. I was married for six years. Gareth and I never had any children. We didn't know why, it just didn't happen and he refused to go to the doctor or anywhere to check out why. Then he started to abuse me. He wasn't violent or anything, he just used to say things about me not being able to have children and so on, and then he wouldn't speak to me for weeks on end. Then he started ignoring me altogether and said he was going away for stag weekends with his mates, although I knew that his mates were still in Bristol. I guess that he had another woman, but I don't know that for certain. I just wasn't interested. We never had sex at all for the last year or so, and I was feeling useless, plain and unattractive; and I thought that no man would ever fancy me again. So, one day I just left him. Packed my suitcase and left. Just like that. I didn't know where to go so drifted back to Downham and stayed with friends for a while in the old town, then found this house to share with Chelsey and Jo-Jo. Then I saw you in Muzzy's that day. I remembered you from when I lived here before. You were quite a handsome and dashing young man then, but far too old for me, of course. I had a crush on you then and used to watch you from my Mum's bedroom window when she wasn't in. I used to get up early to watch you going to work in the mornings and rush home from school just to watch you come in at night. I used to have little dreams about you and me. Silly really, I suppose, but I never told anyone. You were my little secret that no one else could share. Then, when I saw you in the shop and found out that you still lived over the road and that you weren't married, I was really happy. It took you long enough to ask me out, but when you did I felt that life was worth living again for the first time for years. Then, when I made it clear that I fancied you and wanted to' – Mandy took a deep breath – 'have sex with you, you more or less told me to get lost and ran away. I felt terrible again. Unattractive, ugly even, and I was really upset. That's why I never contacted you and it was worse because you never bothered contacting me.' Mandy looked Dave in the eye. 'Right, that's me done. Your turn.'

Dave stared at the floor. 'I think that you're, sort of, you know, lovely,' was all he could manage.

Mandy sighed, a long sad sigh. 'Right,' she said. 'This is what we are going to do. From tomorrow I am working every evening at the pub until Saturday. At 11.15 each evening, you are going to meet me at the door and walk me home, even if you are not out having a pint. You will take me to my front door, where we will kiss goodnight and you will go home. If we are still OK on Saturday, you will take me out for the evening. We will go out for a meal somewhere nice with a glass or two of wine. Then, if it is still OK between us' – Mandy paused and leaned forward, touching Dave's face gently – 'We *will* sleep together.'

Dave's heart was pounding so much. 'We will sleep together.' That's what she said.

'Dave, take that silly grin off your face and say something.' Mandy looked at him as if he was a naughty boy.

'I've had five pints, Mandy, and I'm bursting for a pee.'

Mandy laughed. 'It's the door opposite, and don't be long,' she said, opening the bedroom door for Dave.

After he had finished what seemed like the world's longest-ever pee, he remembered to wash his hands and left the bathroom just as Chelsey, or possibly Jo-Jo, was coming up the stairs. 'That was quick,' she grinned as Dave scuttled back to the safety of Mandy's bedroom.

Mandy gave Dave a huge, happy smile as he re-entered her room. 'Well, have you thought about what I said?' she asked.

'Thanks, Mandy, thanks.' Dave couldn't think of much else to say. 'That would be nice. Thanks.'

'Good. That's settled then. Now you are going home before we both do or say something silly and spoil it. I'll see you tomorrow night at 11.15.'

Dave gave her a quick peck on the cheek before they left the bedroom. Looking over her shoulder he focused on the photograph on her dressing table. Mrs. Barnes stared back at him. Thank God he hadn't noticed that before they started talking.

Seven

Downham Sunday Football League, Knockout Cup, Preliminary Round
Results for Sunday 12th October

The Boar's Head   7   1   Poachers Arms

All other cup results available from D Statham if required

League Table

Team	Pl'd	Won	Drew	Lost	For	Ag'st	GD	Points
Jones Juniors FC	5	5	0	0	24	6	18	15
New Inn, Gorton D	5	3	1	1	17	10	7	10
Poachers Arms	**5**	**3**	**1**	**1**	**12**	**8**	**4**	**10**
Pickled Herring	4	3	1	0	10	6	4	10
AFC Cummiston	5	1	3	1	6	10	-4	6
J G Tanner and Sons	4	2	0	2	9	11	-2	6
Hearty Oak, Downlea	5	1	2	2	15	20	-5	5
Shellduck Inn	5	1	1	3	9	13	-4	4
Downham Churches	5	0	1	4	14	22	-8	1
Lower End WMC	3	0	0	3	0	10	-10	0

Sunday 19th October

Downham Sunday Football League, Division Two
The Shellduck Inn v Poachers Arms
Back of the Shellduck – Kick-off 10.30

THE POACHERS ARMS

1 George Crosswell

2 Steve Tippling   4 Derek Smith   5 Brian Smith   3 Billy Millmore (Capt)

8 Matt Cornwell   6 Vivian Clutterbuck   10 Danny Tomlinson

7 Gordon Gaye   9 Daniel Raisin   11 Gunner Farr

Substitutes
12 Paddy Oakley
13 Wayne Tocket
14 Percy Woodman

Reserves (Please bring boots)
Paul Cornwell
Dave Statham
Barry Plumb

Manager
Dave Statham

All players, substitutes and reserves to turn up at 09.45

Elaine sat at the kitchen table, her anger rising as she thought more deeply about the previous evening. She and Viv had gone out for a drink and a curry at the Taj Mahal Curry and Balti Palace in town. They had decided to stop at the Poachers Arms on the way home and finish the evening with a few more lagers and gin and tonics. As they walked into the lounge bar they noticed Paul and Christine Cornwell sitting alone at the corner table and had naturally joined them. Unusually, the men stayed at the table talking to their ladies rather than standing at the bar: it was late and both men were becoming tired; in fact Paul was as tired as a newt. The conversation was light and cheerful and drifted into talking about Dave and Mandy. Paul had taken great delight in telling the girls how Dave came to them on successive weeks for advice on how to seduce Mandy, and how they had talked about pearl necklaces, which Christine thought was a lovely idea, much to the amusement of the others.

'I'll show you what it means when we get home,' Paul explained, to her look of puzzlement at the laughter. 'But then, be fair,' he continued, his speech slurring slightly. 'Old Vivian here sorted him out. Give him good advice on how to get her going and even sorted out a date for them and explained to Dave what he had to do. Fair play to you, Viv.' Paul raised his glass and drank a lone toast of bitter to Viv.

The more Elaine pondered about what Paul had said, the angrier she became. Viv would not listen to her when she wanted to talk about their sex problem, he refused to discuss it with his own wife, and yet he was quite prepared to offer advice to that bloody daft Dave Statham in the pub. This had to be sorted out.

She stood up and answered the singing of the kettle, making a cup of tea in a large mug. She added two sugars and milk, and stared into the cup for a few seconds trying to calm her mind and let the anger dissipate. When she had gained control, she climbed the stairs and pushed the bedroom door open with her foot. The bedroom smelt of stale lager and just a hint of sweat, not a perfume that Dior would market with any optimism. Elaine moved across the room and opened her wardrobe, quietly taking out a carrier bag concealed beneath shoes and handbags. She turned and looked at Viv sleeping peacefully, his big, tattooed shoulders moving to the steady rhythm of his light snoring. This was going to be one of the most difficult things she had ever had to do and she had to handle it correctly or Viv would just get angry and storm out of the house again. That's why it was better to do it now, whilst he was in bed; it would be far more difficult for him to storm out of the house when he was bollock naked.

She sat on the bed and shook Viv gently. He stirred, turned over and pulled the duvet over his head. She shook him again, a little more forcibly.

'Vivian, love,' she cooed in his ear. 'It's half past and there's football this morning.'

Viv blinked twice, then sat up quickly and looked at the alarm clock next to his steaming cup of tea. 'Bloody hell, 'Laine, it's only half past eight. I've got another hour yet. What's up?'

Elaine paused for a moment then swallowed hard. 'Viv. Your tea's on the side and I've got something for you. Please, please don't be angry with me, but when I leave the bedroom, I want you to look in this bag. Please try not to be angry or shout at me or storm out of the house. I'll be waiting for you in the kitchen with your bacon sandwich when you come down, and we really need to talk. And please remember that I am doing this for us, for both of us, and I love you very much.'

Having finished her speech, Elaine stood up and confidently walked to the bedroom door without looking back at her husband. When she reached the landing, she closed the bedroom door, gripped the banister and released a huge sigh. She was trembling, scared and nervous, yet incredibly elated.

Viv watched Elaine close the bedroom door, looked at the bag and back at the door. He pulled the bag towards him and put his hand inside, pulling out three books. He read the first title: *Coping With Erectile Dysfunction. How to regain confidence and enjoy great sex.* He read it again, and a third time, but he was finding difficulty in interpreting the words into anything meaningful. 'Erectile Dysfunction? Is that what I've got?' he mumbled to himself. 'Nah, I've just been a bit tired, that's all. My todger needs a bit of rest, a bit of a recharge, that's all. I can't have erectile dysfunction, that's for old people and besides I can't spell it.'

Still partially dazed, he looked at the second book: *Sensual Sex. A lover's guide to better pleasure for you and your partner. Complete step by step visual guide to enhanced techniques.* 'What? Me – Vivian Clutterbuck? Sex machine. Needing a guide to shagging? Madness.'

Finally he pulled out a small booklet: *Ann Summers Catalogue*. 'Bloody hell, she wants me to start dressing up in rubber now and using bloody dildos. Bloody hell!'

He finished his tea and flicked through the books and the catalogue. They certainly were explicit and there was more than a hint of pornography in the pictures, but they were written by doctors, so that was probably OK. What to do then, Vivian, old boy? He left the books on the bed as he showered, taking longer than usual and washing his private parts extra vigorously. *It's mine and I'll wash it as fast as I like.* Although his penis hung flaccidly, no matter how fast he washed it.

It was a standard four star hotel room, except that Dave had specified a double bed rather than twin beds. He lay under the sheets, hands behind his head, eyes half closed, remembering the enormity of what he had achieved. He was no longer a virgin. At forty years and a few months, he had had sex. Not alone, but with a woman.

From some odd sense of morality, both he and Mandy had kept their underwear on as they climbed into bed last night. They kissed tenderly for several minutes, Dave happy that it gave him time to relax and control his extreme nervousness. He tried to remove her bra, but found the complicated arrangement of straps and fastenings impossible to fathom. Mandy smiled sweetly and sat up, miraculously bent her arms behind her back and released the bra, revealing her shapely breasts tipped by pretty pink nipples. Dave stared and Mandy softly held him and moved his head towards her. It was an awkward struggle removing her panties under the bedclothes, but she lifted her buttocks to help him and he raised his right leg and hooked them off with his toes. There was one extremely worrying moment when she was removing his underpants and, for a brief second, he worried that he would ejaculate before consummation. But he closed his eyes and thought of a naked Percy Woodman which cooled his ardour sufficiently to prevent an embarrassing early bath.

Vivian dried and took longer than usual to dress. He wandered from the bedroom to the bathroom, looking for any excuse to delay the embarrassing discussion with Elaine, but finally realised that there were only so many times that he could shave, clean his teeth, comb his hair, re-tie the laces to his trainers and check his money. He looked at the catalogue again, studying the nurse's uniform and the skimpy skirts of the French maid, quickly skipping the pages of false penises, which he found strangely disturbing. He opened the books and scrutinized the impossible sexual positions recommended by the doctor authors, carefully turning the page around until he could decipher whose limbs belonged to whom. He suddenly felt better. Perhaps this wasn't all bad. For years he had desired a little more adventure in his sexual life with Elaine, but had never had the courage to mention it. Perhaps this could be a blessing in disguise. But what if his penis let him down again, even if she was dressed in a gymslip and smacked his arse with a ruler?

Slowly he descended the stairs, the smell of sizzling bacon making the journey a little more tolerable, and entered the kitchen. Elaine was sitting at the table and offered him a broad smile, pushing the huge bacon sandwich towards him.

'OK, love, what do you think?' Elaine asked, aware of the strain in her own voice.

Viv sat down heavily in the chair and stared at his breakfast. 'I guess you're right, 'Laine,' he replied without looking up. 'Perhaps there is a bit of a problem that we need to sort out. Tell you what, Babe, give me time to think about it, look at them books and we'll chat again another time. How about that?'

Elaine wanted to scream, to get hold of him and shake him and say, 'No, you big ape. We'll talk now!' but little by little, one step at a time, may be a better way forward. 'Course, Viv. When you're ready, love.'

The bathroom door opened and Mandy entered the bedroom, wrapped in a large white towel with her hair tied up in a white turban. She looked just like the star of a fifties' movie, and he felt as if he were Clark Gable. He congratulated himself on the masterstroke of hiring a hotel room for the night, so much better than squeezing into Mandy's tiny bed or sneaking into his own bedroom, with Tonker snoring and farting in the next bedroom. He watched her walking towards him, not knowing what to say, his mind full of confused emotions of love, longing, pride, lust, comfort and contentment. Mandy broke the silence.

'Come on, dreamer, time you got up. There's a free breakfast waiting for you downstairs. Then you've got to be at your daft football game.'

Dave looked at his watch. 08.45. He salivated at the thought of the breakfast and knew that he would have to get up immediately if he was to have time to eat and make it to the Shellduck by a quarter to ten. He started to get out of bed, but looked and saw Mandy standing in front of him. She was completely naked. She had taken off her turban and her hair hung in little rats'-tails to her shoulders. Her breasts were large, almost too large for her small frame, but beautifully firm and rounded.

'Unless there's something else you'd rather do,' she grinned.

Viv and Paul were standing outside Dave's house wondering where on earth Dave had got to. They surmised several scenarios for his absence, from Dave leaving without them (improbable) to going shopping for his mum (unlikely) to sleeping away from home (doubtful) to being taken hostage by terrorists (implausible). As they were discussing the possibility of him being abducted by aliens (possible), the red sports car raced along Poachers Drive and screeched to a halt in front of them. They watched Barry unfold his bulky frame from the passenger seat and squeeze himself out onto the pavement. He waved a casual goodbye to the blonde driver as the red sports car accelerated up the road and disappeared over the brow of the hill.

Barry watched the car disappear and said, 'Goes like a fucking rocket, doesn't she? And the car as well.' They all chuckled. 'My motor's knackered. Wouldn't start this morning so I had to get her to drop me off. Only just serviced her too.'

'And the car as well,' said Viv, before Barry had a chance to say it.

The three men stood waiting on Dave's drive, reviewing their options. They could take Viv's or Paul's car, or wait to see if Dave turned up. It seemed a difficult decision for a Sunday morning and not one of the three seemed to have the inclination or, indeed, the ability to make the choice. Their indecisiveness was rewarded after a few minutes when Dave's Polo appeared over the brow and tootled down the hill. The lads gathered up their bags and moved to the edge of the pavement as Dave approached. He did not stop, and drove straight past them. They watched the car pass then looked at each other.

'Did you see what I think I saw?' Barry asked. 'Did he have young Mandy in the car? The dirty, lucky bastard.'

After a couple of minutes the Polo returned and Dave parked in the road. 'Get in, lads. Just getting my kit,' he shouted as he jumped out of the car, leaving the engine running. All four veteran footballers were soon on their way and it didn't take long for the ribbing to begin.

'Thanks for picking us up, Dave, only mine needs servicing.' Barry turned round from the front seat and gave Paul and Viv a surreptitious wink 'Yours is a nice little goer, though, isn't she.'

Dave replied innocently that he had no problems with her.

'Mine's useless in the morning, just can't get her going at all,' added Viv. 'What about yours, Paul?'

'Not too bad once she's warmed up. Not as sturdy as Dave's, though.'

'You're a lucky man, see, Dave,' Barry continued. 'Well-built, sturdy little goer, no trouble getting her warmed up, performs well – just the job.'

Dave screwed his face up in concentration. 'I have had a bit of trouble with her exhaust,' he said to the delight of his passengers, who collapsed into giggling fits.

'What?' said Dave. 'What?'

The Shellduck Inn was an old established pub on the southern edge of Downham. It had been built in the 1800s, but had been extended and developed over the intervening couple of centuries so that little of the original building remained. A few stone walls were still in place and some of the gnarled old beams may have been original. It was decorated with horse brasses and modern prints of old paintings showing hunting scenes. They advertised "Real Ale" and home-made food. It was the sort of "Olde Worlde" pub that could be found in towns the length and breadth of the country, and the lads from the Poachers hated it.

'Pretentious bollocks,' Barry described it as they pulled into the car park. 'And don't talk to me about real ale. Just an excuse to sell warm, cloudy beer to folk musicians and computer programmers with scruffy beards and smelly sandals.'

The Shellduck had acres of land at the back, which had been bequeathed to the pub in perpetuity by the original Lord of the Manor, for use and recreation by the citizens of the village. Since "the village" had largely disappeared or been swallowed up by Downham's southern expansion, the land was used as a football pitch and play area. Dave knew that there had been many attempts by the council to buy and develop the land but, thus far, the old bequest had stood firm. The changing area was in the function room, also used for wedding receptions and parties, and retaining a sweet smell of sherry and cake.

There were no hooks in the room, which annoyed Dave as he was unable to lay out the kit as he liked, but the first job was to rearrange the furniture so that he had sixteen chairs placed against the wall, with four trestle tables lined up about two metres in from the wall, four chairs to a table. He laid out the shirts in sequence of 1 to 14 on the table, and placed a pair of shorts and a pair of socks neatly on each of the first fourteen chairs. The remaining two chairs were taken by Paul and Barry. Dave stood back and admired his work as Paul lit up a cigarette. Barry assaulted them with his views on twee country inns and how he would burn them all down and start again, and how could it possibly be home-made food in a pub? It was pub-made food.

The Shellduck players did not have the age diversity of the Poachers' players. They were all twenty-somethings, who used the pub on Saturday nights with their young wives and girlfriends, sipping halves of real ale whilst the ladies drank bottled cocktails and considered themselves sophisticated. In their teens each wag had planned to marry a premiership footballer but had been forced to settle for a player from the Downham and District Sunday League. Some of the girls even came out to watch on Sundays, dressed in designer boots and Victoria Beckham jeans.

'Don't start me on women at football matches. Why the bloody hell…' Dave heard, but was too busy checking that all the team had turned up to listen to Barry's diatribe. Wayne Tocket and Percy Woodman were both a little sulky about being dropped but, as Dave explained, 'Football nowadays is about a squad system and using it to the full, so that no players get knackered and everyone gets to play a part, where every one of the squad is equally important, not just the eleven playing at any one time, and it's important that the squad is utilized to the full, and a rotation system is essential—'

'How come I'm always dropped then?' interrupted Paddy Oakley, who had listened to the speech with great interest.

Dave replied, 'Exactly my point, Paddy, well done,' and walked away leaving the three substitutes bemused.

All players were present and correct as Dave clapped his hands to gain their attention. 'OK lads, listen up,' he began, speaking relatively quietly so that the opposition, changing at the other end of the hall, could not listen in to his tactics. 'This lot look like a load of models from a bloody catalogue, so they won't like a bit of stick. Just let them know that you're there, and you two' – he pointed at Matt and Steve who were comparing love bites – 'that doesn't mean that you can kick seven colours of shit out of them. You've both got suspensions coming up, so be careful. Firm but fair, lads, firm but fair.'

Dave and Paul followed the players out onto the pitch and took up their positions on the halfway line. Dave scanned the opposition as they lined up for the kick-off. They were all disarmingly smart. Their kit was immaculate, with dark green shirts emblazoned with "The Shellduck Inn" in gold lettering on the front. Black shorts, with creases in the front, and dark green socks finished the ensemble. Then Dave noticed their boots. Pairs of shining new boots in red, blue, green, black, gold or silver. He looked at his own team's dress. Dirty boots, some still covered in mud from last week's game, shorts and shirts straight out of the launderette tumble-drier and crammed into an old canvas bag, well worn and wrinkled, like many of the team. 'How come this lot have only won one game?' Paul asked. 'They look fucking good.'

As soon as the match kicked off, Paul had his answer. They were hopeless. For all their designer kit, they didn't have a clue how to play football. They lacked even the basics of ball control; they sliced, hooked, grubbed or missed the ball at every occasion. The mystery was not why they had only won one game, but how they had managed to win one game.

Poachers scored after about five minutes, with the Gordon Gaye cross and Razor Raisin head combination proving far too quick and far too skilful for the Shellduck defence, who posed with hands on hips and looking to the skies as if the goal was a result of divine intervention and not their own lack of ability. Viv began to enjoy his morning, calling for the ball at every opportunity, beating two or three players before going back to beat them again. The Poachers' defenders had lost interest and wandered upfield to try to get in on the action and possibly claim some glory. In spite of the fact that they had lost any semblance of the original formation and were playing a unique 0–4–6, Poachers easily knocked in four more goals through Razor, Gordon, and two for Gunner Farr.

The Poachers' team took up their traditional halftime positions sitting in a bedraggled group, socks rolled down and either swigging from the water bottles or lighting up cigarettes, when Paul pointed out the Shellduck players on the opposite touchline. They were all standing, some combing their hair whilst others were talking to the gaggle of bimbos that had turned up to watch them.

'Did you see that?' asked Paul, his voice raised in amazement and indignation. 'One of their blokes is kissing that girl. Actually bloody kissing her. On a Sunday morning. Must be a bloody sex maniac.' The Poachers' team hooted with derision, whistled and shouted various pieces of advice to the couple cuddling on the side of the pitch. Cries of 'Go on, my son, give her one from me,' and 'Does she play your organ every Sunday?' rang out. The Shellduck players were too busy preening themselves and impressing their young ladies to take any notice of the ragtag army bellowing insults from across the pitch.

Dave was pleased with his team's performance but even more pleased with his new status as a seducer of women and a leader of men. He considered that his pre-match speech to the substitutes had been well received and he felt sure that his new-found inner confidence would allow him to be more decisive and positive. He made a show of studying the teamsheet and furrowing his brow as if trying to resolve some complex conundrum. He finally gained the attention of the players who were more used to seeing him standing amongst them with an air of bewilderment at half-time. 'Listen up, lads, listen up,' he said. 'Substitutes on. Percy, you're on for Big Smithy, Paddy, you're on for Gordon, and Wayne, you're on for Viv.'

'What the fuck for?' Viv was indignant about being removed from a game he was enjoying. 'I'm OK. I don't need to come off.'

Dave smiled the smile of a parent with a wayward child. 'Football nowadays is about a squad system and using it to the full, so that no players get worn out and everyone gets to play a part, where everyone of the squad is equally important, not just the eleven playing at any one time, and it's important that the squad is utilized to the full and a rotation system is essential.'

Viv, Gordon, and Brian Smith looked at each with mouths open. Dave had never made a substitution before unless pressed to do so and today he had made three; and had a little sermon ready to justify the decision. Even Viv was speechless.

Playing three inferior players, particularly out of position, was not a brilliant move and the Poachers struggled to find the rhythm of the first half. Big Smithy had been consistently steady at the back but Percy was thirty-five years old and hadn't played for four weeks. His age, lack of match practice, and a diet of cider and Marlborough cigarettes were taking their toll and he struggled to contain even the limited abilities of these opponents. Wayne was unused to playing in the centre of midfield and kept wandering out of position, leaving a hole in the middle of the pitch which the Shellduck players filled, probably because they didn't really understand where else to go. Paddy was as enthusiastic as ever but had neither the skill nor speed of Gordon Gaye which meant that the main supply route to Razor was stifled. Razor himself was quite happy to stroll about, showing clever little touches of ball control without ever coming close to scoring.

Viv took advantage of his enforced rest to think about what his wife had said that morning. He wandered around the pitch, listening to the Shellduck manager's cries of 'Get across them', 'Work the channels' and 'I want desire.'

'Bugger me,' mumbled Viv, 'Sounds just like the missis.'

As he strolled, Viv continued muttering to himself, 'I've had enough fannying around the problem. 'Laine's right – I'll do something. I'll go home after the match and sort it out, that's what I'll do. Better to test the little fireman once and for all. Nothing ventured, nothing gained,' by which time the mutter had changed to become normal speech. 'We'll go upstairs, strip off with no messing and get down to it, we'll see what happens then.'

'Bloody hell, Viv, don't you ever think of anything else?' Paul's voice disturbed his trance. 'You really are some kind of stud.'

The game became scrappy with the Poachers playing badly and the Shellduck not having the guile or skill to take advantage, and it petered out quietly with no more goals. Dave patted each player on the back, congratulating them all on a good match as Paul caught his eye. 'Time for a quick one here. Get a move on,' he said and made his way out of the function room and into the pub. They were soon joined by Viv, who was first to change following his earlier substitution, Barry, who had run out of things to say about real ale, and Billy Millmore who appeared at Paul's shoulder just as he was ordering a round. The barman pulled five pints and placed them on the bar, the men greedily grabbing the glasses and gulping back the beer. Except Barry, who left his glass on the bar but bent his large frame so that he could study the ale at eye level.

'Excuse me, barman,' he eventually called. The barman came over to the four as Dave, Viv and Billy feared the worst. What was Barry going to embarrass them over this time?

'Yes, mate,' the barman said with a cheery smile.

'Two things, barman.' Barry had assumed an air of importance. 'Firstly, I am a customer and not your mate. You may call me Mr Plumb or Sir. Secondly, would you please fill this glass up to its correct measure of one imperial pint?'

The barman looked at Barry, looked at the pint and said, 'But that bit's for the 'ead, mate, you know, the froff.'

Dave winced. This barman had obviously never met Barry before. 'My good man, can you remember what my friend here ordered to drink?'

'Well yes, five pints of bitter.'

'Precisely, five pints of bitter,' Barry sighed. 'Not five pints of bitter and froth, or even froff, but pints of bitter. And that, barman, is what I want, please. A pint, a full pint of beer. No head, no froth and certainly no froff.' The barman looked like a frightened rabbit caught in headlights, but took Barry's glass and filled it to the brim from the pump, at the same time spilling froth over his hand.

'Thank you, barman. Most kind,' said Barry before taking a long gulp.

'Barry,' said Viv, 'I thought that you didn't like this real ale, so why make a fuss about not having enough?'

'Vivian, Vivian,' replied Barry in his best condescending tone. 'It is a matter of principle. If one orders a pint, one expects a pint. Not froff.'

'Well then,' said Viv, grinning. 'One had better order five more then,' and called the barman for Barry to order a refill.

Although none of the squad liked the atmosphere of the Shellduck they found a table in the corner and spent an enjoyable hour chatting about the game and watching the posers and wags sipping halves and chatting about their designer-labelled shoes, shirts and handbags. Viv came back from the bar after his round and placed three pints on the table before returning with two more.

He looked very serious as he sat down. 'I've just been listening to those blokes at the bar,' he said. 'And we're lucky that we're not playing them next week.'

'Why's that?' Dave asked innocently.

'Because I'm pretty sure that they said something about getting three more players in the week, and they sound pretty good.'

'Who are they?' Dave looked intrigued as Viv called the lads closer into a conspiratorial huddle.

'I distinctly heard them say they were getting George Armani, Ralph Lauren and Ted Baker,' said Viv before leaning back and guffawing loudly. Dave didn't get the joke.

The quick one had soon turned into four pints, and Dave, Paul, Viv and Barry had all bought a round. As they finished their pints, Billy looked at his watch. 'Fuck me, it's quarter past one. We'd better get down the Poachers before they send out a search party,' he said and the men grabbed their various bags and left the bar. Dave realised that he had had four pints and his car was in the car park, but everyone else had also had the same amount, so he had no choice but to drive. As they were carefully cruising through the town towards the Poachers' estate, Paul suddenly said, 'How many pints did we have?'

'Four,' replied Barry.

'And how many of us were there?'

'Five.'

'And who never bought a round?'

'Fucking Billy,' they all shouted in unison.

'And what's more,' said Dave, 'there's absolutely no way that he's going to turn up at the Poachers now. He'll go straight home.'

'Let's hope he gets fucking breathalysed then,' laughed Paul, raising a finger at a police car going the other way.

When they arrived at the Poachers' estate and Dave was parking the Polo, Viv had made a decision. This was D-Day. Do it Day. Today he would put the embarrassment behind him, sit down with Elaine and discuss the issue of his erectile dysfunction. It was a simple problem with a simple solution. The fact was that he had once failed to gain an erection during lovemaking with his wife. Since that time, he had been afraid to try again for fear of repeat humiliation. Those were the facts and he had to do something about it or resign himself to a future without sex. Elaine had offered to help and said that talking about it was the first step on the road to revitalization. She was right, of course, and that was just what he would do. He would sit down with her over the roast dinner and discuss the problem. Then, if things worked out as he hoped, they would retire to bed for a round of sex before picking the children up later.

Viv waved goodbye to the other lads as they cheerily headed for the Poachers Arms. 'Promised Elaine we'd take the kids out this afternoon after we pick them up from her mum's,' he shouted and headed for his house. He stopped at the front door and ran quickly through what he would say before opening the door and stepping inside. He jumped as suddenly he felt a blow on his back and something attacked his legs, almost knocking him to the floor. He fell to his knees and was aware that he was being attacked in his own home – by Batman and Superman.

'OK, Penguin, your money or your life,' he heard as his head was twisted to the left. He looked directly into the eyes of Batman.

'Money, money, Batman,' he cried as his assailant loosened his grip.

'You smell of beer,' added Superman, holding her nose.

As the three lay on the floor and Viv struggled in his pocket for some loose change to pay the ransom, Elaine walked into the hall, wiping her hands on a tea towel.

She beamed. 'Hello, Viv, love. You're home early. Just in time. I was just about to serve dinner.'

'I wasn't expecting Batman and Robin here,' said Viv, handing over a few coppers.

'I'm Supergirl actually,' Emma corrected him as she and her brother raced into the front room to count their ill-gotten gains.

Viv was still sitting on the floor. 'I thought we could talk, actually,' he whispered, 'about, you know, the problem.'

'Sorry, love, but my mum had one of her heads so I picked the kids up early. And I've promised to take them out this afternoon. But we can talk later if you like.'

But "later" did not happen for quite some time.

Downham Sunday Football League, Division Two
Results for Sunday 19th October

J G Tanner and Sons	1	2	New Inn, Gorton Down
Jones Juniors FC	2	2	AFC Cummiston
Shellduck Inn	**0**	**5**	**Poachers Arms**
Downham Churches	4	4	Lower End WMC
Pickled Herring	3	1	Hearty Oak, Downlea

League Table

Team	Pl'd	Won	Drew	Lost	For	Ag'st	GD	Points
Jones Juniors FC	6	5	1	0	26	8	18	16
New Inn, Gorton D	6	4	1	1	19	11	8	13
Poachers Arms	**6**	**4**	**1**	**1**	**17**	**8**	**9**	**13**
Pickled Herring	5	4	1	0	13	7	6	13
AFC Cummiston	6	1	4	1	8	12	-4	7
J G Tanner and Sons	5	2	0	3	10	13	-3	6
Hearty Oak, Downlea	6	1	2	3	16	23	-7	5
Shellduck Inn	6	1	1	4	9	18	-9	4
Downham Churches	6	0	2	4	18	26	-8	2
Lower End WMC	4	0	1	3	4	14	-10	1

Sunday 2nd November

Downham Sunday Football League, Division Two
Poachers Arms v The Pickled Herring
Tenacre Recreation Ground – Kick-off 10.30

THE POACHERS ARMS

1 George Crosswell

2 Steve Tippling   4 Derek Smith   5 Brian Smith   3 Billy Millmore (Capt)

8 Wayne Tocket   6 Vivian Clutterbuck   10 Danny Tomlinson

7 Gordon Gaye   9 Daniel Raisin   11 Gunner Farr

Substitutes
12 Matt Cornwell
13 Percy Woodman
14 Paddy Oakley

Reserves (Please bring boots)
Paul Cornwell
Dave Statham
Barry Plumb

Manager
Dave Statham

All players, substitutes and reserves to turn up at 09.45

Barry could hear Monica clattering about in the kitchen downstairs. More bloody muesli, he thought, as he lay in bed staring at the ceiling, the curtains still drawn to keep out the sight of the cold, November drizzle. She had stayed at his house last night, as usual on Saturdays, and they had had a very pleasant evening, Monica driving them to a small country hotel in the Cotswolds for a meal with Charles Harris and his wife, Caroline. Barry had been a little flummoxed at the menu for a moment, and wished that they had served steak and kidney pie or chicken and chips, but it was not that sort of restaurant. After studying the menu, he was relieved to find that, although there was a surfeit of brulees, terrines and confits, some items were in English. Barry hated eating in restaurants where the menu was in Foreign and had once written a letter to the *Times* on the subject although it had not been published. He finally chose rustic ham soup (can't go wrong with soup) and rib eye steak with flat mushrooms, red onion marmalade and dauphinoise potatoes. He had no idea how the mushrooms had become flat or what a dauphinoise potato was, but steak was a safe option. The sweets did not appeal to his council house tastes and so he settled for a selection of cheeses. He cleverly insisted that Charles selected the wine. 'After all, Charles,' he had said, 'Monica tells me that you are something of a connoisseur on plonk.' Charles laughed but was obviously pleased with the compliment.

As chairman of the local Conservative Association and also of the Magistrates Advisory Committee, Charles had encouraged Barry to apply to become a magistrate. Barry had completed his application, provided by Monica, but was yet to submit the completed form to the Advisory Committee. Both men were feeling the effects of gin and tonics, several glasses of a rich Burgundy and a sweet wine, before Charles suggested that they retire to the conservatory for a cigar with their brandies. 'The ladies won't want to join us. Besides, you and I can have a little man to man chat, young Barry,' he had said as he led Barry away from the dining room.

As they sat in the conservatory, Charles drew on his Cuban cigar and stared at Barry for several seconds. 'Your application. I understand that you've completed it. Put it forward, old boy, put it forward. Can't see a problem, old boy. Ex-serviceman, done your bit for Queen and country, police officer, now a businessman. Really can't see a problem.' Barry nodded seriously. 'Mind you, old boy, it's not just up to me, you know. Committee, you see. Now Monica tells me you've been married and divorced twice, is that right? Only some of the committee might just think that's not quite right, you know. What if you had to sit on cases of a matrimonial nature? Could be a bit awkward if you see what I mean.' Barry did not know what he meant, but nodded anyway.

'Ever thought of marrying again? Might stand you in good stead with other members of the Advisory Committee, if you understand me. Some of them are a bit old-fashioned, you know.' Charles laughed. He put out the remains of his cigar, swigged down the last of his brandy and said, 'Better join the ladies, old boy, can't stay here all night,' before leading Barry into the small lounge next to the dining room where the ladies were finishing a cup of coffee.

'The waiter brought the bill over when you two men were talking man things,' Monica said, passing the piece of paper on a silver dish to Barry. He casually turned it over and struggled to catch his breath for a brief moment. He looked at the bill again to ensure that the total had registered correctly. Two hundred and twenty-four pounds and fifty-two pence. His eyes bulged as he looked again. That was going to be one hundred and twelve pounds each, plus tip; he could say goodbye to a hundred and thirty pounds. For a bloody steak and poncy potatoes.

'I say, that's jolly decent of you, Barry old boy.' Charles was helping Caroline on with her coat. 'We must do it again soon. And thanks again.'

Barry was about to grab Charles, push the bill up his nose and tell him to pay it himself, when Monica stood between them, smiling cheerfully. 'You are very welcome, Charles. Thank you for such a lovely evening.' She glared at Barry as if to say 'Don't say a thing.'

As Charles and Caroline left the hotel lounge, Monica took her purse from her bag, removed an American Express card and placed it on the silver dish. She looked at Barry's face, flushed with alcohol, anger and surprise. 'Because you're worth it,' she grinned.

As they drove home, Monica seemed in unusually high spirits. She had only had one glass of wine all evening and she generally enjoyed a few more than one, so Barry was a little bemused to find her so tranquil. Must be my excellent company, he mused.

'You're quiet,' she said as they carefully negotiated the bends of the Cotswold countryside. 'Everything all right?'

'Of course, darling. Everything's fine. Just feeling happy and relaxed, that's all. And a bit squiffy if truth were known.' Barry felt silly. He had actually said "squiffy" instead of "pissed".

Barry reviewed what Charles had said the night before. Getting married again was a huge step that he really did not want to take, but he wanted that J.P. after his name. Barry Plumb J.P. would prove that he had finally made it into the echelons of the middle classes.

Monica brought a cup of muddy-tasting coffee into the bedroom, smiling broadly and gently humming a pop song that Barry didn't recognize. She placed the coffee beside him and asked, 'Shall I put the television on, darling? It's time for your footer, isn't it?' as she pressed the button on the remote. 'Now you just enjoy your coffee and footer and I'll make you a nice breakfast.'

She leant forward and kissed Barry on the forehead before sashaying across the bedroom and down the stairs. He almost called her back to say that only people who knew nothing about football called it "footer", but realised that she knew nothing about football. Barry was not in the mood to listen to Alan Hansen, so turned the television off immediately and wondered why Monica was behaving so out of character. They'd had a good night out, good food, reasonable company; they'd come home and had good sex. After briefly kissing and petting, he had carried her naked from the waist down into the dining room and laid her on the dining table before taking her rather roughly with her legs over his shoulders. It was certainly not the most romantic sex they had ever had but it was acutely intense and left them both exhausted and breathless. He had laughed afterwards that it was a good job that the table was a good quality, strong and of a solid English make, able to take a severe pounding. She had said that the same thing applied to her.

After pouring the cup of mud into the toilet and taking a quick shower, Barry called out, 'I'll be a couple of minutes,' before dressing ready for the Sunday League match against the Pickled Herring. He slowly descended the stairs and entered the kitchen, empty except for a couple of dirty pots on the work top. 'In the dining room, darling,' Monica called, and Barry turned and strolled into the scene of last night's romp.

Monica was standing by the dining room table, grinning proudly at a huge dish of scrambled eggs with smoked salmon, toast and a fresh pot of mud. The table was neatly laid for two, with plates, cups and saucers, glasses for fruit juice and even serviettes. 'I thought that we should use the table for something other than copulation,' she said as Barry sat down, poured an orange juice and spooned a large portion of the breakfast onto his plate. He buttered a piece of toast and began to demolish the mountain of egg and salmon, wondering why Monica was being so considerate.

'Who are you playing for today?' Monica disturbed his thinking and his eating.

'I am playing *for*, or rather supervising, the Poachers Arms, my love, as I have done every Sunday in the season for the last eighteen years. We are playing *against* the Pickled Herring.'

Monica laughed. 'The who, or what?' she smirked.

'It's one of those new plastic bars in town, near the station, full of estate agents and bank managers from Commercial Road. It used to be called the Porters Arms when I was a lad, when it was a real pub. Now they just sell poofy cocktails and bloody tapas and…'

'That's lovely, Barry,' she said, obviously not listening to a word.

'That, Monica my darling, was absolutely magnificent,' he sighed when the plate was empty, suppressing a belch which, under normal circumstances, he would have released with gusto.

'Because you're worth it.' Monica repeated the adage from the previous evening. They sat quietly for a moment, Barry wondering if he should take the plates out for washing up, but he decided that he should capitalize on Monica's good humour and let her do it. Monica took a deep breath.

'Barry darling, I've been thinking. It's very nice here in your house and I really do enjoy our Saturdays here, but I do have more room at my place. I mean, the Grange has six bedrooms and is quiet and I was wondering if perhaps we shouldn't stay there.'

Barry explained how much he would love to but it was more convenient at his house because of the distance to drive to the Grange after an evening out and because he needed to change for the football on Sundays.

'I'm not just talking about Saturday nights, Barry.' Monica suddenly looked nervous. 'I mean permanently. We've been together for seven months now and we're good together. I don't mean just the sex, although that's really great, but we like the same things, we both want the same things out of life.'

Barry was shocked. He knew that something like this would happen one day, but he wasn't ready yet. He needed Monica to ensure that he was accepted as a magistrate and, in a way, he was very fond of her, but this was a huge commitment.

'I don't mean right away. It's a big step, but I think that we should start planning it for after Christmas. That's only a few weeks away and I don't mean that you should sell this place or anything,' Monica continued. 'Just move in with me and keep your house until you're sure, until we're both sure, that it's right. You could even let the house if you want – a few more pounds won't go amiss. And I've got a really big, strong oak dining table.'

Barry was lost for a moment. 'I-I'm not sure, darling,' he stuttered. 'I've been married and divorced twice before. It's a huge commitment and I don't want to let you down.' Barry's mind began to see the way he could direct the discussion. 'You know how much I think of you. I adore you, worship the very ground you walk on, but I am just a humble council house lad and perhaps I just won't match your expectations. I really am afraid of letting you down.'

Monica stared at the dirty plates. 'But you are everything I want, Barry. You're a strong person, a kind man and I love you.' She paused. 'And I know that you love me.'

'Darling, of course I love you.' Barry's mind was working overtime. 'But I would hate to hurt you. I am a bit of a slob at times, and besides, the business is fairly new and I barely make enough to keep myself, let alone keeping you in the manner to which you're accustomed.'

'Money is not that important. I have enough to keep the two of us in relative luxury for life.'

'But that is not the point, Monica. I'm a proud man and couldn't let you keep me. I just could not live with being a kept man.'

'All you need is one good contract now, to add to all the smaller jobs you've got, and the business will really start to take off. Come on, Barry, what do you say?'

'OK, darling, here's a promise. The minute that I sign the next decent contract, we'll make plans. That's a promise.'

Monica collected the dirty breakfast things. 'It's a deal, Barry,' she said happily as she carried the plates into the kitchen. 'Now you just get ready for your footer game and I'll see to all this.'

Too fucking right you will, thought Barry, as he returned upstairs to collect his car keys, pleased that he had steered the conversation round the way that he wanted. He had no new prospects on the horizon and, with the Christmas and the January sales seasons fast approaching, there was little chance of any retailers wanting their shops disrupted by installing surveillance cameras until well into the New Year. By then he would be Barry Plumb J.P. and if she still wanted him to move in then, it would be too late.

Monica was washing up at the sink as Barry prepared to leave for the football. He was a little earlier than usual, but decided that he was better out of the way and to quit while he was ahead in the game of commitment. He moved up close behind her and put his arms around her, moving his hand up her body and holding her breasts whilst kissing the back of her neck. 'I'll give you a ring later, darling,' he breathed into her ear before releasing her and heading for the door.

'Oh, Barry, I nearly forgot,' Monica called as he opened the front door. 'I've invited Charles and Caroline round to my place for a meal some time after Christmas. Thought I'd ask Gerry and Susan White along as well. I'm not sure that you've met them but they're nice. You'll get on well with Gerry.'

Barry climbed into his newly serviced Audi and drove off towards the rec. As he was early, he took the long way round, avoiding Poachers Drive, and driving along the northern approach road. He passed a row of shops on the bypass, a garden centre, do-it-yourself store and Gerry's Super Saver Discount Store. Gerry's Super Saver, he thought. I wonder if… no, too much of a coincidence.

Paul was sitting, staring at the half dozen footballs in their bag between his feet and Billy was folding up the kitbag. Viv was playing a broken tennis racquet like a guitar and singing, "When I'm cleaning windows", in a very bad impression of George Formby. He finished the song with an equally bad moonwalk for reasons known only to himself.

'That, young Vivian, was fucking awful,' Barry announced as he nodded acknowledgement to the other team members.

'I know,' laughed Viv. 'It's because me banjo's got a broken string. Look,' and handed the racquet to Barry, who saw that it had no strings at all.

'I am not happy, not bloody happy at all.' Dave's voice interrupted Viv's laughter. He was looking disconsolate and stared around the changing room shaking his head. 'Two hooks broken off. Right there, look. I am not happy. It looks like we go from number 4 to number 7, with no 5 or 6. What sort of impression does that give? I ask you. Bloody council. Same last year, never repair the bloody place until the close season when it's too late. Bloody council.'

'It should be a ukulele, Vivian, and don't start me on the council,' said Barry. Dave immediately regretted saying anything about the hooks as Barry launched into a tirade about local councils, rubbish collection, councillors' expenses, parking, road conditions and speed cameras. He broke the invective and stared at Dave who was neatly folding shirts numbered 5 and 6 so that the numbers were plainly visible on top of the small pile of kit. 'You work for the fucking council, Dave, what are you complaining about? It's your own fault.'

Before Dave could attempt any explanation about working for the Social Housing Department whereas the changing rooms were covered by the Parks and Recreation Department, the players began drifting in, deflecting Barry's rant. Dave breathed a sigh of relief and stepped back to admire the layout as Viv grabbed his number 6 shirt and moved next to Gunner Farr to show him his new toy and play "Leaning on a lamp-post" before apologizing for the broken string.

Dave counted the players and clapped his hands loudly. 'Right, lads,' he shouted above the din. 'Pickled Herring this morning. Now we've never played these before, but they must be pretty good. They've only been in the league for four years and just missed promotion last year. They've got the same points as us, so today is a big one. We want effort out there, and remember, firm but fair.' No one was listening.

The players trotted out towards pitch number three, hunching their shoulders and pulling their hands inside their shirtsleeves against the cold November rain. Dave and his crew followed silently as the rain dripped down their necks and their fingers tingled with the cold.

As Dave settled down on his usual position on the halfway line, he was pleased to see that Rabbit was refereeing – at least they may get the benefit of the doubt on any dodgy decisions. It was immediately clear that the Pickled Herring was a good team with some good players and two or three outstanding individuals. The left winger was a short, stocky man with thinning ginger hair and a small moustache, who looked like a younger Captain Mainwaring from Dad's Army. He had obviously once been a fine player, but was now far less mobile than in his heyday and his repertoire was restricted to receiving the ball and controlling it expertly, pushing up the left wing for ten yards or so and delivering pinpoint accurate crosses to his strikers. It was a simple but very effective means of attack. Steve Tippling spent the first half an hour trying to combat this main threat with little success. He had tried every means at his disposal, mainly attempting to kick lumps out of his opponent, but Mainwaring was never where Steve's boot was swinging. Steve was becoming increasingly frustrated, the situation made worse by the winger's politeness and good humour. Luckily for the Poachers, George was in good form in goal and was stopping everything that the Pickled Herring attack could throw at him. On the half-hour, however, even George's brilliance was not enough to prevent the first goal. Inevitably, it came from an accurate cross from the left winger, who shimmied past Steve and curved across the penalty area where a scramble ensued before the ball was finally forced over the line.

The Poachers Arms responded to the setback by launching a wave of attacks, missing out the midfield and hammering the ball for their forwards to run onto. Except that Razor never was much of a one for running, so lounged about disconsolately, moaning that he needed the ball at his feet or on his head. Gordon and Gunner looked cold and fed up and were making only token gestures at chasing the ball, whilst the three in midfield were losing enthusiasm as the ball continually flew over their heads. The half closed with the Poachers' lads trotting off the pitch, cold, wet and frustrated.

As the teas were passed around, Dave filled a plastic cup and marched across the pitch to the referee, standing somewhat forlornly in the centre circle. 'Tea, Rabbit,' he stated the obvious as he handed the cup over.

'Thanks, Dave,' said the referee, pleased to grip something warm and get some feeling back into his hands. 'Good game this morning.'

'Bit tricky in this wind and rain,' replied Dave, 'and they've some bloody good players. That number 11's sharp.'

'Apparently he used to play in the Jock second division for Stenhouse Manure or Cow 'n' Beef or some other team with a silly name. That's why that young full back of yours can't touch him – too bloody clever for him. And that's his lad at number 8. Only sixteen. They reckon that there's scouts watching him all the time.'

Dave scanned the touchline for unknown observers enduring the lousy weather. Apart from the players, officials and hangers-on of both teams, there was the usual motley selection of men avoiding their wives on a Sunday morning and a few kids from the council estate taking advantage of half-time to play in the goalmouth. As he turned, Rabbit tapped Dave on the back and pointed to a lone figure near one of the corner flags, dressed in a smart overcoat and a trilby hat pulled over his eyes against the rain. The man stared at both sets of players and scribbled into a notebook.

'See him,' said Rabbit. 'They reckon he could be from Brentford or Fulham. Now let's get this game under way again. I'm freezing,' and gave Dave a knowing wink. 'And by the way, if I was you, I'd move that tall number 4 to right back, take off your number 2 and bring old Percy on in the middle of your defence.'

Dave sprinted back to his team as Rabbit blew his whistle to call the teams back onto the pitch. 'Steve, you're off, Little Smithy, move to right back, Percy, take Smithy's place, and that bloke in the corner's a scout from Chelsea or Arsenal.'

The players did not have time to think or discuss the changes as Percy peeled off the tattered tracksuit top and followed the other players onto the pitch, his rounded shoulders, grey hair and moustache making him look far more than his thirty-two-odd years. He was still taking a final drag on his cigarette as the whistle blew to restart the game.

'Why me?' asked Steve, a little petulantly. 'I'd 'ave had that ginger this half, easy. I'd have kicked him from ass'ole to breakfast time.'

'Precisely. Rabbit says that one more bad tackle and he was going to send you off and we can't afford for you to be suspended again,' Dave lied. 'You've already got one coming up after that scrap the other week, and you're too valuable to the squad.'

As the second half progressed, the rain lashed down horizontally, whipped across the playing field by the violently gusting wind. Dave loved it. He was warm beneath layers of clothing and his ancient parka, a woollen hat pulled down over his ears. The Poachers Arms was beginning to take over the match, with the front three chasing every ball as if their lives depended on it and every-one working hard for themselves and each other. Each time a player had beaten an opponent, played a good ball, made a timely interception or a strong tackle, he would glance over to see if the stranger had taken note. Fifteen minutes had gone when Wayne Tocket slipped a superb pass through to the inside right position which skidded off the sodden turf and past the opposing defence. Razor moved onto the ball and almost lazily moved it from his right foot to his left before striking a magnificent shot into the roof of the net. He raised one arm and sprinted to the mystery man's corner and turned so that his number was clear to the stranger, and waited for his team mates' congratulations as they engulfed him.

After another fine goal, Razor repeated his celebration in front of the scout and was again mobbed by his team mates. The Poachers' players were lifted by the goals, mounting a wave of attacks which resulted in a fine individual goal from Gunner who cut in from the left and slammed a shot low into the net from fully twenty-five yards. As his team took control, Dave casually strolled over to the stranger in the corner, hoping to strike up a conversation and to see if any of his players had caught the scout's eye. As he approached, there was something vaguely familiar about the man and Dave wondered if he had seen him on the television, perhaps from his playing days or sitting in the Fulham dugout.

'Hello, Dave, awful weather isn't it?' said the man as Dave approached. For a moment Dave was taken aback, wondering how this man had heard of him. Perhaps he was better known in football circles than he had realised. Perhaps premiership managers talked about his knack of bringing on young players or of his tactical awareness. 'It's me, Dave, Peter Cherry, from the Parks and Recreation Department.'

Dave looked under the hat and recognized Peter from the next office. 'Watcher, Pete. What you doing here?'

Peter looked thoroughly miserable. 'New incentive from my boss. Wants us to be more hands-on, more involved, more part of the community, and expects us all to join in something every weekend then give him a ten-minute verbal report at the Monday morning team meetings. Waste of time.'

As he was speaking, Wayne scrambled in the Poachers' fourth goal from close range. 'You wouldn't come every week, I suppose?' asked Dave.

The final whistle blew and Dave followed his players across the playing field and into the changing rooms. The players threw their soaking kit into the centre of the room and in buoyant mood after their four–one success, were clamouring for Dave to tell them about his discussion with the scout. For the first time ever, Dave had the team's complete attention. 'He comes from a leading London league club was all he was prepared to say,' Dave began. 'And he said he was very impressed with some of the players from the Poachers, but he's not allowed to say which ones. However, he said that he would need to come back and watch them again before making any decisions about trials and things.'

Viv, who knew that he was too old to be the subject of any interest, was the first to speak. 'I had a scout watch me once,' he said. 'Watched me for four weeks, every week without fail.'

'What happened?' asked Young Smithy.

'Oh, it never came to anything,' Viv answered. 'He touched my cock at scout camp, so I left the cubs there and then.'

Dave, Paul and Billy stayed behind after the players had showered, dressed and left for the pub. Paul and Dave had a general tidy up, collecting sodden shirts, shorts and socks and stuffing them into the kitbag before gathering up the footballs, first aid kit, water bottles and flasks. Dave had meandered off to find Rabbit. As he entered the changing room, the referees were laughing at something but were strangely silent when they saw Dave. He knew that they had been laughing at the imaginary scout and he felt a little silly as he handed over the twenty pounds fee.

'How did you get on with the scout then, Dave?' Rabbit asked as the other three referees sniggered quietly.

'He wasn't a fucking scout at all,' Dave answered, 'and you know it, Rabbit.'

Rabbit laughed. 'Just a bit of joke, Dave, I haven't got a clue who the bloke is. Anyway, it geed your fellas up a bit, didn't it: played like men possessed in the second half. And what about the team changes I proposed? That worked well and all, didn't it?'

'Certainly did, Rabbit, thanks,' Dave agreed. 'The bloke was a referees' assessor and I told him you'd been really helpful.' Dave left Rabbit with his mouth open and looking decidedly deflated.

At the pub, Paul bought three pints, carefully avoiding Billy who was busy trying to blend into whichever round was being served next, and passed a pint each to Viv and Dave, Viv still holding on to his new stringless instrument.

Dave moved closer to the bar until he saw Mandy and smiled at her, deter-mined to carry off the Hugh Grant look sooner or later. He had even decided to let his fringe grow so that he could push it back off his face in a kind of 'Hey, don't you think I'm a handsome and caring kind of guy' way, although, as yet, his hair had started to stand up at the front. Like a startled chicken, Tonker said.

'Fifteen two and three's five, four one in the end then,' said Tonker as Dave sat down and wondered whether he was expected to respond or whether the whole sentence was some part of incomprehensible cribbage tallying.

He gambled that the 'four one' concerned the football score and nodded. 'Good result. Bound to be in the top three. Could even put us equal top if Jones Juniors get beat at The New Inn.'

'Fifteen two,' said Tonker, putting the seven of clubs on the table.

Dave understood that that was the end of the conversation with his father and turned to Barry. 'Quiet today, old son,' he said.

'Yes, Dave, got a lot on my mind actually. A lot to think about.' Barry gazed thoughtfully across the bar.

'Want to talk about it?' asked Dave, immediately regretting the offer as he knew that Barry could not only complain for England but could also captain the Great Britain Olympic Pedantic Conversation Team when he was in the mood.

'Thirty one for two,' said Tonker.

'Well it's like this,' Barry began, and Dave knew that he was in for a long lunchtime.

Barry explained about the desire to be a magistrate…

'Fifteen two, fifteen four and three's seven.'

…and how he had been seeing Monica for seven months or so…

'Thirty one for two.'

…and how Monica was very friendly with the chairman of the Magistrates' Advisory Committee…

'Fifteen six and six is a dozen.'

…and how Monica had suggested that they move in together…

'Fifteen for five.'

…and how he was worried about making the commitment…

'Fifteen two, fifteen four, two's six.'

…and how he would welcome any advice…

'Twenty four for three and out. And if I was you I'd jump at the chance, Plumby. Ugly fucker like you can't afford to be choosy,' added Tommy.

Downham Sunday Football League, Division Two
Results for Sunday 2nd November

New Inn, Gorton Down	2	2	Jones Juniors FC
J G Tanner and Sons	1	0	Shellduck Inn
AFC Cummiston	5	3	Downham Churches
Poachers Arms	**4**	**1**	**Pickled Herring**
Lower End WMC	3	0	Hearty Oak, Downlea

League Table

Team	Pl'd	Won	Drew	Lost	For	Ag'st	GD	Points
Jones Juniors FC	7	5	2	0	28	10	18	17
Poachers Arms	**7**	**5**	**1**	**1**	**21**	**9**	**12**	**16**
New Inn, Gorton D	7	4	2	1	21	13	8	14
Pickled Herring	6	4	1	1	14	11	3	13
AFC Cummiston	7	2	4	1	13	15	-2	10
J G Tanner and Sons	6	3	0	3	11	13	-2	9
Hearty Oak, Downlea	7	1	2	4	16	26	-10	5
Lower End WMC	5	1	1	3	7	14	-7	4
Shellduck Inn	7	1	1	5	9	19	-10	4
Downham Churches	6	0	2	4	21	31	-10	2

<u>Sunday 16th November</u>

Downham Sunday Football League, Division Two
Lower End WMC v Poachers Arms
Tenacre Recreation Ground – Kick-off 10.30

<u>THE POACHERS ARMS</u>

1 George Crosswell

2 Percy Woodman   4 Derek Smith   5 Brian Smith   3 Billy Millmore (Capt)

8 Wayne Tocket   6 Vivian Clutterbuck   10 Danny Tomlinson

7 Gordon Gaye   9 Paddy Oakley   11 Gunner Farr

Substitutes
12 Paul Cornwell
13 Dave Statham
14 Barry Plumb

Reserves (Please bring boots)
None

Manager
Dave Statham

All players, substitutes and reserves to turn up at 09.45

Billy was annoyed about the telephone call he had received from Dave in the week. The County Football Association had convened a disciplinary meeting on Wednesday and suspended both Wayne Tocket and Matt Cornwell for one month for fighting in the game against Tanner's in October. Razor Raisin was unavailable because of a "family commitment", which probably meant that he was forced into going to see his mother-in-law in Bath, so the team was down to the bare minimum of players and substitutes. He had argued with Dave that more players were needed if they were to mount a serious challenge for the league, but Dave, in his usual languid way, was happy that it would be fine as long as no one else was suspended, injured or henpecked for the rest of the season.

He filled the kettle with exactly two mugs of water and turned it on. Ensuring that Louise had her tea in bed gave Billy an extra twenty minutes of peace. As the kettle boiled, he filled a washing-up bowl with warm water and washed four plates and the cutlery from the previous night's supper, standing them on the draining board before making two cups of tea with one teabag. The teabag was placed in a small dish placed near the kettle as it was just possible to squeeze another two cups out of the bag, and the twins liked weak tea. He picked up the cup and turned to find Louise standing in the doorway with arms folded, staring at him. 'Tea here or upstairs, my sweet?' he asked, forcing a smile and hoping that she would elect to take the tea upstairs.

'On the table,' she grumbled. 'And I've been thinking.' She sat down as Billy continued to clean the kitchen. He always worried when Louise had been thinking as it usually ended up in some hare-brained money-making scheme which broke the rhythm of his easy life. 'We need to make more money somehow. It's all very well saving and being sensible with what we've got, but we need more. Another four years and the girls will be at uni, and that costs a fortune. We need another income source.'

Billy had heard this before. Louise always wanted more money, no matter how much they had tucked away in the bank and savings accounts.

'We do alright, my sweet.' Billy pondered for a brief moment. 'I earn good money, you earn a decent salary, we've got a decent motor, big house, all mod cons. We're doing OK.'

'Well, OK isn't enough,' she snapped. 'Just look at that mate of yours, Barry Plumb. He runs a new Audi and his woman's got a flashy sports car and they've got a house each. She lives in a big manor house in Shepley Overton and she's got a Mercedes as well which she leaves in the garage. He is so jammy. Why has he got so much more than us? He's only a retired policeman, after all. It's about time you earned more money.'

Billy sighed quietly. 'The reason is that she's a widow and her husband was rich. It's that simple.'

'Sometimes, Billy, I wish I was a rich widow. You're not taking this seriously and it's very serious. We need to earn more money and you do nothing. I've tried all sorts of things. I tried writing that book for Mills and Boon, I tried with my own catering business, I tried to get the twins into modelling and what support did you give me? None, that's what. You are useless.'

'But I did help with the modelling,' Billy whined. 'I had my photograph taken with you and the girls for the agency. It wasn't my fault they didn't use us.'

'Useless. It's probably because you were on the photo that they didn't use us. So what are we going to do about it? What are you going to do?'

Billy shrugged and put two pieces of bread in the toaster as he heard the twins patter downstairs and into the kitchen. 'Blimey, girls, you're early. Come and give your old Dad a kiss.' Both girls trotted over and kissed their father on the cheek. He barely had to bend down now, they were growing so quickly.

'Are you two arguing again?' said Ruth. 'What about, this time? Is it money as usual?'

'Your father is useless,' Louise answered. 'He just doesn't understand what it's like to scrimp and save all the time.'

Billy tried to change the subject. 'Why are you two lovelies up so early on a Sunday morning?'

'We told you yesterday,' said Martha.

'And the day before,' added Ruth.

'It's Katie's birthday,' they said together, in high singsong voices.

'Katie and her mum are picking us up at nine o'clock.' Martha began her well-rehearsed synopsis of the programme for the day ahead.

'In her new top of the range Lexus,' Ruth added.

'In her new top of the range Lexus,' repeated Martha. 'Then we are picking up Janine, then we are going to a teashop for elevenses, then we are going ice skating, then we are going to a restaurant for lunch, then we are going riding on Katie's ponies, then we are having tea, then we are having a swim in their pool, and then we are having a small soiree with some other friends.'

'And some boys have been invited,' Ruth added.

Louise stared at Billy as he started to spread the thin layer of margarine on the toast. 'You see what I mean. How can we compete with Katie's parents? Top of the range Lexus, ponies, swimming pool. How can we compete with them if we don't have more money coming in?'

'And they've got a barn they use for parties, with a real bar and a massive widescreen entertainment system and disco lights and everything,' added Ruth, knowing that she was fanning the already flaming argument.

'But I don't really want to compete with them,' Billy offered meekly.

'Exactly the problem. There you are, girls. Your father just doesn't care that we're shown up by not having what everyone else has. He's useless.' Louise turned to Billy. 'You're absolutely useless,' she shouted, and finished her tea with a loud and undignified slurp.

'It doesn't matter, Mummy, really.' Martha looked at her mother with a mock expression of sadness. 'We're used to being the poorest kids out of our group. We'll just explain that you don't earn very much and Katie's mum will understand. She won't hold it against you that we're poor. We're going up to put our make-up on,' said the girls and wandered out of the kitchen, each carrying a mug of weak tea and giggling.

'That's it. You are useless. We have to do something.' Louise's voice was bordering on hysteria.

'The girls are only winding you up, my sweet,' said Billy, trying to cool the situation as he bit into his slice of toast. 'I'll think of something.'

Louise composed herself. 'If we wait for you to think of something, we'll wait forever. And I have already thought of something. This afternoon, I want you to clear out the spare room completely, then decorate it over the next couple of weeks. I'll get the furniture from my old bedroom in mum's house.

142

We'll need new bedclothes and curtains but I should be able to get them in the January sales, and there we have it.'

The impact of Louise's plan hit Billy. 'You mean, let the spare room? Take in a lodger?'

'What's wrong with it?' Louise immediately and automatically went onto the attack.

'Wrong?' answered Billy. 'What's wrong? Absolutely nothing's wrong. It's a brilliant idea. Easy money. We could ask, what, about two hundred a month at least, and it's tax free. Well done, my sweet. Why didn't we think of this before? If it works, we could get the girls to move in together and free up another room. Then, when they go to uni, we could even have three rooms to let. Brilliant, Louise, brilliant.' Louise looked for any hint of sarcasm in his response, but there was none. Billy was genuinely excited about the prospect. 'Well done, my sweet, well done,' he repeated.

'Good. That's agreed then. We'll aim for the New Year to make sure that we can get everything ready, then I'll put an advert in the paper shop window and bingo, we're in the money.'

Dave was studying photographs of Tenerife in Muzzy's shop. He had managed to avoid the moment for weeks but had now run out of excuses and had made the unforgivable mistake of going for his paper fifteen minutes ahead of schedule. He stared at photographs of a swimming pool, of black sand and blue sea, of the hotel from seven different angles, of Muzzy's children in the swimming pool, on the black sand, in the blue sea and in the hotel.

'Fantastic holiday then, Muzzy. Lovely photos. Nice place then, Tenerife?' Perhaps that's where he could take Mandy on honeymoon. A traditional church wedding – he would have to check if that was possible because she had been married before – followed by two weeks in the sun in Tenerife. 'If you've got any details on the hotel, I'd be grateful. You never know, I might go there myself one day.'

'With anyone special?' Muzzy asked, and winked.

Dave became flustered and handed back the photos quickly before jogging back across the road where Vivian and Paul were leaning on his car, Paul drawing deeply on a cigarette and Vivian re-enacting a scene from last night's repeat of Only Fools And Horses.

A car horn blew outside the house and the twins rushed down the stairs. 'That's them. Just look at that car,' shouted Martha, excited about the prospects for the day ahead. 'Please can we have some money, Daddy?'

Billy sighed and pulled the wallet from his back pocket.

'Wait a minute.' Louise stopped him. 'What do you want money for? Katie's mum should pay for everything, it's her party. Just tell her that you were given five pounds each but left the money in the house by mistake when you changed for the party. No, say ten pounds each.'

The girls looked unhappy but knew better than to argue with their mother on matters of finance. 'Now come on, let's get you two into the new Lexus. We can't keep Katie's mum waiting,' and she pushed Martha and Ruth out of the door. Louise ushered the girls down the drive like an experienced sheepdog and opened the back door of the car to allow the twins to clamber in. As she did so, Katie's mother opened the driver's window. 'Thanks awfully, Mrs. Millmore,' she said. 'I'll get them home by ten.'

'Yes. Thank you, Mrs—' Louise suddenly realised that she did not know Katie's' mother's name, but it didn't matter because by this time Katie's mother had closed the window and pulled away.

Louise scurried back into the house as Billy began clearing up from breakfast. 'Did you see that car, Billy? Perhaps we should get one like that when we can afford it.'

'We can afford it now, my sweet,' Billy said. 'We have several tens of thousands of pounds in the bank and in savings accounts. We could buy that car for cash tomorrow if you really want to.'

Louise stopped in her tracks. 'That is just typical of you,' she bawled. 'I work full time, look after two kids, scrimp and save, come up with money-making ideas and you want to spend our nest egg on a new car. You really are useless.' And she stormed out of the kitchen and up the stairs, before shouting down, 'And make sure that you're home by half past twelve today. We're going to Mum's for lunch and I want to check that bedroom furniture.' Billy turned the radio up and continued to wash up quietly.

Lower End Working Men's Club also played at Tenacre Recreation Ground, so it felt like a home game, although Poachers would take changing room number four as the away team. Dave and his crew arrived at the rec at the same time as

Billy, and the four of them unloaded their cars and carried the various trappings of football management into the changing rooms. Lightning stood to attention and greeted the entourage. 'Morning, Mr Statham,' they all replied, aping Lightning's singsong welcome, 'Morning, Lightning.' All except Billy, who whispered, 'Dozy prat' under his breath.

'What number are we today, Assistant to the Groundsman?' Dave asked, ignoring Billy's comment.

Lightning looked at his allocation sheet and said, 'Changing room number four, pitch number three, Mr Statham.' Dave took the key to changing room number four and signed the booking sheet, but noticed that Lightning didn't seem quite his normal self. The happy and relaxed attitude of a man enjoying his work was missing. It was hard to put his finger on, but Dave just sensed that something wasn't right. He made a mental note to go back later.

Dave laid out the kit and the players began to arrive, filtering into the changing room singly or in pairs. The room was soon its usual hubbub of noise and stale smells. There was an air of confidence amongst the team after the result from two weeks ago: second in the league, just one point behind the leaders, and playing Lower End Club who were almost bottom. A freak result last match gave them three points but that didn't alter the fact that they were a poor outfit. Dave ticked everyone off against the teamsheet. 'Where's fucking Plumby?' he shouted. 'Anyone seen Barry Plumb?'

Paddy looked up from tying his laces. 'He was talking to Fat Bryan from the Club earlier on,' he called across the changing room, so Dave went out looking for him. Not that it mattered that much as he would not be called upon to play unless they lost three players through injury, and even then the Poachers would probably be better off playing with ten men. As he passed the office, Dave stopped and had a quick word with Lightning. 'What's up, mate?' he asked. 'You don't seem your usual self.'

Lightning looked confused before replying, 'Is this work or personal now?'

'I think that you've finished the work until the end of the game, so it's personal,' Dave replied tenderly. 'So what's up?'

'I'm not supposed to tell,' Lightning began, but Dave knew that he would tell. 'Mum says that Paul mustn't find out yet until she's had time to tell him.'

'Well, what is it Lightning?' Dave pressed gently.

Lightning looked around, his eyes seeming to work independently. 'Mum's friend Alan keeps coming round and I don't like him and he calls me names when Mum's not there and, to be perfectly honest, Dave, I'm more than a little disturbed by it all.'

Dave felt like laughing at Lightning's strange choice of words, but saw the tears just beginning to form in the corner of his eyes. 'Look, mate,' he said. 'Don't you worry. He probably only calls you names because he's jealous of you, being Assistant to the Groundsman and all. Just try to ignore him and remember that you can always come round my house if you need to get away when he's there.'

Lightning's eyes lit up and looked like he had been given the world. 'What, I can come to your house? To where you live? Thanks, Dave, I will, thanks.' Dave realised that Lightning had probably never been invited anywhere on his own before. Little wonder that he seemed so grateful.

'Guess fucking what. Go on. Guess. You'll never guess. The Boulton twins are home from Afghanifuckinstan.' Dave turned and saw Barry marching towards the changing rooms. 'Guess what lads,' he announced to the team. 'The Boulton twins are back from Afghanifuckinstan.' The Poachers' team groaned and shook their heads.

'Who are they?' Danny Tomlinson's voice piped up from the doorway.

'The Boulton twins, my young friend, are the roughest, toughest, meanest sons-of-bitches this side of the OK Corral.' Viv was enjoying playing a grizzled old sheriff from a 1950s' 'B' movie, but his description of the twins was not altogether inaccurate. Their mother had first produced Thomas, followed by Gerald eleven minutes later. It wasn't known if she was a fan of cartoons, but Tom and Gerry it was. No one had called them Tom and Gerry to their faces since they went to senior school and were teased by an older bully. The bully was found later that evening hanging by his ankles, but otherwise unharmed, from a tree at the back of the school. When he was asked by the police how he had ended up hanging from a tree, he explained that he had tripped. No one teased the twins again. They were both in the Army and rumoured to be SAS, SBS or Paratroopers although no one seemed to know which and didn't know the difference anyway. They were each six feet six, shaven-headed and built, as Viv described them, 'like brick shithouses', with neither carrying an ounce of fat. They were tough, robust and as hard as nails, but honest and fair. As

146

Viv explained, they always apologised as the ambulance arrived to take their opponents to hospital. But the biggest problem with the Boulton twins was that they played for Lower End Working Men's Club. And the Poachers were playing with a severely depleted team.

'OK, lads, listen up.' Dave realised that his dispirited troops needed one of his stimulating pep talks. 'OK, quiet, and listen. We all know the Boulton twins and we've played them before and they're nothing to be afraid of. Firm but fair, remember. Firm but fair.' Dave kept his fingers crossed.

The two teams trotted across the playing field together. Most of the players lived on the Poachers' Estate and many of them had been to school together. Whether you played for the Club or the Poachers was more likely to be decided by where your father preferred to drink rather than by any topographical division. Barry was walking with Fat Bryan and Dave struggled to catch them up, carting his first aid kit, sports bag, flasks and several small water bottles. As he caught them, Barry was smiling and said, 'Go on, Bryan, tell Dave the news, go on, tell him.'

Fat Bryan was always serious and had never knowingly been seen to smile. 'It's not just the Boulton twins,' he explained. 'We've also signed three more of their army mates. And they're all Paras or something. That's why we're behind in our fixtures. After you beat us in the first game, we went to the Sunday League committee and explained that half of our players were fighting in Afghanistan, so they let us postpone a couple of games, but they're all back on leave until after Christmas now. Two of them played last week and we won easy. You wanna see this big black bloke go.'

'Bloody hell,' Dave exclaimed. 'What are you smiling about, Plumby? This is serious.'

'David, I am smiling for two reasons. One: there is more to life than a football result. These lads have been risking their lives in foreign climes to make the world a safer place and I am happy that they're all back in one piece and able to enjoy a civilized morning's sport without worries of being shot or maimed by enemy snipers. Two: I'm not playing against the mad bastards.'

As the teams lined up, Dave and Barry took up their positions on the halfway line. Although the weather was dry, it was grey and cold and the previous week's rain had made the pitch heavy with mud. 'Which ones are the soldiers?' Dave asked Paul who was wandering the line with his linesman's flag.

'Well, you know the Boulton twins,' replied Paul. 'Then there's that big ginger bloke at the back, the big bald bloke in midfield and the big black bloke at the front.'

'We're doomed, we're all doomed,' shouted Viv from midfield.

When the game started, Dave's pessimism soon changed as it became clear that the soldiers were not great footballers. Either because they had little skills to start with, or because months of practice by kicking old bully beef tins in the desert sand had dulled their edge Dave could not tell, but was not unduly worried by what he saw. The first goal came surprisingly from a long upfield punt which was missed by all the tall defenders, allowing Gunner Farr to nip between them and slot an inch-perfect shot past the Club's goalkeeper.

Although the Poachers' team remained a little wary of their opponents and were not fully committed to challenging for fifty-fifty balls, their more skilful approach meant that the majority of the game was played in the Club's half of the field. The equalizing goal came as something of a shock, when the ball was hoofed forward with some desperation from the Club defence and did not seem to be causing a problem as Billy calmly moved back to collect the clearance, when the big black bloke sprinted past him, pushed the ball forward and ran on to thump it into the net.

The Poachers soon recovered their composure and returned to playing the better football, but a little more cautiously than before, aware that the big black bloke could be a danger if he was given space. From a corner, Poachers scrambled a second goal, the ball finally bouncing in off Danny Tomlinson's knee. For the last ten minutes of the first half, it was brain against brawn, inspiration against perspiration, as the Club players, particularly the servicemen, chased every ball, every lost cause, every pass and every tackle. Their vigorous approach was beginning to worry some of the Poachers' team, particularly Paddy up front, never the bravest of players, and the two veteran defenders, Billy and Percy, both of whom were too experienced to be drawn into a physical battle, but their caution was beginning to reveal worrying defensive gaps. The one exception was young Danny Tomlinson who, though only seventeen, was a very clever player and had started to show off his repertoire of skills against his more clumsy opponents, reminding Dave of a matador, teasing and taunting a bull; and the Boulton twins did not take kindly to being teased.

Although leading two goals to one, the Poachers Arms players were not too confident as they slumped around at half-time. As they swigged from plastic water bottles or lit up cigarettes, the talk was of how strong and fit the army lads were, how it was like being tackled by a tank and how they were bruised from top to toe already. Dave was a little flummoxed over how to turn the negative attitude to his advantage and busied himself taking tea to the referee. Barry stepped into the breach.

'This game is easy,' he announced to looks of bewilderment from the team. 'These army lads are easy.'

'What the fuck do you know, Plumby? They're like fucking machines,' said Wayne Tocket.

'What do I know, laddie? I'll tell you what I know. I did my bit for Queen and country, four years in Her Majesty's Royal Air Force, making the world a safer place for erks like you. That's what I know. And I'm telling you, these squaddies have nothing up here' – he pointed to his head – 'nothing between the ears. Nowt. Zilch. And the way to beat them is to keep using your brains. Don't get drawn into a physical battle you can't win. Use your heads and let them run around like mad dogs of war.' Barry was enjoying this and wasn't going to let a mixed metaphor stop him. 'So get out there, play football, use your skills and use your heads and the goals will flow.'

'Well done, Barry, good speech,' said Dave, having returned from tea duties.

'Won't do any good,' Barry responded. 'These blokes are used to yomping across deserts carrying tons of ammunition. They'll hammer us this half.'

Danny, particularly, had taken Barry's words to heart and was enjoying himself in midfield, shouting for the ball at every opportunity. He was beating players with clever dummies, dragging the ball back with his studs and feinting both ways before leaving his opponents floundering in the mud. The Boulton twins were on the receiving end of many of Danny's tricks and were becoming dangerously frustrated, until Danny did one stepover too many and a huge muscled body crashed into him like a train crushing a car at a level crossing. The youngster lay in the mud gasping for breath. The concerned players from both sides stood around the prone body before the big ginger bloke bent down and felt Danny all over with surprising tenderness. He held his eyes open gently with his thumb and forefinger and held three fingers up from his other hand.

'How many fingers am I holding up, son?' he asked in a gentle Scottish accent. Danny answered, 'Three,' still gasping for breath. The big ginger bloke lifted him up then doubled him over then straightened him up until Danny was able to suck in a deep breath.

'He's OK, ref. Just a bit winded, that's all. No permanent damage.'

'Handy having a medic on the team,' Billy said to the big black bloke.

'What, Ginger? He's no medic. He's a para. corporal. Only trained in one thing. To kill with his bare hands. Same as me,' the big black bloke said and laughed at Billy's shocked features.

Within minutes of the re-start the big black bloke pushed the ball past Billy, taking full advantage of his sluggishness in turning, and sprinted on to score a repeat of his first goal. As he trotted back up the pitch past a stunned Billy, he said, 'Oh, and we're trained to score goals. I didn't mention that.'

As the pitch churned up and became heavier, the Club players became stronger and the Poachers' players became weaker. The tackling was somewhat half-hearted with the Poachers' team aware that another accident could be serious when playing against raging army bulls. The Club began to overrun the stretched defence. Two more goals were added before the final whistle, the big black bloke scoring one more to claim a hat-trick and Tom Boulton bundling the ball, George, the referee, one of his own players and a wayward dog over the line for the fourth goal.

As they traipsed off the pitch at the final whistle, the heavens opened and heavy rain was driven into their faces by fierce winds. The players flopped in the changing rooms as Billy scurried round collecting shirts, shorts and socks and stuffing the kit into the old canvas bag, aware that he had to make the twelve-thirty deadline with Louise or he would be in deep trouble.

'Fucking hell, Billy, that's the fastest you've moved all morning. If you'd have moved that fast against that big black bloke, we might have won,' Paul laughed.

When the last of the players had left, Dave and Paul checked the changing room and locked up. Dave returned the key to Lightning, whilst Paul took the car keys and carried the bag of footballs to the car. Viv had already left with Barry to get the beers in so that as little time as possible was wasted. As he ticked the "returned" box on the allocation sheet, Dave said, 'Don't forget, Lightning, any time.'

'Thank you, Mr Statham, er, Dave, er…'

'Dave's fine, now that you've got the keys back, Andrew.' It was the first time that Dave had ever used Lightning's real name.

'What was all that about with Lightning?' said Paul as Dave started the Polo's engine.

'Oh, nothing much; he was just showing me his new form. Nice lad, always polite.'

Paul knew that Dave thought that Lightning was his son but said nothing. It was none of his business.

As they arrived in the Poachers, Barry signalled them over to the corner where two pints were waiting. Tonker looked up from his cribbage. 'Four–two by the Club. Shan't be able to show my face in there for bingo tonight. I reckon your lot bottled it just because they had a few big lads playing. In my day, we'd have given 'em a bloody good whacking. Slowed 'em down a bit.'

Dave ignored the taunt and turned to Tommy. 'Your Danny OK, Tommy?'

'Right as fuckin' rain.' Tommy picked up his cribbage hand. 'Serve the fucker right, pissin' about, showin' off. Might teach the daft twat a lesson.' He threw the six of spades over to Tanner Brown for some reason that defeated Dave.

'By the way, Mandy wants to see you. Says to make sure you see her before you go,' added Tonker. Viv broke out into "Love is a many splendoured thing", but, luckily, only knew the first line. He then left the table and moved to a small group of players who would be more appreciative of his talents, and began telling jokes in the style of Jethro.

After a minute or two of quiet reflection, Barry said that the team really did need more players. Paul and Dave agreed, but where could they find new players halfway through the season? They didn't know any Polish refugees or British soldiers, and would prefer to restrict the team to players from the estate if at all possible.

'What about your lad, Paul?' asked Dave. 'He must have lots of young mates who can play a bit. They don't have to be that good. Just be available when we're short—'

Tonker interrupted. 'In my day, we had players queuing up to play for the Poachers. Had to turn 'em down. 'Course things were different then; wouldn't let a few bloody soldiers intimidate us, would we, Tom?'

Dave caught Mandy at the bar when there was a quiet spell as the men began to leave for their Sunday dinners.

'What's up, Mandy? My dad says you want to see me.'

'I do, Dave. Can you meet me at three when I finish here? It's quite important.'

''Course I can. Look forward to it.'

Dave returned to the corner as Tonker was getting up to leave. Dave finished his pint quickly and said, 'Hang on, Father. I'll come with you.'

'Early today, Dave, anything up?' Paul asked, finishing his pint.

'Not really,' said Dave. 'It's just that it's been a cheap lunchtime without Billy conning drinks, so I'm getting out while the going's good.'

Tonker lit up the last of his pre-rolled cigarettes as they strolled across the road together, took a deep drag and coughed, spitting a large hunk of phlegm into the gutter. By the time they reached home, a matter of less than one hundred yards, he was wheezing hard and stopped at the gate to recover his breath. Dave told him again that he should give up smoking, to which he gave his usual answer, 'My grandfather smoked fifty a day from the time he was thirteen until the day he died. Mind you, he died when he was twenty-four.'

Mandy waved goodbye to the replacement barmaid and came to meet Dave, slipping her coat over her shoulders. He tried to give her a welcoming kiss, but she grabbed his arm and rushed him out of the door and into the rain. Before he could speak, she said, 'Dave, there's no easy way to tell you this. I'm late.'

Dave looked at his watch. 'But it's only five past and I'm in no rush,' he said, puzzled at the abrupt statement.

Mandy smiled and shook her head. 'No, David, not late finishing work. My period should have started on the third of November. It's now the sixteenth. That means that I'm two weeks late. Do you understand?'

They were meandering towards Mandy's house and Dave could feel the rain seeping into his collar and down his back. They stopped under a large chestnut tree near the green at the side of the pub.

'I think so,' he said hesitantly. 'It means that you're up the… in the… well, sort of… pregnant.'

She smiled and shook her head again. 'Not sort of, David. Probably pregnant. I'm always regular to the day and now I'm thirteen days late. It's more than likely, David, that I am expecting your child.'

Dave was stunned. A month ago he was a forty-year-old virgin who had never had sex except on his own, and now he was about to become a father. This needed some taking in.

'What are we going to do?' he asked, his voice croaking, squeaking and quivering.

'That's what we need to talk about, Dave. I really do not know what to do.'

'I will marry you, you know that, don't you?' was all he could think of to say as the rain dripped from the tree, soaking his face.

'Yes, Dave. I think that you really would. But we still have to decide what to do.'

'How did it happen, d'you think?' Dave asked innocently.

'Well, it may have been a stork, or a lavatory seat, or it may have been because we have been having sex at every opportunity for the last month,' Mandy replied, again shaking her head, but this time not laughing.

'No, I know that but, I mean, aren't you taking… tablets?'

'If you mean, you great soft thing, am I on the Pill, then no I'm not. When I was married, we were trying for ages, years actually, and nothing happened, so I thought it was me, you know something wrong. Well, Gareth, my husband, said it was my fault because there couldn't be anything wrong with him, so I just thought that…' Her voice trailed away to nothing.

'Well we can't stop here talking in this weather,' he said, pleased that he sounded strong and manly. 'And we can't go back to your place with your house-mates, so come back to my place and we can talk about it properly.'

'That's great. You can introduce me to your parents. "Mum, Dad, this is my new girlfriend, Mandy. She's up the duff".'

They smiled and held each other tightly.

'Come on,' he repeated. 'The old man's in bed asleep and me mum's kipping in front of the telly. We can go to my room and talk properly.'

They turned and strolled back to Dave's house. He didn't know how he felt. Very happy in one way, very scared in another. Of course he would marry her. He did know that he had never felt so proud of anything in his life. They hurried back to his house through the rain and he opened the front door. As they went in, his mum came out of the front room and stopped dead, staring at them.

'Mum, this is Mandy,' was all Dave could think of to say.

'Yes, I know,' said his mum, and suddenly her face broke into another lovely smile. 'Come in, love, come in, you'll catch your death there. David, take Mandy's coat. That's better, oh and, David, you've got another visitor in the front room.' Dave looked in the front room to see Lightning sitting on the settee with a cup of tea and smiling brightly.

Ten

Downham Sunday Football League, Division Two
Results for Sunday 16th November

Shellduck Inn	3	3	New Inn, Gorton Down
Downham Churches	1	7	Jones Juniors FC
Pickled Herring	0	1	J G Tanner and Sons
Hearty Oak, Downlea	5	4	AFC Cummiston
Lower End WMC	**4**	**2**	**Poachers Arms**

League Table

Team	Pl'd	Won	Drew	Lost	For	Ag'st	GD	Points
Jones Juniors FC	8	6	2	0	35	11	24	20
Poachers Arms	**8**	**5**	**1**	**2**	**23**	**13**	**10**	**16**
New Inn, Gorton D	8	4	3	1	24	16	8	15
Pickled Herring	7	4	1	2	14	12	2	13
J G Tanner and Sons	7	4	0	3	12	13	-1	12
AFC Cummiston	8	2	4	2	17	20	-3	10
Hearty Oak, Downlea	8	2	2	4	21	30	-9	8
Lower End WMC	6	2	1	3	11	16	-5	7
Shellduck Inn	8	1	2	5	12	22	-10	5
Downham Churches	7	0	2	5	22	38	-16	2

Sunday 23rd November

Downham Sunday Football League, Division Two
AFC Cummiston v Poachers Arms
Cummiston Recreation Ground – Kick-off 10.30

THE POACHERS ARMS

1 Gunner Farr

2 Percy Woodman Millmore (Capt)　　4 Derek Smith　　5 Brian Smith　　3 Billy

8 Wayne Tocket　　6 Vivian Clutterbuck　　10 Danny Tomlinson

7 Gordon Gaye　　9 Razor Raisin　　11 Paddy Oakley

Substitutes
12 Jamie Dunbar
13 Majid Ahmed
14 Paul Cornwell

Reserves (Please bring boots)
Dave Statham
Barry Plumb

Manager
Dave Statham

All players, substitutes and reserves to turn up at 09.45

'So what they like, these two mates of yours?' Paul Cornwell asked his son Matthew as they lounged in the kitchen sipping coffee.

'They're fine, Dad, really nice blokes, and they can play a bit,' Matt replied, tearing off another bite of heavily buttered toast with his teeth, 'You'll like 'em both.'

'What's their names again, Jamie and Magic or something, isn't it?'

'Majid. Majid Ahmed.'

'What is he? Indian or Paki or what? Hope he's not a Muslim terrorist. We can't afford to pay the fine if he blows up the Cummiston changing rooms.'

Matthew chewed on his toast. 'Dunno what he is, Dad,' he replied. 'Never asked him. He never went to assembly at school, so he could be Roman Catholic, I suppose.'

'What? With a name like Magic. No – the Catholics are all Seans or Josephs, O'Flahertys or Murphys. Some of them's Poles, though, but they're all called Tchaikovski or Knockabollockoff or something. Probably a Hindu. Hey, Matty, what's a Hindu? Lays eggs, gettit?'

Matthew looked confused and continued, 'We went to school together, then I lost touch a bit. I don't think he drinks, so I don't see much of him. What's that make him then, if he don't drink? A Muslim, I suppose.'

'Bloody thirsty, I would think,' said Paul without smiling. 'And what about this other lad, Dunbar, Scottish is he?'

Matt smirked behind his mug of tea. 'Something like that, yeah. Big ginger lad, wore a kilt to school, we used to call him Jock.'

Paul looked at his watch. 'Pillock.' he said. 'Ah well, better get off. Lots to do with Dave to sort things out for this morning. Paperwork, balls and stuff. You coming out this morning?'

Matt was always embarrassed when his father left the house on Sunday mornings because he knew that he was going to see that woman in the flats behind the shops. Of course, he never said anything to his mother, but he had known for years. Everyone on the estate knew, except his mother. 'Yeah, I'll be there later. Bloody frustrating not being able to play.'

'Then watch that temper of yours in future. I'm always telling you.'

'See you, Christine,' Paul called up the stairs to his wife who was in the bathroom washing her hair. 'Leave me dinner in the oven if you like,' and he closed the front door, breathing in the cold November air before opening the garage.

He parked prominently in front of the shops and marched into Muzzy's to buy his usual provisions: newspapers, cigarettes and chocolate. As he left the shop he paused and looked at the sky. It was low and grey and miserable, but calm and still, typical for a November morning. There was no wind and the clouds hung like a heavy blanket, blocking the sun but also insulating against the worst of the winter weather. Paul pulled up the collar of his thick, padded jacket, looked around him and strode around the back of the shops towards the flats.

Linda was sitting at the kitchen table, smoking her fourth cigarette of the morning when Paul let himself in. She ground the cigarette out in the ashtray and stood up to flick the switch on the kettle and press the lever to lower the bread into the toaster.

'You OK, Lin?' Paul asked as he sat down at the table. 'You look sort of different.'

'Yeah, I'm fine, Paul, thanks. I've just spent twenty quid on getting my hair done and you noticed that I'm sort of different. Thanks,' she replied, pouring the boiling water into a large mug with "World's Best Mum" decorating the side. Paul had bought the mug the previous Mothers' Day and given it to Lightning to pass on to his mother.

'Always observant, me,' said Paul, accepting the tea and toast and passing Linda's cigarettes, chocolate and ten pound note across the table.

'Please, Paul, put the money back in your pocket. I don't need it, honest,' Linda said as she passed the note back across towards Paul.

Lightning stumbled into the kitchen, his eyes flicking from side to side and his fists clenched in front of him. 'Mum, Mum, disaster, disaster,' he yelled. 'Oh, good morning, Paul, and how are you today? Mum, Mum, disaster.'

'Sit down and calm down, Andrew.' Linda spoke very firmly. 'And tell me what's up. Quietly and calmly.'

Lightning sat down and looked around him, panic in his eyes. 'Disaster,' he yelled again.

Linda held up her hand towards Lightning. 'Quietly and calmly, Andrew, please.'

Lightning took three deep, well-practised breaths, looked at his mother and said, 'I can't find the changing room key. It's gone, I've lost it. What can I do, Mum?' Tears appeared in the rim of his eyes and he was shaking.

'OK, sweetheart. We'll find it. Don't worry. Now, when was the last time you had it?'

Lightning's face twisted in concentration, and he replied, 'Yesterday.'

'Good, well done. And was your bicycle key with it?'

Lightning grimaced again with the effort of trying to remember, before answering, 'Yes'.

'Did you lock your bicycle up in the passage like I've told you?'

There was another pause whilst his mind travelled back to the previous evening. 'Yes, definitely.'

'That's good, because that means that the keys must be here or you couldn't have locked your bicycle, so nothing to worry about. Now, did you bring the keys up to the flat after you locked your bicycle?'

Lightning nodded, paused, then shook his head, but by now he looked relaxed and confident that the investigation was moving in the right direction. His eyes narrowed as he concentrated. 'Not sure, Mum.'

'OK, so the first place to look is in your bicycle lock. Perhaps you left them there. If not, all we need to do is trace your steps after that and we'll find them.'

'Right,' Lightning agreed and nodded enthusiastically.

'Well, go on then, look on your bike.'

Lightning rushed out of the door happily, enjoying the detective work, and Paul enjoyed watching the special interaction between mother and son.

'They'll probably be there,' said Linda. 'It's my fault, I usually check, but last night I was, sort of, busy. He usually leaves them there. Too much to think about – locking his bike, remembering the keys, finding out what's for tea or what's on the telly.'

Paul smiled and was about to ask what it was that she was busy with, when Lightning burst back into the kitchen. He looked triumphant and held the keys up in the air. 'Mission accomplished. Well done us,' he announced before disappearing into his bedroom. Two minutes later he returned, wrapped up like a polar explorer. 'Better get off,' he said. 'Them changing rooms won't open themselves,' and opened the door to leave the flat.

'Got the keys?' asked Linda as he was about to leave.

Lightning felt in his pockets. 'Whoops,' he said and re-entered his room, before returning through the kitchen, keys held high, and opened the door.

'Bye, Andrew, see you later,' Paul shouted as Lightning skipped down the stairs. Then he asked, 'What's with the hair-do then, Lin?'

'Well…' Linda began slowly, searching for the right words. 'I've met someone.'

Paul looked bemused, before saying, 'Yeah, you've met someone. So what about it? I mean, we meet people every day, don't we?'

'I've met someone, well, special. You know, a man. We're, in a way, we're, sort of, going out.'

Paul was stunned. Many years ago, Linda had had a couple of boyfriends when Lightning was growing up, but not for years. Why would she want a boyfriend? Where did that leave him? He blurted out, 'Who is he?'

'I met him at work,' Linda began, 'and he's a really nice person. He's taking over from my boss, temporary for the moment but it may be permanent if it works out. He's forty-two, divorced with two children, a boy and a girl, and has just moved here from Reading after he split with his wife. Says it was too painful to stay in the same town as her. He's tall, going a bit thin on top but that's OK, very smart, and plays squash and badminton. He doesn't like football or cricket and doesn't drink alcohol except for wine with his dinner. He's very sophisticated. And he's invited me to play badminton at the sports centre tomorrow evening and I really, really like him.'

Paul stared into his tea, trying to make sense of what he had just been told and the significance to himself. He suddenly felt angry and jealous, but was unsure what he was jealous of. Was it jealousy of the other man or the possible effect on his relationship with Linda or the fact that it may change his comfortable way of life?

'What do you think then?' Linda interrupted his thoughts.

'Why do you want another man?' he whined. 'You've got me. What's wrong with me?'

Linda had prepared for this line of questioning and had practised her response. 'Paul, I am very, very fond of you. What we have is something special and nothing can break it, but it's not a relationship in the full sense of the word. I mean, I love seeing you a couple of times a week, but we've never actually gone out together and we've never had… well, had relations, so we're not an item or anything – just friends. You do understand, don't you?'

Paul pushed his toast away and tried to think of the right words. Communication had never been his strong point, but this was impossible.

'We could have been more than just friends,' he said, looking at the floor. 'But I never tried it on because it didn't seem right somehow.'

'I know, Paul. There were times, years ago, when I thought that perhaps you and me would get together, especially just after Andrew was born, but then you married Christine—'

Paul interrupted. 'I had to marry her. I had to when she was in the club. I just had to.'

Linda was touched by Paul's old-fashioned, if misguided, sense of honour, as she explained, 'I understand that, Paul, but I need something else, I need the companionship of a man, I need to be treated as a woman, not just as a friend, I need… other things in life.'

'What's he after then? Just divorced, two kids. And if he doesn't like football, there must be something wrong with him. You ought to be careful, Linda. He's after something.'

'Of course he's after something, Paul. He's after what I'm after: a little company and fun and enjoyment and romance. He's a single man after all and I'm a single woman. We're after the same thing.'

'And bloody sex I suppose,' Paul blurted out without thinking.

Linda looked shocked then answered angrily but calmly, 'Yes, Paul. And sex. I haven't been with a man for over ten years. Do you understand what that's like? Of course you don't. You go home to Christine every night and I'm here, alone. Every bloody night for ten bloody years.' Her voice started to rise as the anger and emotion she felt began to pour out. 'Ten bloody years and you see me two or three times a week with some fags and chocolate and the odd few quid and think that's all I need. Paul, I am not one of your mates down the pub, I am a woman.'

Paul too was angry. Angry that he was in danger of losing the woman he wanted to protect for ever. 'Well we could have had sex if that's what you wanted but you never said anything to me. We could still have sex if that's all you want.'

'That is not all that I want, Paul. Don't you ever listen? I need someone to take me out, someone to say I look pretty, someone to buy me flowers…'

'And what about Andrew, have you thought about him?' Paul knew that this was not playing fair but he was becoming desperate.

'Don't you dare bring Andrew into this,' shouted Linda, by now in full flow. 'I have single-handedly brought that boy up for eighteen years with all his difficulties and done a bloody good job. He's never wanted for anything and has grown into a wonderful young man, so don't you dare use him to get at me.'

Paul was stunned. He got up quickly from his chair and headed for the door. 'Do whatever you bloody want to,' he shouted. 'It's none of my business.'

'That's right, it is none of your business,' Linda yelled as Paul walked out of the kitchen.

As he was leaving, Paul turned and shouted, 'And if he doesn't like football, he must be bloody queer,' and slammed the door behind him.

Paul's hands were shaking as he tried to light a cigarette on his way back to the car. He had left Linda's flat earlier than usual and knew that Dave and Viv would not be ready for another ten minutes or so, so he decided to drive to Cummiston alone. As he pulled out into Poachers Drive from the row of shops, Barry uncurled himself from the red sports car stopped outside Dave's house and held out his hand towards Paul's car as if hailing a London cab. Paul drove straight past, almost hitting Barry in the process and forcing him to leap onto the pavement where he slowly dropped to the ground and ended up sitting on the kerb in an ungainly heap. Monica missed the incident and was speeding up the road behind Paul. As Barry tried to lift his sixteen-stone frame from the pavement, a few pennies dropped onto the pavement next to him. 'There you go, mate, get yourself a cup of tea,' said Vivian, and went to lean on Dave's car.

Paul drove quickly through the country roads leading through Cummiston village and into the Sports and Social Club car park, where he sat in his car smoking another cigarette. He was angry that, after all these years, Linda could simply announce that she had a bloke, just like that. As he was turning over what she had said in his mind, Dave's Polo turned into the car park and pulled in alongside

Paul's car. Barry was first out and rapped on Paul's window. Paul wound down the window, stared at Barry and said, 'What?'

'You fucking mad bastard, Cornwell.' Barry launched into a tirade. 'What the fuck were you doing, you stupid prick? You could have fucking killed me, you prat. You need to take fucking driving lessons before you *do* kill someone, you dick.'

Paul opened the car door. 'Fuck off, Plumby,' he said and marched into the changing rooms.

Barry looked at his companions in the car. 'No need to be rude,' he said.

Dave never liked the Cummiston changing rooms. They were housed in an old wooden village hall behind some old age pensioners' bungalows and, for reasons unknown, always smelt of pee. Viv always maintained the smell drifted over from the pensioners. The changing rooms were well maintained, as the football teams were the hub of village life. The saving grace for playing at Cummiston was that opposite the changing rooms was a small wooden hut, perched on a bank high above the pitch and known as the "Wendy House". It contained a small but well-stocked bar and seemed unaffected by any licensing laws, except those imposed by Goggy the barman. That is, Goggy opened up when he felt like it. Luckily for Dave and the other spectators, he always felt like it on Sunday mornings. Dave studied his clip-board and started to tick the names of the players, who were in various states of undress. 'Right, lads, listen up, this is important today. We've got two new lads just signed on, friends of Matty and Tommo. They are,' he checked the sheet on his clip-board, 'Magic Ahmed. Where are you, Magic?'

Majid was sitting quietly in the corner and raised his hand shyly. 'Majid,' he said. 'My name is Majid.'

'Well done, Magic,' Dave continued. 'And, we've got young Jamie Dunbar. Come on, young Jock, where are you?'

From the seat next to Majid, a colossus rose slowly and bashfully waved his hand. He was six feet four and as black as the ace of spades.

'Bloody hell,' said Viv. 'You Jocks must have had some sun up in Scotland.' Luckily for Viv, Jamie laughed alongside everyone else.

'Right now, settle down lads. Magic and Jock are subs today, but I'll probably bring them on sometime anyway, so no sulking if you get pulled off at half-time.'

'Sulk?' said Viv. 'I'd love to be pulled off at half-time. I only get a cup of tea normally.'

'And one more thing.' Dave ignored the laughter from the ranks. 'This is the last game before the Christmas break and if we win, we will be second in the league at the halfway stage, so everything to play for.'

'What if we lose?' Gunner Farr asked innocently.

'If we lose, we could still be second, providing that the New Inn and the Pickled Herring don't win.'

'And what if we draw?'

Dave checked the league tables on his clip-board. 'If we draw and the New Inn lose, we stay second.'

'But what if we draw and the New Inn wins?'

'Then they go second and we go third.'

'What if we lose, the New Inn wins and the Pickled Herring wins?'

Dave checked again. 'Then we go third unless the Pickled Herring wins by an avalanche, then we'll be fourth.'

'But what if the New Inn loses, the Pickled Herring wins by an avalanche and we lose by an avalanche? What then?'

Dave looked up to see the whole team trying to suppress laughter.

'Just bloody well make sure we win,' he said. 'And remember...' Everyone joined in. 'Firm but fair.'

The outlook from the bank overlooking the pitch offered an excellent view of the game and Dave, Barry and the three substitutes decamped to a position there, level with the halfway line. Paul accepted his usual role as linesman but with less grace than normal, snatching the flag from the referee and, given his instructions 'Just flag for offside, goal kicks, corners and throw-ins, I'll manage the rest,' muttering, 'I know what I'm fucking doing.'

The game started badly for the Poachers, with the young Cummiston winger dancing past a clumsy tackle from Percy Woodman, cutting in from the left wing and letting fly with a scorching drive which left Gunner rooted to the spot, the ball hitting the net with a resounding thump. The Poachers responded by slowly but surely gaining control of the game with the danger coming, as usual, from the speed of Gordon Gaye on the right wing. On the other wing, Paddy Oakley had been threatened with a broken leg or worse by the broad-shouldered, red-faced yokel playing full back, and had decided that cowardice was the better part of valour and retreated into his own half of the field, ensuring that he saw as little of the ball as possible.

On the end of several indignant shouts from the players and obscene shouts from the Cummiston villagers was Paul, who was running the line and keeping up with play but flagging at bizarre and random times. He missed at least two obvious offside decisions when Gordon's enthusiasm led to him bursting forward too quickly. He had given the advantage to the wrong team at throw-ins on several occasions.

'What the hell's up with him this morning?' Barry asked no one in particular. 'First he nearly kills me in his car, then he was most discourteous in the car park and now he's acting like he's never seen a football match before in his life. If he carries on like this, he'll be refereeing in the Premiership in no time.'

Dave tried to get away because he knew that Barry was about to begin a rant. The signs were there. He had uncovered something to rant about and, once he had started, he would not stop. 'Did you see that clown on Match Of The Day this morning, or last night for you bastards with no lives? Did you see him? Tall bloke, shaven head. Why they all try to look like Yul Brynner I'll never know. Spend more time shaving their bloody heads than learning the rules of the game. The problem is the football authorities, you see. Apparently you've got to be reffing for twenty years before you stand a chance of getting on the Premiership list, which means that ex-pros don't have time if they want to become refs when they've finished playing, so all refs in the league are, by bloody definition, the fat blokes and tossers that were no good at football when they were younger. Mind you, you could have some interesting refs if they had ex-footballers. I mean, could you imagine that Paul Gascoigne refereeing, or that Joey Barton. Be interesting that if they were referees…' Everyone had managed to slip away from Barry during his speech leaving him lecturing on the vagaries of refereeing to a toothless local who knew no better.

The referee at this particular game was becoming more and more confused with Paul's waving of the orange flag, particularly when a long-range shot from Razor Raisin sailed harmlessly over the bar and Paul signalled a corner.

'Bloody goal kick, linesman, what's up with you?' the Cummiston goal-keeper yelled in frustration, only for Paul to shout back that the goalkeeper had definitely touched the ball and if he didn't like the decisions he could go and fuck himself. Approaching half-time, the Cummiston left winger again waltzed past Percy and drove a hard cross into the goalmouth where it was deflected into the Poachers' net.

The Poachers' players were pleased to hear the referee's whistle for half-time and traipsed back to their halfway line encampment on the bank for tea and sympathy. Paul stayed on the line, arms folded and flag gripped tightly in his right hand, staring at the empty playing field.

The usual half-time disorder of tea being slurped, water being guzzled, cigarettes being lit and blame being attached was subdued as the team discussed the performance of their linesman. 'What's up with your old man, Matty?' Dave asked. 'Is he all right or what?'

Matt shook his head. 'Dunno,' he replied 'He was fine this morning before he went out to meet you, then something's happened. What happened at your place, Dave, sorting out the kit and stuff?'

Dave glared at Barry and Viv who were about to interject by saying that Paul was on his own earlier that day. 'He did seem a bit preoccupied, but we didn't think anything of it, did we, lads?'

Matt could tell from his voice that he was lying but respected his attempt to cover for his father. 'Dunno what it is then,' he said, knowing that something had happened at Linda's.

Dave decided to bring the two new lads on for the second half in place of the tired and ageing Percy and the invisible Paddy. 'Magic, can you play on the left up front. Just skip past that big farmer at full back and get the ball into the middle for Razor's head. Paddy, you need a rest. Well done.'

'Majid, my name is Majid,' said the young lad quietly.

'That's it, Magic, just aim for Razor's big head.'

Paddy was pleased to be coming off before the big farmer scythed him in half as promised. Dave resumed. 'And Percy, you can take a rest too and, Jock, you can play at full back. Just give that winger a bit of stick. He's too bloody dangerous.'

'Och aye the noo,' replied Jamie.

Dave wondered whether his substitution was a wise move when Majid took up his position on the left wing. He looked like a little skinny lad with kit that was two sizes too big, and was balanced on what seemed to be a larger person's feet. He reminded Dave of the photographs that he had seen in the *Sunday Times* of starving refugees from Pakistan, alone, scared and lost. Within minutes of the kick-off, Majid received a long pass from midfield on the left touchline and killed the ball expertly before taking half a dozen paces forward on his outsized feet. As the big farmer lurched towards him, Majid hit a long pass infield, failing to connect with Razor's head by inches and jumping over the scything tackle, leaving the full back in an ungainly heap on the touchline. As they took up their positions following a scramble in the Cummiston goalmouth, the farmer whispered in Majid's ear, 'Do that again, sunshine, and you won't need a lift to get home. You'll be flying to fuckin' India on the end of my fuckin' boot.'

Minutes later, Majid received the ball again and was aware of the full back thundering towards him. He looked up, feinted to cross again before pushing the ball outside the full back and sprinting down the wing to deliver an inch perfect cross that Razor met with his forehead, the ball sailing over the advancing goalkeeper into the net.

The defender began to mark Majid tighter and continued his threats but the young winger was able to deliver some telling crosses and passes. Although he was caught heavily two or three times by the red-faced farmer, his slight body seemed to ride the tackles easily and avoid any injury. In defence, Jamie seemed to have a sixth sense when the ball was played towards the young Cummiston winger and intercepted it easily, never having the need to commit to a tackle or, indeed, to break sweat.

With ten minutes left, Paul's erratic performance as linesman reached new heights when the Cummiston forwards played a series of short passes before launching a long-range effort which floated over Gunner's head and into the net. Paul immediately raised his flag to signal for offside and the referee blew for a free kick to the Poachers. The Cummiston players were incensed and surrounded the referee, before charging over to complain to Paul. As a Cummiston player pushed his face into Paul's and said something about a cheating bastard, Paul pulled back his head and lurched forward, cracking the player across the eye with his forehead, causing cuts to immediately open on both men's heads. In the aftermath of vitriol and blood, the Poachers' players managed to separate the combatants and hold Paul down, which had the added benefit of keeping him from the baying mob of angry country boys. The referee stood back and allowed the scuffle to cool down before calling Paul over. As players from both teams stood around chatting amicably about the peculiar incident, the referee straightened his back and said, 'You are my referee's assistant, and I do not believe that you are allowed to head-butt players. I shall send you from the field of play,' and held the red card high in the air. 'Now tell me. Was it offside?'

'No idea, ref,' Paul replied meekly. 'I wasn't watching.'

'OK, thanks for that. Please can I have my flag back?'

Matt ran forward and volunteered to finish the game as linesman, the referee handing him the flag with some relief.

Paul made his way morosely to the Wendy House and, as he and Matt crossed, Matt said, 'You want to watch that temper of yours, Father.'

Much to both teams' amazement, the referee then signalled a goal for Cummiston and restarted the match. The second Poachers' goal came from another fine centre from Majid which evaded Razor's head but was met with a vicious dipping drive from Gordon running in from the opposite wing. With just a couple of minutes to go, Jamie, gaining in confidence as the game wore on, broke on the right, and cracked the ball into the centre and past the goalkeeper where Majid was able to run the ball into an unguarded net. As Majid turned, his arm raised in an understated and slightly embarrassed celebration, the big full back stared at him as if he was contemplating which type of death to administer for maximum pain.

The Wendy House was full of players from both sides by the time Dave made it, and he ordered two pints before finding a spare corner to sit. Paul and the player he had headbutted sat together comparing cuts, neither of which needed more than a butterfly stitch, administered by Goggy between pulling pints. Barry was ranting on about the lack of sensible and pragmatic refereeing, pillorying every match official he could think of, except of course the Russian linesman in the 1966 World Cup final. Without warning, the natural light in the hut dimmed as the doorway was blocked by the bulk of the red-faced full back. The Wendy House went quiet as he said, 'Where is he? Where's that little Paki?'

Dave could see Jamie move quietly forward to protect his friend, and Matt and Steve immediately took up a position where they could be into the action as soon as any trouble started. The full back moved menacingly across the small room and stood in front of Majid, his huge frame making the newcomer look even smaller and more vulnerable. He pushed his hand towards Majid. 'Well done, Tiddler,' he said. 'I'm glad I don't have to play against you every week.

What do you want to drink? Hey, Goggy, get my mate here another orange juice and pull three pints for me.'

Dave met Mandy outside the pub at three. Although dull, the Sunday was not cold, so they decided to walk through the park, taking the long way round to her house. He was pleased to feel her arm link into his as they strolled in silence.

'I've been awake all night thinking, and I know what I'm going to do.' Mandy's abrupt start to the conversation made Dave nervous, worried that the decision would not be that she wanted to get married and live happily ever after. 'I'm going back to Bristol for a while.'

Dave heard the words clearly, but didn't understand what they meant. 'Going back to Bristol? Why? What for? Bristol. Bloody hell, Mandy, I don't want you to go anywhere. I want you to stay with me. I never want you to leave. Please, Mandy, don't go.'

'I've got to, Dave. I've got things to do there.' Mandy spoke very softly as they reached her front gate. 'I've arranged to stay with my friend in my old flat, so I'll be OK.'

'But the baby? What if there is a baby? Mandy, what are you going to do?'

'I'm sure that there is a baby, Dave. That's why I must go to Bristol. But, Dave, I'll phone you when I get there, and don't worry, I'll come back some-time after Christmas.' She put her arms around Dave and held him closely for a moment, before turning and walking to her front door without looking back.

Eleven

Downham Sunday Football League, Division Two
Results for Sunday 23rd November

New Inn, Gorton Down	4	2	Downham Churches
Shellduck Inn	2	2	Pickled Herring
Jones Juniors FC	4	0	Hearty Oak, Downlea
J G Tanner and Sons	2	1	Lower End WMC
AFC Cummiston	**3**	**3**	**Poachers Arms**

Results for Sunday 30th November

Lower End WMC	2	2	J G Tanner and Sons

Results for Sunday 4th January

Pickled Herring	1	0	Lower End WMC

League Table

Team	Pl'd	Won	Drew	Lost	For	Ag'st	GD	Points
Jones Juniors FC	9	7	2	0	39	11	28	23
New Inn, Gorton D	9	5	3	1	28	18	10	18
Poachers Arms	**9**	**5**	**2**	**2**	**26**	**16**	**10**	**17**
Pickled Herring	9	5	2	2	17	14	3	17
J G Tanner and Sons	9	5	1	3	16	16	0	16
AFC Cummiston	9	2	5	2	20	23	-3	11
Hearty Oak, Downlea	9	2	2	5	21	34	-7	8
Shellduck Inn	9	2	2	5	15	24	-10	8
Lower End WMC	9	2	2	5	14	21	-13	8
Downham Churches	9	0	2	7	24	42	-18	2

Sunday 11th January

Downham Sunday Football League, Division Two
Poachers Arms v Jones Juniors FC
Tenacre Recreation Ground – Kick-off 10.30

THE POACHERS ARMS

1 George Crosswell

2 Jamie Dunbar   4 Derek Smith   5 Brian Smith   3 Billy Millmore (Capt)

8 Wayne Tocket   6 Vivian Clutterbuck   10 Danny Tomlinson

7 Gordon Gaye   9 Razor Raisin   11 Majid Ahmed

Substitutes
12 Matt Cornwell
13 Paddy Oakley
14 Percy Woodman

Reserves (Please bring boots)
Paul Cornwell
Dave Statham
Barry Plumb

Manager
Dave Statham

All players, substitutes and reserves to turn up at 09.45

It was undoubtedly the worst Christmas that Dave had ever had. From his first memories as a child, he had looked forward to the festive season; he enjoyed the build-up, the shopping for presents, the corny films on television, the sound of Slade and Roy Wood's Wizzard wherever he went, and the over-indulgence of food and drink. This year's Christmas routine was the same as the previous years, but the excitement and enjoyment were missing. He could not get Mandy out of his head. She had called him on Christmas Eve, but the number was withheld so he couldn't ring her back. She had wished him a happy Christmas and promised to be in touch again, but he had heard nothing since. In fact, he felt that the last month had been the worst of his entire life. He had lost his first and only real girlfriend and there was no Sunday League football. He looked at his clock. 08.10. Twenty minutes ahead of schedule, Dave slowly clambered out of bed, pulled back the curtains and stared out of the window. There had been an overnight frost leaving a white carpet sparkling on the small lawns at the front of the houses in the road. He wondered if the ground would be considered dangerous and the game against Jones Juniors postponed. That really would make it the most miserable time he could remember. Things could not get worse. He heard Tonker coughing and the bathroom door slam. Tonker had made it into the bathroom to unload last night's beer and curry and puff away on an Old Holborn roll-up. Things *had* got worse.

Jones Juniors FC was the long-running passion of a local builder and builders' merchant called Allan Jones, who had started the team for his sons in the Downham under-elevens league. As his sons had grown up, so the team advanced in leagues, through the various youth teams to full Sunday League members. The team was now run by Allan's sons, Aaron and Buddy Jones, who were less than popular in league circles due to their arrogant, win-at-all-costs philosophy. Dave didn't hold out much hope of beating Jones Juniors this morning but, like most clubs in the league, would relish the opportunity of snatching a point from the overbearing, pompous brothers.

He studied the team again, satisfied that there was a chance, albeit a small one, of holding its own this morning. With his new signings Jamie and Majid showing tremendous promise, the Smith brothers holding the back four together, Viv and his two young apprentices, Wayne and Danny, controlling midfield, and Gordon and Razor continual threats to any defence, he felt that this was a strong, well-balanced team. He did not enjoy disappointing players by not playing them, but was helped by a second suspension for Steve Tippling for previous bookings and Gunner Farr working on annual stocktaking. Matt Cornwell had cried off earlier in the week with a groin strain, saying that he would be happier to be a substitute, so the team all but picked itself. The only fly in the ointment was Percy Woodman, but he should have been aware that the effects of a high daily intake of cider and cigarettes were not conducive to elongating the sporting life of a finely tuned athlete, which he certainly was not.

As Dave pondered the team and studied the latest league table, he heard Tonker coughing as he left the bathroom, so he braved the foul atmosphere and rushed in to relieve himself, trying to hold his breath for as long as possible. This practice was self-defeating because the long period without breathing caused him to take a huge breath, thus sucking in a large gulp of offensive, fetid air. He contemplated reporting Tonker to the council on Monday morning for breaking the Clean Air Act, but decided that he would be better off if he bottled the air from the bathroom and sold it to a Middle East dictatorship for use as a weapon of mass destruction.

He dressed and heard his mum clattering about in the kitchen. His mouth watered at the prospect of the full English breakfast that would be served in a few minutes. He gathered his papers and his football kit, placed everything carefully in his bag and trudged downstairs.

'You're early this morning, David love,' Dave's mum said, a happy, beaming smile creasing her shiny pink face. 'Sit down and I'll make you a cup of tea. Breakfast won't be a minute.'

'Where's Dad?' Dave asked casually as he glanced at the back page of the *Sunday Mirror*, delivered from Muzzy's.

Dave's mum delivered the cup of steaming tea to the kitchen table. 'Just popped out into the back garden for some air, I think' she replied.

'I reckon he's got another woman,' Dave said, carelessly folding back the paper to look at the previous day's football results.

'So long as it's not that Mrs. Barnes with her big thingummybobs,' laughed Dave's mum, then immediately regretted the joke. 'Sorry, love, I didn't think. I forgot that Mandy's given you the whatsit,' and returned to her frying pan. Dave said nothing.

Having finished his breakfast, using the last of his toast to wipe the last of the HP sauce, bacon and sausage grease from his plate, Dave stood up and carried his plate to the sink. 'You sit down, Mum, I'll do the washing up today,' he announced.

'You will not,' his mum insisted. 'That's my job. You go and get ready for your whatsname and leave this to me.'

'Mum, you're the best ever,' Dave said and hugged her tightly for a moment. Tonker returned, coughed and rolled another cigarette.

By the time Dave had been to Muzzy's to buy his paper and Hamlet cigars and chat about Tenerife, Viv and Paul were waiting by his car. Viv had metamorphed into Lee Evans, or it could have been Norman Wisdom, and was telling jokes complete with the full repertoire of wild actions, whilst Paul stared into space or, more accurately, stared in the direction of Linda's flat.

'Get a fucking move on, Mr Grimsdale, we're freezing our bollocks off here,' was Viv's friendly greeting on seeing Dave return from Muzzy's. Dave grinned. At least he now knew that it was Norman Wisdom.

On Dave's return, the mates threw their kit into the boot of the Polo and Dave backed carefully off the drive. 'No Barry this morning,' he said as he pulled away from the house and moved up the hill. Viv, sitting in the front, turned round to look in the back of the car and jumped in mock surprise.

'Fuck me, you're right, Dave. No flies on you. Did you notice that, Paulo, no Barry this morning? Sharp as a marble, our Dave here.' Dave felt happier now that he had Viv mocking him. It was putting the worst Christmas ever behind him and getting things back to normal.

Lightning was standing to attention as the men arrived in the rec changing rooms. 'Morning, Mr Statham,' he said and twisted his face strangely at Paul, one eye squeezed shut and the other blinking rapidly.

'You OK, Lightning,' asked Viv. 'Or you got something in your eye?'

'I'm very well, thank you,' Lightning replied continuing to twitch and grimace. Paul knew that Lightning's attempted wink was meant for his benefit. Dave took the key, signed below "Betty Swollocks" and opened up the changing room. The room was freezing and the men's breath was clearly visible as they blew into their hands in a futile attempt to warm up. Paul dumped his bag of footballs on the cold concrete floor and made an excuse about going back to the car to collect something. He accepted the keys from Dave and returned to Lightning's office.

'What's up, Andrew?' Paul asked.

Lightning looked around carefully and called Paul closer. He checked around again, then whispered, 'Mum says sorry about the argument and you can come round again if you want to but not in the week and please ring first so that she can tell you if it's all right thank you.'

Paul felt in his pocket and pulled out a small paper bag, sealed with sellotape. He passed it to Lightning, saying, 'Thanks, Andrew, tell your mum thanks. We'll see. And here's a late Christmas present for you.'

Lightning's face lit up as he opened the bag but looked confused when he studied the contents, a key ring in the shape of a football, attached to a chain and a clip.

'Look here,' Paul explained. 'You can put your keys on this ring, then put the clip on your belt here. The chain and keys go in your pocket so that you can never lose your keys because you can still use them when they're clipped on, see?'

Lightning grinned broadly and nodded as Billy went past into the changing room. Billy could not wait to tell what he had seen. '…I'm telling you, he was giving him a present and whispering to him. I've always known that that half-wit's his boy. Never any doubt but that proves it. Why else would he give him a present?' Billy was revelling in what he had observed and was tempted to ring his wife at home to tell her, but the cost of a mobile phone call made him change his mind. The changing room was soon its usual hubbub of noisy, half-clothed footballers as Dave was checking that everyone was present. The only persons not ticked off on Dave's teamsheet were Barry, but that was no great loss, and Majid. 'Magic,' Dave called out. 'Anyone seen Magic?'

A quiet voice was heard from the corner of the room. 'Majid, my name is Majid and I'm here.'

'Well done, Magic,' Dave continued. 'Now listen up, everyone. This is the big one. Jones Juniors are good but we can beat them. Get the ball out to the wings whenever you can, and you two, get those crosses over into the centre.

Defence, no heroics, just concentrate and play it simple. No overlapping or pushing up too much. Oh, and remember to let them know you're about early.' Dave was pleased with the team talk even though no one listened.

'You forgot something, Boss?' Viv spoke up and immediately the room was quiet. Dave looked quizzically at Viv as the whole team shouted, 'Firm but fair.'

As the players and officials made their way to pitch number three, Dave was feeling much happier than any time over the previous few weeks. He was still aching from not having seen Mandy and wondering if he would ever see her again, but was looking forward to the morning's contest. As he and Paul carried their kit across the playing field towards pitch number three, they were joined by the Jones brothers.

'Morning, losers.' Aaron patted Dave heavily on the back. 'Ready for a stuffing this morning, are you?'

Dave just shrugged and smiled. 'We'll see,' he said, trying to look casually confident.

Paul was not so subtle. 'Fuck off, Jonesy, you wanker,' he replied, satisfied that he had cleverly made his point.

'Ooh, listen to 'er.' Buddy Jones joined the conversation. 'Fancy a little bet this morning then, gents? Say a fiver each on the final score.'

Dave did not gamble and Paul hated the idea of giving the Joneses his hard-earned cash, so both men mumbled something about not being gamblers, but if they were, they'd bet more than just a fiver.

They caught up with Paddy Oakley who had been ambling slowly towards the pitch. 'Hear that, Paddy,' Aaron called. 'These two mates of yours are thinking of betting us a tenner each on today's game, but I think they're going to shit out and not bet. Whaddya reckon to that?'

'I'll take that bet,' announced Paddy confidently. 'You give me the draw and the bet's on.'

'You are on, my son, a tenner each it is. That's a score from you if your bunch of fat tossers lose. D'you want to pay us now?'

'Just get your tenners ready, Jonesy,' Paddy said pleasantly as he trotted off to join his team mates at the pre-match kick-about.

Paul just had time to collect his linesman's flag from the referee before the game started and the Jones Juniors' forwards immediately laid claim to the Poachers' half of the pitch. The Poachers' defence was holding out well with the three younger players producing heroic, if somewhat desperate, tackles and clearances, whilst Billy used his twenty years of experience and positioning sense to stop the ball reaching the right winger. The forwards and midfield were being pushed deeper and deeper into home territory as the game took on the appearance of a siege. After twenty minutes or so there was no score, and whilst the game was being played almost exclusively in the Poachers' half of the field, there was an air of control and confidence growing in the home team. The Juniors' captain was pushing his men forward, continually talking. 'Come on lads, this lot are rubbish; they can't play, they're crap. This is easy, lads, once we get one, we'll get six.'

An awkward challenge on the hard, frozen ground in midfield flattened young Danny Tomlinson, who sat on the halfway line holding his knee. The referee blew his whistle and Dave rushed on with his bucket of water, sponge and the rarely opened first aid kit. He splashed cold water on the knee, which was beginning to swell. The treatment had little effect although it was the only first aid that Dave knew, so it was decided that Danny should go off. As Dave helped him off the field he called out to Paul to send his boy Matty on as substitute.

'Right, Matt, get changed, you're on. And watch that temper of yours. These lads are good and they'll try to wind you up.'

Matthew just smiled. 'I'll have that fucking captain,' he said, ignoring his father's advice completely, and ran on to replace Danny.

The game continued in the same vein for the rest of the half with Matthew Cornwell adding a little more steel to the midfield. The Poachers even broke out on a few occasions into the Jones Juniors' half, without seriously challenging the goal. Meanwhile, the occupying forces of Jones Juniors could not break down the stubborn and rugged Poachers' defence. With George Crosswell again in superb form in goal, stopping everything thrown at him, or kicked and headed at him, the half drew to a close with no goals.

At half-time the Jones brothers could be seen on the opposite touchline berating their players, arms gesticulating wildly as they urged their team on to greater effort, pointing left, right and centre, and then clenching their fists in belligerent demands for more drive and aggression. Dave watched them for a moment, before calling for the attention from his own team. 'Look at them Joneses,' he said, pointing across the pitch. 'Worried or what? Just keep it up.' It was probably the best team talk he had ever given.

Matt Cornwell had taken a couple of wild swings at the Jones Juniors' skipper during the first half, and his father knew that he would have another go at him whenever the opportunity was available. He didn't have to wait long. Immediately from the kick-off, as Paul was stamping out a cigarette before taking up his position as linesman, the skipper received the ball and, striking a pose reminiscent of Bobby Moore at his cool and controlled best, sprayed an accurate pass to the right wing, saying, 'This is easy…' before Matt cracked him heavily across the knee with a two-footed lunge. As they fell, the skipper's elbow flashed towards Matt's nose. The referee never saw the initial foul, but turned in time to see the elbow and both players drop like stones, one holding his knee, the other his nose. He called Paul across.

'Did you see what happened, referee's assistant?' he asked.

'Not really,' Paul replied. 'Just something of nothing, I think.'

'Did you see your number 12 tackle the opposition number 4 late or any other infringement?'

'No, I didn't see anything,' Paul answered truthfully, although he could have a fair guess as to what had happened.

'Thank you,' said the referee, before turning back to the skipper, taking a red card from his pocket and raising it high in the air. As number 4 trudged off the pitch still shaking his head, the referee turned to Matt. 'I've got a feeling you got away with a late tackle, number 12, but I never saw it. I'm going to keep an eye on you. Now carry on and watch it.'

Matt took up his position, trying to control a smirk, his face and nose surprisingly showing no signs of assault. Paul returned to the halfway line and was immediately accosted by Dave.

'That's a turn-up,' Dave smiled. 'How's your boy's face?'

'Bloke never touched him,' Paul answered. 'Matt just fell over. Fucking acting. I can't stand fucking acting. I'll give him a bollocking when I see him.' Paul paused for a few seconds. 'Unless we win,' he added, 'then I'll buy him a pint.'

As the game continued, the Poachers' team gained in confidence. The Juniors' team were shaken and pulled out of position, with a couple of their players spending more time trying to exact retribution from Matt than concentrating on the game in hand. As the game settled down into a routine, the ample figure of Barry Plumb was seen hurrying across the playing field, half running and shouting loudly. Dave turned and said to Percy, 'I thought I'd gone deaf 'smorning, but Barry's here now.'

'Dave, Dave, hurry, hurry,' were the only words that the small group could understand as Barry approached.

'Hurry, what for?' said Percy. 'BBC's probably given a poof comedian another few million just for being a nancy. No wonder Plumby's upset.'

The men laughed and turned their attention back to the match. Barry Plumb finally, and painfully, arrived, blowing hard with his face the colour to match his surname. He bent over and took in three or four deep gasps before panting, 'Dave. Your house. Ambulance. Serious. Fuck off quick. Go now. Emergency. Hurry.'

Dave was stunned for a moment. 'What's happened, Barry?' he asked beginning to panic.

'Heart, I think. Hurry. Fuck off now.'

Dave left his kit and ran back across the rec towards his car. He turned back and shouted, 'Thanks, Barry, thanks,' before continuing his sprint to his car. As he started the engine, backed out of the parking place and began to drive home, his mind was a confused and foggy mess. 'That's why Tonker wasn't at the match this morning. Cigarettes, that was the problem. Smoked since he was twelve. Over fifty years of inhaling tobacco smoke. Come on, lights, change. Heart, Plumby said. Oh shit, there's the ambulance. Oh shit, there's someone being carried out on a stretcher. Oh shit, shit, shit.'

Dave pulled up in the road behind the ambulance as the stretcher was being loaded into the back of the ambulance. He leapt out of the car and noticed that there were tubes and wires hanging from a stand and swinging wildly, even though the paramedics eased the stretcher very gently into the vehicle. The paramedic looked at Dave. 'You David?' he asked. 'We've been expecting you. I'm really sorry, David. We'll do what we can.'

Dave was stunned as he looked towards the house. Sorry? Sorry? Does that mean...? Oh shit. Mum, I must see Mum. He rushed towards the house, just as Tonker came out drawing deeply on a cigarette. Tonker had obviously been crying, his eyes red and tears slowly running down his yellowed, wrinkled old face. Dave ran up to him and wanted to hug the old man. He just held his arm tightly.

'She just went down. Just like that. One minute, washing up. Said something about her chest and went down. Tommy called the ambulance. Didn't even have time to finish his tea. I didn't know what to do. Good job Tommy phoned for me. What do we do now?'

The paramedic called out, 'Quickly, if you're coming in the ambulance, Mr Statham,' and Dave led Tonker into the ambulance. 'I'll follow in the motor, Dad,' he said before the ambulance sped away.

'I stopped when I saw the ambulance and had a word with the ambulance blokes,' Barry explained to Percy. 'Pretty serious, apparently. His mum was on the kitchen floor and they were trying to revive her. Poor old Tonker didn't know what to do. Just stood there with a fag on asking if anyone wanted a cup of tea. Then I rushed up here to get Dave. Good job I was late, I suppose.'

Percy just nodded and said, 'Serious, then.' He didn't know what else to say.

The game continued in similar fashion throughout the second half, with the Poachers' team defying every Jones Juniors' attack with brave defending, tough tackling and far more than their fair share of luck, until the referee blew his whistle for full time with neither team managing to score. The players left the pitch with the Poachers' lads happy and satisfied with one point, the Juniors' team not overly concerned about the loss of two. This was more than could be said for their management team. Aaron and Buddy Jones were fuming as they walked across the pitch at the end of the game. Paddy was waiting for them, arm outstretched in a gesture of goodwill and to collect his twenty pounds. 'Well played, lads, unlucky,' he offered as the men met.

The brothers were not gracious in defeat. 'If that bloody sub 'adn't 've dived, we'd 'ave pissed it,' Aaron complained, handing over a ten pound note.' Give the man your tenner, Buddy. Pay up and look big.'

Buddy continued moaning about Matt's dive, but handed over his ten pounds just the same. 'Double or quits when we're 'ome,' he suggested to Paddy.

Paddy shrugged nonchalantly. 'Too early yet, boys,' he replied. 'I need to input the data into my PC and see what it predicts.' The Jones boys stared, mouths agape, wondering if a computer really could predict football scores.

As Paddy, Paul and Barry reached the changing rooms there was pandemonium. All the Poachers players were surrounding Lightning, who stood clutching his clip-board, his eyes flicking wildly from one person to the next and in a state of obvious distress.

'What's going on here?' Paul asked as he entered the building.

'Lightning won't give us the spare key,' replied Viv. 'Dave's gone home with it and Lightning says he's not authorized to give out the spare one.' He turned to Lightning. 'Come on, Lightning, you know me, give us the key for fuck's sake.'

Lightning clutched his clip-board even tighter and opened his mouth but no sound emerged. Suddenly, Billy pushed his way to the front. 'Listen, you fucking idiot, give me those keys or else, you half-witted, brainless moron.'

Paul spun round and grabbed Billy by the neck, pushing him backwards until he hit the wall. 'Don't speak to him like that, you… you…' – Paul ran through his mental thesaurus of insults – 'you… you cunt,' he shouted, pulling his fist back ready to thump Billy. His arm was held firmly, stopping him throwing the punch.

'You want to watch that temper of yours, Dad,' said Matt, releasing his arm.

Lightning was looking even more like a startled chicken, tears welling in his eyes until Barry stepped in.

'Now, Andrew,' Barry said, using his best police voice. 'Now it appears to me that you are quite right not to give up that key and I appreciate that. Well done. However, we do need to get into the changing room, so if you open the door for us, you will maintain ownership of the key and we get in to get changed. Fair enough?'

Lightning nodded, the tension flowing from his strange face, and moved between the players towards changing room number 3. He removed a bunch of keys from his pocket, held firmly by a chain attached to his belt, and opened the door. He pushed the door open and stood to one side, allowing the players to enter, most of whom patted his arm and said, 'Well done, Lightning.' Except Billy, who mumbled, 'Dozy half-wit,' under his breath.

In the Poachers Arms, the players' happiness at taking a point from the morning's match was tempered by the news about Dave's mum.

'Fuckin' good job I was there,' explained Tommy, the crib game postponed for the day out of respect and because there were only three players. 'I phoned the fuckin' ambulance, see. Dialled nine nine fuckin' nine straight away. Knew it was a fuckin' heart attack, straight away. My old man nearly fuckin' went the same way. Having it off late one Saturday; gets chest pains; me old mum calls me; I goes round; fuckin' heart attack. I called the fuckin' ambulance then an' all. He recovered thanks to me. Quick fuckin' mind, see, me. Back as good as ever a month or two later, only for his prostrate to get him. Survives a fuckin' heart attack and dies of fuckin' prostrate cancer.'

'Prostate. It's prostate,' Barry corrected him.

'Yeah,' Tommy continued. 'Fuckin' prostrate killed him. Survived the heart attack though, thanks to me.'

The subdued drinking continued, small groups of men standing or sitting round quietly chatting about illness, fate and the fickle world in which they lived. Paul's mobile rang and everyone stopped to look as he answered.

'We drew nil–nil. Yeah, it was a good result, wasn't it? His knee's OK now, should be fit for next week. Matty? He's OK; the bloke never touched him. I don't approve of diving, mind, but that skipper deserved it… yeah… yeah… see you later… OK.'

Paul switched off his mobile and looked up. 'Dave's mum died on the way to hospital,' he said calmly.

Twelve

Downham Sunday Football League, Division Two
Results for Sunday 11th January

Pickled Herring	2	4	New Inn, Gorton Down
Hearty Oak, Downlea	4	5	Downham Churches
Lower End WMC	3	1	Shellduck Inn
Poachers Arms	0	0	Jones Juniors FC
AFC Cummiston	7	2	J G Tanner and Sons

League Table

Team	Pl'd	Won	Drew	Lost	For	Ag'st	GD	Points
jones Juniors FC	10	7	3	0	39	11	28	24
New Inn, Gorton D	10	6	3	1	32	20	12	21
Poachers Arms	**10**	**5**	**3**	**2**	**26**	**16**	**10**	**18**
Pickled Herring	10	5	2	3	19	18	1	17
J G Tanner and Sons	10	5	1	4	18	23	-5	16
AFC Cummiston	10	3	5	2	27	25	2	14
Lower End WMC	10	3	2	5	17	22	-5	11
Shellduck Inn	10	2	2	6	15	27	-12	8
Hearty Oak, Downlea	10	2	2	6	25	39	-14	8
Downham Churches	10	1	2	7	29	46	-17	5

Sunday 18th January

Downham Sunday Football League, Division Two
New Inn, Gorton Down v Poachers Arms
Gorton Down behind the New Inn – Kick-off 10.30

THE POACHERS ARMS

1 Gunner Farr

2 Steve Tippling   4 Derek Smith   5 Brian Smith (Capt)   3 Matt Cornwell

8 Jamie Dunbar   6 Wayne Tocket   10 Danny Tomlinson

7 Gordon Gaye   9 Razor Raisin   11 Majid Ahmed

Substitutes
12 Billy Millmore
13 Paddy Oakley
14 Percy Woodman

Reserves (Please bring boots)
Paul Cornwell
Barry Plumb
Vivian Clutterbuck

Manager
Dave Statham

All players, substitutes and reserves to turn up at 09.45

Vivian dragged himself from the settee and stumbled towards the kitchen, his eyes barely able to open, his head thumping and his throat feeling like sandpaper. He carefully took a glass from the cupboard, filled it with cold tap water and took a long, thirsty drink. He tried to focus on the kitchen clock, squinting through sore, bloodshot eyes at the numbers swimming in front of him. Both hands were wavering around the seven or eight, but he was struggling to decipher which hand was which. He filled the kettle and switched it on, blearily spooning instant coffee into a mug. He looked at the clock again, the hands becoming clearer. It was twenty to eight. He took the coffee to the kitchen table and slumped onto a chair, holding his head in his hands.

Stupid bloody Dave Statham. Why the hell did he come round here last night? Just as he was about to give her one for the first time in bloody months and bloody Statham knocks at the door. The kids were at the in-laws and he and Elaine had decided that they would have a night in. There was a cold easterly wind ripping through the estate and icy rain sporadically lashed against the window. 'Not much fun out there tonight, 'Laine,' he said, 'Why not rustle us up a nice steak and we'll open a bottle or two of Rioja and have a cosy night in on our own? Whaddya say?'

Elaine did not need persuading. She enjoyed her Saturday nights out but was far happier staying in and having Viv all to herself. Whenever they did go out, there was always someone Viv knew to talk to. After a few beers it always became the Vivian Clutterbuck Comedy Hour, with Viv running through his repertoire of bad jokes and even worse impressions, which people seemed to find hilarious. Except Elaine, who lived with Jethro, Frank Spencer and Tommy Cooper all week.

Elaine had showered and dressed and Viv had bathed, shaved and put on one of his best Ben Sherman shirts and white Chinos. He was even using aftershave as he trotted down the stairs to where Elaine was preparing the evening meal. As she was slicing the tomato for the side salad, he had sidled up to her, put his arms

188

around her and hugged her tightly, kissing her on the neck. The trouble with Viv was that he couldn't do anything gently and he almost squeezed all the breath out of her, but she felt happier and more relaxed than she had done for some time. The unforeseen show of affection from her husband had also made her feel attractive and excited, and she was aware of a slight sexual arousal, anticipating what could happen after the meal. Viv had retired to the settee with a glass of cold lager, watching football on Sky, whilst Elaine busied herself in the kitchen. Steak, chips, side salad, and an M and S cheesecake. If that doesn't get him going, nothing ever will, she thought, singing softly as she laid the dining table in the lounge-diner. She carefully placed plates, cutlery and wine glasses, and opened a bottle of their favourite wine before carrying another lager in to Viv. She neatly folded two serviettes and placed them in the glasses, lit two candles and dimmed the lights. She carried the two steak dinners in from the kitchen and called, 'Your dinner's ready, handsome.'

Viv switched off the television, pulled himself off the settee and turned towards the table. 'Bloody hell, 'Laine, that looks fantastic. Just what the medical practitioner ordered,' he said and took his place at the table.

One hour and two bottles of Rioja later, the couple was sitting on the settee, Viv's big arm around her shoulders, sipping brandy and talking in a lazy, slightly drunken way about their children, their home and their plans. The conversation led inevitably but easily to the subject of sex and, for the first time, Viv was relaxed enough to be able to discuss his sexual glitch with no embarrassment.

'I've had a really good look at that Ann Summers catalogue,' he slurred, 'but I don't think that it's for us. The nurse's uniform will never fit me and them other attachments won't fit our hoover.'

Elaine giggled. 'I don't need an attachment when I've got you,' she purred and stretched up to kiss his cheek. 'In fact, I think that I'm going to put your big attachment to the test right now.'

Viv had a slight moment of panic, but before he could say anything or move, Elaine had forced him down onto the settee and was holding his shoulders firmly. She lay on top with her legs astride him, her groin pressing against his and gyrating gently. She held him down and kissed him passionately, almost violently, forcing her tongue into his mouth. Viv was big enough and strong enough to have pushed her off, but found the situation oddly erotic and felt an erection beginning. 'Stay there and do as you're told,' Elaine commanded firmly. 'And don't you dare move until I say you can.'

Viv nodded meekly as she eased herself off him and he felt her hands undo first his belt and then slowly unzip his Chinos. 'Stay exactly where you are,' she warned him again and gently took his stiffening penis in her hand, her fingers slowly and tenderly moving up and down the shaft. 'If you're a good boy, I may just…' she began as the doorbell rang loudly.

Viv would have leapt off the settee in shock except that Elaine's weight was still partly pinning him down. Elaine said, 'Who the bloody hell? Just leave it, Viv, it can't be important.'

'But it might just be. It could be something wrong with the kids or…' The doorbell rang again. 'I'd better go.'

Viv pushed his way past his wife, zipped up his Chinos and opened the front door.

'Hello, Viv, hope you don't mind, but I need to talk to you about the match tomorrow.' Dave's voice sounded weak and feeble as he looked up at Viv from the doorstep.

Viv stood aside. 'Yeah, you'd better come in, mate,' he said and stood aside to allow Dave to enter.

'It's only Dave, 'Laine,' he called as she straightened her clothing. 'Needs to talk about tomorrow's game.'

Elaine stood up as the men entered the room. 'That's OK, Vivian. I was going to bed anyway. Make yourself at home, Dave.' Dave took Elaine's place on the settee and Viv sat opposite in the armchair. As Elaine left, she fixed Viv with a 'just wait 'til I get you alone' stare.

'What's up then, mate?' Viv asked, trying to ignore Elaine's venomous glare.

Dave sat and stared at the coffee table. There was a large bottle marked "Cognac" in front of him. 'Is that brandy?' he asked.

'Fuck me, Dave, there's no flies on you tonight, is there. Do you want one?' Viv asked, taking another glass from the cabinet. 'Now what's up?'

'Well, what with me mum and the funeral and that, I haven't picked the team for tomorrow and haven't printed the teamsheet or anything, so I was worried that no one would turn up for the game, you know, what with the funeral and that.'

Viv handed Dave a large glass of brandy. 'No need to worry about that, Dave. All the players have got a fixtures list. They all know that we've got the New Inn away and they'll all be there. We can pick the team tomorrow. Look, what say we meet in your place at, say, half eight, pick the team, you type it up and everything's hunky dory.'

'Well yeah, but I don't know who to pick.' Dave downed his brandy and held out the glass for a refill. 'Only we've got all those players signed on and no injuries and no suspensions. I don't want to upset the new lads, they've done great, but how can we leave anyone out?'

'Let's sort this out tomorrow. Tell you what. I'll text Barry now and call Paul in the morning and the four of us can have a quick get-together at your place tomorrow. OK?'

Dave held out his glass for a second refill. 'Only what with the rush for the funeral and that, I've not really had time.'

Viv filled his glass and looked at Dave properly for the first time that evening. He looked rough. The dark rings under his eyes looked as if he had just been in the ring, and the pub, with Ricky Hatton; his skin was a pale yellow and drawn in at the cheeks, with red spots erupting on his nose, cheeks and chin. Viv poured himself another brandy and prepared for a long night.

Dave looked for his tracksuit in his wardrobe but it wasn't there. He sat on the bed and tried to remember where it was the last time that he had worn it. Last Sunday. Was it really just a week ago when his mum had passed away? It seemed so long ago. He bent down and found his tracksuit under the bed, pulled it out and looked at it. It was a mess, creased and bedraggled like an old rag. It was always washed and hanging in the wardrobe when his mum was there. Dave put it on anyway. Perhaps he ought to organize something for the washing and ironing, now that his mum was gone, but he just had not had time. The crema-tion had only taken place the day before, just six days after his mum had died in the ambulance. He was lucky that he knew Carol Manners in the Parks and Recreation Department at the Civic Offices. For some reason that Dave could never fathom, the crematorium was under the administration of the Parks and Recreation Department. As he knew Carol so well, he was able to act as an intermediary between her and the Co-op, who were arranging the cremation. Tonker said that he wanted it to take place as soon as possible. 'Get it over with, like. Sooner the better. We can't bring her back now,' he had explained, dragging on another roll-up. Dave had seen Carol on the Monday afternoon after spending the morning with the funeral directors.

'You're lucky, Dave love,' she told him. 'They do work on a Saturday in the winter at the crematorium: lots of old folk passing on with the cold. Can't afford heating nowadays, you see. First time they've been warm for months when they're incinerated. And we've got a cancellation for this Saturday.'

Dave wondered how there could be a cancellation at a crematorium until Carol explained. 'Apparently the family changed their minds. Thought they'd go for a traditional burial,' Carol explained. 'If you ask the man from the Co-op to call me direct tomorrow, I'll fix it up. Meanwhile I've pencilled your mum in for eleven o'clock, Dave love. And I am sorry, pet.'

The organization for the cremation took some time but had gone well and Dave was too busy organizing to be upset. He had kept his emotions in check through-out the week leading to the service and felt sure that he would maintain control throughout the day on Saturday. And he would have done if it hadn't have been for the Poachers Arms' regulars. As he arrived in the funeral car following the hearse, the whole team, supporters and pub regulars had lined the drive leading to the little chapel and applauded Dave's mum as the hearse crawled slowly between the two lines of people. Each one of those men, and many of their wives and girlfriends, had given up their Saturday off to pay respects to his mum. That's when he broke down.

After the service, he and Tonker walked along the line of people waiting outside, shaking hands and hearing their words of condolence. The mourners reviewed the wreaths and flowers, all of which were eclipsed by a huge wreath in the shape of a red and white football, with a message attached, simply saying "To Dave's Mum from the Poachers Arms F C."

As the gathering broke up and people made their way slowly to their cars, Dave noticed a familiar, small car pulling out of the car park. He stared as Mandy turned and waved at him, her beautiful smile temporarily erasing the pain and upset of the moment, then he raised his arm in a weak attempt to signal for her to stop before she pulled out of the car park and was gone.

The Poachers had laid on a good spread. 'Done your mum proud,' said Tonker. 'Pity she's not here to see it. She loved a good buffet.' He headed for the door and another roll-up as the guests made the most of the free food and settled in for a good afternoon's wake. Dave was being presented with so many pints that he couldn't possibly drink them all and they were lined up on the table, but there was no need to worry: Billy was close by to help and was drinking as if his life depended on it.

'Can't see 'em go to waste,' he said cheerfully as he took another pint, and his wife, Louise, returned from the buffet with two plates stacked high with ham sandwiches, sausage rolls and prawn vol-au-vents.

The Match Of The Day theme played in Dave's pocket and he quickly downed the dregs of his pint and found a quiet corner to answer his mobile.

'Hi, Dave, it's me.'

'Mandy. What? Where? You came. Thanks. Why? Where are you now? We're in the pub—'

Mandy interrupted him. 'Dave, calm down. It's not right that I see you now, not appropriate. Today's for your mum, so I'll see you tomorrow at three as usual outside the pub. Oh, and Dave. I've really missed you.' She hung up. Dave returned to the throng and continued drinking with the lads until late afternoon, feeling, if not happy, then content and relaxed. He knew that the cremation had drawn a line under part of his life and he could not look back. It didn't stop him loving his mum, he always would, but now was the time to look forward, especially to tomorrow at three o'clock. He returned to find his remaining pints had disappeared, along with Billy.

A pall of blue smoke hung over the untidy kitchen as Dave, Viv and Paul sat round the table and Tonker stood by the hob amongst discarded food wrappings, poking at a smouldering frying pan, a roll-up stuck to his bottom lip. Dave had laid out the kitchen table with four sheets of Downham Borough Council headed notepaper and four pens, in order to give the impression of a proper meeting. 'We might as well get going,' he said. 'Can't wait for Plumby all day. Now are we sure that there's no injuries?'

Paul shook his head and Viv stared into the blue fog through bloodshot eyes but said nothing. 'OK, then, it looks like we've got a full squad to choose from so it's probably easier if we say who's definitely in first. Then we'll sort out the awkward positions later.

'George in goal, the Smith brothers in the middle at the back, Billy at number 3, Viv in the middle, Gordon and Gunner up front with Razor. Agreed? Right that's eight agreed; just three to pick out of the remaining eight players. Any ideas?'

'To be fair, I wouldn't mind standing down today. Give the kids a chance. Shame to drop anyone really,' Vivian offered, his head still thumping and feeling nauseous from the smell of Tonker's culinary efforts.

'That's good of you, Viv, well done. Good club man isn't he, Paul? Well done, Viv,' said Dave, pleased that the offer had removed one less obstacle. Viv felt embarrassed at the false plaudit but was relieved that he wouldn't be playing. Dave continued, 'I think that the two new lads, Jock and Magic, should stay in. They've both done good so far and it'd be a shame to drop them now. Agreed?' Paul nodded. Viv really didn't care.

'Right, that means that we've got to decide who plays up front because one of the forwards will have to drop back into midfield and it leaves Steve, Percy, Wayne, Matt, Tommo and Paddy for two midfield positions. Now Paddy doesn't mind being sub and Percy's crap, so that leaves Steve, Wayne, Tommo and Matt to choose from. Steve can only play full back, but then young Jock reckons he can play midfield, so we could play Steve at right back and push Jock up, leaving Wayne, Tommo and Matt for one midfield position. They're all good lads, that's the problem, so what do you reckon?'

'Up to you,' Paul replied, none too helpfully. Viv felt that he had lost the will to live.

'Well, we could drop Billy, he wouldn't mind too much, put Jock back to left back. Paul, you can tell your Matt that he's sub because he won't argue with you and Bob's your uncle.'

Dave continually crossed out names on his teamsheet and scribbled in new names and sat back looking at the team with some satisfaction. The front door opened and Barry burst in. 'Bloody coppers. What a bloody shower. Sorry I'm late, lads. Just got stopped for speeding. Instant fine of sixty fucking quid. Pardon my French, Tonker. Forty-eight miles an hour on the bypass and a bloody plod jumps out with a radar gun. Fucking sixty quid. Something's wrong with the police in this bloody country.'

'Hang on, Plumby.' Paul looked perplexed. 'You were a copper for twenty years, weren't you?'

'Bloody right I was. I was a copper when it was a proud occupation, upholding law and order and catching criminals, not leaping out of a bush to stop a law-abiding citizen going about his lawful business. And I know the little prat. I trained him. Not to catch motorists, obviously, but to catch muggers and burglars and rapists. I said to him, "You should be out catching real criminals," but he laughed at me. "I am, Plumby," he said. "You." Wouldn't have happened in my day. Real coppers we were. On the beat, catching scum on the streets, in my day.'

'Fuck me, Plumby, you've only been out the force two fucking years,' Tonker stated as he turned away from his smoking pan.

Barry barely stopped for breath. 'And you know what made it worse? He's bloody Rabbit's boy, the copper. With a referee for a father, what do you expect? Whole country's gone to pot. Let's have a look at this team then.'

Barry studied the teamsheet. 'No good,' he said after a suitable amount of time looking somewhat studious and diligent. 'George can't play. Phoned me on Friday. Going on another bloody leadership weekend or some such nonsense. No wonder the country's in such a state.'

'Oh, bloody hell,' Dave exclaimed, perhaps a little over dramatically. 'Right, if we put Gunner in goal, that means we can move Magic forward; no, wait a minute, he's already forward. We could put Matty in, if he doesn't mind playing in the centre, but we don't want to upset Tommo, so…'

'Dave, why don't you just go and pick a team and I'll tell everyone who isn't playing that if they don't like it, they can piss off,' Paul said firmly.

'Right, good idea, do we all agree that…?'

'Just fuck off and do it,' Viv shouted, the noxious smell from Tonker's cuisine beginning to stick ominously in his throat.

Dave rushed upstairs to his PC to create the teamsheet as Tonker carried the frying pan over to the table. Onto a waiting plate, he tipped out some smoking brown/black lumps in a viscous brown liquid, and said, 'Eat up, lads, do you good,' just before Viv raced upstairs for the bathroom.

Gorton Down was a small village which nestled tidily in the folds of the hills to the south of Downham. It was a pretty village with stone-built thatched cottages, a small post office, and general store and a pub. The New Inn was typical of many pubs in the countryside where the brewers tried to be all things to all men and succeeded in being nothing to anyone. The old public bar remained, with its small bar, dartboard and yellow-stained ceilings above half a dozen old tables of different styles and eras. The lounge bar was modern antique with stripped wooden floors, beams and old black and white or sepia photographs of the village in bygone years. At the back was a new extension and conservatory, creating a restaurant serving "home- made" foods: steak and ale pies, game pies, shepherd's pies, wild boar pies and jugged hare pies. In fact anything that the cook could fit into pastry had appeared on the menu at one time or another, although it was often difficult to distinguish between the tastes of the different offerings as they were all drowned in the cook's favourite Bisto gravy.

The overall effect was that the New Inn was unsure whether it was a café, a pub, a restaurant or a pie shop. But they had always had a fair football team, which was the pride and joy of the landlord who often slipped better players boot money to make the weekly trip into the country worthwhile.

The changing rooms were in two large wooden buildings behind the pub, overlooking a private pitch which was used as a camping and caravan park in the summer, the wooden sheds converted to entertainment venues for the campers. The ground was somewhat uneven after having four-by-fours dragging their heavy vans over the pitch all summer, but the changing rooms were comparatively luxurious with several showers and toilets. This was a great advantage on Sunday mornings when one toilet was often shared between many footballers, the majority of whom had drunk twelve pints and forced down a greasy kebab the previous night.

Dave counted in the players and was pleased that everyone was there except George Crosswell. Although Paul had promised to announce the team, he handed the job over to Barry, who was more confident in public speaking and better equipped with a loud and commanding voice.

'Here is today's team,' he proclaimed, holding Dave's teamsheet like a town-crier, and shouting out the names and numbers of the selected players and substitutes. He finished by saying, 'I understand that some of you may be upset by not being selected this morning, but Paul here has given this some thought and has agreed to act as a counsellor to any player who may need, er, counselling. So, Paul, you have some advice for those who may be upset by the team selection, I believe.'

He moved away and pushed Paul to the front, as the players waited for Paul's words of consolation. 'If you don't like it, piss off,' he announced.

Paul's words had somehow removed any signs of discontent and the players were in good spirits as they prepared to take the field. Just before they left the changing room, Viv dragged himself to his feet. 'Lads, listen up a moment,' he shouted. 'One more thing to say. You know that yesterday was a sad day for our secretary and manager. I don't have to tell you that today is for him, for Dave. Go out and play for his mum and make him proud.'

'Firm but fair,' the team shouted back and set off with an unusual determination.

What Dave saw when he took up his position on the halfway line was surreal. The Poachers were playing with an enthusiasm, determination and vigour he had rarely witnessed from a team, certainly not on a freezing Sunday morning in January in a windswept field behind a pub. Even Razor, who rarely broke into a trot normally, was chasing and harrying the New Inn defence, whilst the team shouted and encouraged each other, and began playing with a confidence based on a knowledge that they were all playing for more than just a result. The New Inn, usually a solid and workmanlike side, were overawed by the Poachers' resolution and soon conceded the first goal, a predictable run and cross by Gordon and a centre which Razor stretched to toe-poke past the goalkeeper. Two more goals were added in the first half, a fine turn and shot by Razor, and a goalmouth scramble, finally forced over the line by Danny Tomlinson.

Although being on the receiving end of a severe reprimand by the landlord, New Inn could not cope with the pace, skill and resolve from the Poachers' team and conceded another four goals in the second half. Majid scored with a clever lob from the edge of the penalty area; a blast from Gordon, which could have been a cross or shot, thumped in off the underside of the crossbar, although no one questioned his intent; and a powerful header from Big Smithy from a corner made it six. The final goal was the icing on the cake, with the confident Poachers Arms passing the ball from goalkeeper to defence to midfield to the strike force, through a dispirited New Inn team enabling Wayne to run the ball into an empty net.

Bundling balls, buckets and other accoutrements into his car boot at the end of the game, Dave, Paul, Viv and Barry were in a reflective mood. 'If only we could play like that every week, we'd walk this league, and probably Division One as well,' Dave gloated, stuffing his hands into his pocket against the chill of the freezing wind. 'Anyone fancy a quick one here before we go back to the Poachers?'

'Yes please, Dave. Just a quick one, mind, I've got to take Louise to her mum's again.' Billy appeared as if by magic at Dave's shoulder. 'Get them in and I'll be there as soon as I collect the kit.'

As Billy sprinted into the changing rooms, Viv looked at Paul and smiled. 'He needs to keep on the mother-in-law's sweet side so that he gets the house when the old girl kicks the bucket, but what the fuck,' he said. 'If I had to go home to a missis like his, I'd need more than money to make life worth living. I'll buy the tight scrote a pint,' and the men jauntily strode into the lounge bar via the back entrance.

'Five of your very best pints, landlord,' called Barry. 'And have one yourself. Call it a consolation prize.'

Viv looked round at the blackboards advertising the pub's wares. 'I expect you'd rather call it "consolation pies",' he said. 'That's the only sort of pie you haven't got, by the look of it.'

The landlord laughed at Viv's poor joke and replied, 'Thanks. I hope you lot get stopped by the police on the way home.'

'Don't start me on the excuse for a fucking police force in this country,' Barry exploded, as the other three moved quietly into a corner leaving the landlord to listen to Barry's ranting.

As the team filtered into the Poachers, there was an uneasy air. Tonker was playing crib in the corner as usual, but the players and pub regulars seemed uncomfortable about being seen to be enjoying themselves the day after Dave's mum's cremation. As Dave arrived, Tonker shouted across, 'Oy, Dave, get us four pints and ask that pillock behind the bar if he's got any sandwiches left from the funeral. I'm starving.'

'Bugger that, Dad, they was curled up yesterday. Better get home and find that bit of old cheese behind the fridge,' Dave called back and the atmosphere immediately relaxed. Tonker still left the pub at one thirty, even though there was no roast to go home to, but he was a creature of very strict habit and wandered out at his normal time, lighting his last cigarette as he went. Dave checked his watch and remembered Mandy for the first time that morning. He had been so busy with his team selection, clerical tasks, managerial duties and the game of football that Mandy had been pushed into the back of his mind. She was going to be there in just over an hour. Dave suddenly felt very hot and began to sweat.

'You all right, Dave?' asked Paul. 'You've gone all red.'

'Yeah, fine, Paul, just remembered that I ought to see Tonker's OK,' said Dave. He finished his pint quickly and rushed out of the pub and over the road to his home. He never noticed the pots and pans piled in the kitchen, the dirty plates left on the dining table or the discarded food littering the kitchen worktop as he rushed upstairs and undressed before jumping into the shower. He heard Tonker shuffling about in his room and wondered if he was hungry with no roast await-ing him on his return from the pub. After showering, shampooing and shaving, Dave searched his ancient wardrobe and chest of drawers for clean clothes. He had never accumulated a large collection of clothes, believing that more than enough was too much, and had certainly never followed any fashion trends. Most of his clothes seemed to be piled on the chair in the corner of the room or hiding beneath his bed, but he managed to find a clean, if very old, shirt, and reclaimed the jeans he had been wearing every evening for the last week from the floor. He put on his only trainers, his old leather jacket and hurried out of the house and across the road to the Poachers. He stood in the lobby of the pub, shielding from the cold wind which was carrying the first traces of icy sleet. The lobby door opened and Mandy stepped inside. Dave looked at her and opened his mouth but there were no words to express what he felt, so he just stood there, staring at her with mouth agape. Mandy stared back, her head slightly to one side and a smile playing on her lips. 'Well?' she asked. 'Aren't you going to kiss me, then?'

Dave knew that he should rush forward and take her firmly in his strong arms, planting a long, lingering kiss on her beautiful moist lips, at which time everything would become black and white, the train would pull away in a great hiss of steam and the credits would roll leaving them to live happily ever after.

'Er, right,' he said, leant forward and kissed her gently and courteously on the cheek.

She giggled a little and shook her head. 'You, David Statham, are not the most romantic man in the world.' she said. 'How you ever managed to father this child inside me, I shall never fathom. Now kiss me properly.'

After kissing her properly, they retreated from the weather to Dave's house, barely speaking as they walked arm in arm across the road. As they entered the hall, Mandy sniffed. 'What is that smell, David?' she asked, moving slowly towards the kitchen. When she saw the detritus of a week's fried dinners and takeaway Chinese food cartons, she stopped and stared in disbelief.

'I am not talking about our future until this mess is cleaned up. Just remember that this is your mum's kitchen and she would be ashamed to see it like this. Run some hot water, get me a rubbish sack, and we'll sort this out now,' she stated positively.

'Firm but fair,' said Dave.

Dave was amazed how quickly and easily the kitchen was returned to normal with Mandy at the helm, whilst he followed her orders. Within half an hour, all the rubbish had been placed in the sack, the washing-up had been completed, crockery and cutlery dried and put away and work surfaces wiped down. Mandy inspected their work and nodded in satisfaction.

'That'll do for now, but just make sure that you keep it like it,' she ordered. 'Now put the kettle on and make a cup of tea. We have things to discuss.'

They sat on the settee in the lounge with their tea on the coffee table. Mandy did not offer any explanation on how she had spent the previous month, and it was better not to ask any questions, but to let her tell him in her own time.

'Well, aren't you going to ask me any questions?' she said eventually, convincing Dave that he would never understand a woman's mind.

'Well, yes,' Dave began, thinking intensely for a moment. He took a deep breath, and then blurted out, 'Where have you been? What have you been doing? Why didn't you call me? Is there a baby? Do you know what sort it is? Are we keeping it? Shall we get married?'

Mandy put her finger lightly on his lips. 'Slow down, Dave,' she said quietly. 'I wish I'd never asked. But OK. Here goes. I went back to stay with my old girlfriend in Bristol to sort out a lot of things. I spoke to Gareth, you know, my husband. At first, he was angry. Well, he stayed angry, really, but he has agreed to a divorce and that's going through now.' Dave sat in open-mouthed wonder, barely daring to guess what was coming next. Mandy continued, 'Please close your mouth, Dave, you look like a fish. Gareth also agreed to buy my share of the flat and that has been completed. I sold it to him cheaply and made nothing out of it, but it was worth it to break that link.'

Dave nodded, ensuring his mouth was closed.

'I have sorted out my will and some insurance policies and bank accounts which were all linked to Gareth, so, as soon as the divorce is absolute, I will have no ties whatsoever with Gareth or Bristol. I have been to my doctor and confirmed that I am now three months' pregnant and, as you are the only man I have been near for about a year, you can take it that you are the father. I think that we should now have the baby and see how we feel then. I'm living back in the house with the girls for the time being, but it's not really suitable so I've made enquiries about rooms in the area and I'm looking at a few next week—'

'You can stay here, with me…' Dave interrupted.

'Thanks, Dave, I knew you'd say that, but it's too soon. After all, we've still only known each other three months and what with your mum just passing on, it's just too soon, but we'll see how things go. And that, Father-Of-My-Child, is about it.'

'Great. That's fine,' was all he mustered by way of response.

'There is one more question you haven't asked.' Mandy held his hand as she spoke.

Dave's mind discharged all previous thinking and moved into blank mode. 'What's that, Mandy?' he asked innocently.

Mandy smiled and stood up, keeping hold of his hand. 'Shall we go to bed?' she asked.

Thirteen

Downham Sunday Football League, Division Two
Results for Sunday 18th January

New Inn, Gorton Down	0	7	Poachers Arms
Lower End WMC	3	1	AFC Cummiston
Hearty Oak, Downlea	2	2	J G Tanner and Sons
Pickled Herring	1	5	Jones Juniors FC
Downham Churches	0	3	Shellduck Inn

League Table

Team	Pl'd	Won	Drew	Lost	For	Ag'st	GD	Points
Jones Juniors FC	11	8	3	0	44	12	32	27
Poachers Arms	**11**	**6**	**3**	**2**	**33**	**16**	**17**	**21**
New Inn, Gorton D	11	6	3	2	32	27	5	21
Pickled Herring	11	5	2	4	20	23	-3	17
J G Tanner and Sons	11	5	2	4	20	25	-5	17
AFC Cummiston	11	3	5	3	28	28	0	14
Lower End WMC	11	4	2	5	20	23	-3	14
Shellduck Inn	11	3	2	6	18	27	-9	11
Hearty Oak, Downlea	11	2	3	6	27	41	-14	9
Downham Churches	11	1	2	8	29	49	-20	5

Sunday 25th January

Downham Sunday Football League, Division Two
Poachers Arms v Hearty Oak, Downlea
Tenacre Recreation Ground – Kick-off 10.30

THE POACHERS ARMS

1 George Crosswell

2 Steve Tippling   4 Derek Smith   5 Brian Smith (Capt)   3 Matt Cornwell

8 Jamie Dunbar   6 Wayne Tocket   10 Danny Tomlinson

7 Gordon Gaye   9 Razor Raisin   11 Majid Ahmed

Substitutes
12 Vivian Clutterbuck
13 Gunner Farr
14 Billy Millmore

Reserves (Please bring boots)
Paddy Oakley
Percy Woodman
Paul Cornwell
Barry Plumb

Manager
Dave Statham

All players, substitutes and reserves to turn up at 09.45

It was unusual for Barry to wake up so early on a Sunday morning. It was unusual for Barry to wake up without a degree of a hangover on a Sunday morning. It was unusual to wake up in Monica's bed on a Sunday morning and it was very, very unusual to wake up on a Sunday morning as an engaged person. He rolled over carefully and climbed gingerly out of bed, passing the en-suite and slipping quietly into the family bathroom next door to relieve himself. He looked at his watch under the glaring light of the bathroom and squinted until his eyes adjusted to the brightness. It was half past seven. As he returned to the bedroom, he left the door open a fraction so that a narrow shaft of light from the landing entered the bedroom; just enough illumination to allow him to collect his clothes and carry them quietly outside and back into the bathroom. He showered as quickly and quietly as possible before drying himself in the thick, king-sized bath towel and dressed, ready to make an early escape. He needed time to consider his options after last night; he needed to remember exactly what had been said. He shuffled silently down the stairs and looked into the huge kitchen, with its expensive handmade units surrounding a heavy, wooden farmhouse table. He went to the fridge and poured an orange juice from the carton before sitting down to review the previous evening in his mind.

He had always been nervous about dinner parties, hoping that he wouldn't make a *faux pas* which would show him up to be a member of the proletariat that he had worked so hard to leave behind. He was proud of his rise from his council house background and was never reticent about explaining to anyone how he had climbed from being one of the great unwashed to a position of standing in the community, first as a sergeant in the local constabulary and now as a successful businessman running Downham Security Services. He drove a top range Audi, lived in a four-bedroomed detached house and was, if things went as he planned, about to become a magistrate. He was also about to host a dinner party for a man who was the chairman of the local Conservative Party, a Justice of the Peace and chairman of the Advisory Committee for the local magistrates. The other guests he had not met before but Monica described them as a very wealthy local businessman and his wife. Barry's rise up the social scale did not stop him worrying about using the correct cutlery, dropping his peas onto the floor, getting too drunk on red wine or making inappropriate comments about the guests' wives' breasts.

He had arrived at Monica's imposing country house at seven o'clock, in time to make an effort in preparing for the guests, but too late to do any of the hard work. As he let himself in, Monica was putting the finishing touches to the impressively laid out table in the large dining room, ensuring that all cutlery, plates and glasses were positioned perfectly. Her "lady-who-does" was in the kitchen, checking and rechecking pots of steaming food and sauces and slicing something at the kitchen worktop. Barry surveyed the scene and felt proud and contented, like the lord of the manor awaiting a royal visit, his servants preparing a grand banquet in his honour.

Monica rushed towards him and kissed him on the cheek, saying, 'Oh, Barry, you're early. Thank you. You are a wonderful man; now please can you check that everything's right on the table, get the drinks ready – not just the beer – and check that Mrs Williams has everything she needs in the kitchen. And make sure she doesn't burn anything. Oh, and make sure we have ice and you know where the bottle opener is, and open a couple of bottles of red now. And put some decent music on, something classical. I think that's it. I'm just going up to change. And, Barry, you look lovely.'

Barry felt good as he wandered into the kitchen and sat down at the table. He smiled at Mrs Williams. 'Evening, Tracy,' he said. 'What's for dinner?' Barry had known Mrs Williams since she was Tracy Cunningham during his schooldays. Mrs Williams returned his smile.

'Hello, Baz. Starter's French onion soup, then it's baked oysters and spinach, then roast loin of venison with gravy and loads of veg. My Terry gets the venison from somewhere but I don't ask him where. How are you anyway? Come up in the world since school, haven't you?'

'Not really, Tracy,' Barry replied, trying to sound casual but pleased that Mrs Williams had commented. 'Just worked hard, that's all. And now Mrs Bond – Monica and I – are sort of an item, you know.'

'I know all right, Baz. Got pots of money, they reckon, since her old man went. I mean, they had plenty anyway, but they reckon she had him insured for thousands, millions even. Course, me and my Terry do all right. Got a nice house off the council in the village. We was very lucky because his family's local. Village family, otherwise we wouldn't have got the house. Still, I always knew you'd do alright for yourself. I wasn't a bit surprised when you and her ladyship started courting, like. Hey, do you still see that daft Dave Statham?' Tracy leaned forward conspiratorially. 'He was always after a quick hand job,' she laughed. 'Not like you. Always wanted to go all the way, you did,' she whispered before returning to her pots, laughing.

'Tracy, keep it down and don't say anything to Mrs Bond about the past. OK?'

'You're not ashamed of me are you, Baz?' Tracy teased. 'You wasn't ashamed of me when you used to take me behind the garages.'

'Tracy, please, that's enough. If Mrs Bond ever found out…'

'If Mrs Bond ever found out what?' Monica said as she walked into the kitchen.

Barry froze. Mrs. Williams coolly replied, 'We was just saying, Mrs Bond, that my Terry gets the venison from somewhere that might not be exactly, you know, legal, as it were, and Mr Plumb says that you're not to find out because you might not approve.'

'Oh, Barry,' Monica laughed, 'you really are a sweetie, but I don't mind where it comes from so long as it tastes as good as it smells. Now, how do I look and have you done your jobs yet?'

'You look absolutely stunning, Monica, and I've nearly finished my chores,' Barry lied, moving into the dining room to find the wine. Monica followed him and gave him his orders for the evening. 'Do not start ranting about Scotsmen, foreign footballers, homosexuals, policemen, antisocial behaviour, or any so-called comedians called Carr. Stay calm and stay sober.'

The guests arrived together by taxi and Monica greeted them at the door before leading them into the dining room where Barry was pretending to study the label on the bottle of red he had just opened. 'Barry, you know Charles and Caroline,' Monica said, moving to one side as Barry shook Charles firmly by the hand and pecked Caroline on each cheek. 'And this is Gerry and Susan.'

Barry repeated his greeting and was almost overcome by the mixture of expensive perfume and cheap aftershave. After an aperitif or two, the three couples sat down to a magnificent repast. Mrs Williams stayed in the kitchen, only appearing to dispense the food and to collect the dirty plates between deliveries. As she brought in each superb course she winked at Barry, and he hoped that no one else noticed. He also hoped that she had washed her hands thoroughly since going behind the garages with Dave Statham.

The meal was truly excellent, with the delicious, tender venison standing out as a wonderful main course. Two bottles of chilled white wine, followed by three bottles of red and one of sweet to complement the walnut chiffon pie, had left all diners in a satiated and mellow condition. Barry was, however, as sober as a judge, or a JP, drinking water between small sips of wine, aware that presenting a sober and responsible impression for Charles was essential to guarantee his approval as a magistrate. After the meal, as Tracy looked in to clear the final remnants from the table, Monica, who had been cool, calm and efficient through-out, said, 'You may go home now, Mrs Williams. We'll see to the rest of this. And, gentlemen, why don't you go into the lounge and pour yourselves a large brandy. I'm sure that you have some business or something to discuss.'

Barry poured one small and two large brandies as his guests slumped into the sumptuous leather armchairs. 'Now, Barry, I understand you're an expert on retail security systems,' Gerry said, slurring his speech slightly. Barry raised one eyebrow and shrugged, trying to look modest yet confident. Gerry sipped his brandy and continued. 'Only I've got seven stores, y'see. Gerry's Super Saver Discount Stores. You probably know them, and I'm losing a small fortune to pilfering. The problem, Barry, is that my stores cater for the, shall we say, lower social economic end of the market: mainly families with smaller incomes, single parents, the unfortunates of society who need help, who need an outlet like mine to provide them with the consumer goods they deserve, at prices they can afford. And they're nearly all thieving bloody pikeys.'

'Not a problem, Gerry. I could fit the latest surveillance cameras, electronic tags on the goods, scanners at the point of sale, that sort of thing. And the impor-tant thing is that we can introduce a system that will provide enough information to get convictions. Nothing reduces pilfering like reading in the local paper about someone getting convicted for shoplifting. I can also hold staff training sessions to help your people identify and apprehend felons and record incidents in a manner that will hold up in court.'

'Sounds expensive, Barry,' Gerry drained his glass and held it out for a refill. Barry did not like being treated like a waiter, but this was business so the glass was duly recharged.

'Of course it is, very expensive,' he said, returning the full glass, 'but not as expensive as continually losing stock to the, er, unfortunates. I've got a computer model which will show you just how much you'll save, if you're interested.'

Barry gained in confidence as the conversation remained on familiar ground and Gerry and Charles became increasingly incoherent. He was sure that, if he could have produced a contract there and then, Gerry would have signed up immediately for the top of the range retail security package, which he was yet to devise.

The ladies joined the men in the lounge, Monica carrying in a tray of coffee. 'This sounds like business talk,' she said. 'I hope that it's not too boring.'

Charles stirred from a semi-comatose state. 'Not at all,' he mumbled. 'It looks like young Barry's just sold a retail security system to Gerry. Things are looking up for you, Barry, what? Big contract with Gerry round the corner, meeting of the Advisory Committee next week to consider your application. All you need now is a good wife, what?'

'Well, Barry.' Monica was talking to Barry but addressing the whole room. 'You did say that if you are accepted next week and could gain another big contract, perhaps it was the right time.'

Barry was feeling relaxed, confident and off-guard. 'I did indeed say that, Monica, and perhaps Charles is right, perhaps I do need a good wife.'

'Oh, Barry darling,' Monica cooed. 'Is that a proposal?'

Barry suddenly realised what he had said and five pairs of eyes stared at him, waiting for a response. He thought quickly and there appeared to be no way out. 'Monica darling,' he said, 'when I do propose to you, it will be on one knee and made with the full commitment and love I feel for you.'

'Go on then, get down on one knee and do it, you romantic young thing,' Charles blurted out, enjoying the scene unfolding before him. Barry hesitated, but realised that he had no choice, dropping to one knee and formally proposing whilst professing his love for Monica. He hoped that no one had noticed that he had his fingers crossed.

Dave stirred and blinked in the semi-darkness and felt Mandy's warm, damp breath on his face as she lightly nuzzled his ear. What a wonderful way to be woken up. They touched lips very lightly before parting and staring at each other. Mandy whispered quietly. 'I must go before your dad gets up. We don't want him to know that I stay overnight just yet,' she said, 'and before you ask, the answer's no.'

'How did you know what I was going to ask?'

'Because you're a man. And anyway, I've got lots to do today. I'm going to see a room which sounds really nice this morning and I want to be away before your dad wakes up.'

'Where's this room?' Dave asked quietly, still unhappy that Mandy would not move in with him permanently.

Mandy went to her bag and fished around before bringing out a cutting from the local newspaper. She tossed it on the bed and continued to get dressed as Dave read the advertisement:

Large room for rent in family house
Fully furnished with en suite bathroom
Excellent location in quiet cul-de-sac
£200 per month
Meals by arrangement

'Why has it only got a mobile number?' Dave asked, a little concerned. 'Be careful, love.'

'Of course I will, Dave. Must rush. Bye. Love you,' she whispered as she crept out of the door and down the stairs.

'See you later, Mandy,' called Tonker from his bedroom.

Dave dressed quickly and turned on his computer. He double-clicked his team-sheet and stared at the names for a few moments. He was very worried that he had upset too many players, but decided that the magnificent performance of the previous week warranted keeping the same team. The only change was George Crosswell coming back for Gunner Farr who was relegated to substitute. Gunner was upset, complaining that he was dropped because he had agreed to play in goal instead of up front so was penalized for doing Dave a favour. Viv had complained that he was dropped because he did Dave a favour by dropping out voluntarily last week. Percy was upset because he seemed to be permanently excluded from the team. Paddy moaned that he was always being dropped. Billy was unhappy because he was dropped and still had to do the laundry and that wasn't fair, although he may have to put up the price of the laundry to compensate.

Dave did not enjoy the confrontations but Paul had handled the complaints in his usual diplomatic manner. 'If you don't like it, piss off,' he had delicately explained in the pub on Friday night.

Dave printed two copies of the teamsheet before pulling on his crumpled tracksuit and searching for his football socks which he finally located under the wardrobe. He found his trainers under the settee in the lounge and pulled them on before venturing out to Muzzy's for his newspaper. As he opened the door, the cold wind brought a blast of snow which stung his face and made his eyes fill with tears. He ran across the road and into Muzzy's. He pushed the paper shop door open and walked in, wiping his eyes as he looked for the sparse pile of *Sunday Times*. He took the newspaper to the counter and Muzzy reached for his packet of Hamlet without being asked.

'Good morning, David. Is it an important one this morning, a top-of-the-table clash again?' Muzzy tried to hide his sparse knowledge of the game by reading phrases from the *Mail on Sunday* and repeating them.

'Not really, Muzzy, although all games are important at this stage of the season, but it's not a six-pointer.'

Muzzy nodded but obviously had no idea what Dave was talking about.

Dave really fancied eggs and bacon, but looked in the cupboard which bore a startling resemblance to that of old Mother Hubbard. He made a cup of tea and sat looking at the paper and moping until Viv and Paul knocked on the door.

As they drove to the rec in Dave's Polo, Viv kept up an incessant chatter. 'Dropped. Dropped after all I've done for this club. Bloody dropped because I did the manager a favour last week. What's reckon then, Paulo, dropped? Me, a man of my ability and skills. A man amongst men, a superstar in football circles, a legend in me own lunchtime. Dropped. What d'you think then, Paulo?' Viv slipped into Kenneth Williams mode. 'Infamy, infamy, they've all got it in for me.'

Paul was enjoying the show. 'If you don't like it…'

All three started to laugh and shouted, 'Piss off,' at the top of their voices.

They arrived at the rec, parked in Dave's spot, grabbed the kit and hurried through the cold into the changing rooms.

'Morning, Lightning,' Dave shouted. 'Are the games still on in this weather? Have you cleared the snow off the lines?'

'What do you think he is, a railway maintenance man?' shouted Viv, confusing Lightning altogether.

'Mr Bridges assures me that all games are playable, in spite of the inclement conditions,' replied Lightning, handing over the key to changing room number three and thrusting his clip-board forward for signature. 'Please sign here under Ivan Ardon,' he requested politely.

As Dave and Viv opened up, Paul stayed with Lightning. 'How's your mum, Andrew?' he asked quietly. 'Is she still seeing this man?'

Lightning cocked his head and replied, 'I think she's seeing him all right, Paul. He stays in the flat but I don't like him. He still calls me names and says that it would be better if I fucked off, but I don't like swearing, and I don't want to go anyway. Can't you tell him to go away, please, Paul?'

Paul wanted to do more than just tell him to go away and felt his anger boiling inside before consciously reducing the pressure and letting his rage subside. 'There's not much I can do, Andrew mate,' he explained. 'Only it's your mum's choice and not really my business. But just tell her that I'm thinking of her and, Andrew, you should really tell her what this man says to you, you know.'

'I think I will, Paul. And I'll tell her that you're thinking of her,' said Lightning, looking relieved and happier now that he had been told what to do.

'Chatting with Lightning again, Paul?' Billy stated loud enough for the others to hear. 'Any problems at home with him, or what?'

Paul ignored the taunt and lit up a cigarette, determined to bide his time for revenge. He didn't have to wait too long.

As the players arrived there were few grumbles from those who had been relegated to substitute except, surprisingly, from Gunner Farr, one of the most reliable and solid members of the squad. He took Dave outside into the corridor and explained. 'Look Dave, if I was playing bad, I wouldn't mind, but you asked me to play in goal, so I did to help you out. Then you dropped me. If I'd have played up front as normal, I'd be OK. And this Magic lad's OK but he's only played a couple of games. I've been playing for The Poachers for five years and I've never been dropped before.'

Dave tried to win Gunner round, explaining the rationale behind his selection and promising that he would be playing next week. Dave continued to cajole and sweet-talk him, telling him that he was important to the team and had only been left out because Dave felt that he was mature enough to understand. As Gunner was begrudgingly beginning to accept the justification, Paul put his head out of the changing room door.

'Come on, Dave, time to get this lot geed up a bit. Tell him that if he don't like it he can piss off.'

Gunner looked startled at Paul's bluntness. 'If that's your fucking attitude, I will,' he shouted and walked out of the building. As Dave returned to the changing room, the players had changed and were squeezing out ready to trot off to pitch three. Paul looked at Dave and held his hands out. 'What's up with him?' he asked. 'It was only a joke.'

Dave and Paul followed the players out and were joined by Rabbit, strolling to referee a different game on pitch four. 'Who you got today, lads?' Rabbit asked, not really interested in the answer.

'Hearty Oak, Cummiston,' Dave replied. 'Should be straightforward enough,' when they heard Barry bellowing behind them, 'Hang on a minute, Rabbit, hang on, I want a word with you.'

Rabbit stopped and turned round as Barry arrived wheezing and panting. He took a few seconds to regain his composure and breath. 'Your boy,' he gasped, 'your boy bloody nicked me last week for speeding. Call himself a copper. In my day—'

'Was you speeding, Mr Plumb?' Rabbit interrupted politely.

'Well yes, but I was unlucky—'

'And how fast was you going, Mr Plumb?'

'I was doing forty-eight, but—'

'And where was you doing forty-eight, Mr Plumb?'

'On the bypass, but what's that—?'

'Then my son was correct to book you. The speed limit is forty and you was guilty, Mr Plumb, and not unlucky. The little bastard nicked me on the same day for doing forty-two. Now that's bloody unlucky,' and Rabbit hurried off to take charge of pitch number four.

The game kicked off at a frantic pace with the unskilled but enthusiastic Hearty Oak players whacking the ball in the direction they were facing then chasing hell-for-leather after the elusive orb before clumping it forwards, or backwards, or sideways, beginning the chase once more. The young and inexperienced Poachers' team, buoyed by their victory from the previous week and aware that this success was achieved in part by hard work and passion, tried to match the Hearty Oak in the headless chicken stakes. The result was a somewhat chaotic game of "chase the ball". The thin covering of snow and the icy wind did not help and players were slipping and sliding on the frozen ground as they waited for the ball to land from its latest launch site.

The referee blew his whistle at half-time with neither side managing a shot on target. Dave poured a generous helping of hot tea into a plastic cup and asked Barry to take the warming beverage across the pitch for the referee, who was standing alone and forlorn in the centre circle, desperately wishing he had never passed his referee's examination. He accepted the cup gratefully and said, 'Barry Plumb, isn't it? Sergeant Plumb? Remember me – Constable Winkfield? We worked together in Salisbury years ago.'

Barry looked carefully at the referee. 'Fuck me. It is you. Wee Willy Winkie. How the bloody hell are you? How long you been at this game?'

Constable Winkfield slurped his tea gratefully. 'Been refereeing about ten years, but just got transferred to Downham from Salisbury. The missis wanted to move to be nearer her mum, so we—'

'Funny thing. Me and the lads have just been discussing modern policing. I was saying that in my day, well in our day, we had bloody discretion. If a villain needed a whack in the nuts then he got one. Not like today. Can't touch 'em today. All they need is a good hiding, some of these youngsters, but there's too many rules against it…' Barry was away and Wee Willy never managed another word before he finally had to ignore Barry and blow his whistle to start the second half.

Dave knew that he should change the team to bring on Billy or Viv and try to calm things down, but the substitutes were none too keen to strip off their snug clothing and expose their nicely warmed skin to the ravages of a winter morning's wind and sleet. Although the halftime team talk had stressed the need for a more composed style of play, the Poachers were too involved, too entrenched in the frantic battle of effort over style to change. The Hearty Oak had played this fast, frenetic football all season and were better at it than the usually composed Poachers' players, with the result that they gradually gained command, forcing the Poachers' defence further and further back towards their own goal. Had it not been for the magnificent form of George in goal, the Hearty Oak could have scored half a dozen goals. The fact that the Hearty Oak forwards couldn't shoot straight also helped. Finally, even George's heroics were not enough and the ball squeezed through a packed defence of eight Poachers' players crammed into the penalty area, and was forced over the line.

With only ten minutes left, Viv braved the cold and stripped off his tracksuit, a sweatshirt and two T-shirts before telling Dave to call young Majid off. He was going to save the day. Dave called, 'Magic, Magic. Off you come, lad. You done great, but we just need to get Viv on for the last ten minutes.'

'My name is Majid, Majid,' said Majid as he gratefully accepted the sweat-shirts, T-shirts and tracksuit, all of which were several sizes too large, but Majid was just happy to be cocooned in layers of warm clothing.

'Suppose it doesn't get this cold where you come from, Magic,' Barry said, passing Majid a cup containing the dregs of the halftime tea.

'That's right,' said Majid. 'It's usually hot and sunny in Harvest Close. I think it's probably the proximity of Pete's chippy that does it.'

Viv sprinted on to the pitch and reorganized the team immediately. 'Danny, push up front to support Razor. Jock, get out of defence and fill this gap in midfield. Wayne, push to the right and forward more. Defence, slow down and look for me every time. Feed me whenever you can. Gordon, when I get the ball, start your run forward and I'll pick you out. Razor, get in that middle and prepare for Gordon's cross. Come on, lads, we'll win this one.'

Spirits were immediately raised as the Poachers Arms heard the call to arms and realised that their saviour had arrived. The team re-formed and immediately looked and felt better balanced. The first Hearty Oak attack was calmly broken up by a fine interception from Big Smithy, who looked up and drove a hard but accurate pass towards Viv in the centre circle. Viv was aware of the whereabouts of his team mates without looking. Gordon had moved wide onto the right wing and was ready to sprint down the touchline, anticipating the imminent pass. Razor was on his toes, ready to move forward into the opposing penalty area to receive the cross. Support was primed from Wayne, Danny and Jamie. As the ball hit Viv, he killed it skilfully, dummied to the right, losing his marker with expert aplomb, spun to his left and fell over holding the back of his right leg in pain. As he sat down, grimacing and trying not to scream out, the opposing skipper gathered the unattended ball and lofted it forward. It sailed over the heads of the defenders pushing up towards the halfway line and over George, who was on the edge of the penalty area urging his team forward. The ball bounced twice and nestled gently in the back of the net as Viv cursed his luck.

Walking into the Poachers Arms public bar, Dave was surprised that the team was so happy. Warmed up and with a beer in their hands, the game was all but forgotten as they joked about Viv's glorious entrance into the fray and his immediate and somewhat inglorious exit.

'Never warmed up, that was the problem,' Viv explained to four team members pinned against the bar. 'Too keen to get on to sort you useless buggers out. Like a load of kids chasing the ball in the playground,' he continued before lapsing into Tommy Cooper and repeating old jokes that even the youngsters had heard several times before.

Dave's despondence was immediately lifted as he saw Mandy behind the bar. He ordered his pint, plus a round for the cribbage corner and a round for Paul and Barry. He asked Mandy how the house visit was that morning.

'I'll tell you later,' she answered secretively. 'I can't tell you now, but it's very interesting.'

Dave was intrigued as he ferried drinks between the bar and the old men's corner, finally seating himself next to Tonker and opposite Paul, Barry and Billy.

'Fifteen two and a pair's four. Two nil, then,' Tonker said without looking up from the cards.

'Yeah, we was useless, played like a load of kids.'

'I know that. Thirty one for two. Me and Tommy was watching from behind the goal. Twenty four for three. Best bit was when Viv came on like the cavalry to save the day, then went over like a sack of shit. Eighteen for two.'

'Made us fuckin' laugh. Charges on like the fuckin' cavalry, givin' out fuckin' orders and falls over first time he gets the fuckin' ball.' Tommy joined in the discussion before Viv hobbled over to take up his seat in the corner. 'Here, Viv, that impression you done just now was fuckin' great. Really fuckin' funny.'

Viv was pleased at the recognition and beamed. 'What, the Tommy Cooper?' he asked happily.

'No, before that, at the rec,' giggled Tommy 'When you was Charlie fuckin' Chaplin.'

They all broke down in laughter except Viv, who just looked baffled.

As the pub began to clear, Mandy wandered over to collect some glasses and sat down in the seat vacated by Billy who had left just before it was his round. 'Listen to this Dave,' she whispered, leaning forward as all the men stopped chatting to hear what she was saying. 'That room this morning. It was very nice. Clean, with a lovely en-suite. Well-furnished and in a lovely cul-de-sac.'

'You taking it then?' Dave asked.

'I don't think so.' Mandy shook her head. 'I'm not too sure about the couple who run the place.'

Dave looked puzzled. 'Why, Mandy? I said to be careful. What's wrong with them?'

'Well, nothing wrong exactly. But it belongs to that mate of yours. You know, the one that was sat here and never buys a round. His photo was all over the place with his sour-faced wife and daughters. There's no doubt about it.'

The lads looked stunned for a moment and Paul started to say, 'The tight-fisted, money-grabbing—' until Viv interrupted.

'This, gentlemen, is a miracle. The Lord has shined his light upon us. Hallelujah and praise be. David, my boy, before I go home today, please can you supply me with a few sheets of official Downham Borough Council headed notepaper? For the Lord has shown me the way.'

Fourteen

Downham Sunday Football League, Division Two
Results for Sunday 25th January

Poachers Arms	**0**	**2**	**Hearty Oak, Downlea**
Lower End WMC	3	3	New Inn, Gorton Down
AFC Cummiston	2	4	Pickled Herring
J G Tanner and Sons	4	0	Downham Churches
Jones Juniors FC	4	1	Shellduck Inn

League Table

Team	Pl'd	Won	Drew	Lost	For	Ag'st	GD	Points
Jones Juniors FC	12	9	3	0	48	13	35	30
New Inn, Gorton D	12	6	4	2	35	30	5	22
Poachers Arms	**12**	**6**	**3**	**3**	**33**	**18**	**15**	**21**
Pickled Herring	12	6	2	4	24	25	-1	20
J G Tanner and Sons	12	6	2	4	24	25	-1	20
Lower End WMC	12	4	3	5	23	26	-3	15
AFC Cummiston	12	3	5	4	30	32	-2	14
Hearty Oak, Downlea	12	3	3	6	29	41	-12	12
Shellduck Inn	12	3	2	7	19	31	-12	11
Downham Churches	12	1	2	9	29	53	-24	5

Sunday 1st February

Downham Sunday Football League, Division Two
Poachers Arms v Downham Churches
Tenacre Recreation Ground – Kick-off 10.30

THE POACHERS ARMS

1 George Crosswell

2 Steve Tippling 4 Derek Smith 5 Brian Smith 3 Billy Millmore (Capt)

8 Jamie Dunbar 6 Wayne Tocket 10 Matt Cornwell

7 Gordon Gaye 9 Razor Raisin 11 Majid Ahmed

Substitutes
12 Paddy Oakley
13 Percy Woodman
14 Vivian Clutterbuck

Reserves (Please bring boots)
Paul Cornwell
Barry Plumb
Dave Statham

Manager
Dave Statham

All players, substitutes and reserves to turn up at 09.45

It was a busy day for Billy Millmore. He ran through the list of tasks in his head as he was scrubbing his fingers with a nail-brush, trying to remove the thick, black bicycle chain oil. Job one was completed and the twins' bicycles would be in a serviceable condition for the foreseeable future. He had cleaned them, oiled them, mended one puncture and tightened one chain. The twins would still moan that they were the only girls without new bikes, but new bikes cost money, so a good service now and then would do. Radio Four chatted quietly in the background as he cleaned the oily tide mark from the sink and refilled it with more hot water, just enough water for his needs. He washed up the plates, mugs and cutlery, dried them and put everything away. After wiping down the worktops, he stood back and admired his handiwork, the kitchen gleaming and the taps sparkling as they caught rays from the low winter sun sneaking through the window. Louise flounced into the kitchen and inspected the results of Billy's labour.

'Where's the hockey today, my sweet?' he asked, trying to sound interested. 'Is it an indoor or outdoor game?' Louise did not answer but busied herself making tea.

'Well,' Louise said suddenly. 'Have you decided what to do about it yet, or are you just going to do nothing and hope it goes away?

'Well, what are you going to do?' she repeated, taking an envelope from the worktop and throwing it at Billy. He opened the envelope slowly and re-read the letter from Downham Borough Council.

Dear Mr and Mrs Millmore,

It has been brought to our attention that you are advertising a room (or rooms) in your home as available for rent. It is the policy of Downham Borough Council to ensure that such availability is first offered to residents of the borough currently on the official housing list, in accordance with recent Home Office legislation (HO18473/08/D).

The council will, of course, reimburse you for the room(s) at the government recommended rate of £27.50 per month, plus an additional £17.50 per person. In your case, we would recommend that the room is suitable for four to five persons. Please note that we have notified the relevant tax authorities on your behalf.

At the moment, we have over 7,000 residents on the housing list and we are extremely pleased that you are able to relieve the suffering of the more unfortunate members of society. Whilst we cannot guarantee who will be chosen for your home, the below list can be used for you to select your preferences.

- Persons claiming political asylum (usually Eastern European or North African)
- Financial migrants seeking employment (European Union or Commonwealth countries)
- Young one-parent family (mother with between two and five children)
- Travellers seeking a permanent home (Gypsies and young travellers)
- Young offenders (guilty of serious crime but seeking rehabilitation)
- Drug offenders (usually the young and vulnerable)
- Alcoholics (senior citizens with drink and incontinence problems)
- Any other vagrants or homeless persons

Please number the above in your order of preference and return to me at the Civic Offices.

Thank you again for your help in this matter and we look forward to introducing some of our many clients to your home as soon as possible.

Tanya Golightly
(Senior Officer, Private Home Placement)

Louise snatched the letter from Billy and returned it to the envelope. She was ready for confrontation and Billy could not escape. She started with a full attack, blasting away at her defenceless husband.

'You are useless. It's no good reading the letter over and over again; just decide what you're going to do about it. I want you on that phone first thing Monday and sort it out. Ring this Tanya woman and tell her it was a mistake. And do it from work – it may take some time to sort out and I don't want you wasting money on our phone.'

Billy tried a diversionary tactic. 'But I'm not even sure that it's genuine. I mean, it might be a joke, someone taking the pee.'

Louise was on the offensive and was not going to let her prey go easily. 'And who knows about it, you stupid man? The advert didn't quote our address or home telephone number; just my mobile, and only four people know that number, you, the girls and mum. So unless it's you taking the pee, it must be Martha, Ruth or mum. Do not be so damn ridiculous, and sort this out.'

Billy's counter was weak but he was desperate. 'But someone could have found out. What about the people who have viewed the room?'

Louise was determined not to let Billy off the hook. 'We've only had three enquiries and none of those are exactly prime suspects. It could have been that Indian family who spoke no English and turned it down because there were no cooking facilities in the room, or that young lad with spots and a nose ring who I turned down because I didn't want him near the girls, or that woman who came when you were at football.'

Billy whimpered, in a last minute plea for clemency, 'It is possible it was her. I still think it might be a joke.'

Louise was not to be prevented from scoring an overwhelming victory. 'Then ask that dopey Dave Statham if he's ever heard of this Tanya woman. He works at the council. Then we'll know if it's genuine or not. I'm going now. And remember: get this kitchen cleared up, make sure the girls are OK to go round Mum's, and do not be late round there for lunch at one thirty. Got that?' Louise gave Billy one last glare as if to say 'don't you dare say anything,' and walked out of the kitchen door. Billy put his head in his hands, defeated and cowed with no hope of recovery through a second leg or a replay.

The weather was surprisingly pleasant as he left the house, cold but calm and dry. He retrieved the girls' bicycles from the garage, and sent them on their way with a barely touching kiss on the cheek. He read the letter again, stuffed it into his sports bag and loaded the car ready for the morning's game. He hoped that he would fare better in the next battle than he had done in the earlier one that morning.

As he drove to the rec, Billy was unsure what he felt most nervous about: the severe dressing down from his wife which was likely to continue for the rest of the day at least, or the thought of a family of drug-addicted, incontinent, foreign rapists barbecuing stolen swans in his back bedroom. After parking at the rec, Billy mulled over his concerns for a few minutes before forcing himself out of his car. A huge shadow blocked out the weak wintry sun as he reached into the boot of his car to extract the football kit. He turned his head to see Barry standing over him.

'Want a hand, Billy?' Barry asked, leaning over and grabbing a corner of the laundry bag. 'I'm bloody knackered. Been up half the night. There was a raid on a supermarket in Chippenham and I had to go in to sort out the CCTV for the police. Seems a load of bloody Eastern European immigrants broke in and stole half the store. Bloody typical. Anyway, we finally identified the gang and got them banged up. Seems that they lived just round the corner. Rented a room from some poor old lady for next to fuck all a week, and twelve of them lived there. Never even paid the old girl the rent. Problem is that she had lodgers in the war, evacuees from the smoke, and was still registered with the council so she had to take them. Apparently that's the law now. Bloody nerve.'

As the two men lugged the laundry bag into the changing rooms, Dave and his crew were chatting to Lightning and signing for the key to changing room number three. As they passed, Viv looked at Lightning carefully. 'Something wrong with your eye, Lightning?' he asked.

When the men had opened up the changing room and dropped off their bags, Paul surreptitiously returned to Lightning's office and asked, 'What's up, Andrew?'

Lightning looked around to make sure that no one else was about, an easy job with each eye looking in a different direction anyway. 'Mum says please can you call round next week because she needs to talk but this is top secret so no one else must know.'

Paul's heart sank. He guessed that the relationship with her new boyfriend would be moving on and the possibility of more permanent living arrangements may have to be faced. He knew that he would be one of the first to be told. 'Do you know why, Andrew?' he asked nervously.

'Nope,' was the only reply forthcoming, as other team managers began crowding round to collect their keys.

In changing room number three, Billy's mind had been taken off his immediate problems with Louise and potential lodgers as the opportunity for gossip could not be missed. 'See that, see that,' he called to Dave who was laying out the players' kit. 'Paul just sneaked out to talk to Lightning. Something's up there. Trouble at mill, I'd say. Obviously turns to his dad when there's a problem.'

Barry ignored Billy's snide comments and continued his questioning of the moralities of immigration. 'The bloody problem is that they don't even speak English. And they don't bloody work. Just over here to milk the system and they get put up in decent rooms for next to fuck all. What's that all about, Dave, what's that all about then?'

'It's law, Plumby. New legislation. We've got a new woman, started in the housing department about two weeks ago, making sure that every fucking pikey from all over the world has a nice place to live while they claim the dole. We call her the rottweiler. Once she's got her teeth into you, she never lets go. Sits near me and you want to hear her getting digs for everyone. Mind you, to be fair, it's not just foreigners; she'll find a nice gaffe for any druggie, alky or gyppo too fucking lazy to do a day's work.' Dave stood back and admired the neat layout of kit, not daring to look at Barry for fear of losing control and bursting out in laughter.

As each team member entered the changing room, they were caught by Barry and told about the unfortunate, imaginary old lady with a dozen forced evacuees. 'And what's more,' Barry raved, 'the law reckons they'll get away with it because they're all waiting for their bloody families to join them from Ajpakistania or wherever. Then there'll be fifty of them in the old girl's house and she'll be sleeping in the fucking shed.'

Dave clapped his hands loudly and called for the attention of his men. 'Right, lads, listen up.' The hubbub barely subsided as he began his team talk. 'Bit of a slip-up last week. Bit naïve, that's all, but we still did well and we're still in with a great chance of promotion. Remember that half this lot will bugger off later on to go to work, so keep battling to the end. Magic and Gordon, get them crosses over, accurate. Midfield, nice and safe, easy balls to the wing and tight marking. Defence, whack 'em early and let 'em know you're there. Steve and

Matty, watch them fucking tempers. Billy, keep your eye on the kids. Firm but fair, lads, firm but fair.' No one listened.

As Dave approached pitch number three, he was surprised to see that the Downham Churches' team looked decidedly under strength, both in terms of their physical size and the number of their players. The Churches' trainer was, like Dave, struggling with his cargo and the two football officials laboured together like a couple of overworked pack mules as they passed the time of day.

'Your lot look a bit, well, under strength, this morning,' Dave commented.

'You are so right. We've only got nine men and half of them's boys. It's all Geoffrey's fault. Geoffrey's a lovely vicar, but he can be headstrong at times. He insisted that we sign all these Polish and Ukrainian chaps, helping to integrate them into society here, he said, doing God's work, he said, and what happens? First they have to go off to work before the games finish and now they can't afford to live in the UK any more so they've gone back to Poland or Ukrania or wherever. They reckon that with prices going up every day here, it's a better standard of living over there now. We've only got a few lads from the church choir and youth club. It's too late in the season to sign any more players so we'll just have to make do and pray. I'm sure God is listening, but I've a feeling He's not much of a football fan.' And the trainer toddled off to the far touchline where he stood alone, a rather sad and forlorn figure.

'Good luck anyway, mate and, er, God be with you. At least you'll have a bit of company if he is,' Dave shouted but the trainer was too wrapped up in his worries to hear.

From the kick-off, the difference in strength was vast and obvious. The church lads tried hard and ran vigorously about the pitch, but were outplayed in every aspect of the game. After just five minutes, Gordon had zipped through the inadequate defensive line, scoring one goal and pulling the ball back for Razor to add another. From each kick-off, the ball was almost immediately returned to the Churches' half and only spirited defending, bad luck and a lazy attitude from the Poachers' players stopped the score reaching double figures at half-time. As it was, Razor, Wayne, Matt and Majid had all added to the score and the players loped off at half time, barely out of breath and six–nil to the good.

Percy and Paddy were keen to join the action and were cajoling Dave into making "tactical" substitutions. Paddy tried to embarrass Dave into making changes. 'Come on, Dave, we've been standing on the touchline all season in rain, snow, and sleet. Never complained, have we, Percy? Just put up with it for the sake of the club. Come on, Dave, give us a run out.'

Dave looked round at his troops, idly chatting, sipping tea or drawing hard on their cigarettes. They had all played well enough and pulling anyone off would seem like an insult even though he agreed that the substitutes deserved a game. 'Anyone fancy coming off to let Percy and Paddy have a run?' he asked finally, trusting that a couple of players would save him the embarrassment of making a decision.

'I'll come off,' Razor volunteered with a sly wink to the rest of the team. 'Getting a bit knackered out there anyway.'

'Me too,' Matt offered. 'My leg's playing up a bit.'

Big Smithy joined in. 'Me and our kid got to see family straight after the game, so we'll come off now, thanks, Dave.'

'And me. I could do with a break.'

'Me too, I'll come off.'

'I'm really shagged. I had ten pints, a curry and a session with Randy Rose from the Blue Parrot last night.'

'No, no. Let me have a rest. I had a few shots last night. Come to think of it, I think I had Randy Rose as well.'

Dave stood in the middle of his players, bewildered as to his next move. His mind cranked round slowly, trying to work out the best way to decide without upsetting anyone. The fact was that the players really didn't care whether they played or not given the ease with which they were winning. Viv, so often Dave's saviour, stepped in. 'Jamie and Magic, you can come off and let these two old bastards have half a game, can't you? Do the old boys a favour, and we can save you for next week.'

Far from being upset, the two newest signings felt honoured that they had been selected to be saved for next week, and gladly gave up their positions, allowing Percy and Paddy to enjoy their forty-five minutes of glory.

The second half was a repeat of the first, with the Poachers' eleven scoring almost at will against the increasingly dispirited youngsters from the Churches. Paddy was like a spring lamb, running, jumping and generally enjoying himself, gambolling around in the crisp winter sunshine. Percy lurched about the field in his usual ungainly but effective manner, before wandering off with a couple of minutes to go to be sick behind the goal. The Poachers added seven more goals without reply, with Razor, Gordon and both Smith boys knocking in easy chances. The glory went to Paddy who scored three excellent goals including a spectacular thirty-yard drive.

As the teams strolled back to the changing rooms at full-time, Dave felt sorry for the Churches' trainer and made a point of seeking him out and offering words of consolation. 'Unlucky, mate. Some of your youngsters are going to be good in a couple of years. Just keep at it.'

'I'm not so sure,' the trainer lamented. 'Geoffrey's going to be quite annoyed. Thirteen–nil. Bit of a hiding, wasn't it? He will be angry.'

Viv trotted alongside the pair and gleefully joined in the conversation. 'I'm sure that it's not the first time the vicar's taken a hiding, is it? Tell you what, next time you're in church, you ought to grab him by the organ and say that these choirboys should be taken into the bell-tower and tolled off. Or talk to him alone. Tell him that it's his fault. Take him up the apse and give him what for.'

The trainer nodded disconsolately. 'Perhaps you're right,' he said, shaking his head. 'Perhaps I should be harder with him.'

Viv snorted loudly and trotted off giggling to himself.

Billy was aware of his orders about dinner at one thirty sharp as he walked into the pub. He was also aware that, if he had not spoken to Dave about the letter, his dinner would not be worth eating under the savage abuse he would receive from Louise and her dragon mother. But Dave was collecting subs and Billy was aware that he also needed to try to avoid paying his subs and buying a round, so he lurked quietly in a corner chatting to Matt and Steve until Dave had finished his cash-gathering. Billy accepted a pint from Matt before squeezing through the crowded bar towards the old men's corner. His concerns on how to raise the subject of his enforced occupation were resolved by the presence of Barry, who was maintaining his tirade against any person, living or dead, who hailed from anywhere east of Ramsgate, particularly if they had settled in England's green and pleasant land. His eyes bulged and face reddened as he warmed to his task and propounded his theory that the last thousand years of English civiliza-tion, where we had saved the world countless times from barbarism, Fascism, socialism, and any other "isms", was about to collapse because we were allowing in vast swathes of immigrants who would destroy our culture and weaken our gene pool. And the devastation was being assisted, even encouraged, by the pinko, lefty, vegetarians who were mis-running the country.

'This is the tip of the iceberg,' he barked. 'Today they insist on taking our spare rooms; tomorrow they'll take our jobs and our women—'

'They can 'ave my job and my fucking missis,' interrupted Tommy. 'Fifteen four and a pair's six.'

Barry was momentarily distracted, and before he could guide his crusade back on track, he paused, allowing Billy to ask, 'So, do you know this woman well then, Dave, the one who's allocating rooms to people?'

'Not that well, really,' Dave replied. 'She's not been there that long. All I know is that she's like a bulldog when she finds a room to let. Never lets go. That's why we call her the pitbull.'

'I thought you called her the rottweiler,' a confused Billy stated.

'Ah, yes, some people do. She's only been there a week or so and already she's got two or three nicknames because of her aggressive nature. All I'm sure of is that I wouldn't want to cross her.'

'What's her name again?' Billy asked.

Dave had made a point of remembering the name under threat of death from Barry and Viv. 'Tanya, Tanya something,' he replied, trying to appear casual whilst his heartbeat increased noticeably. Lying was not his forte. 'Golightly, I think. Tanya Golightly.'

Billy visibly blanched, finished his beer quickly and said that he had to leave for family reasons before scooting quickly out of the pub. He did not connect the roar of laughter as he left with the discussion about the fictitious Ms Golightly.

Still sniggering and pleased with his performance, Dave strolled to the bar to order another round. Since Mandy had resumed working in the Poachers, Dave had spent as much time at the bar as in "his" seat and volunteered to go for almost every round, including serving the cribbage school. The old men's corner secretly agreed that he was a soppy, lovesick fool but were grateful for the waiter service so said nothing. Dave ordered the round, when George tapped him on the shoulder.

'Can I have a quick word, Dave?' he asked, looking somewhat uncomfortable. 'Only thing is this. You know that I've had a few weekends away lately, training courses sort of thing. Well, I've been offered a promotion at work. Team Leader of the support group. More money. Need it with my tribe growing fast.'

Dave was genuinely pleased because George was a nice lad, and the best goalkeeper in the league. 'Well done, George,' he offered. 'Congratulations. Want a drink to celebrate? Another pint here please, Mandy.'

George appeared even more embarrassed. 'No, no, wait a minute, Dave. That's not all. It means that I'm on call twenty four seven. Every day, including Sundays, so I shan't be available to play from next week, being on call, like.'

After the jubilation of a thirteen–nil win and the deception over Billy, Dave suddenly felt dumbfounded. As much as he wanted George to do well, his mind raced into football mode, mentally re-planning his team selection without George. That's OK, just put Gunner in goal – only five games to go, he won't mind. Gunner! Paul had told him to piss off last week and he hadn't been seen since. No goalkeeper. Promotion in the offing and no goalkeeper.

'You OK, Dave?' George's voice broke into Dave's planning.

'Yeah. Er, no. You can't not play. We need you, George, we can't do it without you. Please, George, you've got to play.'

'Sorry, Dave, I really am, but this is money and I need it. Anyway, I've accepted the job now so it's too late.'

'But just because you're on call doesn't mean you can't play. I mean, you can have your mobile with you. Or I'll have your mobile and give you a shout if you get a call. George, we can get promotion this year.'

'I know, Dave, and I realise what it means to you but I can't play with a mobile in my hand and if you answered a call, I'd get hung, drawn and quartered or even worse, sacked.'

'Georgie, Georgie mate. Try it. Let's try it for next week. After all, what are the odds of being called out. Go on, what do you say? Let's just try it.'

'You fuckin' brewing' that fuckin' beer yourself or what?' shouted Tommy.

Fifteen

Downham Sunday Football League, Division Two
Results for Sunday 1st February

Hearty Oak, Downlea	3	4	New Inn, Gorton Down
Poachers Arms	**13**	**0**	**Downham Churches**
AFC Cummiston	2	1	Shellduck Inn
Lower End WMC	4	1	Pickled Herring
J G Tanner and Sons	2	7	Jones Juniors FC

League Table

Team	Pl'd	Won	Drew	Lost	For	Ag'st	GD	Points
Jones Juniors FC	13	10	3	0	55	15	40	33
New Inn, Gorton D	13	7	4	2	39	33	6	25
Poachers Arms	**13**	**7**	**3**	**3**	**46**	**27**	**28**	**24**
Pickled Herring	13	6	2	5	25	29	-4	20
J G Tanner and Sons	13	6	2	5	26	32	-6	20
Lower End WMC	13	5	3	5	27	27	0	18
AFC Cummiston	13	4	5	4	32	33	-1	17
Hearty Oak, Downlea	13	3	3	7	32	45	-13	12
Shellduck Inn	13	3	2	8	20	33	-13	11
Downham Churches	13	1	2	10	29	66	-37	5

Sunday 8th February

Downham Sunday Football League, Division Two
J G Tanner and Co. v Poachers Arms
Tanner's Sports Ground – Kick-off 10.30

THE POACHERS ARMS

1 George Crosswell

2 Steve Tippling   4 Derek Smith   5 Brian Smith   3 Billy Millmore (Capt)

8 Jamie Dunbar   10 Vivian Clutterbuck   6 Wayne Tocket

7 Matt Cornwell   9 Razor Raisin   11 Majid Ahmed

Substitutes
12 Paddy Oakley
13 Percy Woodman
14 Paul Cornwell

Reserves (Please bring boots)
Gordon Gaye
Barry Plumb
Dave Statham

Manager
Dave Statham

All players, substitutes and reserves to turn up at 09.45

Paul took a deep breath and tried to stop his hands shaking as he reached up and pressed the doorbell. The flat door swung open and he was suddenly engulfed by a powerful hug that squeezed the breath from his body and smothered his face in a blanket of warm, dry pullover. He managed to pull his face from the suffocating wool and gasped to suck in some air before he collapsed, but the arms still held him so tightly that he could not move.

'Andrew, put him down.' Paul heard Linda's voice from somewhere behind the grizzly bear that was trying to crush the life from him, and he was abruptly freed to see Lightning's face, grinning wildly in front of him, eyes rotating like a chameleon. Linda was sitting at the kitchen table, holding a mug of tea, blue-grey smoke rising from the cigarette burning in an ashtray. She stared at Paul for a moment and said, 'Don't just stand there, you gormless-looking blighter. Come in and shut the door. Andrew, please go and get ready for work now. Paul and me have got things to discuss.'

Lightning slapped him heavily on the shoulder and both men stood staring at each other with silly grins until a delayed reaction from the blow knocked Paul sideways, waking him from his starry-eyed trance. Lightning walked backwards out of the kitchen towards his bedroom, still beaming, as Paul steadied himself and moved towards Linda. She rose slowly from the table and threw herself into Paul, planting a huge kiss on his mouth and holding it there. He stood rigid and shocked, arms dangling lifelessly by his sides, wondering what to do next. Luckily, the decision was taken away from him as Linda broke the kiss, reached for his hands and squeezed them tenderly before resuming her place at the table. She squashed the cigarette in the ashtray and immediately lit a new one, passing the packet on to Paul. He sat down and lit his own cigarette, glad of something to do rather than open the conversation.

'I've really missed you, Paul,' Linda began as tears formed in the corners of her eyes. She took a man-size tissue from its box and blew her nose loudly, then dabbed her eyes. She stared at Paul for a moment, making him feel extremely uncomfortable, and said, 'I've given him the big E. This bloke, I've dumped him.'

Paul hoped that he had heard correctly. From thinking that Linda may be pregnant, getting married or leaving the area, she had announced that there was again no one else in her life. He searched for the right words to express his joy, not only to show that he understood and that he sympathised with her, but to reassure her that it was probably for the best although she may be feeling hurt and vulnerable. 'Any chance of some toast?' he asked, hoping that he could buy time to think of something more compassionate.

As Linda placed the bread in the toaster, she began to explain, knowing that Paul could never ask the right questions. 'At first it was great. We went out, for meals and that, and got on really well. He was kind and attentive and bought me little gifts and told me that he loved me and that he had left his wife and wanted to settle down with me. Then he started staying overnight, you know, sort of sleeping here, with me. And things changed. I heard him call Andrew names a couple of times, you know, thick and stupid, that sort of thing. But I thought I loved him and didn't do anything about it. I thought that he would stop and everything would be OK, but it got worse. Then he stopped taking me out and stopped the little presents. He just used to come round here at night, stinking of stale wine or brandy and, you know, stay the night. I started to hate him coming round and then, one night, I said that it was all over and he laughed. He bloody well laughed at me. He said that that was fine with him, that he'd got what he wanted and why should he want to stay with a woman with a nutter for a son and that he was going back to Reading to his wife anyway. Bloody hell, Paul, I've been so fucking stupid.'

Paul stared into the ashtray. He felt so angry that he wanted to find the man and beat the bastard until he cried for mercy. Paul could feel his face burning and felt his eyes bulging and watering as the thumping in his chest felt like a traction engine pounding out of control. His fists were tightly clenched and his ears were ringing, a red mist enveloping him completely.

'I think you need a cup of tea as well,' said Linda, removing the toast from the toaster and passing the slices to Paul.

He looked up to see her smiling at him as if the previous conversation had never taken place, before she calmly filled the kettle from the tap.

'Where is he now? Just tell me where he is and I'll sort this out. I'll rip his bloody head off, I'll—'

'Keep calm, Paul. Everything's OK now. I've had a week or so to think about this and I've come to terms with it. He was a complete shit, I know, but he's shown me that what I've got here is worth more than a few meals out and some tatty jewellery. He's actually done me a favour in the long run. I don't need anyone. It's been just me and Andrew for twenty years now and we're doing OK.'

'I could, sort of, take his place, if you wanted,' Paul heard the words but was surprised that they had come from his mouth.

Linda passed the hot buttered toast and a cup of tea across the table. 'You know, if you'd have said that any time up until a few weeks ago, I'd have jumped at the chance, I really would. We both know what we mean to each other and I'm selfish enough not to worry about anyone else, Christine, Matthew, Andrew. But these last few weeks have taught me a lesson. There's only room for one man in my life, Paul. I love Andrew so much and there's no love left for anyone else. But thanks, anyway. Thanks for everything over the years and thanks for the offer, but the answer's no. Andrew and me are kind of special and I'll never, ever do anything to change our relationship, ever again.'

Paul munched on his toast in silence as the kitchen door opened and Lightning entered the room, looking like he had just appeared from the cover of a tin of sardines. He was swamped by an outsize cape and giant sou'wester, his large feet flapping around in the biggest Wellington boots Paul had ever seen. 'Bloody hell, Andrew,' he laughed. 'You off to catch some cod in the North Sea, or what?'

Lightning looked puzzled. 'No, Paul, just off to work as usual,' he explained seriously, 'and it's swishing down with rain out there.'

'Take that kit off, mate,' said Paul. 'I'm taking you to work today, and no arguments.'

Mandy was looking out of the bedroom window as Dave was putting the finishing touches to the revised team sheet. He had received a call from Gordon Gaye on Thursday to explain that he had "pulled something" in training for his Saturday team and would be unable to play this morning, although he could go as a reserve and play for the last few minutes if it was desperate. No one had heard from Gunner Farr since he had walked out and George Crosswell had finally agreed to play even though he was on call, 'just this once to see what happens'. Paddy and Percy both reluctantly agreed to act as substitutes, notwithstanding their fine performances the previous week, and Dave had all but promised to bring them on in this game, calling them a pair of super-subs, which satisfied their egos.

Mandy gazed out of the window at the rain lashing down over the Poachers' Estate towards the shops and pub opposite. She stared at the flat above Muzzy's where she spent her childhood, and down to the Poachers Arms, where she now spent Saturday evenings socially, and other evenings and Sunday lunchtimes working. She felt relaxed and at home in the simplicity of life on the estate.

'I do love staying here on Saturdays, Dave,' she finally whispered, 'but it's getting a bit awkward, what with your Dad and everything. I mean, I'm sure that he finds it a bit awkward and I'll have to rush off in a minute before he gets up even though he knows that I stay here every Saturday night. Isn't there anything we can do to make it easier for all of us?'

Dave finished preparing the team selection and pressed the print button. The printer made clacking sounds, whirred a couple of times and spewed two copies of the teamsheet onto the desk. 'Don't really know, Mandy, like what?'

'Well, I don't know. Something that means we can stay together here at night without trying to hide it from anyone, especially your dad. And maybe so that I don't rush off in the mornings. And perhaps so that we can spend more nights together. Dave, there must be something we can do.'

Dave re-read his teamsheet, neatly folded the two copies and placed them in an envelope, then put the envelope into his sports bag. 'Well, I suppose we could come home earlier while he's at the pub, then get up earlier so that he doesn't realise.'

'David Statham, will you listen to me? Take your eyes off that computer screen and listen.'

Dave was a little taken aback at the abrupt orders from Mandy and was unsure how he should react, so he turned round on his computer chair and faced Mandy, wondering what was coming next. He was surprised to see that she looked a little angry. And she had called him David, which was not a good sign.

'Do I have your full attention, David?'

Dave nodded.

'Do you understand that I am with child, your child?'

Dave nodded.

'Do you love me?'

Dave nodded.

'Do you want me to sleep with you regularly?'

Dave nodded.

'Are we committed to each other as a couple?'

Dave nodded.

'Do you want everyone to know that we are committed to each other?'

Dave nodded.

'Do you want this current embarrassing situation to continue?'

Dave nodded, then realised his error and shook his head.

'Do you want us to live together?'

Dave nodded.

'Then what shall we do, David?'

'Well, I dunno really. Um. I suppose you could move in here permanently.'

'Oh, Dave,' Mandy squealed in delight. 'Do you really mean it? You want me to move in with you? It's a big commitment, Dave, but of course I will. I'll get my things, such as they are, when you're at football and move in today. Oh Dave, you really are very sweet. Thanks.'

They heard Tonker shifting across the landing for his morning ablutions. 'About bloody time too,' he shouted through their bedroom door.

Dave grabbed his bags and went to the front door where Viv was waiting, sheltering from the rain.

'You OK, Dave? You look sort of in a bit of a dream.'

'Fine,' Dave replied. 'Fine. It's just that I think I may have done something rather scary but very exciting this morning. I just hope it doesn't backfire on me'

'Took her up the wrong 'un, eh, Dave? No worries. Me and Elaine do it all the time. One up the bum, no harm done, as the old saying goes. And if she backfires now and again, that's only to be expected.'

Tanner's Sports Ground was, by any amateur football standards, upmarket. By Downham Sunday League standards, it was nothing short of absolute luxury. It was located next to the Tanner's factory, a series of large red brick and cream-painted buildings with assorted entrance gates, chimneys and rows of windows in each building. The rain had eased a little during the journey and, as they pulled into one of the side gates, Dave remarked how he was always reminded of L S Lowry whenever he looked at the buildings.

'Ellis who?' asked Viv.

'Lowry, L S Lowry the painter,' Dave stated resolutely. 'One of the finest English painters of all time.'

'Of course,' Viv responded knowledgeably. 'I think he done my gran's house in Omdurman Street. Same colour cream as he done this place. Not very neat on her back wall.'

Dave sighed in frustration. 'Not that sort of painter, Vivian. He was an artist.'

'Yeah, my gran said he was on the piss a lot when he done her place.'

Dave shook his head and decided not to continue the conversation. After a moment's silence, Viv added, 'Mind you, Lowry had a very interesting and individual outlook, and his subjects of Manchester and Lancashire street scenes were interpreted naively, with imperfect technique but with real imagination.'

Dave was speechless until Viv added, 'Mind you, he still fucked up my gran's back wall.'

Dave followed the large sign "J G Tanner and Company Ltd. Sports and Social Club" and pulled into the ample car park next to building number 2. He parked next to the changing rooms, facing the pitch. The men sat in the car for a moment and gazed over the green sward in front of them. Behind the changing rooms was the football pitch in the centre of a full athletics track, where some very keen local athletes were braving the rain and wind, stretching, jumping and jogging around the athletics arena. At the back of the changing rooms was a grandstand, directly overlooking the pitch. Beyond that was the cricket square, roped off against the destructive studs of straying Sunday footballers. The whole site was surrounded by huge, mature trees, naked of leaves and swaying in valiant defiance of the late winter wind and rains.

'With these dramatic skies and billowing clouds, we could be looking at a scene from Suffolk captured by the English romantic painter, Constable,' said Viv as he opened the car door. 'Mind you, he should be out arresting criminals, not fannying about painting pictures.'

Dave loved the spacious changing rooms at Tanner's. There were just four separate rooms for teams and one for the referees, each one magnificently tiled in white and dark green, and furnished with dark wooden benches, always immaculately varnished. There were twenty large, ornate hooks evenly spaced around each room. The screw heads holding the hooks had been covered so that removal was impossible, ensuring that none were lost to the many players who took the opportunity to pillage whatever they could from opponents' changing rooms. No windows were broken, the floors were tiled and clean, and there were neat, wooden lockers under the benches, each with a fastening to allow padlocking. There were no individual showers but two large tiled baths, the size of small swimming pools, which were always topped up with steaming hot water at the end of the games. As Dave laid out the kit, he imagined that this must be what life was like for managers of Premiership sides, except that Sir Alex may have someone to lay out the kit for him.

As the Poachers' team drifted into the changing rooms in ones and twos, most looking like they had tried to drink the town pubs and clubs dry the previous evening, Paul sat quietly in the corner, staring at the floor tiles and trying to control the anger he felt. The cheerfulness of the troops preparing for battle as they boasted and joked, was increasing his anger as he tried to blank Linda's seduction from his mind.

'…she had next to bugger all on, anyway, in that weather. I thought, here we go, Matty-boy, another notch on the old bedpost. Went back to her place, parents in bed, straight on the settee, wham bam thank you ma'am. Home by two. Didn't even ask her name.' Matthew was laughing as he swaggered in, with Jamie and Majid listening in awed silence, their mouths agape.

'About time you got fucking changed, never mind all that shite,' Paul shouted at his son and stormed out of the changing room, slamming the door behind.

The room fell immediately silent and Matthew shrugged. 'PMT,' he said, and carried on boasting about his Saturday night conquests, much to the delight of his audience.

Dave checked his men for the final time. It was time to deliver a battle cry to send his team into combat with enthusiasm and pride, prepared to die for the cause. He tried to recall some of the speeches he had heard on the History Channel and stood before his troops, arms folded. 'Lads, lads, this is a big one. Just four games to go and we are in a great position for promotion, so, er, do your best, eh? Oh, and firm but fair.'

Paul put his head round the door. 'And watch your fucking tempers this time, you two wankers,' he shouted at Matthew and Steve, who responded with a one-fingered salute.

Dave gathered up his cargo and staggered to the stand where the substitutes, reserves and a few odd supporters were sheltering from the rain. He took up his position in a dugout marked "AWAY TEAM" and waited to be joined by his right-hand men. But everyone else had realised that the rain was gusting into the dugout and that the grandstand offered shelter from the worst of the weather. Dave had made his move and could not be seen to retreat into the grandstand, so sat alone trying to hide himself from the blasts of icy rain. As he squeezed himself into one corner, a familiar face looked into his shelter and grinned. 'Just when you thought things couldn't get worse, look who's referee today. Me,' said Rabbit Warren.

'Alright, Rabbit?' Dave replied, trying not to show that he was freezing to death. 'Didn't know we had you today.'

'Change of schedule. You was supposed to have Mr Benfield, but he's got the flu and I didn't have a game, so I volunteered for this one. Must've been fucking mad in this weather.'

'You can always blow early, make it thirty-five minutes each way if you like. I won't say anything. Besides, we can get down the pub earlier if you do.'

'Now now, Mr Statham. Rules is rules and I must stick to them. The rules say forty-five minutes each way and forty-five minutes it will be. But we'll see how it goes. See you later,' and Rabbit turned and sprinted against the elements to the centre circle and gave a loud blast to summon the team captains for the toss.

Dave was facing into the corner of the dugout, trying to light a Hamlet, when he felt the bench shudder and heard a loud exhalation of air. He turned to see Barry sitting next to him, dripping wet and his face the colour of beetroot. Barry gasped a few times and Dave worried that a heart attack was imminent, until Barry began a tirade. 'Bloody council. Bloody council workers. Bloody Tommy, your dad's mate, and his bloody pickaxe-wielding maniacs. Bloody council.' Dave knew better than to ask what was wrong but guessed that he would be told anyway.

'I left the motor in the road last night. She had her little sports car in the garage because of this bloody rain and the other garage is full of stuff, so I had to. Leave it in the road that is. I was careful. You know me, David, always law-abiding in every way, so I put the car in the corner of the cul-de-sac, tucked out of the way, not blocking anyone in, causing no harm, ready to pull out this morning. I come down after breakfast, breakfast she calls it, bloody sawdust and rabbit shit I call it, what's wrong with a good old fry-up anyway, anyway, where was I? That's it, so I come down, I go to get in the car and bloody Tommy and his merry men have dug a trench around the car, so I can't get the bloody car out. "Come on, Tommy," I says, "I'm off to football, what the fuck are you doing?" "Looking for gas," he says. "Reported gas leak and you've parked right by the gas main where we've got to dig." "Why today, why fucking Sunday?" I asked him. Do you know what he said? Do you know what he said, Dave? He said it was to prevent inconvenience to the public. "What am I then?" I says. "I am the fucking public." He says why didn't I park in my garage anyway and I says none of his fucking business and I says, well fill the trench in so I can get out and he says he fucking can't until the gas engineer's been so I said he should go fuck himself. I swear, Dave, I swear that if he hadn't been holding a big pickaxe, I'd have knocked him into the fucking trench, but in the end I just walked away. She wasn't ready, so I had to wait for her to put her bloody face on and do whatever women do in the bathroom and she got snotty and said it was only football, and I would have told her to go fuck herself too but I needed the lift. Bloody late. I hate being bloody late. Nearly missed kick-off and all because of the bloody council. Trouble is, Dave, with the council, you've got councillors and they're either fiddling cash or on big ego trips, that's the bloody problem with the council, Dave, councillors. And red tape. And health and safety. And lazy bloody council workers. Fuck me, Dave, it's cold in here. I'm going up in the stand.' With that, Barry moved out of the dugout and disappeared behind Dave to assail some other poor unsuspecting innocent with his tales of woe.

Dave turned his attention to the game which had started with the Poachers Arms winning the toss and electing to play with the gale at their backs. The gusting wind and rain made control difficult and passing impossible as both teams tried to keep the ball with short passing movements which inevitably broke down as the ball skidded off the greasy surface. Most of the play was taking place in the Tanner's half, the monotony broken by the occasional wild shot from a Poachers' forward flying high or wide past the goal. Tanner's occasionally broke out of their half, only to be forced back again by a combination of wind, rain and inaccurate passing. Although frustration was beginning to show, both teams remained constrained and tempers were held in check. Eyes watered, cheeks reddened, and knees turned a mottled blue as the weather looked to be the only winner on the day. Paul patrolled the line as usual, but seemed lost in his own world, missing several offsides and awarding throw-ins randomly.

As the half-time whistle went, all twenty-two players sprinted for the brief but welcome shelter of the stands. The warming tea was poured from the flasks and players gratefully cupped the plastic beakers in numb fingers and slurped the hot contents greedily. Dave tried to think of appropriate words of encouragement but was struck momentarily speechless by the cold and by the fact that his players always ignored him anyway. The Tanner's manager seemed in a similar situation, more inclined towards trying to keep players alive than to offer meaningless words of support. Both sets of players looked like cold, sodden refugees seeking sanctuary, as they muttered and whined about the cold, the rain, the wind, the greasy pitch and even the tea. A small but powerful lobby was growing to abandon the game and retreat to the bar.

Rabbit had also sought refuge in the stand and accepted a tea from Dave with an appreciative smile. He took a sip, sat back on his seat and said loudly, 'Well done, all you lads out there.'

Both teams stopped their whingeing, moaning and groaning and turned to face the unlikely source of encouragement. Rabbit looked around at his surprised audience and continued. 'It's times like this morning when I know that the country is in good hands. The youth of today get a bad press, but just to see you lads out there giving everything, in this weather, just for the pleasure of playing the game, warms my old heart. Well done to all of you, you can all feel proud. Now let's get on with it, lads, and keep up this fine spirit and sportsmanship. Let's go.' With that, Rabbit finished his tea, threw the empty cup towards Dave and sprinted across the pitch to restart the game. The players immediately followed, with renewed vigour and a sense of pride reflected in their determination to see the game through in the spirit of sportsmanship and endeavour.

As Poachers kicked off the second half, their uphill task became immediately evident as a long pass to the wing from Viv caught a gust of wind and the ball was blown back deep into the Poachers' half where it remained except for the odd punt out which was inevitably and immediately returned.

Majid had been patrolling his left touchline alone for a full twenty minutes, without once touching the ball, his small shoulders hunched against the weather, looking forlorn and miserable, when a stray pass from the Tanner's midfield landed at his feet. He seemed surprised to have such close contact with the ball, looked up and began to sprint towards the opposing penalty area. The Tanner's defence, which had all but forgotten his existence, began a charge from where they had been encamped on the edge of the centre circle. Majid seemed to cut through the fierce storm as the bigger, heavier and very much slower defenders sprinted bravely but vainly in his wake. The goalkeeper, who had been ineffectively trying to shelter behind a goalpost, came out far too late and Majid was able to place the ball neatly past him and into the Tanner's net. Majid looked embarrassed as he was engulfed by his team members, or at least the few who could battle the elements to reach him.

As Poachers attacked with more energy, Tanner's were forced to defend even though the weather continued to support them. From defence, a desperate clearance was banged upfield, chased by eager Tanner's forwards. The Poachers' defensive line stopped as a man and raised their arms with a call of 'offside.' Rabbit, emerging from the edge of the Tanner's penalty area through a ruck of players, looked for guidance from Paul, who kept his flag firmly by his side and sprinted up the touchline in line with attacking players who were able to draw George Crosswell before slipping the ball in for an equalizer.

Matthew Cornwell stood, hands on hips, glaring angrily at his father. 'That was fucking miles offside, what's up with you?' he shouted.

'Onside,' Paul responded. 'Now just get on with game.'

But Matt was not prepared to let it go. 'You must be fucking blind. It was fucking miles off.'

'Don't you fucking use that language with me, boy, or I'll—'

'Or you'll what?' screamed Matt, unable to control his temper. 'It's about time you watched what's fucking happening here instead of thinking about your other fucking family.'

Paul looked stunned and took steps towards Matt. Suddenly father and son were facing each other throwing punches on the edge of the pitch whilst everyone else watched in amazement. Surprisingly, Barry was first on the pitch and forced his way between the combatants who continued to snarl insults and trade blows, most of which were landing on Barry. The threesome wrestled, punched and kicked as the rain lashed down until players from both sides eventually managed to tear the two apart and Rabbit blew his whistle for full-time, a good ten minutes early. 'That'll do for today, lads. Good draw. Well played,' he said as he led the way into the dressing rooms.

The players were in a frivolous mood as they frolicked in the steaming, muddy water of the large bath. Grazes were stinging as the hot water soaked into the minor injuries and fingers throbbed as life returned, but the fact that they had emerged from the bitter weather and finished the game, albeit early, with a satisfactory draw was cause for celebration. Viv had tucked his genitalia between his legs and was parading around the edge of the bath to somewhat inappropriate shouts of 'Get your tits out for the boys,' whilst the team splashed and played like schoolboys on a seaside outing.

Dave and Barry sought out Rabbit who had bathed and changed and was chatting quietly with the manager from Tanner's. 'Sorry about the fuss, Mr Warren,' Dave apologized. 'Don't know what caused that little scene, but sorry anyway.'

'What scene was that?' said Rabbit, looking genuinely perplexed. 'I've just been talking to my friend here from Tanner's and he didn't see anything either. I just blew the whistle for full-time and noticed your lads celebrating, shall we say, enthusiastically.'

'Yes, of course, Mr Warren, that's fine then. So the result stands and nothing more to report, then?' Dave confirmed his understanding.

'What else was there?' Rabbit asked as he made his way to the bar with the Tanner's management.

Barry wiped blood from his mouth and felt the swelling on his left cheek and slapped Dave on the back. 'Time for a pint, Mr Statham,' he said, dribbling blood down his chin.

As Matt left the changing rooms, bathed, changed and dried, he saw his father sitting quietly in his car. The car window opened slowly and Matt felt a wave of panic spreading through him. Paul stared for a second, and said, 'I always told you to watch that temper, Matthew. Now get in the car. We've got somewhere to go together before the pub.'

Matt climbed in the car and Paul pulled out of the car park, neither man talking as they drove away. By the time they reached the rec, Lightning had completed his Sunday tasks, locked the changing rooms and was waiting for his lift, shielding beneath the changing room porch against the unrelenting rain. Lightning opened the door and climbed into the back of the car. As neither Matt nor his father spoke during the journey, Lightning also said nothing. They arrived at Muzzy's and parked the car. 'Come on, Matthew, there's someone you should meet,' Paul said as he opened the car door. 'Then we can go for a beer.'

Lightning took the start of the conversation as his prompt for speaking. 'Phew, what a morning I've had,' he said. 'What with the rain and the mess and the football and everything. Phew, what a morning.' Paul and Matt looked at each other and smiled. Phew, what a morning indeed.

The men climbed the stairs and followed Lightning into Linda's flat. She was standing at the kitchen sink, preparing something green; cabbage or sprouts or lettuce, guessed Matt who had never eaten anything green except tinned peas. She looked surprised as the three men walked in, but calmly said, 'Go and get changed, Andrew, there's a good man. Roast lamb for lunch,' and turned to face Paul and Matthew.

Paul suddenly wondered what he had done and why he had brought Matthew to see Linda and stuttered, 'Linda, this is—'

'I know Matthew,' she interrupted. 'I used to help out at the school, remember. How are you, Matthew?'

Matt was more confused than anyone. 'All right, I suppose,' he answered and shrugged his shoulders.

Linda looked from one to the other. 'Were you fighting over me and Andrew?' she asked.

'How did you know…?' a stunned Paul muttered.

'Because I'm a woman and we know these things. Besides, you don't get black eyes like that at football normally.' The men looked at each other and realised that they had identical swollen eyes, just beginning to turn a dark purple. 'And now, you want to explain about us, Paul. Is that right?'

Paul tried to speak but could only manage a sort of low grunt.

'Right, Matthew, here's the truth. Andrew is not your half-brother; he is not your father's son. His father was your dad's best friend who died while I was pregnant. Since then, your dad has been kind to me and Andrew, very kind, but we have never had an affair. We are good friends, and only good friends, despite all the rumours on the estate over the years. He loves you and your mum. Now go off both of you and have your beer.'

Paul nodded. 'Thanks, Lin. But how did you know that was what we came here for?'

Linda smiled and shook her head. 'I told you. Because I'm a woman.'

As they climbed down the stairs, Matthew put his arm around his father's shoulders. 'My round then, Dad,' he said.

Barry immediately made a beeline for Tommy who was dealing the cards ready for the next game of cribbage. 'Is my car free yet, Tommy?' he bellowed.

Tommy coolly turned round. 'Fuckin' engineer's been. Fuckin' repair team's been. Fuckin' 'ole's filled in,' he replied, returning to his cards.

'Why the bloody hell did you have to do it on a Sunday and block me in? Bloody ridiculous. Why a bloody Sunday?' Barry was still unhappy and time had not mellowed his anger.

Tommy swigged his beer. 'I didn't fuckin' *have* to block you in at all,' he explained slowly. 'In fact I had a fuckin' ramp in the fuckin' van I could have put down to allow you to drive over the fuckin' 'ole, if you'd have fuckin' asked and not gone off on one. And as for Sunday, well, the report only come in Saturday night and that said "Very Urgent". I got the docket here, look. Urgent – smell of gas reported by some bloke called Barry Plumb.'

Sixteen

Downham Sunday Football League, Division Two
Results for Sunday 8th February

AFC Cummiston	P	P	New Inn, Gorton Down
J G Tanner and Sons	**1**	**1**	**Poachers Arms**
Jones Juniors FC	2	0	Lower End WMC
Shellduck Inn	4	2	Hearty Oak, Downlea
Downham Churches	0	7	Pickled Herring

League Table

Team	Pl'd	Won	Drew	Lost	For	Ag'st	GD	Points
Jones Juniors FC	14	11	3	0	57	15	42	36
New Inn, Gorton D	13	7	4	2	39	33	6	25
Poachers Arms	**14**	**7**	**4**	**3**	**47**	**19**	**28**	**25**
Pickled Herring	14	7	2	5	32	29	3	23
J G Tanner and Sons	14	6	3	5	27	33	-6	21
Lower End WMC	14	5	3	6	27	29	-2	18
AFC Cummiston	13	4	5	4	32	33	-1	17
Hearty Oak, Downlea	14	3	3	8	34	49	-15	12
Shellduck Inn	14	4	2	8	24	35	-11	14
Downham Churches	14	1	2	11	29	73	44	5

Sunday 15th February

Downham Sunday Football League, Division Two
Poachers Arms v Shellduck Inn
Tenacre Recreation Ground – Kick-off 10.30

THE POACHERS ARMS

1 George Crosswell

2 Steve Tippling   4 Derek Smith   5 Jamie Dunbar   3 Billy Millmore (Capt)

8 Wayne Tocket   10 Vivian Clutterbuck   6 Daniel Tomlinson

7 Gordon Gaye   9 Paddy Oakley   11 Majid Ahmed

Substitutes
12 Percy Woodman
13 Paul Cornwell
14 Matthew Cornwell

Reserves (Please bring boots)
Barry Plumb
Dave Statham

Manager
Dave Statham

All players, substitutes and reserves to turn up at 09.45

O8.15. Another fifteen minutes and Dave would have to get up. He wondered where Mandy was, but he was too warm and too cosy to drag himself out of bed to find out. Tonker said that she had a habit of disappearing for hours at a time during the day when Dave was at work, so Dave assumed that that was just what women did.

08.16. The Match Of The Day theme tune played loudly on his mobile phone and he jumped out of bed immediately, fumbling with his clothes which had been left in a crumpled heap on the floor. After unsuccessfully checking the trouser pockets, his shirt pocket, his shoes and under the bed, he found the offending mobile on his bedside cabinet, happily singing, 'da da da dah, da da da dada'. He grabbed the phone and pressed the green button, grunting, 'Hello, hello, Dave Statham, Poachers Arms F C here.'

'Dave. Sorry to disturb you. It's Brian Smith here. Can't play today, I'm afraid, Dave. Bloody flu or something. Feel like shite.'

Dave began to panic. 'You sure, Brian? I mean, you are key to the team and even if you're not fully fit, you're still better than playing, say, Percy,' he said, whilst thinking he could move Jock to centre half and put young Danny in at number six, then…

'I'll take that as a compliment then, Dave,' Brian coughed in his ear. 'But honest, mate, I can't make it. Probably be OK next week though. See you.'

Dave looked at the silent phone for a moment before pulling on his pants and turning on his computer. Names, numbers and positions were racing round his head but he knew that he just had to sit at the PC screen and he would be able to rearrange the team without too much trouble. That was the joy of a PC. Cutting, copying and pasting, spreadsheets, letters and reports were all made so much easier, and the Internet offered a good selection of pornography as a bonus.

Dave double-clicked on the file named "team" and the Poachers' line-up flashed up on the screen. He added a note against Brian Smith's name and ran through the squad:

254

Brian Smith – not available due to illness
Matthew Cornwell – dropped for fighting
Joseph Farr – left club?
Daniel Raisin – not available due to work

Four of his best players unavailable was a slight worry but the Shellduck were a poor side so Dave was not unduly concerned. He moved the players round on the screen until he produced a line-up he was happy with. He stared at the screen, satisfied with his selection before realizing that he was bursting for a pee and Tonker may be about to go to the bathroom for his post-beer and curry clearance, with an Old Holborn roll-up. Dave pressed the *print* button and rushed out of the bedroom, across the landing and into the bathroom. As he stood against the toilet, urinating loudly, a familiar smell from the past played around his nostrils. He sniffed. His mouth watered and he almost dribbled onto his naked chest as the scent of bacon wafted enticingly around him. A fry-up, the little love's only gone and done a Sunday morning fry-up.

He tried to force the urine through quicker as he almost tasted the sausage, bacon and egg, but much of last night's beer remained in his system and refused to be rushed. A loud knock on the door made him jump slightly as he splashed the toilet pan. 'Get a bloody move on, David, I'm busting for a piss. And it smells like we've got ourselves a fry-up,' Tonker shouted from the landing.

Dave completed his urination and decided that Tonker's need was greater than his at that moment and turned and opened the bathroom door without washing his hands. 'About bloody time too,' Tonker grumbled as he rushed into the vacant space desperately holding his crotch.

After dressing quickly, the men left their rooms at the same time and hurried down the stairs. As they walked into the kitchen, both were suddenly hit by a strange and emotional feeling that they could not explain. The kitchen table was laid as it had been laid on Sunday mornings for many years, Mandy was standing at the hob as their breakfast sizzled and spat in the frying pans. Tonker let out an audible gasp. Father and son said nothing as they sat at their usual places and waited to be waited on. Mandy filled two plates with the mouth-watering fare and smiled as she carried the plates to the table. She placed a plate in front of each man, alongside a large, steaming mug of tea, looking quizzically at them.

'Haven't you ever seen a fry-up before?' she asked. 'Now get on with it while it's hot. You really do look like you've seen a ghost, you two.'

Mandy sat with the men and ate a smaller version of the breakfast as they cut, dipped, chewed and swigged in a state of absolute bliss. When they had finished, Tonker and Dave pushed their plates away from them and sat back in their chairs. Tonker began rolling a cigarette. 'Thanks, Mandy, that was great. Think I'll go up for a… to the toilet now,' he said and stood up from the table. Mandy reached forward and took hold of the new roll-up. She smiled very sweetly.

'I don't think you need this to go to the lavatory, Eric,' she stated firmly. 'You can smoke it outside when you come down.'

Tonker stood with his mouth agape, looking at his freshly rolled cigarette in Mandy's hand. 'Yes, dear, right then, that's fine then, right, see you in a minute, after my, you know,' he muttered and left the kitchen in a state of bewilderment.

Dave laughed. 'Well done, Mandy,' he congratulated her. 'It's about time he stopped making that foul smell in the bathroom. And stopped smoking his roll-ups as well.'

'I know. I'll talk to you both about that later,' she said. 'After I've got ready and after you've washed up.'

Dave stopped laughing as Mandy left the kitchen, leaving him surrounded by the remnants of the repast. Twenty minutes later, Dave had finished washing up and clearing the kitchen and was about to leave to collect his *Sunday Times* from Muzzy before setting off for the rec. Tonker was standing forlornly outside the kitchen door sucking on a damp roll-up and feeling very sorry for himself. Mandy entered the kitchen and called Tonker in from outside, giving concise orders that he should put his cigarette out first. 'Please can you both sit down?' she asked, smiling sweetly. Both men took their usual seats at the dining room table.

'I've got to get off, Mand, football, you know, Viv's waiting outside, I expect, and I've got to get my paper and that…'

'Then the sooner you let me speak, the sooner we'll all be able to get on, David. We really do need to talk about some of the things that go on in this house. I've put up with your ways for the last week and, to be honest, some of them are disgusting. It's not much, honestly, and it'll make all our lives a lot easier. Eric, please can you not smoke in the house and especially in the toilet.'

'But I've always smoked on the bog, since I was first married and I don't see why I—'

'Eric,' Mandy interrupted. 'When was the last time you went into the garage?'

Tonker was puzzled. He never went into the garage. He didn't have a car and the garage was simply used as a convenient place to store anything that was of no use but couldn't be thrown away. Somewhere in there was his old bicycle that he bought in 1966. He remembered because it was the year that England won the World Cup and he cycled to his mother's house to watch the final. It now had only one wheel, no brakes and no saddle, and the chain was seized with rust, but it may come in handy one day, if he could ever find it beneath two old lawn mowers, three old beds, several boxes of newspapers, a broken garden fork, four suits (one with flared trousers and wide, very wide, lapels), two old car batteries, a disused push-chair, a garden gate (broken), a washing machine (broken), a box of old shoes saved for gardening, a car tyre, a radiogram, a Singer sewing machine, a house plaque saying "Dunroamin", a spin-drier and several boxes of vegetable seeds from the mid-eighties.

'I don't know,' Tonker answered, 'but what's that got to do with anything?'

'Go into the garage. Now, please.'

Tonker got up from the table and, still mumbling, went out of the kitchen door towards the garage back door.

'David, you have to share the chores a little, but as you are pretty useless, being spoilt all these years, we will restrict it to washing up and keeping the kitchen tidy to start with. You are very good at that and it's your responsibility from now on and no one else is allowed to interfere. Apart from cooking, the kitchen is your domain.'

Dave was just about to protest, trying to think of a logical reason why he could not assume responsibility for the cleanliness of the kitchen, when Tonker burst back in through the kitchen door. 'My garage. What have you done to my garage? And my stuff? My stuff that was in the garage. Where is it? It's gone.'

'All that old rubbish is now on the council tip if you want to go and collect it,' Mandy replied. 'Why, Eric, aren't you happy with what I've done?'

Dave was bemused. 'What has she done, er, have you done?'

'Your father now has his own smoking room,' Mandy explained. 'I've cleared out the garage and put in a settee, a telly and a fridge. And a carpet and some odds and ends. Now Eric, take David out and show him your smoking room.'

Tonker and Dave walked slowly out and disappeared into the garage.

'Bloody hell, Dad, it's like a little palace in here,' said Dave, genuinely surprised as he scanned the converted garage. 'Look, that's our old sideboard. It's clean and been polished and everything. And isn't that your old chair in the corner? And the walls have all been painted. And there's an electric fire. Bloody hell, Dad, tell you what, I'll swap and you have my room. I'll move in here.'

'What do I want with your room? I'm not happy about this, but I suppose I'd better make the most out of it to keep her happy,' Tonker replied, staring at the transformation.

'David, Vivian's here waiting for you,' Mandy called from the kitchen.

Viv was sipping a cup of tea at the kitchen table as they re-entered the house. 'Before you go, there's one last thing.' Mandy looked at the father and grand-father of her unborn child. 'For obvious reasons, we must clean this place up. We cannot bring a new baby into this house with it like it is.' At the mention of a baby, Viv nearly spat his tea over the table. 'From now on,' Mandy continued, 'both of you will wipe around the toilet when you have finished and not leave pee on the seat, the floor and anywhere else where your bad aim takes it. I have put a toilet brush in there – Vivian, no jokes about preferring toilet paper – which you will use every time that you've been. And there is a toilet spray which will be used after each visit. Understood?'

The men nodded quietly. 'And, Vivian, if you mention one word about what you've heard here this morning, I will tell everyone exactly what I know about you. If you know what I mean. Now go. All of you.'

Dave and Vivian left by the front door for football and Tonker slouched out of the back and into his smoking room. Mandy let out a long sigh of relief and sat down until she had stopped trembling, and wondered if Viv really did have any skeletons in his cupboard.

As they left the house, Barry was waiting next to Dave's Polo. 'Hello Plumby,' Viv shouted, throwing a mock punch towards his midriff. 'Tommy blocked your car in again?'

'No he bloody hasn't. And if he ever tries that bloody trick again, I'll sue him… and the bloody council. The problem, you see, Vivian, is fear engendered by a left-wing fascist government and fed by the media. Everyone is afraid to stand alone and challenge diktats from those who purport to govern us. They are scared to use common sense in case it upsets some politically correct communist bureaucrat at the town hall. Thus, if the likes of Tommy are told to dig a hole in a certain position at nine o'clock on a Sunday morning, he will dig it there at that time, no matter whether it makes sense to do so or not. We, or rather they, are brainwashed into thinking that using their initiative will mean a potential loss of their job so that they can't afford a flat screen TV or a visit to Froggie Disneyland or something. The issue, you see, Viv, is that this constant left-wing introduction of more and more petty rules, supported by the right-wing desire for material goods is not conducive to a compatible philosophy, and brings neither satisfaction nor happiness in one's life. We were all far happier when life was freer, simpler and we had no rules and the barest of possessions. Possessions can only bring unhappiness—'

'You had a racing bike before anyone else when we were young. And your own telly in your bedroom,' Dave interrupted.

'That's why he's such a miserable fucker then,' Viv laughed as the men drove away from the estate towards the rec; and they never found out why Barry wasn't using his own car.

Following his and Tonker's earlier reprimand, Dave and crew were a little late as they entered the rec. Someone had taken Dave's normal parking slot and he was forced to leave the car at the back of the car park, where he knew he would be blocked in. This was annoying but inevitable, and could mean a five-minute delay in getting to the pub after the game. For the first time that day, Dave noticed that the sun was shining, causing the overnight frost to melt, and water dripped with irregular plips and plops from the bushes and trees around the changing rooms.

Dave wandered up to the Assistant to the Groundsman, who was studying his key allocation sheet with great concentration. He looked up as Dave approached and said, 'Good morning, Mr Statham. Your key has already been collected by Mr Cornwell, see, he's signed for it next to Changing Room Three, just below Ben Doon and Phil Macavity.

Dave wasn't too pleased to see that the shirts had been laid out by the time that he had arrived. At this stage in the season there were only half a dozen coat pegs remaining, so Billy had decided to place all the shirts, number up, on the benches which ran around the room. The shirts were also placed on the benches where Billy knew that the players would change – and not in strict numerical sequence. Dave wondered whether to exercise his authority and re-arrange the kit, but decided that discretion was the better part of valour and left well alone. Paul sat in one corner lazily blowing up an old, scratched football whilst Barry continued to explain the faults with consumerism to a totally disinterested Vivian. Billy sidled up to Dave and spoke very quietly. 'I've been trying to ring the council on and off for the last three weeks and I can't get hold of this woman, this Tanya Golightly. No one seems to have heard of her. What's it all about, Dave?'

'Top secret, Billy, that's why,' Dave explained. 'Apparently the government don't want the public to know that they're being spied on, what with all this bollocks about filling your bins too much and putting stuff in the wrong boxes and so on.'

Billy smiled and nodded. 'Thanks, Dave,' he said.

As the team members arrived, Dave pointed out the team changes pinned on the dressing room door, although the players took little notice and continued their usual Sunday morning changing room banter. When they were changed, Dave called for order, a call which was largely ignored until Barry boomed out, 'Will you lot fucking listen for once, thank you,' in his best ex-police sergeant voice.

Having achieved a modicum of silence and attention, Dave began. 'Today, lads, is important. Today, we can take a giant step towards promotion if we beat the Shellduck. We need total concentration and everyone just needs to do their job properly and efficiently with no heroics, OK? They're not a bad side, so hard work and control, that's the thing today. Defence, nice and tight. Midfield, keep feeding Gordon and Magic, and...'

By this time, the footballers had started their own conversations again and Dave's quiet voice was drowned in the hubbub. Again, Barry's voice boomed above the din. 'And remember. They're all nancies so give them a good whack early on.'

'Firm but fair,' they all shouted in unison.

As they left the changing rooms, George passed his mobile to Dave, who wondered whether or not he should switch it off, before deciding that he would leave it on and simply ignore any calls.

The referee was unknown to any of the Poachers' crew, a tall, red-haired man whose skin had taken on a translucent blue hue decorated with big orange freckles. He also had thick, rubbery pink lips and his pale blue eyes bulged and watered as they caught the low winter sun. He seemed to move his long, gangly limbs in a kind of slow-motion as he loped around the pitch. He looked like an exotic tropical fish grazing on a coral reef.

The game began to settle into a pattern with Poachers pushing the ball around neatly, and patiently waiting for an opportunity to release Majid and Gordon. The Shellduck eleven were running frantically in circles trying to understand the coaching calls from the touchline, accompanied by squeals and even sillier calls from the attendant girlfriends. Dave and his touchline crew were surprised to see the Shellduck manager sitting on a fold-up chair and scribbling in a small note-book. This had little effect as the Poachers strolled into a two-goal lead, with one each from the wingers, both converting crosses from the opposite wing: Gordon with a fierce volley and Majid running the ball into the net around a stranded and bemused goalkeeper. As the first half wore on, Poachers' players had lost interest and were content to perform little cameos, backheels, dummies and flicks. Their casual play was punished when, through hard work and enthusiasm rather than following the increasingly obscure instructions from the coach, the Shellduck managed to scramble the ball over the line. George blamed his defence, the defence blamed the midfield and the midfield blamed the forwards for the lapse and, whilst they were still arguing, the buoyant Shellduck players attacked en masse and forced the equalizer over the line from close range. The attitude of the teams changed as the Poachers' team seemed more concerned with arguing amongst themselves than using their superior skills to beat the opposition, and the Shellduck players, spurred on by the shrieks from their adoring groupies, made more and more effort before cracking in a third goal just before half-time.

Dave was frantic as the fish-referee blew for half-time and his players left the pitch, still quarrelling amongst themselves. As Dave was trying to devise his half-time talk to re-instil the missing enthusiasm and to encourage his boys to pull together, he noticed that the Shellduck manager had erected an easel and whiteboard on the opposite side of the pitch. Dave watched in awestruck disbe-lief as the manager then produced several magnetic discs and placed them on the board which appeared to have a football pitch marked on it. As his own players swigged from water bottles, slurped hot tea and lit their cigarettes, the opposing team gathered around the whiteboard and watched intently as the manager drew lines and moved the discs around. They were listening attentively, pausing only to comb their hair or squeeze the hands of their girlfriends.

Dave raised his voice to try to ensure attention. 'Have you seen what's going on over there?' he shouted. 'Look at them, fucking load of fashion models being coached with a blackboard, fannying about with tarts at the same time. Their manager reading from a little notebook and scribbling on the blackboard. And you know what makes it worse? They're fucking beating you. Now stop fucking arguing and go and kick their asses. OK?'

'Whiteboard,' said Little Smithy.

'What?' Dave turned, surprised by the response.

'It's a whiteboard and you said blackboard.'

'He's right,' young Tommo confirmed. 'That board is definitely white.'

Dave looked confused. He had expected the men to rise as one and charge back into battle, encouraged and enthused, but all they wanted to do was discuss the colour of a board.

'That's racism, that is,' Jamie added. 'Us blacks get blamed for everything and that proves it. That board is not black.'

'Bloody right, Dave. You could get done by the police for racist remarks. I've read about this sort of thing in the *Sun*.'

Within seconds the whole team were united in condemning Dave as a racist bigot and how calling a whiteboard a blackboard could start race riots across Downham. Dave looked genuinely confused and upset as the team began laughing at his embarrassment and slapped each other enthusiastically before trotting happily back onto the field of play.

The Poachers' players took complete control of the game as the Shellduck team, keen and fit as ever, were confused by the lines scrawled across the whiteboard. They grouped in ever tighter knots of players and tried to remember the lines zigzagging across the roughly-drawn plan and how they should convert the lines to the actual field of play. Gordon took full advantage of the bewilderment; after two or three close misses, he was able to break clear and hit the ball cleanly past the Shellduck goalkeeper to level the score. Two more goals came from a chip by Wayne Tocket – a collector's piece he described it afterwards – and a fine individual effort from Jamie Dunbar.

As Paddy chased a long ball into the opposing half, he was challenged by a Shellduck defender. The two players went down in a tangle of legs on the icy surface and there was a sickening crack. Both players lay for a few seconds as they, and the watching team and supporters, recognised the telltale sound. The Shellduck player slowly disentangled himself and stood warily. Paddy stayed down, his right leg twisted at an awkward angle, his head back and his mouth open, as if caught on a still photograph in mid-scream. But no sound came from it, a huge void in his white, twisted face. The referee arrived in seconds and immediately summoned Dave across the pitch. 'Broken. Call an ambulance now,' he commanded, and helped Paddy to lay down. 'Stay there, son, and don't move,' he added. 'And, manager, give me your coat.'

The fish-referee seemed to have everything under control and Dave was grateful that he took responsibility. 'OK, lads. Call it a day there. I was about to blow anyway. You go and get changed and me and the manager here'll look after number 9,' he said authoritatively.

The Shellduck defender involved in the innocuous tackle bent and patted Paddy on the shoulder. 'Really sorry, mate. If there's anything I can do…' and his voice trailed off as he shrugged and walked slowly to the changing rooms with the rest of his team. After several minutes, when the other games on the rec had also finished, the small cluster of men forming a circle around Paddy looked lost and lonely, standing in the middle of the large recreation ground which minutes before had been a hive of footballing activity, with three games being played and shouts of encouragement mixing with the groans of those on their way to defeat. It was reminiscent of the aftermath of a First World War battle where the few survivors stood dazed and shell-shocked amongst the post-battle carnage. Except that this time the carnage was just one broken leg; and even that made Dave feel sick.

They heard the ambulance first as its siren echoed around the playing field. Then it came into view, cutting a muddy swathe across pitches one and two and pulling up next to the abandoned little group of men. The paramedics, both short, plump men, leapt from the ambulance and peered at Paddy, who was shivering violently, his face the colour of the grey/white clouds which had moved across to block out the watery sun.

'That don't look too good. Don't worry, mate. We'll soon get you sorted,' the first paramedic said as they unloaded a stretcher from the back of the ambulance. They cautiously lifted Paddy onto the stretcher and fixed his leg in position with what looked like a miniature lilo. Finally, the stretcher and its live cargo were loaded into the ambulance before it slowly crawled towards the exit of the rec, this time carefully avoiding the playing pitches and the raucous whine of its siren at odds with the sedate progress across the slippery grass.

A freezing Dave and the fish-referee made their way to the changing rooms as Dave realised that his warm outer garment was travelling in the ambulance with Paddy. Gordon broke the silence during the eerie march across the battle-field. 'I'll go up the hospital to see he's OK. I'll get his clothes and go up, Dave. No point in all of us going. I'll give you a ring when I know anything.'

Dave tidied the changing room, gathered his manager's kit and returned the keys to Lightning before slowly strolling to his car. Apart from the Polo, the car park was empty. The cloud had now covered the sun and a chill wind began to gust across the rec as Dave surveyed the desolate scene. He felt for a pocket to stuff his hands into against the cold and realised that he was not wearing his coat. Car keys. The thought hit him like a hammer. The car keys were in his coat and his coat was somewhere in the hospital. He still carried on walking towards the car in the forlorn hope that some miracle may happen and the Polo open its doors and start itself up without the need of a key. He stood next to the car for a moment and then pulled the door handle. He was shocked to find that it opened. And the keys were in the ignition. 'Well done, whoever did this,' he said out loud as he threw his bags onto the passenger seat and sat down to start the engine. He began to pull away slowly when, suddenly, there was a scream like a tortured animal behind him and Dave gripped the steering wheel, almost leaping up to the roof, and his heart thumped as if it would burst from his chest. His foot slipped from the clutch, the car leaping forward before dying and coming to a halt. He turned to see Viv leaning forwards behind him, his face contorted, his mouth twisted in agony and his eyes staring madly. 'About bloody time too. I'm busting for a pint,' Viv said quietly and clambered into the front passenger seat.

Once Dave's pulse had settled back to normal, he was able to restart the car and they pulled slowly away from the car park. 'You are a daft bugger sometimes, Vivian,' Dave scolded. 'I nearly shit myself.'

Viv giggled, 'Only nearly? Smells like you did. Good old Paddy stopped the ambulance to give the keys to Lightning and he gave them to Paul and he gave them to me. I had to wait on my own because the others said you weren't worth missing a pint for.'

Mandy pointed at two pints waiting on the corner of the bar as Dave and Viv walked in. They each grabbed a glass and downed the beer greedily. Two more were waiting as soon as they had drained the glasses and they accepted these with a little more restraint before wandering across to the old men's corner to take up their customary positions. Tonker was missing, standing in the pub porch smoking a roll-up as Tommy and the cribbage players waited impatiently for his return.

Tommy leaned forward. 'Your fuckin' old man been telling us that your fuckin' woman's built him his own little smoking room in the fuckin' garage then, Dave. He's chuffed to fuck. Says we can go round any time for a beer and a game of crib. Get some ale from Tesco's, half the fuckin' price, a good session and a game of crib. Chuffed to fuck, he really is.'

'I hear that you like your smoking room then, Dad,' Dave said as Tonker returned to take up his position, rubbing his hands to try to bring life back to his fingers after standing out in the cold for ten minutes.

'It's all right, I suppose,' Tonker replied. 'At least I can have a fag in peace without some busybody bloody politician saying that I haven't got the right to kill myself how I choose and where I choose. Bloody government'll fine us for farting next.'

'Good idea, that,' Viv joined in. 'Pound a fart, two pounds for a silent-but-deadly, and a fiver if you follow through.'

Barry nudged Dave's arm and nodded towards the bar. Billy was chatting with someone who looked familiar. 'Isn't he the chap that tackled Paddy this morning?' he asked.

'Could be,' Viv said. 'It is if he's wearing Channel Number Five socks and a Jimmy Choo jockstrap.' As they watched, the Shellduck footballer passed Billy a small envelope and both men walked slowly towards the door.

'Looks like a drugs score to me,' Barry announced. 'I've got a nose for these things after all my time in the police. Take it from me, Billy's just bought a load of crack or H.'

'Not with his own money he hasn't,' said Dave. 'He won't even buy a pint with his own money.'

The stranger patted Billy on the shoulder and they left the bar together.

Minutes later the man returned without Billy and he looked around the bar until he noticed Dave and his crew in the corner. He nervously approached the corner. The men stared at him curiously; even the cribbage players pausing in counting their hands.

'I'm really sorry,' the stranger said. 'Not just about your player; I mean, I am sorry about him, but about the money as well.'

'Money, what money?' Dave asked.

'The whip-round from our lads, from the Shellduck. The money I gave to your skipper at the bar ten minutes ago. Only I found another tenner in my pocket, so I should have given him that too. Really sorry. But I changed the small change to this tenner and must have forgotten to put it back with the rest of the cash, like,' and he handed the ten pound note over to Dave.

Dave thanked him and asked how much he had given to "the skipper". 'It must have been forty quid,' he answered, 'because I collected forty-one from the players and our manager made it up to a round fifty from club funds. I'm really sorry but that tenner must have got separated somehow. I hope it helps your mate, short-term like, until things get sorted.'

'Don't apologise, mate, that was very thoughtful. I'll make sure that Paddy gets the money straight away. Thanks.'

The Shellduck player smiled sheepishly and left the pub as the regulars in the old men's corner winked and nodded. There was no sign of Billy or the forty pounds.

Seventeen

Downham Sunday Football League, Division Two
Results for Sunday 15th February

New Inn, Gorton Down	1	0	J G Tanner and Sons
AFC Cummiston	0	3	Jones Juniors FC
Poachers Arms	**5**	**3**	**Shellduck Inn**
Lower End WMC	7	1	Downham Churches
Hearty Oak, Downlea	2	4	Pickled Herring

League Table

Team	Pl'd	Won	Drew	Lost	For	Ag'st	GD	Points
Jones Juniors FC	15	12	3	0	60	15	45	39
Poachers Arms	**15**	**8**	**4**	**3**	**52**	**22**	**30**	**28**
New Inn, Gorton D	14	8	4	2	40	33	7	28
Pickled Herring	15	8	2	5	36	31	5	26
J G Tanner and Sons	15	6	3	6	27	34	-7	21
Lower End WMC	15	6	3	6	34	30	4	21
AFC Cummiston	14	4	5	5	32	36	-4	17
Shellduck Inn	15	4	2	9	27	40	-13	14
Hearty Oak, Downlea	15	3	3	9	36	53	-17	12
Downham Churches	15	1	2	12	30	80	-50	5

Sunday 22nd February

Downham Sunday Football League, Division Two
Pickled Herring v Poachers Arms
Tenacre Recreation Ground – Kick-off 10.30

THE POACHERS ARMS

1 George Crosswell

2 Steve Tippling   4 Derek Smith   5 Jamie Dunbar   3 Billy Millmore (Capt)

8 Matthew Cornwell   10 Vivian Clutterbuck   6 Daniel Tomlinson

7 Gordon Gaye   9 Daniel Raisin   11 Majid Ahmed

Substitutes
12 Paul Cornwell
13 Percy Woodman
14 Wayne Tocket

Reserves (Please bring boots)
Barry Plumb
Dave Statham

Manager
Dave Statham

All players, substitutes and reserves to turn up at 09.45

Viv opened his eyes and stared at the morning light framed by the bedroom window. He tried to turn over to relieve the unusual stiffness in his arms and legs, but his movement was restricted. He tried to raise himself up from the bed but succeeded only in lifting his head. He panicked, with thoughts of paralysis scampering around his brain until he noticed that his wrists were securely locked to the headboard. He looked again and blinked, forcing his eyes to focus correctly. He was secured by handcuffs. He tried to move his legs and feet but they too were fastened to the bottom of the bed. He guessed from the feel of the hard metal around his ankles that handcuffs had been used here too. He was secured tightly in a star position, legs and arms spread wide… and his wife was missing from his side. *Where the bloody hell was she? Had they been broken into during the middle of the night by terrorists and she had been kidnapped? No, that was just too silly. Besides, they'd need a JCB to carry her out.* He immediately regretted the cruel thought.

'Elaine, bloody hell, Elaine, where are you?' he shouted. There was no reply.

'Come on, Babe, stop messing about, I know it's you,' he called, still struggling in vain to free himself from his manacles. No reply. He began to panic. What if it wasn't Elaine? Or what if it was her, and she'd left him. Left him to die of thirst and hunger. After all, he'd treated her pretty badly lately. They had had no sex for months and she was a healthy young woman who would have certain needs in that quarter. And just last week, he had accused her of telling the neighbours about his problem. She denied it of course, and she did seem genuinely upset that he would even consider the possibility of her discussing their private life with anyone else. 'Elaine, where are you?' he shouted, louder this time, but again there was no reply.

Viv stared at the ceiling, trying to make sense of what was happening, when the bedroom door opened slowly. Viv raised his head once more and stared ahead. The door was pushed completely open with a sudden rush which made Viv start. He looked at the figure standing in the doorway. It was a woman. It was so obviously a woman. She stood there silently, her ample body framed by the light from the landing. She flicked on the bedroom light and walked slowly, very slowly, towards the bed, one steady pace at a time. Viv's eyes took time to adjust to the sudden brightness and he tried to focus on the figure moving stealthily towards him. She looked a little like Elaine and walked a little like Elaine, but this was not Elaine. This woman had long, straight, black hair and a red mask. She was wearing a bright red plastic basque, laced tightly at the front with black ribbon and her large breasts were beginning to tumble over the top of the bra. She stopped at the end of the bed, her legs slightly apart, staring at him. His voice was strained and low as he asked, 'Elaine, is that you, love? Come on, 'Laine…'

'Shut up!'

Her voice was that of Elaine, but harder, stronger and with a quiet power and authority he had never heard before. 'You miserable wretch. You will speak only to answer my questions from now on,' she continued and pulled the duvet slowly from the bed. Viv felt the chill air, his legs and arms akimbo, naked on the bed. It was then that he noticed that the woman had a whip in her right hand.

'But, please…' he began.

'I will not tell you again,' said the woman, and flicked the whip so that the tip rested on his chest. 'One more word and I will flay you until you are barely alive.'

As Viv stared at the ceiling he felt the whip being pulled slowly down his body until it rested on his genitals. The whip was moved so that it was beneath his penis and then used to slowly raise the member from its resting position. The whip stopped and was moved away. His head jerked forward as the woman in red pulled him roughly by the hair and placed two pillows beneath his neck so that he could see what was happening both in the room and to himself. He immediately noticed that he had the beginnings of an erection.

The woman walked away from him, bending to pick up the whip which had fallen to the floor. He stared at the glorious rounded orbs of her buttocks beneath the tight fitting outfit. The woman stood up and looked at him. Her eyes travelled down his body, settling on his stiffening penis.

'You like that, I see. You dirty little man. You will pay for being so disgusting,' she said and raised the whip threateningly in her right hand. Viv looked at her with mock terror until she brought the whip down across the top of his thighs, stinging like a hard slap. The terror was no longer mock.

271

''Laine, that hurts, now a joke's a joke but—'

The whip lashed down again, this time across his belly. 'I think that you had better apologise, you worm, and you call me *Mistress*,' the woman demanded sternly.

'Look, sorry, er... sorry, Mistress, but that hurt and really I…'

The whip cracked across his chest. She walked around the bed as Viv's eyes followed her, wondering what she would do next. Wherever he looked, Viv could not help but catch sight of his own penis, swollen and erect. Amongst the many emotions he was feeling, pride in his erection seemed to be uppermost. 'You dirty, dirty little creature,' she growled. 'I will have to make you pay for being such a disgusting little maggot,' and she climbed onto the bed. She sat astride Viv and held his penis for a moment before carefully guiding it into her, and began to slowly move up and down. She leant forward until her large bosom seemed as if it would escape from her basque and smother him. As she moved faster, all the while denigrating Viv with insults, her voice rose with the speed of her movement until she was screaming at the top of her voice. Viv too became loud with months of pent-up sexual and mental frustration culminating in a deafening roar as the two ground into each other with a strength and force that made the bed rock and crash against the bedroom wall, adding to the cacophony of lovemaking.

Dave was sitting at his computer as usual at that time on a Sunday morning, somewhat bemused at the clamour emanating from his neighbour's house. He tried to concentrate on putting the final touches to his teamsheet, with Big Smithy still not fit following his bout of influenza and Wayne Tocket ringing in to say that he had a knock and would be better going sub. Mandy pushed the bedroom door open and carried in a big, steaming mug of tea, placing it on Dave's desk.

'What on earth's going on next door? It sounds as if Viv's trying to kill Elaine,' she commented. 'Is this normal?'

'Never heard them before,' Dave answered. 'And it sounds more like Elaine's trying to kill Viv to me. We all know they're at it all the time, like rabbits on honeymoon, Viv reckons, but I've never heard them before. I'm sure that Viv'll give me all the gory details on the way to the match.'

Mandy patted him on the shoulder. 'Well, keep it to yourself then. I don't want to know about that sort of thing,' she said. 'On second thoughts, perhaps you should tell me, just so that I know Elaine's all right. And breakfast's in ten minutes.'

As she left, Tonker was leaving his bedroom. He looked very embarrassed and mumbled, 'Bloody hell. I thought that was you two trying to kill each other. I suppose that it's just that randy bugger next door,' and disappeared into the bathroom.

'Remember to clean the toilet when you've finished,' Mandy called and skipped down the stairs laughing at the strange life she was creating for herself.

Viv lay on the bed and rubbed his wrists and ankles which ached from being constrained for so long. The intense thrashing of a few minutes before had put extra strain on his arms and legs and now they were painful as he massaged and flexed, trying to force some life back into the joints. The woman had climbed off from her position on top of him and left the bedroom, to return a minute or two later with the key to free him. She also brought a small bowl of hot water, a flannel and towel, but said absolutely nothing as she unlocked the handcuffs and washed his genitals with the steaming water. She dried him and gathered the toiletries and cuffs before walking from the room without a word or backward glance. Viv felt drained but euphoric. It was certainly the most powerful sex he had ever experienced, such that in the final few seconds he had almost passed out as he exploded with a bellow like a rutting stag.

The bedroom door moved open a little and Elaine's head poked around. 'Ah, you're awake, good,' she said as she entered the room. 'I was worried that it's getting a bit late and you've got football this morning.'

Viv stared at his wife. Her hair was its normal short, blonde style and she was dressed in jeans and a sweater with her fluffy slippers. She went over to the window and opened the curtains. 'What do you fancy for breakfast this morning?' she asked as Viv slowly pulled the quilt over himself, feeling very exposed and self-conscious displaying the red weals on his chest. 'I'll just do your usual then, shall I?' Elaine continued as she left the room.

His ankles hurt as Viv lowered himself cautiously onto the floor and limped painfully across the bedroom and into the bathroom, after checking that Elaine was not watching him cross the landing. The hot water in the shower stung his chest like a thousand pinpricks before the pain gave way to a wonderfully warm caress. He began singing at the top of his voice. 'Chains, mah baby's got me locked up in chains,' but knew no more than the first line so repeated it several times. He quickly dried himself, pulled on his Sunday football clothes and happily trotted downstairs into the kitchen. He still felt a little awkward and looked for any sign from Elaine to acknowledge what had happened earlier. She handed him a cup of tea and his usual bacon sandwich. As she did so, she was almost nonchalant in explaining, 'I'm not picking the kids up from mother's until tea time, so try not to be late for dinner, Vivian.'

A car horn outside interrupted Viv's thoughts and he stuffed the remainder of the sandwich into his mouth and gulped the last of his tea. He picked up his sports bag and moved towards Elaine, pecking her cheek. 'See you about, what, one thirty then,' he said, still expecting some reaction from Elaine about the morning's activities.

'That's fine, Vivian,' was all she said, and returned to the sink and her washing-up.

Dave was sitting in his car on his drive, studying the football results in the *Sunday Times*. He glanced up as Viv opened the back door, threw his bag onto the back seat and took his place in the front passenger seat. Dave had a wide grin, almost splitting his face in two. 'What's up with you?' Viv asked as Dave pulled away, still grinning.

'Good bit of horizontal jogging this morning, Viv? Nearly woke up the whole street, you randy bastard.'

'David, what goes on in a husband and wife's bedroom is private and personal,' Viv replied, feeling secretly pleased that Dave had commented on his prowess.

Viv seemed especially cheerful as the men drove out of the estate and was singing, 'Chains, my baby's got me locked up in chains,' repeatedly, using a voice which seemed to mix Elvis and Al Jolson with a touch of Amy Winehouse. 'Chains, mah baby's got me locked up in chains…'

'And they ain't the kind that you can see, whoa, it's chains of love got a hold of me, yeah,' Dave stated flatly with no pretence at singing. 'Had it on an old Carole King LP.'

'Chains, mah baby's got me locked up in chains, yeah, it's chains of love got a hold on me, and they ain't the chains that you can see,' sang Viv, this time using a high falsetto to mimic a woman's voice, although he had never heard of Carole King.

Dave decided to leave Viv to his song and turned his mind to the morning's game. The Pickled Herring were only two points behind the Poachers Arms in the league and a win today was essential to maintain the challenge for promotion. A defeat would mean Poachers slipping to third or fourth and, with the last two games against Jones Juniors and the New Inn, all ideas of promotion would become nothing but a pipe-dream. He felt unusually nervous as they pulled into the car park. Paul's car was already there, and he would be chatting to Lightning, they guessed. He then remembered the fifty pounds that he had paid Paddy Oakley's wife on the previous Sunday evening from the Shellduck players' collection. He knew that he had to ask for the money from Billy Millmore that morning and was not looking forward to the possible embarrassing exchange. He had considered not challenging Billy and simply writing off the loss as his own, but realised that this was one time when Billy could not be allowed to get away with his shenanigans, and a confrontation was inevitable. They entered the cold block building and accepted the key for room four from Paul, who reached backwards with the key as he was explaining to Lightning that the manager of the White Hart was not really Mike Hunt and that P. Dophile did not really run Downend Police FC. They let themselves into the changing room and smelt the dank, cold tang of late winter. The rooms had been in use for five months of a typical British winter and the smell of sweaty bodies and rubbing oils had mixed with the clammy air, without heating or ventilation, to create a smell unique to local recreation ground changing rooms. Viv threw his chest out and took a deep breath. 'Just take a whiff, Dave,' he said loudly. 'Sweat, smelly feet and farts. Can't beat it on a Sunday morning. This is what life is all about. This is what makes Britain great. Where else in the world could you soak up this atmosphere?'

Dave secretly agreed with the prognosis, but said nothing. 'Chains, my baby's got me locked up in chains,' sang Viv as Paul and Billy walked in together.

'Paul, Viv, can you lay the kit out, please. Me and Billy's got to talk about this year's dinner dance,' Dave mumbled and indicated to Billy that they should talk outside. As they stood in the corridor, Dave wished he had decided not to challenge Billy about the money. 'Bit awkward really, Billy,' he began, 'only there should be fifty quid from the Shellduck that they collected for Paddy, and we, well, we never sort of, we never got it, and I paid it out of my own money,' he muttered, glad that the corridor was dark enough to hide his reddening face.

'Forty quid!' Billy snapped back. 'It was only forty quid. I've been meaning to take it round Paddy's all week, but I've been so busy, you know how it is. But look, I've got it here,' and he pulled his wallet from his back pocket and took out four ten pound notes. Dave wondered why it was four crisp, new ten pound notes from a collection and why it wasn't in the brown envelope he had seen handed over the previous week.

'I'll take it then, shall I?' Dave said, accepting the money and really hoping that his suspicions were not valid.

As they returned to changing room four, other players were beginning to drift in. Viv was still singing but Billy noticed that the number 10 shirt was not laid out in sequence but tucked away in the far corner of the room. Not only did this offend Dave's ordered eye, but made him wonder why Viv of all people would want to hide himself away from his team members. He was usually wandering about naked, putting underpants on someone's head or a sock over his own penis or farting loudly in someone's face. The clamour suddenly stopped as Matty Cornwell spun Viv round and shouted, 'Fuck me, Viv, what the fuck's that on your chest?' and everyone turned to look at the bright slashes decorating Viv's upper body, amongst the old and fading tattoos.

'Cat,' Viv stuttered. 'Missis just bought a cat. Dug into me in the night. Couldn't get it off.'

'Cat, my bollocks,' Matt continued, delighted that he had forced the exuberant Vivian Clutterbuck into deep embarrassment instead of Viv being the protagonist. 'That's scratch marks all right, and not caused by a pussy. Not directly, anyway. Your Missis must have been going wild to do that.'

Viv turned quietly back to face the wall as the players hooted in coarse laughter. 'Gentlemen,' he said, just loud enough to be heard, 'when you have grown up, you will realise that a gentleman does not discuss his private life,' a comment met by more hooting and laughter. Viv was enjoying playing the part of the heroic gentleman, saving the blushes of his concubine, whilst allowing his compatriots to enhance his reputation as the local Casanova. Dave's team-talk was lost in the ribald comments about Viv's love life, so he confined his comments to a brief 'Firm but fair,' and decided to leave the players to their own devices.

Dave checked that he had everything as he stared around the empty changing room: first aid kit, water bottles, flasks, mobile phone, George's mobile phone, wallet with an extra forty pounds, and keys. He loaded up, managed to free one hand to lock the door and struggled out through the narrow corridor into the dull February morning. As he toiled across the playing field, he was joined by Barry. 'Late on parade, sir, sorry,' Barry said as he came alongside Dave. 'Had a few last night with some important people. Late night and too much vino and brandy. You know what it's like when you're entertaining.'

Dave's arms were aching under his cargo of bottles, flasks and boxes. 'Not really. I've never been that entertaining myself. Now grab hold of these bottles, will you?'

Barry took the bottles and continued. 'You see, some of us, Dave, people like you and me, are prepared to put more into society than we take out. You run this football team, giving these youngsters direction, a target in life, and someone to look up to.'

Dave wondered just what Barry was talking about. No ranting, no raving, no mention of football pundits, Scots, immigration, homosexuals, hoodies, local councillors or any so-called comedian with the surname Carr. Dave was amazed that, once the kit had been unceremoniously dumped by the halfway flag, Barry stood quietly, applauding the players of both sides and not once looking for a victim to regale with condemnation of one or more of the world's minorities.

The game began well for Poachers with a goal just two minutes after the kick-off. Some scrappy interchanges in midfield finally ended with the ball slowly making its way towards the Pickled Herring goal area where young Daniel Tomlinson appeared from nowhere and unleashed a fine drive past the goalkeeper. The only weak spot in the team was Viv, who appeared in pain throughout the opening twenty minutes, frequently stopping to exercise his wrists, bending to rub his ankles or carefully stroking his chest. He seemed unable to keep up with the pace of the game and was caught in possession several times and, when he did manage to keep possession, his passes were weak and inaccurate. The Poachers took control of the game, in spite of Viv's obvious discomfort and inability to complete the simplest of football tasks. When the Pickled Herring manager signalled to the referee that he wanted to make a substitution, Dave was disappointed to see two players come on that he had forgotten about; one, a young lad and the other an older, balding chap. 'That's a bummer,' he said to no one in particular. 'Remember them. Captain Mainwaring and son. Both shit-hot players.'

Paul sprinted back from his position further along the touchline. 'See that, Dave. Bloody Captain Mainwaring's coming on. And Viv's playing like a wanker. Better get him off and put Tocks on. I'd move Steve into midfield as well to have a go at Mainwaring.'

'Just what I was going to do,' said Dave, and waved to the referee. 'Tocks, you're on. Play right back and tell Steve to mark that Mainwaring.'

'And emphasise the mark bit. Mark him up and down his shin if possible,' chuckled Paul, looking forward to the impending battle.

Viv was happy to be called off. He was old enough and experienced enough to realise when he was playing badly and his joints were painful every time he moved. He accepted the tracksuit cast off by Wayne Tocket and settled to watch the rest of the game with comparative pleasure. Steve was even happier to be given licence to kill and had a short conversation with Matt Cornwell before the game was restarted. Almost immediately, Mainwaring took control of the match, losing his marker and picking out his team mates with ease. The only good thing for the Poachers was that he appeared to have a slight limp and did not venture outside the centre circle. As he conducted the game, Steve and Matt were confusing each other and neither was able to get within yards of Mainwaring. The first half fizzled out with Poachers retaining their one goal lead, but with the Pickled Herring looking the more likely to score.

The players returned to the pitch after half-time, a resounding dressing-down ringing in their ears from Viv. Although replaced at half-time for being totally ineffectual, he had managed to turn his replacement into an act of selfless sacrifice. 'If I am prepared to come off for the good of the team,' he told them, 'then the least you can do is to put in the effort to make it worthwhile. Midfield, stop trying to kick the old ginger boy and simply cut off his supply – no, Steve, not by removing his jugular with your boot – but just make sure that you stop the ball reaching him. How? By positioning, that's how. Position yourselves to remove him as a target. And you all need to consolidate positions. Defence, you must hit the wings. Midfield, support your strikers. You front lads need to turn their back four.'

As the players took up their positions, they looked to their experienced captain, Billy, for guidance. 'What was Viv on about?' asked Jamie.

'He just meant run around a bit more,' Billy explained and the players nodded, the first instruction that they had understood.

The team did indeed run about a bit more and their efforts were matched by the opposition who must have had a similarly enlightening team talk at half-time. The result was that both sides lacked for nothing in effort but the game became fast and frenetic, with only Mainwaring trying to restore order out of the chaos. There were openings at either end but poor shooting and good goalkeeping kept the score at one nil. With minutes to go, the Pickled Herring were awarded a corner from a sliced clearance and as the winger bent down to place the ball, George Crosswell's mobile began to ring in Dave's pocket. He took out the offending telephone and stared at the screen. It said *work calling*. Dave wondered whether he should answer the call, switch the mobile off or call George, but the decision was made for him by the distinctive ringtone carrying to George who was busily trying to organize his defence and signalled to Dave to let him have the phone. The corner floated into the packed goalmouth whilst George was on his way across the pitch towards Dave and the ball bounced off an attacking player in the direction of the goal. It seemed like a slow-motion action replay as the ball arched forward and began to drop towards the goal. It was about to cross the line when Jamie Dunbar leapt elegantly to his right and pushed the ball over the crossbar with his fingertips.

Through the resulting chaos, the referee had little choice but to show Jamie a red card and award a penalty. The ball was placed on the penalty spot and Mainwaring was in position to begin his run up, but there was no goalkeeper. The referee blasted his whistle and looked around him, but no goalkeeper appeared. George, meanwhile, was ambling back towards the goal, speaking loudly into his mobile: something about databases, unintelligible to normal people.

'Get a move on, keeper. I could book you for leaving the field of play without permission, you know.' The referee was fast losing patience.

George was a little uptight after the call. 'No you couldn't,' he argued. 'I never left the field. Just went over there to get my phone.'

'Well, get back in goal, then. It's a penalty against you. And turn that phone off or give it to someone else, will you?'

Dave had sprinted around the pitch and was standing, gasping for breath, behind the goal. 'Give us the phone and just save this fucking penalty,' he wheezed, praying that George would do just that and promising himself that he would give up smoking Hamlets from now on. George shouted into the phone, 'Ring me back,' and threw Dave the phone before turning to face the penalty.

Captain Mainwaring stood patiently with arms folded watching the debacle in the Poachers' ranks with a confident smile, waiting for the whistle, the ball sitting neatly on the spot. The referee reviewed the scene. All was ready at last and he blew his whistle loudly. Mainwaring took two steps to the side and began a purposeful run towards the ball. He was about to strike the ball when the sound of 'Is this the way to Amarillo?' reverberated around the goalmouth. It was too late to stop the kick but Mainwaring was distracted enough to blast the ball over the crossbar, and George turned and called for his phone.

The Pickled Herring players surrounded the referee who explained that there was nothing he could do because there was no law against a spectator receiving a phone call on a public recreation ground, even with the call signal of an old pop record. The game restarted with the Poachers' players buoyant, the Pickled Herring team despondent, and George cheerfully congratulating his computer operators for resolving the failure. It ended a few minutes later with the score remaining at one–nil.

Dave, Paul, Barry, Viv and Billy had taken up their positions in the old men's corner of the Poachers Arms public bar. Dave's quickly invented lie about discussing the end of season celebration had reminded the senior team members that it was time to organize the bash which, for several years, had taken place in the upstairs room at the Lower End Working Men's Club. As Tonker and his pals shuffled, dealt and pegged away at the next table, the men debated whether the Club was a suitable venue if promotion were to be gained. Billy was particularly keen to try somewhere new and, as he put it, more in keeping with the club's success and the standing of its players. 'Let's face it, the young lads aren't going to enjoy the club much. They're used to wine bars and night clubs, so a night out in a dingy room above the club is hardly going to excite them.'

'They've got a skittle alley there. We could always arrange a skittles competition to brighten the evening up,' Paul suggested, much to the disdain of his fellow committee members.

'Billy's right,' Barry added. 'The Club is a bit, shall we say, down-market and, be honest, we are not really "working men" per se, are we?'

'I dunno about per fucking se, but I fucking work in a factory. If that don't make me working class, I don't know what does.' Paul was becoming annoyed at what he saw as delusions of grandeur amongst his peers.

'I think Paul may be right,' Dave agreed, 'and besides, we get the Club for free. They're only worried about selling more beer and they certainly do that with our lot.'

Viv was even more supportive. 'And it's only just down the road. No cars to worry about and we can get pissed without worrying about getting home.'

But Billy was determined. 'Look, this could be an important year for us if we get promotion. A few pints and a game of skittles in a scruffy attic that smells of stale beer and piss is hardly the way to celebrate. Dave, this club deserves better, you deserve better. You've built this club up to be a force to be reckoned with. We all have. We've worked hard to make it what it is today. A success. Let's celebrate that success in a fitting way. Why not a nice hotel somewhere, with a nice buffet, a good disco and even rooms to stay the night, to get over the driving problem?'

The men sat and thought about what Billy was saying. 'Go and get some beers in while you're just sitting there, David,' Tonker whispered from the next table. 'Four pints of bitter, son.'

Dave fetched the beer for the cribbage players and ordered five pints for the football committee. He was also warming to the idea of an hotel.

'That's not a bad idea, you know, lads,' he said as he re-took his place at the table. 'Perhaps we do deserve something better this year.'

'Count me out, fucking cost a fortune. Where am I going to get money for a hotel on top of what it costs for the do?' Paul grumbled.

'Not for me either,' added Viv. 'I like the Club.'

'I'm not sure.' Barry re-joined the conversation. 'The Club is part of our long and distinguished tradition.'

'But look.' Billy was not to be dissuaded. 'Paul, tell your missis that it's going to be a posh do and she'll need a new dress and that she deserves a special night out. Make out you're doing it for her and she'll pay out of the housekeeping. And Barry, a man with your position in the community is more suited to a hotel dinner dance. I mean, we'll insist on suits for the blokes. Tell you what, we could all hire dinner jackets and make it a really smart do.'

Paul and Barry mulled over Billy's suggestion. 'It does make sense. I think I'm coming round,' Barry announced, imagining himself in a dinner jacket proposing a toast to the Queen and announcing, 'Gentlemen, you may now smoke,' except that they wouldn't be allowed to smoke, of course.

Paul was still unsure, until Billy played the first of his aces. 'Of course, a hotel will hold a lot more, so we could invite people not directly part of the football club. Like Rabbit the referee, perhaps, or even Lightning from the rec and his mum; you know, sort of open it out a bit.'

The bait was too much to resist and Paul gobbled it up. The thought of an opportunity to go out openly with the two women of his life was too much to resist. 'I suppose so. Yes, let's give it go,' he said, trying to curb his enthusiasm for the project and not once considering the complications that the evening would undoubtedly bring.

Viv was still not convinced until Billy played his second ace. 'Of course, with a big do, we'll need someone to act as MC. You know, give out the Player of the Year trophy, Clubman of the Year, that sort of thing. We'd need a volunteer for that.'

'I suppose you all expect me to take that on, then,' Viv announced without appearing too eager, and without pausing. 'Go on then, if it helps I'll do it.'

Billy smiled smugly and downed his pint, waiting for someone to offer to buy another round.

'It's going to take a lot of organizing.' Dave's natural pessimism brought him down to earth. 'I don't have time and it's getting late to book a hotel, and—'

'Don't worry, lads,' said Billy. 'I'll sort it all out. I've got some contacts through work, so leave it all to me. What about the end of March, just after the last game? Is that OK? Just leave it all to me. Mine's a pint, whose round is it?'

Viv's wrists and ankles were throbbing and his chest stinging. 'Not for me, lads, thanks,' he said. 'I'm home for an early lunch,' and left the pub, singing, 'Chains, mah baby's got me locked up in chains.'

Downham Sunday Football League, Division Two
Results for Sunday 22nd February

Jones Juniors FC	2	2	New Inn, Gorton Down
Shellduck Inn	2	4	J G Tanner and Sons
Downham Churches	3	3	AFC Cummiston
Pickled Herring	**0**	**1**	**Poachers Arms**
Lower End WMC	5	0	Hearty Oak, Downlea

League Table

Team	Pl'd	Won	Drew	Lost	For	Ag'st	GD	Points
Jones Juniors FC	16	12	4	0	62	17	45	40
Poachers Arms	**16**	**9**	**4**	**3**	**53**	**22**	**31**	**31**
New Inn, Gorton D	15	8	5	2	42	35	7	29
Pickled Herring	16	8	2	6	36	32	4	26
Lower End WMC	16	7	3	6	39	30	9	24
J G Tanner and Sons	16	7	3	6	31	36	-5	24
AFC Cummiston	15	4	6	5	35	39	-4	18
Shellduck Inn	16	4	2	10	29	44	-15	14
Hearty Oak, Downlea	16	3	3	10	36	58	-22	12
Downham Churches	16	1	3	12	33	83	-50	6

Sunday 1st March

Downham Sunday Football League, Division Two
Jones Juniors F.C. v Poachers Arms
Gas Board Social Club – Kick-off 10.30

THE POACHERS ARMS

1 George Crosswell

2 Steve Tippling   4 Derek Smith   5 Brian Smith (Capt)   3 Jamie Dunbar

8 Matthew Cornwell   10 Vivian Clutterbuck   6 Daniel Tomlinson

7 Gordon Gaye   9 Daniel Raisin   11 Majid Ahmed

Substitutes
12 Wayne Tocket
13 Billy Millmore
14 Percy Woodman

Reserves (Please bring boots)
Paul Cornwell
Barry Plumb
Dave Statham

Manager
Dave Statham

All players, substitutes and reserves to turn up at 09.45

Judge Barry Plumb, resplendent in scarlet gown and long white wig, looks down at the dock, his piercing blue eyes striking fear into the miserable worms on whom he is about to pass sentence. He surveys the courtroom for one last time before placing the black cap atop his wig. 'You have been found guilty of the serious crime of being yobbos,' he begins, pointing a long bony finger at the group of quivering prisoners, 'and there is but one sentence I can pass. You will all be taken from here to a place of execution and hanged by the neck until you are dead. Take them down.'

The court gasps at the severity of the sentence but breaks out in spontaneous applause, knowing the decision to be brave and just.

Alan Hansen is placed in the dock alongside Gordon Brown, Billy Connolly and the Krankies. Judge Plumb, hero of the people, fixes Hansen with a steely glare. He begins: 'Scotch people are taking over this fair country and the spread of this cancer must be stopped immediately. You are sentenced to serve penal servitude in the colony of Australia for a period of no less than one hundred years.' He leans down to his clerk of the courts. 'That should sort the bloody Aussies out as well,' he winks. 'Now what about comedians who can't tell a joke without saying "fuck" and everyone who's ever been on "Never Mind the Buzzcocks"? Shall we do them now?'

'Why not, sir, we have plenty of room left on the convict ships or perhaps we should let them dance on the end of a rope…'

'Penny for them, darling.' Barry jumped in surprise as Monica whispered in his ear. 'I've been watching you for the last half an hour. You've been talking to yourself in your sleep. Or you've been awake and talking to yourself. What are you thinking about?'

'Oh, just this JP business. It's a big responsibility, you know, and I really want to do the job properly. I was thinking about what Charles was saying last night and getting my mind around it. You know, I really feel that my whole life has been geared towards this moment, towards this position of responsibility in the community. Tolerance and understanding, that's what Charles said. Tolerance and understanding. That's what a magistrate needs and I believe that my life and career up 'til now has prepared me for this role. And being non-judgemental. He said that too. I must be non-judgemental. Non-judgemental just about sums me up. And impartial. I am, and always will be, impartial.'

Monica slipped both legs out of bed and stood up. She stretched and moved towards the window where she drew the curtains allowing muted light to seep into the room. 'There's a couple of youngsters in hooded tops hanging round your car, darling,' she said.

Barry leapt out of bed. 'Bloody hoodies,' he shouted. 'Bloody vandals, I'll bloody swing for 'em.' He looked out of the window towards his parked car. No one was near it. He scanned the road looking for miscreants.

'Non-judgemental and impartial, darling, non-judgemental,' Monica laughed, and moved swiftly into the en-suite bathroom as a pillow hit the door behind her. Barry slipped back under the warm duvet.

Judge Barry Plumb, JP, and hero of the people, looks down upon the court once more. He stares at the small group of teenagers in the dock. 'You scum have been found guilty of standing near my car and of having greasy hair and acne. You will be called up into the army and sent to the Middle East for the next twenty years until you learn how to behave.' There, that's sorted them out. The pretty lady clerk of the courts stands before him. 'And you misled me, young lady, a man of justice. You are sentenced to perform an act of oral love upon me until I beg for mercy.'

Monica stepped naked from the en-suite bathroom, her skin pink and glowing from her early morning shower. Barry smiled his most charming smile. 'Why don't you get back into bed for a while, darling?' he asked. 'We've got half an hour before we have to get up. Let's just have a nice romantic little chat here in bed.'

'Barry, if you are going to lie to me about your intentions, please try to disguise that rather large bulge under the duvet, will you?'

Barry looked down at the rather large bulge under the duvet. 'Fancy a shag, then?' he said, more in hope than expectation.

'Don't be crude, please, Mr Non-judgemental Tolerant Barry Plumb, Justice of the Peace,' said Monica before returning to bed.

The unappetising bowl of rabbit cage scrapings was hardly touched except for the constant stirring from Barry's spoon. He was reading the letter again: '…and are pleased to tell you that your application has been successful…'

'Have you told your friends at the football club about your new position, yet?' Monica asked as she busied herself at the kitchen sink. 'And I don't mean that new position you had me in earlier this morning.'

'No, no, not yet,' Barry replied. 'It's sort of awkward. Most of them won't understand what a JP is and their only experience of magistrates will be from appearing at the juvenile court. I don't want to scare the youngsters. I am a sort of father figure to them as you know. They look up to me as a leader, as someone they all aspire to be. Apart from that Steve Tippling and Matty Cornwell. Bloody yobs, those two.'

'Well, I think that you should tell them today,' Monica said firmly. 'After all, they will all be as pleased as you are and it could even increase their respect for you.'

Barry continued to stir his muesli, his stomach rumbling but unable to face forcing the tasteless bran and lumps of dried banana into his mouth. 'I think I'll get off early for the game this morning, Monica,' he stated suddenly. 'You're right, I should tell people. I should follow etiquette and tell Dave first. It's only right that he's told first, so I'll pop round his house now.'

'It's only half past eight, sweetie. Isn't that a little early?'

'I'll take the letter as well. I should tell him first,' Barry added, ignoring Monica and pulling on his warm overcoat as protection against the cold March wind. He grabbed his sports bag and hurried to his car, starting the motor and pulling away quickly before Monica could delay him further. Ten minutes later he was knocking on the door of Dave's house. As soon as Dave opened the door, the delicious smell of bacon wafted out to greet him, increasing the hunger pangs.

'Morning, Dave,' he called cheerfully, entering the house without being invited and heading straight for the kitchen. The table was laid with three places and Mandy was standing at the hob with two huge frying pans sizzling in front of her.

'Hello, Barry,' she said, without turning from her culinary duties. 'You're early this morning.'

'Yes, I am. I've got something important to share with Dave. Well, with all of you actually. It's quite important so I didn't even wait for breakfast. I need to chat to you all about something important. And I've had no breakfast.'

'So, no breakfast, eh,' Mandy sighed. 'You must be starving.'

'Well, I am as a matter of fact, Mandy. But talking to you and Dave with important information is more important than mere food, of which I have had none this morning'

'I'll tell you what, Barry. Pull up a chair and sit at that table. No point in being uncomfortable as well as hungry, is there?'

'No, no, I suppose not,' Barry replied, his mouth watering.

'Come on, Mandy, stop teasing.' Dave joined in the conversation. 'We can't leave Barry with nothing. I'll make him a cup of tea while you, me and Dad eat that lovely fry-up.' Mandy giggled and looked at Barry's face which reminded her of a small boy who had been told that Christmas had been cancelled.

'I expect we can rustle up a bit of breakfast for you as well, Barry,' she offered, unable to resist his sulking face any longer. 'Take your coat off and sit down. Now, what's this important information?'

Barry removed his coat and took up a position at the table, smiling happily as he accepted cutlery and a plate from Dave. He pulled the well-thumbed letter from his pocket and passed it to Dave, who read it carefully.

'Blimey, Mandy. Our Barry here's been made a Justice of the Peace. Well done, mate, well done. Do we call you Sir or M'Lord from now on?'

Barry smiled patronisingly. 'No need for that, Dave,' he said. 'It won't change me, you know that. It's just that I felt you should be first to be told because of your position in the club.' Mandy heard 'in the club' and froze. For a second she wondered whether her news about the baby had finally slipped out. 'Only the football club is dear to all our hearts and I do have a certain status amongst the team and the supporters, so I felt that you should know before I make a general announcement.'

Tonker opened the door and came into the kitchen after finishing his first roll-up of the day in his smoking room. Dave repeated the news. 'Dad, Barry here has just become a Justice of the Peace and came round to tell us first.'

'That's right, Tonker. Only I do have a certain respect and status, both within the club and with its supporters, so I thought that Dave should be the first to know. That's why I'm here this morning,' Barry added in his best Justice of the Peace voice.

'And so that you can have a decent bloody breakfast for a change, Plumby,' said Tonker, taking up his position at the table.

Barry looked hurt. 'There is that an' all,' he agreed. 'I'm bloody starving.'

The talk over breakfast turned from Barry's news to the morning's match: Jones Juniors FC, away. 'They've only dropped four points all season,' Dave said, wiping the last of his fried egg from his plate with a piece of bread and butter. 'And if we lose this one and the New Inn win their next two, which they should do, they'll have four more points than us going into the last game, so we've got to win today.'

'A draw will do us,' Barry countered. 'That means that it will all be on the last game and our goal difference is far better than theirs.'

'Thanks to the hammering we gave them early on.'

'But we must get the draw today, at least. Unless New Inn drop points in their next two games, which is unlikely.'

Mandy coughed loudly. 'You boys will be late going out to play if you don't hurry up,' she said.

Barry looked at his watch. 'We've got ten minutes yet, Mandy. No worries.'

Mandy gave one her sweetest smiles. 'Just enough time to clear up and do the washing-up, then.'

'I'm off to my room for a fag,' said Tonker.

Dave and Barry were joined in the Polo by Viv as they headed for the Gas Works Social Club Ground. It was an old ground with just one football pitch, and a large wooden club house. Many years previously it had been the social club for workers at the gas works which stood opposite, but the gas works was now a housing estate, and the club was in private hands. The club and ground was owned by Allan Jones, life chairman of Jones Juniors FC and his two sons who ran the team. It was ripe for development and worth a small fortune as land for housing, but the Joneses didn't need the money and enjoyed being lords of this very small sporting manor. All other clubs hated playing at the gas works ground, including everyone at Poachers Football Club. The pitch was uneven and closed in by the backs of old terraced houses on two sides and a B&Q shed at the far end. The top end was close to the road, and the whole was surrounded by a twelve feet high fence to protect the surrounding buildings and traffic from wayward footballs, and the club from wayward teenagers. As they pulled into the small car park, the three men felt a sense of anti-climax at the drab surroundings with the strong wind blowing a white plastic bag across the pitch, adding to the dilapidated feel of the ground.

The changing rooms felt and smelt cold as the wind whistled through cracks in the window frames. The men knew that the home dressing room was well sealed and warm, with a gas heater creating a cosy atmosphere; all part of the Jones Juniors' plan to gain the upper hand before the game started. Billy limped in with the kit, injured in an over-thirties six-a-side match earlier in the week, and he and Dave began to lay out the kit. The team arrived and all seemed subdued except Viv who was in an exceptionally buoyant mood. He was dancing round the changing room talking to everyone and offering words of encouragement, saying how Jones Juniors were scared of them after they were so close to beating them last time (a lie) and that he heard the manager saying that Poachers was the best team they would face (a lie) and that they would need to be on top form to scrape a point (a lie). He said that he had spoken to some of the Juniors team during the week and they were not confident (a lie) but were not worried because they had already won the league with points to spare (possibly true). He added that the game was a formality and Poachers should win easily (absolute bollocks).

'Right, lads, listen up,' Dave called for attention. 'If we win today, or even get a draw, promotion is a real possibility. The worst that can happen is that we then go into the last game needing to beat the New Inn and we've already thrashed them seven–nil this season. If, however, we win today and New also win, then that means we'll have…' The hubbub in the changing room continued with Dave's speech drowned by laughter, shouts and jokes. And Viv, for some reason, was carrying out a very bad impression of Ricky Gervais dancing.

Barry's deep and loud voice boomed out, suppressing all other sounds and demanding attention. 'Bloody listen for once, will you?' he thundered. 'Jones Juniors have already won the league so won't be geed up for this one. They won't want to get too involved because most of them have got important games coming up on Saturdays in the senior leagues. So get stuck into 'em. Hard as you like. Fuck the firm but fair; give them stick.'

'Kick anything that fucking moves.' Paul added his constructive contribution.

Barry's following announcement that he was to become a Justice of the Peace was drowned by the excited cheering that followed.

The referee, a portly, bespectacled old boy called Dai Reese and, quite naturally, known as Taffy to all and sundry, started the game with a loud whistle which was almost lost in competition with the shrieking wind. Dave and his touchline crew ignored the jibes from the Jones brothers, except for Paul who raised two fingers towards their rendition of 'We are the champions.' Taffy looked and shook his head, muttering, 'Not what one usually expects from the referee's assistant.' A light, cold rain began to sweep across the pitch as the kick-off was taken by Jones Juniors. They played the ball carefully for three or four passes before hitting a long ball out to their left winger who was calling for the ball near the halfway line. As he turned to face his own goal and collect the ball, he was clattered in the back by Steve Tippling, his legs flying up in the air before landing unceremoniously in a heap, the ball trickling gently out of play. Taffy signalled a throw-in and Steve trotted quietly back to take up his position at right full back. The throw-in was directed along the touchline to the same winger, who was again unceremoniously kicked up in the air by Steve on receiving the ball. Shouts for a free kick were ignored, and the referee allowed the game to continue whilst wiping rain from his glasses with the tail of his black referee's shirt which was then left flapping in the wind. The left winger never called for the ball again during the match and retreated to take up a position closer to his own full back.

The swirling wind and rain made control difficult and the Jones Juniors' frustration was amplified somewhat by being kicked, pushed, barged and blocked by the eager Poachers' team. Infringements were largely ignored by Taffy who continually indicated free kicks or throw-ins which seemed to bear little connection to the actual incidents on the pitch. The Jones brothers were loudly animated on the opposite touchline as Barry took to moving up the pitch, in line with the play, and roaring instruction to the Poachers' team to assault, assail and attack the opposition at any opportunity. The Juniors' forward line had lost all spirit and spent the first half picking themselves up from the ground and complaining to Taffy, who continued to ignore their pleas for protection against the battering they were receiving. The half ended in a confusion of bodies, arms and legs as the Poachers' goalkeeper was unceremoniously bundled over the line by Razor Raisin, before he, in turn, was barged over by a large defender, leading to a skirmish on the goal line involving half a dozen players from each side. Taffy watched the scuffle for a minute or two before scrutinising his watch closely and blasting his whistle for half-time. The players immediately broke from their tussles and returned to their respective touchline encampments for a break and a warming cup of tea.

Barry called the team around him, having assumed the mantle of team coach for the morning. 'Gentlemen. The tactic of aggression is working well. They are obviously rattled and don't want to get involved. Just keep it up and keep on top of them. Don't give them an inch of space and whack them whenever you get the chance.'

As confidence grew in the second half, Poachers pushed forward and wingers Gordon and Majid began to pepper the Juniors' area with accurate crosses which Razor, supported by the midfield, was meeting with head, foot and body, causing Jones Juniors to defend desperately. It seemed as if the Poachers' half was designated out of bounds as the ball was restricted to an area between the halfway line and the Juniors' goal. A break from Jones Juniors took everyone by surprise, including their left winger who had tried to distance himself from the action to prevent injury from the ever-aggressive Steve. But the ball found its way to him through a misdirected punt and he was clear in the Poachers' half with no opposition as he raced towards the goal. In hot pursuit were the Poachers' defence and Taffy, who guessed that the ball was somewhere near the blurred, lone figure racing goalward. Paul was alongside the attacker with legs, arms and flag pumping as he attempted to keep up, and Barry was in hot pursuit of Paul, screaming instructions to the beleaguered defence to hack their quarry down. George Crosswell had been a spectator for most of the game and was cold and wet and more interested in listening out for his mobile phone than concentrating on events happening a hundred yards away. Before the defence could reach him, the left winger struck a firm shot from the edge of the penalty area which flew past George and crashed against stanchion supporting the net. The winger jumped in the air, arm raised in celebration, whilst the ball bounced out into the grateful arms of the goalkeeper. As the Jones Juniors' team caught the forward and celebrated their breakaway goal, Taffy caught up with play, his short legs steaming like pistons and shirt tail flapping. George held on to the ball, wondering whether or not to simply play on or concede the goal. As he reached the scene, Taffy looked at Paul for guidance but Paul stood impassively and did nothing.

The Juniors' players turned to Taffy and insisted that it was a legitimate goal and should be awarded, but the referee held the whistle close to his lips, not knowing whether to blow it or to wave play on. He again looked across at Paul, who had by now been joined by a puffing Barry. Taffy blew his whistle, stopping both the play and the celebrations and yelled across to Paul. 'Was it in?' he shouted. 'Was it a goal?'

Paul shrugged. 'I couldn't see, to be honest, ref,' he replied, almost surprising himself with his honesty.

'Definitely not in,' Barry blurted out. 'I was close enough to see. Definitely hit the post, definitely.'

'Well, if you're not sure and I'm not sure, I can't give it, can I? After all, I can't see a bloody thing,' Taffy said before turning and shouting at George to play on.

The miscarriage of justice strengthened the Jones Juniors' resolve and Poachers were lucky to survive as the match changed to become a series of non-stop attacks on their goal. But survive they did and Taffy finally blew his whistle for a repeat of the no-score draw earlier in the season.

On leaving the pitch, Barry was aware that the Jones' brothers were making a beeline for him. As they approached, he could see that they were not approaching him to exchange pleasantries.

'Oy you, fat bastard.' They blocked his route to the changing rooms and Aaron poked a large finger aggressively into his chest. 'Did you tell that fucking ref that the ball never crossed the line? You lying—'

Barry pulled himself up to his full height and assumed an air of superiority and control. 'My dear Mr Jones, I am Barry Plumb, JP, a magistrate and a Justice of the Peace. One of the many requirements for my position is that of impartiality. Now, are you accusing me of being dishonest?'

Aaron was not easily put off and continued to rant until his brother Buddy held his hand up and intervened. 'Well, if you're a JP, then of course we believe you, but please forgive my brother, only it did look like a goal.'

Barry looked down on the two brothers and sensed that they were beginning to feel uncomfortable. 'Impartiality, gentlemen, is my middle name, as I'm sure you'll find when you next come to renew your drinks' licence for this club. Impartiality. And, after all, your fine side has already won the league, so it doesn't really matter too much, does it?'

Aaron looked at his brother and smiled. 'Of course, Mr Plumb, we understand completely,' he said and offered his hand. Barry shook each man's hand in turn and strode across to the changing rooms. He was going to enjoy being a JP

The changing room was a riot of songs, sweating bodies and spotty buttocks as the Poachers' players and officials realised the impact of their well-earned draw. No matter what happened in the New Inn's last two games, the second promotion spot behind Jones Juniors would be decided on the last day of the season. Dave watched the antics of his team with a mixture of paternal pleasure and maternal disgust as they cavorted around half-naked, in Viv's case totally naked, shouting, swearing and singing as if promotion were guaranteed. He had tried to call them to order several times without success and shouted across to Barry, 'Barry, can you get these idiots to shut up for a minute?'

Barry banged loudly on the changing room door and bellowed into the small, steamy confines of the room. 'Listen up, will you. Dave has got something serious to tell you,' and with an extravagant gesture of his arm, pushed Dave in front of him. The team, in various stages of dress or undress turned to listen to their manager.

Dave felt nervous even about public speaking on this small scale and smiled uneasily before beginning. 'Two things, lads. Important things. A: remember that there's no game next week so that the postponed games can be played. Our next game is the big one against the New Inn in two weeks. B: Billy's arranged the end of season do for the twenty-ninth of March and he'll pin all the details up in the pub next week. C: don't forget to pay your subs.' He was immediately swamped by dirty, wet football socks.

The five senior football club members sat in the pub's old men's corner, trying to warm up after the morning's sport, excited by the prospect of promotion and the forthcoming dinner-dance. The cribbage players were shuffling, dealing, playing their cards and rearranging matchsticks up and down the crib board in a confusion of movement and patois that locked them into their own world, until their beer glasses were empty. Dave had managed to phone the manager of the New Inn and announced to the assembly that the New Inn had managed to scrape a two–one win over the Pickled Herring, which left them equal on points with the Poachers Arms but with a game in hand. Win, draw or lose the game in hand, he had explained, the final league position would depend on the last game of the season. 'I'll have a pint of bitter to celebrate, Paul,' said Billy and began to describe his plans for the "do".

He explained, 'I've managed to book the Post House. Four-star hotel. A wedding reception was cancelled. Apparently the future bride found her fiancé in bed with her mother so cancelled the wedding. No sense of humour, women. Anyway, I got the room free and a buffet at only twelve-fifty per person; and they said we can have a special room rate of only thirty quid for a double. I mean that's only fifty-five quid for the night, plus beer money. Bargain or what? It took a lot of negotiating skills to get these rates, I can tell you. Had to use all my charm. I've got the quote here, look.'

Billy passed the quote around the table and each man studied it carefully looking for signs of forgery or subterfuge, whilst wondering why Billy had gone to so much trouble for no personal gain. But all seemed in order. The headed notepaper seemed genuine. The quote seemed genuine. Perhaps Billy had turned over a new leaf.

Downham Sunday Football League, Division Two
Results for Sunday 1st March

New Inn, Gorton Down	2	1	Pickled Herring
Jones Juniors FC	**0**	**0**	**Poachers Arms**
Shellduck Inn	2	6	Lower End WMC
Downham Churches	3	2	Hearty Oak, Downlea
AFC Cummiston	4	5	J G Tanner and Sons

Results for Sunday 8th March

AFC Cummiston	1	1	New Inn, Gorton Down

League Table

Team	Pl'd	Won	Drew	Lost	For	Ag'st	GD	Points
Jones Juniors FC	17	12	5	0	62	17	45	41
New Inn, Gorton D	17	9	6	2	45	37	8	33
Poachers Arms	**17**	**9**	**5**	**3**	**53**	**22**	**31**	**32**
Lower End WMC	17	8	3	6	45	32	13	27
J G Tanner and Sons	17	8	3	6	36	40	-4	27
Pickled Herring	17	8	2	7	37	34	3	26
AFC Cummiston	17	4	7	6	40	45	-5	19
Shellduck Inn	17	4	2	11	31	50	-19	14
Hearty Oak, Downlea	17	3	3	11	38	61	-23	12
Downham Churches	17	2	3	12	36	85	-49	9

Sunday 15th March

Downham Sunday Football League, Division Two
Poachers Arms v New Inn, Gorton Down
Tenacre Recreation Ground – Kick-off 1030

THE POACHERS ARMS

1 George Crosswell

2 Percy Woodman   4 Derek Smith   5 Brian Smith   3 Billy Millmore(Capt)

8 Paul Cornwell   10 Vivian Clutterbuck   6 Dave Statham

7 Gordon Gaye   9 Daniel Raisin   11 Majid Ahmed

Substitutes
12 Barry Plumb

Reserves (Please bring boots)
None

Manager
Dave Statham

All players, substitutes and reserves to turn up at 09.45

299

'Why couldn't you have told everyone that they had to pay for the hire of the hotel ballroom and we could have kept the money?' Louise asked in her usual aggressive manner, her face grimacing like a church gargoyle. 'Sometimes you really are just plain useless, Billy.'

Billy turned and faced her, forcing a smile. He sighed loudly and began to explain again. 'Because Dave wants invoices and receipts for everything, that's why. He gets an accountant mate of his at the Civic Offices to audit the club accounts and they are sticklers for getting it right. They'd have been bound to find out. Anyway, we'll do OK, don't worry about that. I did a great deal with the hotel. If we get more than ten bookings for staying overnight, we get our room free. And we get a free evening meal on the Saturday from the vouchers I've saved from using the hotel at work—'

'But we've still got to buy drinks. That could cost a small fortune at the hotel,' Louise interrupted, still grimacing and refusing to be swayed by Billy's argument.

'But we can buy a cheap bottle of vino and down that in the room before the free dinner, which includes another bottle of plonk anyway. Then we sidle into the do and tag onto anyone who's buying a round. If we leave it until about nine o'clock, most of the lads'll be too drunk to notice. If I do get caught for a round, say that you're not thirsty and I'll just have a half. When it's anyone else's round, you have a large one and I'll have a pint. Easy. I reckon we'll do the whole night for about a fifteen quid max, including a meal, the buffet, drinks, a night in a posh hotel and breakfast. That can't be bad, can it?'

'You two talking about money again?' a bleary-eyed Martha yawned as she pushed open the door to the kitchen and slouched in.

'Just making sure that we don't waste your inheritance, my darling,' replied Billy, glad of the intrusion in case Louise took him to task on his failure to generate cash from organizing the end of season dance. 'Where's Martha?'

The pretty face peered up under a tousled head of blonde curls. 'I am Martha, Daddy, and you know it. Ruth's staying in bed for a while. It's her turn with the iPod and she says she wants to enjoy her music in peace.'

'I suppose she's got some awful modern popular music boyband on, has she? Who is it? The Westlife or Boys Aloud? Or is it one of those screeching American women? Britney Ferries, or that one from the egg factor, Fiona Lewis?'

Martha shook her head sadly, shrugged, and grabbed the toast that Billy had just thinly covered with spread. 'I'm going back to bed as well,' she mumbled and returned to her sister, munching on the toast.

Billy had hoped that the conversation was over, but Louise was not yet to be silenced. She had been hatching plans whilst Billy was teasing their daughter. 'What if we sold the meal vouchers? They must be worth about fifty pounds. And then there's no need for us to pay for the do. I mean, no one's going to realise if we don't pay. And you could always under-estimate the number of people there. If, say, there's forty people, you collect forty lots of twelve pounds fifty and then say that you only sold thirty tickets. If anyone queries it, say that some people turned up without paying but you'd rather not say who. Sort of play the injured party. We should still be able to have a good night out and make ourselves about a hundred pounds.'

Billy was worried that this could lead to a full-scale row, a row he knew he would lose. He explained.

'It's not that easy, my sweet. I can't sell the vouchers because they're in my name and non-transferable. As for the tickets, Dave collects all the money for this sort of thing.'

'OK, OK. But just make sure that the evening costs us nothing. Absolutely nothing. Understand? And try to think of a way that we can come out of this with a profit, will you? Useless, you are useless.' And Louise flounced out of the kitchen, up the stairs and into the bathroom.

'I understand that you have the big one this morning, Dave,' Muzzy smiled as he handed over the change from Dave's ten pound note. 'Vivian was in earlier and tells me that you only have to gain a winning game to achieve promotion to the Premiership. You must be one nervous manager.'

Dave really did not feel nervous that morning. He felt eager, elated and excited, but nervousness was not the overriding emotion. He was confident that his team could win against the New Inn and it would take an accident of serious proportions to stop the Poachers Arms Football Club, managed by David J Statham, from being promoted to the Downham Sunday League, Division One. Not quite the Premiership, but a distinguished achievement nonetheless.

'That's right, Muzzy, a win against a team we beat seven–nil earlier this season. And they only scraped a draw last week against mediocre opposition, although that makes no difference to today. If they'd have won, we would still have finished above them if we win today because of our better goal difference, even though we'd be level on points. So that made no difference except that their confidence will be knocked.'

Muzzy looked bemused as the intricacies of points and goal difference in football had always evaded him. He changed the subject. 'I also understand that you are having a ding-dong at the Post House in two weeks to celebrate your success and that I am invited.'

'Correct, Muzzy,' Dave confirmed. 'You are indeed invited to attend this extravaganza. Only twelve pounds fifty each and a special room rate of just thirty pounds for a double.'

'Thank you, thank you, David. I shall attend the celebration with my dear wife, but I will reject your kind offer of a room. I have to be up at five o'clock to receive the newspapers, so it is better I am home. I shall look forward to my first ever promotion dinner-dance.'

Dave bade Muzzy farewell, tucked the *Sunday Times* under his arm and jauntily strode across the road to home and breakfast. He looked across at the Poachers Arms and smiled to himself at the memory of all his young team members sitting quietly in the bar the previous evening sipping shandy and preparing for an early night. 'This is a big one,' he told them. 'If you want to test yourself against the best, this is your chance. Don't bugger it up. Just a couple of beers and then home for an early night. Be ready for tomorrow.' The lads had all nodded and agreed that they would have just one more before taking his advice and going home early.

As he entered the hallway, he saw the large figures of Barry and Viv sitting at the kitchen table, places set before them. Barry was pointing his fork at Viv and explaining his position on religion and marriage. 'It's not that I don't want to marry the woman. It's just that she'll want it in a church and I'm afraid that I cannot go through the charade of a religious ceremony. I mean, if there was a god – which there isn't, Viv, there isn't – then how could he allow the suffering and injustices that happen in this world? And what about the several billions of years of the world before man, how do you explain that then? You see, it's not the marriage as such I don't want, it's the church and all that nonsense.'

'What the bloody hell are you two doing here?' Dave asked with good-humoured indignation. 'Just come round for a good fry-up, I suppose.'

'Not at all, dear boy, not at all,' Barry replied. 'I am here to help you with anything that you may require to ensure that we leave no stone unturned in this morning's preparations. M'colleague Vivian is also here for the same reason.'

'That's right.' Viv entered into the discussion. 'I am also here to make sure we leave no turn unstoned and to help you through this most auspicious of mornings. And if there's some of that eggs and bacon going, I'll help you out with that as well.'

Tonker joined them and Mandy busied herself at the hob, wondering how four grown men could get so excited about twenty-two footballers kicking a bag of wind. Four large fry-ups were soon presented to the waiting diners and the carefree repartee barely disguised their anxiety. There was a loud knocking on the front door which the men conveniently pretended not to hear. Mandy stared at each of them in turn before accepting the inevitable and going to answer the door for the third time that morning. She had barely opened the door when a flustered Paul pushed his way in, his face red and sweating and his eyes bulging above dark bags. He looked as if he had been badly made up for an amateur dramatics presentation of Frankenstein.

'They're all inside. All of them. Inside. Give us a fag, Tonker. They're all in-bloody-side.'

'Who is? Inside where?' Dave asked, unable to fathom what Paul was rambling about.

Paul took a deep drag from the roll-up offered to him by Tonker and stared at the assembled group. He composed himself. 'Our Matt, Stevie, Wayne Tocks, young Tommo, Jock Dunbar. All locked up. In the nick. Bloody idiots. Scrapping. Inside. All of 'em.'

Everyone stared open-mouthed at Paul, waiting for the punchline. It didn't come. Instead, he stood there, drawing deeply on his roll-up and his head shaking slowly. Dave looked at Barry; Barry looked at Viv; Viv looked at Tonker. They all looked at Paul and began to talk at once.

'What d'you mean, inside? Who's been scrapping with who? When did it happen? How long for? When are they coming out?' Dave felt his hands involuntarily and uncontrollably begin to shake.

Paul regained his composure and spoke slowly and clearly. 'I had a phone call in the night. Don't know what time. Four, five o'clock perhaps. From the police station. Said that our Matt had been locked up for scrapping and I had to go up there. So up I goes, praying they wouldn't breathalyse me 'cos I'd had a few. When I gets there, I sees Tommo, Steve's dad and a big black bloke who turns out to be Jock's old man. So there's not just our Matty, but the other lads as well. All locked up. Apparently they was in the Blue Parrot last night and a punch-up starts. Steve Tippling whacked some bloke because he called Jock a black bastard and all hell lets loose. This bloke had a bunch of mates who starts on Steve. 'Course all the boys joins in and knocks seven colours of shit out of them, then the law turns up and nicks them all. Bloody state they're in and all. Blood everywhere…'

'But I told them last night. I told them all to go home and get an early night. They said they would. They all said they would,' Dave exclaimed, his voice rising an octave.

'Well they didn't. They went up town, clubbing. And now they're locked up in the police station. The sergeant says he's not sure what's going to happen. Sometimes they have a special court on a Sunday to deal with things if Saturdays nights have been rough, but he says that even if they can't convene a hearing, he wouldn't think they'll be out much before this afternoon.'

No one knew what to say. Paul was so obviously upset that it looked as if he might burst into tears at any moment and none of the men wanted that to happen. Finally, Mandy took control, passed Paul a cup of tea and said, 'We're really sorry, Paul. You must be devastated with your lad in trouble like that. If there's anything we can do, anything at all, you only have to ask.'

Paul looked down at her with tears beginning to form in the corners of his eyes. 'Thanks, Mandy,' he said softly. 'You are a good girl.'

'What are you going to do now, Paul? What do you want us to do?' she asked gently.

'Well,' Paul began, 'I can play right back in place of Steve. Billy'll have to play at number 3, bad leg or not, and Percy's OK to play in midfield. Dave, I reckon you'll have to play this morning as well.'

'Unless Barry plays in goal and George comes out on the field,' suggested Viv.

'No, keep George in goal. I'll just be sub,' said Barry, satisfied that his heroics earlier in the season would be a fitting end to his career.

Dave summarized. 'Right. Billy, Paul, Percy and me will play. Barry sub. We'll sort out the final positions when we get to the rec. OK?'

Paul's face took on a look of steely determination and he smiled. 'Thank Christ that's that sorted then. I'll just get off and get my kit and see you there.'

Mandy shook her head in total disbelief.

The players were gathered in changing room number three at Tenacre Recreation Ground. Just the odd coat hook remained. The team had finally managed to get changed after some confusion over shirts and waited, heads lowered, as Dave explained the situation and offered words of encouragement to his beleaguered squad. 'We'll play four-four-two today. After all, we can't afford to be too cavalier and we can't afford to concede. With only two up front today – that's you, Gordon, on the right wing and Razor in the middle – we'll all have to move up to support the front line so, Magic, you've got to work your bollocks off on the left wing, supporting the defence and midfield and then getting up to give Gordon and Razor a hand. Viv's going to have to work like buggery to help me and Paul out. The rest of you know what's needed, and heads up, lads, it's not as bad as it looks. We got a good mix of youth and experience and we can win this one. Remember, if we win, it's promotion. That simple. Oh, and don't get injured. We've only got Barry as sub.'

Barry stood up to address the team. 'I shall take over as manager, trainer and linesman for the duration of the match,' he announced. 'And I would pray except that, as we all know, God is simply a figment of the imagination of the poor, the ignorant, the gullible. I will tell you now that—'

'Firm but fair,' shouted the whole assembly, drowning Barry's sermon.

The team left the changing rooms to take up their positions on the field, leaving Barry to carry the bags and bottles as part of his newly assumed position of responsibility. He panted across the recreation ground towards pitch number three with a strong sense of foreboding, stopping only to make a call on his mobile. This was the most important game that Poachers had played in years, and half the team were in police cells, nursing their bruises and headaches from the excesses of the previous night. To add insult to injury, a big crowd had turned up to watch the Poachers' glorious drive for promotion; a drive which looked like it was about to stall quickly and ignominiously. An old man with a scraggy dog, pleased that Barry seemed otherwise engaged with his bags, bottles and boxes, took up a position behind one goal. Tonker and Tommy were in position behind the other goal, their bicycles unceremoniously and untidily abandoned next to them. The council house kids and a scruffy couple in stained, quilted anoraks were joined by various other small groups of supporters in twos and threes, plus a large contingent who had hired a bus from Gorton Down for the occasion. After a quick check, Barry reckoned that there were close to a hundred people watching. In the far corner was the lonely figure of Gunner Farr.

The sky was a pale blue and the daylight bright as Rabbit looked around at the Poachers team. Billy arrived in the centre circle for the toss-up and awaited the arrival of the New Inn captain. 'Motley crew you've got out today, Billy. I hear on the grapevine that half of your blokes are in the nick,' Rabbit said as Billy rubbed his hands in nervous anticipation.

'Bloody yobs, Rabbit. Bloody yobs. Caught scrapping in town apparently. We're struggling a bit today. Even got Statham and Cornwell playing, today of all days. Need to win to get promotion today, Rabbit, so any help would be very much appreciated.'

'Come on, Billy, you know better than that. You'll get no favours from me,' Rabbit stated as the New Inn skipper lumbered to the halfway line and held out a hand that looked like a large pink ham.

'Morning, skipper. Motley-looking crew you've got out today. That's your manager stripped off ready for action, isn't it? You look more like a geriatric eleven.' Billy smiled ungraciously, but could think of no riposte. The Poachers' eleven did indeed look geriatric.

Having lost the toss, Poachers were about to kick off when Dave was aware that his tactical plans were somewhat awry. Unused to a four-four-two line-up, his players were assembled somewhat randomly around the pitch and Razor stood with the ball at his feet with no one to pass to. Gordon had assumed his position on the right wing as ordered and there was no other player forward. Rabbit blasted his whistle to signal the kick-off and Razor stood bemused and alone. Dave looked around him at the players lining up as instructed, and decided that there was nothing for it but to take up a forward position himself to accept the first pass from Razor. As he trundled forward, one of the Gorton Down charabanc members hollered, 'Come on, Grandad,' which soon developed into an orchestrated rendition of the Clive Dunn song 'Grandad, granddad, we love you' accompanied by boisterous laughter. A red-faced Dave reached Razor, who gratefully eased his embarrassment by pushing the ball a couple of feet forward and to his left, where Dave trapped it carefully before realizing that he had no idea what to do next. In a state of some panic, he tried to hit an ambitious ball out to Gordon on the right but succeeded only in scuffing the ball a few yards to a surprised New Inn forward. This led to an all-out onslaught on the Poachers' goal, a position which was relieved only by a huge boot upfield by Big Smithy. Dave had just made his way back to assist the defence when he found himself being urged to run back in the direction of the opposition half. Billy called for the defence to move out and, as the defence by this time consisted of everyone but Razor, the whole team moved forward. Except Dave, who was exhausted.

As the Poachers' team, urged on by Billy, attacked the New Inn half, the ball was pumped back again and, much to his surprise, landed once again at Dave's feet. Again, panic set in as he took a mighty swing at the ball, succeeding only in slicing it out of play for a New Inn throw in. He bent with his hands on his knees gasping for breath. Billy ran up to him and patted his back. 'You OK, Dave?' he asked, keeping one eye on the ball and one on Dave. Dave stood up straight, gulped in air and gasped, 'Just getting my second wind. I'll be OK in a minute.' For the next quarter of an hour, Dave spent much time and energy running between attack and defence but, thankfully, never had need to touch the ball again.

Percy was struggling at right back, having not played for some weeks and having consumed several pints of cider, twenty cigarettes and a lamb vindaloo the previous evening. This fact had slowly dawned on the New Inn team and they began to direct the play towards their left wing to put Percy under increasing pressure. Paul was playing at half back in front of Percy and he, too, was a little ring rusty, having not played a competitive match for two or three years, and the play was concentrated on the weak Poachers' right. Dave decided to stay on the left.

Surprisingly, however, Dave's tactics seemed to be paying off. The defensive line-up was restricting the New Inn to few scoring opportunities, crosses from the vulnerable right were being intercepted and cleared by the Smith brothers, and the midfield was working hard in supporting the defence. The New Inn was a steady and workmanlike rather than a creative force, and lacked the guile to break down the Poachers' spirited defending. The play had become so predictable that even Percy and Paul had adjusted to the positioning and pace of the game and began to take control of their particular patch. It was a reflection of the stalemate that the first half ended with no goals and with neither goalkeeper called upon to make a serious save.

There was an air of optimism as the team decamped at half-time. The players were spread around, gulping water and congratulating each other on a hard fought and uncompromising half with no goals conceded. Billy was pleased with the performance but felt uneasy. His plans for a free evening at a four-star hotel with the possibility of making a little extra depended on the team's end of season celebration and it had been taken as read for the last few weeks that promotion would be gained, giving good cause for the festivities. If promotion was not achieved, he was concerned that the impetus may be lost and, if enthusiasm waned, the party may not go ahead. No one had yet paid any cash over, so there was no obligation. There was also no encouragement or ideas forthcoming on how to break the deadlock and a draw was no good: the Poachers Arms needed to win.

Dave, Paul and Barry were standing happily in a little group at the edge of the encampment, all breathing heavily from their exertions, especially Paul who was drawing deeply on a cigarette. They were happy with the fact that they had not conceded a goal and that the action was going to plan. Billy approached them.

'We've got to do better this half,' he blurted out. 'We're getting nowhere in attack and we need to win. We can absorb the pressure all day, but we don't look like scoring.'

The senior commanders were suddenly brought down to earth. Billy was right and their feeling of satisfaction with the morning's travails rapidly vanished as they realised that, to win the game, they would have to do more than defend. They would have to take chances in attack. It would have to be, as Paul eloquently described the situation, 'shit or bust.' But none of the three seemed to be able to rise above their personal input to the game and suggest a course of action. Billy realised that he had to take command if his plans were to bear fruit. He decided to take positive action.

'Right, this is what I think we should do. Dave, you're doing no good in midfield so go up front and just create a diversion to give Razor more space. Get Magic to push forward a bit more. I can sort out their right wing easy, especially as they're pumping the ball out to the left all the time. Paul, if you go back to partner Big Smithy in the middle of the back four and push young Smithy into midfield where he can be more effective. Gordon's hardly had a kick first half so get the ball out to him or Magic and get some high balls over for Razor. And we must stop this attitude that stopping them scoring is OK. It isn't. We want to win.'

'Sounds good to me,' Paul agreed. 'Go and sort it out, Dave. I'm finishing this fag.'

Dave was a little confused and tried to relay the plan to the team but gave up after confusing his right and left and called on Billy to explain. The team took the field for the second half with a new formation and a renewed determination to win. The plan looked good. Good, that is, until the New Inn attacked Percy who was now unprotected and allowed the New Inn winger past him to cut in and score with a superbly placed, if somewhat speculative, drive from twenty-five yards. It was the sort of shot that George would normally stop with ease, and he may well have stopped this one with ease if he had not been answering his mobile phone.

As the New Inn players congregated in a rather untidy and unsavoury heap to celebrate the goal, George ran to Dave.

'Got to go, Dave, sorry,' he said. 'Whole system's gone down. Database is fucked by the sound of it. Sorry, mate. Got to go.' Without further ado, he sprinted for the changing rooms, leaving the Poachers with ten men and a deficit of one goal. Rabbit blew his whistle and trotted over to Barry who had assumed control for the morning. After listening to Rabbit, Barry called Billy over to him. They were joined by Dave, who was looking for inspiration on what to do next.

'Did one of your players just leave the field of play without permission?' Rabbit asked rhetorically. 'Well I'm going to caution him,' and Rabbit raised his yellow card to George who was sprinting towards the changing room a hundred yards away. 'Anyway, let's get this game underway again, shall we?' he stuttered.

'Can't for a minute, Rabbit.' Dave also looked confused. 'Only we haven't got a goalie. Are we allowed to play without a goalie?'

'No, come to think of it, you're not,' said Rabbit scratching his head with his whistle. 'You'd better get one quick.'

Dave and Billy looked around, panic beginning to take over.

'I'll do it. I'm still signed on, aren't I?' Gunner Farr quietly approached the group. 'I've got my kit here. Only be five minutes.'

'We haven't got five minutes,' said Rabbit. 'What you'll have to do is play with ten men but put one of them in goal until laddo here is ready, then bring him on and change goalkeepers. Come on then, lads, let's get on with it.'

Viv, understandably, volunteered to be the temporary goalkeeper and Poachers packed the defence, hoping to hold out until Gunner could take over. The New Inn became so eager to increase their lead that they lost all discipline and simply whacked the ball goalward at every opportunity. Balls rained down on the goal but none were accurate enough to cause Viv any problems. Poachers needed to score at least two goals and a brave rearguard was of no use. After withstanding the barrage, Dave took the opportunity to call the team together as Gunner arrived, fully kitted, to replace Viv in goal. It was agreed that the formation should be changed again to the old-fashioned four-three-three and that all-out attack should be executed to enable the Poachers to snatch a glorious victory. The flaw was that no one had told the New Inn about the new plan and, encouraged by their noisy band of supporters, they too were attacking in droves. The game seesawed from one end to the other, with desperate attacks being repelled by even more desperate defending. Rabbit was exhausted, sprinting from one goalmouth to the other with no let-up, the game being played with such enthusiasm that the occasional free kicks and throw-ins were taken immediately, Rabbit barely having time to blow his whistle. During one particularly intense New Inn attack, nineteen of the assembled throng was packed into the Poachers' penalty area, the ball ricocheting around like a pinball, before a frantic but hefty boot from Big Smithy lofted the ball out to the halfway line. A lonely Majid, who had obeyed his instructions to stay on the wing and attack, picked the ball up and skipped around a lumbering challenge from the only defender. He raced forward, his skinny legs a blur and, as the goalkeeper sprinted towards him, cracked the ball from twenty yards into the net. He turned and looked around him, wary of celebrating in case the effort had been disallowed for some reason, and appearing embarrassed before a great cheer arose as he was swamped by his team mates.

The goal led to a change in momentum whereby the play moved almost solely to the New Inn half as the defenders became acutely aware that one more goal would end their dream of promotion. Balls now rained down on their goal as

Gordon and Majid were given almost free rein on the wings and all clearances were played straight back again by the commanding Poachers' defenders. Razor climbed magnificently to meet one cross and his following header smacked the crossbar, which quivered under its power. Viv let fly from the edge of the area, the ball crashing against the post with the goalkeeper beaten. Successive corners were delivered into the penalty area to be scrambled away, shots were whistling past the post, being cleared off the line and being tipped, caught and punched away by an inspired goalkeeper. Throughout the siege, Dave had fulfilled his responsibilities to the full, running around the penalty area, causing confusion in the defending ranks, without once touching the ball. Until five minutes from the end.

A New Inn defender managed a clear kick away from goal and immediately called his colleagues out to follow the clearance and relieve pressure. The players sprinted back into no man's land where the ball was rolling gently towards Gunner's penalty area. Gunner had spent his time since coming on waiting on the edge of the area, doing little but shout encouragement, but now he was called into action. As the ball approached him, followed closely by a hoard of thundering attackers, he thumped the ball high and hard back towards the opponents' goal. As it sailed over the heads of almost everyone, they turned to see it land at the feet of Dave, alone in the New Inn half. Ignoring cries for offside, he hoofed the ball towards the goal and set off in pursuit. The ball landed on the edge of the New Inn penalty area as Dave arrived with defenders in hot pursuit and the Poachers' team moving slowly forward and screaming at Dave to shoot. He looked up and saw the goalkeeper coming out to meet him and heard the rumble of players behind him. He remembered to take his time. He remembered to stay cool. He remembered not to panic as he placed his left foot alongside the ball and began to swing his right leg, imagining the ball sailing majestically into the goal to win the game and promotion. What he had not remembered, however, was that he was an unfit forty-year-old who hadn't kicked a ball in anger for years and was knackered after spending the last eighty-five minutes running his heart out. The ball was neatly teed up and his leg swung strongly enough but, unfortunately, the point of impact of his boot was some way distant from the position of the ball. The impetus of the kick caused him to end up in an inelegant heap whilst the ball bobbled softly into the hands of the goalkeeper, much to the delight of the visiting fans. There were to be no more chances for either team as they succumbed to the inevitable draw.

The mood in the pub was sombre. Players stood in small groups chatting and shaking their heads or stood alone staring into space, clutching their pint glasses as comforters. Dave was obviously embarrassed although most people were kind enough not to say anything. He knew that, as it was the last game of the season, he should say something, but what could he say? 'Sorry, lads, we'd have got promotion if I hadn't fucked it up' did not seem appropriate.

A murmur rose in the pub, becoming louder as the inmates looked out of the window and saw five embarrassed young men climbing out of a large Kia driven by an equally large black man. Jamie Dunbar's father had been called to pick up the prisoners from the police station whilst the game was being played. As the youngsters entered the pub, they were swamped by their team mates as they swapped stories of the morning's happenings. With Barry and Paul, Dave sat quietly in the corner and was reminded of a wildlife documentary where African wild dogs return to their den after a hunting trip and are greeted by the rest of the pack. He just hoped that the men didn't start sniffing each other's arses. He was also very grateful that the intrusion had taken the attention away from him.

One by one, the young men broke away from the group and moved across to stand at the table in front of Dave, Barry and Paul, until all five stood before him.

Jamie coughed and looked at the floor as he spoke. 'Dave. We're very sorry about last night. We're sorry that we let you down, and, um…'

'We promise that we won't ever let you down again,' whispered Daniel in his ear.

'And we promise that we won't let you down again,' repeated Jamie.

'And we're really sorry about the game this morning,' added Steve. 'We know just how much promotion meant to you and that, but we'll all play next year, if you want us, and we promise we'll win you promotion. Honest.'

Dave looked at the self-conscious young men standing in front of him, heads down and genuinely remorseful. The rest of the pub looked on silently waiting for Dave's response and even the cribbage school had stopped.

He considered standing to deliver his speech, but decided to stay seated. 'Thanks, lads,' he began. 'You're right; I was upset about missing out on promotion. I've dreamt about this moment for years. I worked so hard this season and really, really felt that this was our year. I believed we'd get promotion.'

'Why the fuck did you fuck up that fuckin' shot then,' mumbled Tommy, but no one heard. The miscreants shuffled in self-conscious silence.

Dave looked at each one in turn. He continued. 'But then I thought, do we really want to play teams like the Boar's Head every week and get hammered or are we happier in the second division, and I thought we're better off where we are for one more season, so all's well that ends well, boys. Mind you, you can get me a pint. I'm too bloody stiff to get up.'

'Make it five fuckin' pints,' Tommy added.

The lads returned with the beer and Jamie sat down with the old men and explained what had happened that morning. 'We was in the cells, really worried about ever seeing daylight again, when this sergeant, grumpy bastard, lets us all out, returns our stuff and tells us to piss off. Said we was being released with a police caution. Said something about being lucky to have friends in high places.'

Barry sipped his pint quietly and said nothing.

Billy had returned home straight after the game, partly because he could not wait to tell the gossip to Louise and partly because she had instructed him to do so. She opened the door and said, 'Disco,' as he stood in the porch. 'Who's doing the disco at the do?'

'Not finalized it yet. Probably ask DJ.' Dave replied without thinking. DJ was the son of Louise's brother and his name was Daniel James, always called DJ. He was twenty-one years old and scraped a living running a mobile disco, trundling round in old Ford Transit badly painted in black with an equally badly painted sign in red and yellow saying "DeeJayDeeJay's Mobile Disco" on the side.

'Exactly,' said Louise. 'And how much does he charge?'

'For me, he'll do it for a few pints.'

'Exactly. And how much will you tell them he charges?'

The light flickered in Billy's brain. He smiled. 'Well done, my sweet,' he grinned. 'Fifty pounds seems fair to me.'

'Exactly. Now get down that pub and sort it out,' and the door slammed in his face.

Billy was surprised to see the pub in such a jolly state. The uncomfortable and sullen mood he had left in the changing room had magically changed to one of laughter and merriment. The young jailbirds were in high spirits as they exaggerated the previous evening's brawl, each one embellishing his own part in the affray; the other team members were laughing about Dave's brave attempt to score and joking that he had missed deliberately because he didn't want promotion; Barry had ambushed some unfortunate strangers who had called in the pub on their way back from church and was pointing out how science had disproved the existence of God many times over; Dave was happily chatting to Paul and laughing about the morning's game; and Viv was telling anyone who would listen that 'Dave always was a brilliant player off the ball, just fucking useless on it'. Billy sidled over to Dave's table, hoping to be included in the next round.

'Sorry to bring this up now, Dave,' said Billy, keeping one ear open for anyone going to the bar, 'but we need to re-cost the do. Only we haven't thought about the disco. You see, it's going to cost at least fifty for a disco and we need to add that cost in, so that'll make it another couple of quid each, so instead of twenty-five per couple, it'll be about twenty-eight. Is that OK?'

Dave was still giggling at Viv's telling of his new joke. 'No problem, Billy,' he laughed. 'Why not round it up to thirty per couple and anything over we can put to club funds.'

Billy accepted a pint from Paul before leaving the pub a very satisfied man.

Twenty

Downham Sunday Football League, Division Two
Results for Sunday 15th March

Poachers Arms	**1**	**1**	**New Inn, Gorton Down**
AFC Cummiston	0	3	Lower End WMC
Jones Juniors FC	4	0	Pickled Herring
J G Tanner and Sons	1	2	Hearty Oak, Downlea
Shellduck Inn	3	5	Downham Churches

League Table

Team	Pl'd	Won	Drew	Lost	For	Ag'st	GD	Points
Jones Juniors FC	18	13	5	0	66	17	49	44
New Inn, Gorton D	18	9	7	2	46	38	8	34
Poachers Arms	**18**	**9**	**6**	**3**	**54**	**23**	**31**	**33**
Lower End WMC	18	9	3	6	48	32	16	30
J G Tanner and Sons	18	8	3	7	37	42	-5	27
Pickled Herring	18	8	2	8	37	38	-1	26
AFC Cummiston	18	4	7	7	40	48	-8	19
Hearty Oak, Downlea	18	4	3	11	40	62	-22	15
Shellduck Inn	18	4	2	12	34	55	-21	14
Downham Churches	18	3	3	12	41	88	-47	12

The Poachers Arms Football Club
Annual Dinner Dance

The Post House, Marlborough Drive, Downham
Saturday, 29th March

Dancing to DeeJayDeeJay Disco

From 7.30 pm to 01.30 am
(buffet at 9.30 pm)

Price: £15.00 each

Special offer: Double Room with breakfast: Just £30.00

Gentlemen: Dinner jackets or lounge suits please

Please see Dave Statham or Billy Millmore for tickets

or ask behind the bar

Dave Statham, Secretary

Before she had gone to town shopping, Mandy had left Dave a list of household tasks to complete: empty the dishwasher, clean the oven, tidy the kitchen. But he still mooched around in a languid state of slothfulness, inventing reasons why the duties could not be fulfilled. The time slowly moved on until the hands on the kitchen clock pointed in parallel towards the ceiling. Dave opened the garage door and called out to Tonker, who was sitting on the settee, partly hidden by a fog of blue/white smoke, watching a loud American cartoon.

'Coming over the road for one, Dad?' Dave craved company, even Tonker's.

'No thanks, David. Tommy and the boys are coming round later for a game of crib,' replied Tonker before taking another drag from his roll-up. 'It saves us a small fortune. Tommy's missis gets the beer from Safeway's at half the price in the pub. And we can have a smoke.'

Dave shrugged, and ambled across the road into the pub. As he walked in from the cold, damp street, the smell of the pub surrounded him. It always reminded him of a wet dog, a kind of stale, musty tang, a combination of stale beer, urine and disinfectant. The bar was empty apart from Paul, who was sitting at the bar, studying the *Racing Post*. Mandy was behind the bar, having completed her shopping, and greeted Dave with a huge smile. The drab, dull, boring day was immediately brighter and Dave wanted to leap across the bar and hold his mistress tightly and smother her in kisses. The two lovers stood and grinned at each other like lovesick teenagers.

'I'll have another pint while you're doing nothing,' said Paul and pushed his glass towards Mandy. 'And get Romeo one before he falls over.'

Dave pulled up a stool and sat next to his cohort. 'Thanks, Paul,' he said. 'Ready for tonight?'

'Certainly am, Dave. Missis got a new frock. Under strict orders to be home by three at the latest today to give me time for a long kip this afternoon. Then a shave, shower, shampoo and shit, and I'll be ready to go.'

'Don't be so disgusting, Paul.' Mandy passed two pint glasses across the bar. 'I've got a new dress as well. Sale in Debenham's. It's long, sleeveless and back-less, in navy with sort of glitter on the top. You'll love it, Dave, you really will.'

There was silence for a moment.

'I'll probably just do a Yankee today. Got three horses picked out; just can't sort out the fourth,' said Paul, tapping the *Sporting Life* with his pen. They sat and drank quietly for a moment, the peace broken by the crashing of the double doors opening as Viv danced in singing, '*Dancing Queen, only seventeen, da da da deen*'. He put a huge arm around the shoulders of the two drinkers and gripped them tightly, continuing to sing, '*You can dance, you can jive, having the time of your life, shag the dancing queen.*'

'Fuck off, you mad bastard, you made me spill some beer,' grumbled Paul, wiping the bar with the sleeve of his pullover.

As Mandy passed him a pint, Viv said, 'I understand that you girls have been talking then, Armadillo, and have a nice little surprise for us gentlemen, is that right?'

'What's that then? Nobody's told me anything.' Dave looked confused.

'Well, my little amigo. When they were in town this morning, our ladies decided that we are going to the hotel early. Make use of the pool and jacuzzi and stuff before the do. We're off at two-thirty apparently.'

Dave looked at Viv then at Mandy. 'Is that right, Mand?' he asked.

'Well, Elaine and me were talking in town and she said that she thought the rooms are available from three, so she phoned up and they are, so it seemed a shame to waste them so we thought we might go for the afternoon and get ready for the do there. If that's OK with you, Dave, I'm sure we'll find something to do for the afternoon,' she said.

Dave felt himself reddening as an afternoon in a double hotel room with the light of his life and without Tonker coughing and spluttering in the next room, sounded very appealing. 'Yes, yes. Sounds OK to me. I've got a few things to finalise with the hotel. Arrangements for the buffet and so on. Yes, good idea,' Dave said, trying unsuccessfully to sound cool.

With overnight bags waiting on the drive, the two couples felt in holiday mood. Dave opened the boot of the Polo and placed his case neatly inside and made a move towards Viv and Elaine's case. Viv, still singing 'Dancing Queen', quickly grabbed the handle. 'That's OK, Dave. I'll do that,' he said and swung the heavy case into the boot, where it landed with a loud metallic rattle.

The four set off, excited and happy except for Viv's singing, '*Sat'dy night and the lights are low. Looking for a place to go, da da da da dumdy do... dancing queen...*'

The afternoon was spent in a state of relaxation and absolute bliss. Dave and Mandy made love, had a swim, made love, sat in the jacuzzi, would have made love again except that the football results were on the television, and took a long bath together before getting dressed in readiness for the evening's revelry. Dave had hired a dinner jacket and, with dress shirt, bow tie and shiny patent leather shoes, looked like a shorter, fatter version of Fred Astaire, except that he couldn't dance. He admired himself in the full-length mirror several times before turning to Mandy. 'It's no wonder you couldn't resist me this afternoon,' he stated. 'Am I not the dog's whatsnames in this whistle?'

'Bollocks,' said Mandy, shocking Dave with her language. 'The words you are looking for are the dog's bollocks. And you certainly are, David Statham.'

Dave was embarrassed. 'You look lovely too,' he blurted out.

'David, I am sitting in my underwear, putting on my make-up and trying hard to disguise that fact that I am several months' pregnant. I do not look lovely.'

'You're always lovely to me. And always will be.' Dave left the room quickly before his blushes showed. As he trotted happily from the lift to the function room to check the final arrangements, he glanced into the hotel dining room. In the far corner, partly hidden behind a screen, he glimpsed familiar faces: Billy and Louise attacking huge steak dinners, just a few hours before the buffet. Something was amiss and Dave was trying to work out what as he veered round and made for reception ensuring that he was not seen by his team mate. The receptionist was a very pretty girl who, he guessed, made up for in beauty what she lacked in brains.

Dave's logical mind was in overdrive. 'Hello, Miss,' he opened. 'I'm David Statham and I'm in charge of the function in your ballroom this evening. My colleague, Mr Millmore, is in the dining room with his wife and I don't want to disturb him now, so could you let me have his room number, please?'

The receptionist stared at her computer screen and replied, 'I'm afraid that I can't do that, sir. I can put you through to his number.'

'But you see, he's not there at the moment, he's in the dining room and I just want to know his number for later because we still have things to arrange for this evening.'

The receptionist shrugged. 'Well, I suppose that'll be alright. Mr Millmore is in an executive suite, number 311.'

'Thank you,' said Dave, fishing for more information. 'I remember now that he said he'd pay extra for an executive suite.'

'Oh, no,' replied the receptionist. 'He's got a complimentary room because he booked the function this evening. I was here when he booked it. Him and the manager had quite a row about it at first, until he said he would cancel the do and not use the hotel for business any more neither. And he's got vouchers for a free dinner as well. Including a bottle of house wine.'

'Yes, I know.' Dave lied. 'And his drinks are free this evening too, aren't they?'

The receptionist referred to her screen again. 'Oh, no. After the meal and the room, he has to pay for everything else just like anyone else. Mind you, he's doing alright as it is, I reckon.'

Dave grinned. 'He certainly is, Miss, he certainly is,' and he skipped happily off to the ballroom.

Dave and Mandy knocked on Viv's door and were shown into their room, a mirror image of their own. Dave explained what he had found out and there was a general feeling of anger mixed with inevitability. 'The tight sod had to be getting something out of it, I just couldn't think what,' Viv opined angrily. 'I've got a good mind to, to…'

'Just leave it, Viv,' advised Dave. 'After all, he's not done anything illegal and it doesn't really affect us. Let's just enjoy the evening and forget it. I certainly will. In fact, I have now wiped it from my mental databanks.'

His companions agreed and they left the room and called the lift to descend to the ground floor. They strolled into the function room, each couple arm in arm, and were captivated by the room. Dave had only seen it in daylight, but now the main lights were dimmed, and there was a glow from candles on each table as the early birds sat around chatting and drinking. That is, the ladies were sitting around chatting at the tables and their men were standing at the brightly lit bar, swilling back pints and sharing crude jokes or discussing the day's football results. There was a brighter light at one table tucked away in a corner. Dave's eyes slowly focused to see that it was Tonker and the crib school, concentrating on adding their cards up in fifteens, pairs and runs. Dave nudged Viv and pointed to the crib table.

'Daft old buggers think that they've found a nice quiet spot to play crib,' he explained. 'What they don't know is that they're sitting right next to a bloody big speaker, so when the disco starts blasting away…' In a few minutes, the disco started blasting away, the signal for the crib players to adjourn to the hotel lounge.

'Don't forget to call us when the grub's ready,' were Tonker's last instructions to his son as they left the room, partially deaf.

The evening's entertainment proceeded predictably, with the disco banging away and being largely ignored. The ladies were sitting and talking and the men drinking at the bar. Dave's table was enhanced by the presence of Barry and his ladyfriend. Monica did not want to be there and only attended under duress and with the promise, albeit dubious, that Barry would attend church the following summer to prepare for their future life together. However, she found herself warming to both Mandy and Elaine as the evening, and the gin and tonics, wore on. The ladies were surprised to see Paul and his wife, Christine, joined by Linda and her son Lightning, although they were careful to call him Andrew. As the girls sat and gossiped, Lightning was sipping a lemonade, his eyes bulging and looking at both sides of the room at the same time, mesmerized by his first ever adult party. Paul was running around like a mother hen, ensuring that the table was continually replenished with drinks and worrying about the course of the conversation between the ladies. After their blowout dinner, Billy and Louise had ensconced themselves near the buffet table, in the company of some of the young bucks, and were accepting drinks from all and sundry whilst carefully avoiding the need to buy a round.

At nine o'clock, the disco stopped, the house lights were raised and DeeJayDeeJay called for Viv to present his speech and the season's trophies. This was Viv's moment of glory. He knew that he had a captive audience who had drunk enough to laugh at anything, and he had spent hours on his speech. That said, he was still nervous as he leapt up onto the small stage. Temporarily blinded by the lights, he panicked as he felt for his speech in the wrong pocket and he almost wished that he had not accepted the role, but he then found the papers, his sight adjusted to the light and he was away. A brief summary of the season's achievements, interspersed with some bad jokes, was skated over as the assembled throng awaited the presentation of the trophies. Viv put on his best Gary Lineker voice, adopting a bad Leicester accent and wearing false ears.

'The first presentation is for the top goal scorer, our own golden boot award, which goes to Daniel Razor Raisin with fifteen goals.' Razor sheepishly climbed onto the stage and took the miniature golden boot trophy and refused the offer to say a few words before returning to his seat.

Viv was beginning to enjoy himself. 'And the next presentation is for the player of the year. There were many nominations for this prestigious award but after some consideration and many late night discussions in the Poachers, the committee has decided that the award goes to' – Viv paused for effect – 'me.' The crowd booed and banged their glasses in mock anger although no one would have objected if Viv had been awarded the trophy.

He scrutinized his speech more closely and held up his hand.

'Sorry, ladies and gentlemen. I misread the winner. In fact it is' – another pause – 'our own flying winger, Gordon Gaye.'

Gordon grinned widely as he accepted the tiny plastic statuette of a footballer, and was about to take the microphone to offer thanks, but Viv was now on a roll and wasn't going to give up the mike easily, so Gordon shrugged and returned to his place at the bar.

'And now, ladies and gentlemen, two very special awards. The first goes to someone who has been a member of the club for over twenty years and, this year, came to the rescue of the club when he was needed, at great expense to his health and his underpants. For Club Man of the Year, step forward Barry "Mr Placid" Plumb.'

Barry was genuinely surprised as he climbed the stage to receive his award, a large gold-coloured trophy and a bottle of cheap champagne.

'Now, Mr Plumb' – Viv was shouting into the microphone as he handed the cup over to Barry – 'I believe that you have some other news for us. Come on, Barry, don't be shy, tell everyone your news,' and held the microphone at Barry's chin.

'Well, I do have some very important news actually,' Barry began, unable to suppress the grin spreading across his face 'It has been officially announced that I am about to become a—'

Viv snatched the mike back and shouted, '—husband. That's right, ladies and gentlemen. Barry is taking the plunge with his delightful new lady here, Monocle. Monocle, stand up and give us all a wave.'

Barry looked stunned and gazed down to the table to see Monica standing and offering a regal wave to the assembled throng. She returned Barry's gaze before matching his broad smile and raising her glass to her lips. Barry forced a smile and felt sick as he descended the stage and returned to his fiancée, to rapturous applause from the room.

'And finally,' Viv boomed, 'last, but by no means first, we have an extra special award. To our manager, secretary, treasurer and all round boss of Poachers Arms Football Club, I bring you Mr David Statham.'

Although Dave had expected something, he hated going onto the stage and had to be pushed forward by Mandy and several footballers. He stood on the stage, looking down and wondering just what sort of trophy Viv would hand him. Viv was enjoying himself immensely.

'We have a very special award for Dave. Something that he will require over the next year, something that no one thought Dave would ever need, but need it he does. Paul and Andrew, bring it up, please.' From outside the room, Paul and Lightning carried a huge box, and stumbled through the cheering tables of footballers and onto the stage. Dave was bewildered as to what sort of trophy could be in such a huge box.

'Come on then, Dave, open it up,' Viv called into the mike as the whistles and shouts from the floor added to Dave's confusion and embarrassment. He began to open the outer wrapping, thinking that it would be a parcel which takes an age to unwrap, layer after layer, only to finally find a small gift inside. Having removed the paper, he opened the box and stood looking in disbelief.

'Get it out then, Dave, as the actress said to the bishop, get it out.' Viv seemed more excited than anyone.

Dave leant into the box and pulled out a carrycot, followed by packs of nappies, a baby's bottle, babygros, several fluffy toys, a baby bouncer and a plethora of other baby-related paraphernalia.

Viv was chuckling at Dave's obvious bafflement. 'That's right, ladies and gentlemen. Downham's worst-kept secret. For those of you a bit slow on the uptake when you handed over the cash for Dave's collection, Mandy's growing bump is not caused by too many pints in the Poachers. Our Dave here finally worked out what to do with it and him and Mandy are going to be parents. Come on up, Armadillo.'

The room exploded into cheers as Mandy joined Dave on the stage, tears running down both their faces. After regaining composure, Dave took the microphone from a beaming Viv. 'Thanks, everyone, thanks a lot. And I'd just like to say that I've put a tab of two hundred and fifty pounds behind the bar to celebrate, so get stuck in, 'cos once it's gone, that's it. Oh, and don't forget the buffet's ready now.'

Amongst the cheering crowd, Billy was wondering whether to rush to the bar to take advantage of the free tab or rush to be first in the buffet queue.

The buffet was cleared away and the disco was pumped up to maximum volume. Barry, still stunned from the public announcement of his forthcoming nuptials, was making excuses not to dance. Monica was insistent and he was eventually forced to submit to the inevitable and moved his not inconsiderable bulk around the dance floor creating a fair impression of a hippopotamus having an epileptic fit. Monica finally relented and led him from the floor to his seat, allowing him to flop down and concentrate on finishing his pint to recover from the exertions. Monica decided that, as Barry's dancing left much to be desired, she would dance with Lightning, and walked across to his table, lightly held his hand and took him to the dance floor where they danced together, Monica rather smoothly and sexily, and Lightning producing an indescribable series of movements which seemed to consist mainly of stamping his feet augmented with vigorous arm waving. Monica was soon replaced by other wives and girlfriends, as the ladies were happy to dance with a man whilst their menfolk lounged about the bar. Lightning became the most sought-after man in the room.

As the night and the effects of the beer wore on, the footballers slowed their drinking and, almost as one, took their partners onto the dance floor for the final half an hour or so of shuffling round to "Lady in red" and "I'm not in love". The Erection Section, Viv called it. Paul stayed with Christine, holding her extra tightly but always keeping an eye on Linda who was commandeered by Majid for the final dances.

Dave and Mandy barely moved, standing in the middle of the floor oblivious to the people and sounds surrounding them, not even leaving the dance floor when the music stopped between numbers. Viv and Elaine had surprisingly made an excuse about being very tired and retired to their room at midnight.

Dave was sitting in his hotel room, showered and dressed and reading the sports pages of the *Sunday Times*. His head felt a little fragile and there was a slight, nagging ache over his left eye. That apart, he had no effects from the previous night's excesses. He looked up at Mandy, pink and shining and fresh and beautiful as she applied a light covering of lipstick and massaged her lips together in that odd way that women have.

'Stop staring and telephone Viv and Elaine. I'm starving and there's a big breakfast with my name on it downstairs,' she chided him. Dave reached across and dialled Viv's room number.

'Mr and Mrs Clutterbuck. Your colleagues in the room next door await your company at breakfast, so shift your bums and let's go,' he stated plainly and hung up without waiting for a reply.

Barry was staring at the television and watched Monica as she stepped from the bathroom, clad in a large white towel. He knew that she did this to tease him, but was not about to complain. 'The answer's no. I want my breakfast,' she said without waiting for Barry to ask. She turned her back to him and dropped the towel, ensuring that he had good sight of her bottom as she moved across the room to collect her underwear. He smiled contentedly as he gazed at her well-rounded buttocks.

'I know what you're thinking, Barry Plumb,' she said without turning round. 'And the answer's still no.'

'I was just thinking how much I love you,' Barry said absent-mindedly, surprising himself by the statement.

Viv and Dave joined Barry in the corridor, waiting for the lift.

'Which one of you lot had the film on last night?' Barry asked as the lift lights slowly moved down from the fifth to the second floor. 'The noise seemed to be coming from near your rooms. Horror film or something, wasn't it? Lots of clanking chains and screaming.'

'I heard that too,' Mandy added. 'Sounded a pretty awful film. Groaning and banging. I had a job to sleep, but of course Dave had his beer tranquillizers so he slept OK.'

'No idea,' Elaine answered 'We were asleep early, weren't we, Viv?'

Viv nodded, none too convincingly.

The six squeezed into the small lift to travel down two floors to the dining room, where the young men looked pale and quietly pushed pieces of bacon around their plates. The older men, Paul, Barry, Viv and Dave had brought their complementary newspapers and were still catching up on the football results, whilst tucking in to the full monty. Many years' experience of boozy nights and hotel living had taught them when to stop drinking, something the youngsters were yet to learn. Paul was being attended to by his harem, who supplied him with tea, toast and eggs and bacon as he read the results out to Lightning.

Replete, Dave and Mandy slowly left the dining room, visiting each table in turn to thank the occupants for attending and for their contribution to the presents. Viv called to them to get a move on and they left the room with a final wave just as Billy and Louise rushed into the dining room. 'They're here late to hoover up all the scraps and leftovers,' observed Viv.

'And to fill her bag to take home to the girls for their breakfast,' Barry added with a look of disgust.

'I knew he'd be last out from breakfast,' said Dave. 'I was relying on it.'

Having paid the bill, Dave and Viv carried the bags to Dave's car and breathed in the cool spring air. Barry strolled across the car park with Monica to say their goodbyes. 'Well, that's it for another season. Thanks for everything, you two, a great night to end a great season,' said Barry, shaking hands with his friends, 'and thanks for the drinks, Dave. Two hundred and fifty pounds behind the bar. Very generous of you, very generous indeed.'

Dave shrugged as they shook hands. 'Not that generous really, Plumby,' he said. 'I put the two hundred and fifty quid on room 311. Billy's room.'

Firm but fair, they all agreed, firm but fair.

Play Football

Steve Rossiter

"A wonderfully illustrated guide for a child, teenager or adult beginner keen on learning the basics of football."

Play Football is a full-colour guide to football techniques and skills full of clear illustrations. It is intended for players of all ages but is particularly helpful for beginners, and adults wishing to coach beginners.

Covers all facets of the game: passing along the ground, kicking through the air, controlling the ball with your body, dribbling skills, moving the team in play, shooting skills, goalkeeping skills and many more.

Includes foreword by Bruce Grobbelaar.

Size: 298mm x 210mm   Pages: 148
Binding: Paperback   ISBN: 978-1-906050-16-0   £9.99

St Thomas' Place, Ely, Cambridgeshire CB7 4GG, UK
www.melrosebooks.com   sales@melrosebooks.com

PLAY FOOTBALL
A guide to techniques and skills

STEVE ROSSITER

foreword by

BRUCE GROBBELAAR